Diane Bell has been writing and telling stories for as long as she can remember: as a child for "The Argonauts", an Australian radio show of the 1950s; in her late teens and early twenties as a primary school teacher in Victoria and New South Wales; with her two children, now story-tellers in their own right; and, after earning her Ph.D. in anthropology from the Australian National University (1981), as an ethnographer of the exotic and the mundane. After nearly seventeen years in the USA, most recently as Professor of Anthropology and Director of Women's Studies at The George Washington University, DC, she has returned to Australia to live, write, and engage with social issues that have been at the forefront of her research: women, Indigenous peoples, religion, politics, higher education, law and justice. No doubt the list will grow as she settles into her new home in Ngarrindjeri country in South Australia and her new office at the University of Adelaide.

EVIL

A NOVEL

DIANE BELL

SPINIFEX

Spinifex Press Pty Ltd
504 Queensberry Street
North Melbourne, Vic. 3051
Australia
women@spinifexpress.com.au
http://www.spinifexpress.com.au

First published 2005
Copyright © Diane Bell
Copyright © on layout, Spinifex Press, 2005

This is a work of fiction. It does not portray real places or events or living persons.

Edited by Janet Mackenzie
Cover design by Deb Snibson
Typeset by Claire Warren
Printed and bound by McPherson's Printing Group

National Library of Australia Cataloguing-in-Publication data:

Bell, Diane, 1943– .

Evil : a novel.
ISBN 1 876756 55 1.
I. Title.

A823.4

CONTENTS

PROLOGUE

Evil. That's what it was. Elusive, but evil nonetheless. Having named it she felt fortified. It wasn't the obvious evil of bombing innocent civilians but a more subtle, pervasive thing. It lurked in dark places, shelves of musty black robes, folded not hung. Had they ever seen the bright light of the hard noonday sun or, like the bodies they cloaked, were they, too, denied? Evil oozed out of the closets, into the hallways, onto the table set for dinner: red meat, heavy wine, creamy sauces, stewed brussels sprouts. The alcohol smell lingered the next day. Evil had a particular odor, she decided. Part decay, part deceit. This thing she now acknowledged as evil was visceral, palpable, not an abstract conceit at all. It confused, angered, and tantalized her. Decoding its shape, texture, taste and yes, smell, had become almost a full-time job. She needed to write of this thing to make sense of her intense years of fieldwork with this strange tribe of non-reproducing males.

1

MEETING THE NATIVES
January 1995

In the beginning, she had not realized it would be her anthropological training to which she would turn to plumb the strange new world in which she had landed. She had been recruited, after an international search, to fill a prestigious position at St. Jude's, one of the outstanding Jesuit liberal arts colleges of the northeast United States. The move was heartbreaking: winding up her affairs in Uganda, where she had been doing fieldwork; saying goodbye to friends and colleagues; selling most of her furniture; culling her books and papers so that what remained was her essential library. It was all an aching blur now. She hated parting with her books almost as much as parting with people who were dear to her. Her books sustained her, nourished her, kept her moving when it would have been so easy to give up. She was counting the days until the remaining two hundred boxes arrived from her home base in Australia.

So much of what she did as an academic required access to reports, court transcripts, short-lived newspapers, correspondence, tapes of oral histories, marginalia. She had an eye for the bizarre and unusual, and often charmed the colleagues with whom she shared her finds. Much of what she cared about was not part of the received wisdom of her times. "Subvert the dominant paradigm" said the bumper sticker on her sensible little compact. That was a good starting point, but she longed for more. Her passion was for social justice – a cause she shared with her ex-husband, but Bruce was in Australia. *Damn him*, she thought. *It had been so good, could still be so good.* Sure, they had their problems, but together they had campaigned for self-determination for Indigenous peoples, for a world in which the voiceless were heard and the weak were empowered. In part, it was the possibility of pursuing these goals that had drawn her to St. Jude's with its mission of being "In the service of others." She hoped that in the United States she would be at the epicenter of global affairs, and she lived to be part of the action. And, if she was going to be brutally truthful and hold herself to the same standards she advocated for research, she had to admit she was hoping for some respite. It was not the hard work so much, but the emotional drain of always being on call, of always being responsible as she had been for the last twenty years as Director of Global Research Inc., an Australian-based consultancy firm she had established with her husband.

But here she was alone and cold, on this miserable January day in 1995, moving into an apartment that hitherto had known only Jesuits. Her place was on the ground floor of one of the wooden, triple-decker houses common in this part of the country. The living room and kitchen were of generous proportions, but the two bedrooms were tiny, the plumbing basic. She had no furniture. She planned a visit to the local thrift shop but for now was making do with a futon borrowed from a colleague. There was a sorry-looking saucepan in the compartment under the oven. It would suffice for boiling water until she could go shopping. Using the Red Zinger tea she always carried with her, she made a cuppa, sat on the rolled futon, and decided that this would be her sleeping place for now. The unpacking and cleaning could wait until tomorrow. She drank in the fragrance of the tea, but the smell of the apartment was still there. She worried that no matter how hard she scrubbed she wouldn't be able to get rid of the smell. It was a strange damp and moldy smell, like rotting vegetation on the forest floor, and something else she couldn't quite identify. She stacked a couple of boxes in the cold stairwell at her back door to take to her office and made a mental note to buy a heavy winter coat as soon as possible. And flowers? Something aromatic to mask the smell.

The phone rang. It was Hannah calling from London. "How's it going, Mum? What time is it there?"

"Only 5 pm, but it's dark and I'm ready for sleep, if I can."

"Oh god, Mum, still not sleeping are you? Call me when you're settled. I just wanted to make sure you'd arrived safely."

"Oh, I'm safe all right, it's just the smell."

"Of what?"

"Ecclesiastical decay? I don't know."

"Call housekeeping in the morning," said the ever helpful and resourceful daughter. "Night. Love ya."

"Thanks. Love you too."

She made her bed near the heater. Listening to the hot water gurgling through the pipes of the ancient system, she snuggled down to reread Bruce's last letter from Australia. She thought about her role in their break-up, divorce, and reconciliation. He'd called her "flighty." Said couldn't stay the course, said she just moved on when things got too tough. *Not fair*, she thought. *I finish one job and then move onto the next challenge. I'll show him who has staying power, but first I need sleep.* She thought about her daughter and son-in-law in London, and Ned, her son, who was in South-East Asia. She snuggled closer to the heater, fantasized that she was warm and comfortable, and finally fell into a troubled sleep. This was like being in the field on the first night: so much to anticipate, so much to be done. *Will the natives be friendly when I wake?*

Early next morning, eager to escape the gurgling and gushing crescendos of the dry-caked heating system, she took a box of books, stacked a few extra on top and walked across the campus to her office in the Religious Studies Department in Coyle Hall. She was feeling less hopeful that this was the place where she would make "her stand," and was beginning to regret her decision to uproot and move to Resolve, Connecticut. None of the college buildings was labeled: as she would be told later, if you didn't know where you were, you shouldn't be there. Her hopes for respite from a hostile world were evaporating fast. And, if her chronic insomnia – well, she liked to call it wakefulness – was kicking in again, her life would become even more stressful. "Just stay still," Bruce had said. "You'd be able to sleep if you'd just slow down." But she didn't want to slow down. She wanted others to move faster.

She struggled up the stone stairs of Coyle Hall and paused on the sixth floor. *Which way do the numbers run?* She was there before the faculty and the secretaries, but she was not alone. Along the hallway she could just make out the form of a woman, not tall, light of foot, walking quickly towards the landing. A bunch of keys hung from her wrist. *The housekeeping staff?*

"Room 606?" she inquired and leaned forward to read the name embroidered on the pocket of the blue rayon uniform. "¿Magdalena?" The soft 'd' rolled off her tongue as naturally as if she were a native Spanish speaker.

"*Sí, Señora*," Magdalena responded with the formality appropriate when addressing a stranger and added hastily "Yes," as she spun her key ring to the one labeled 606.

"*Buenos días*, Magdalena. I'm Dee." She smiled and bowed slightly. "I arrived last night but I could hardly sleep, so I thought I'd get an early start. Looks like you were up earlier than me, though."

Balancing a box of books on one hip, Dee moved to shake hands, but instead the books on the top of the box fell forward and copies of her favorite current reading cascaded down the stairs. Magdalena had the office door open in a flash and together the two women began to retrieve the books and shuffle them onto one of the two over-stuffed chairs. "Hum, smells like fresh paint," Dee sniffed. "Recently painted?"

"Couple of days," Magdalena replied and busied herself with the books. Dee noticed that she was reading the titles – Iris Murdoch's *The Nice and the Good*, Jane Smiley's *Moo*, Umberto Eco's *Foucault's Pendulum*, and a clutch of Amanda Cross mysteries – as she picked them up. "The office was all closed up for a while."

"Why? It's such a wonderful space, so much light," Dee said, looking out the corner window across three of the seven hills of Resolve and down to the sprawling town.

"Oh, if these walls could talk." Magdalena stood looking at the floor-to-ceiling bookshelves. Then, realizing Dee had turned and was about to ask another question, she moved towards the door. Dee tossed the last of the paperbacks onto the chair. "*Murder in a*

Tenured Position – my favorite Amanda Cross novel." Dee began to sort the books onto the shelves but saw that, although Magdalena was anxious to get going, she was eyeing the books in a covetous fashion. "Want to borrow one?"

"I don't get much time for reading. Long hours, kids, my aunt needs care, no car, you know."

"Maybe on the bus?"

"You sure?"

"Of course."

"*Gracias.*"

"*De nada.*"

Dee picked up the nameplate that was propped against her phone and slipped it into the slot on her office door. "Professor Dee P. Scrutari". It looked good – gold letters on a black background. Someone had an eye for style.

Dee turned her attention to the stack of papers on her new desk. Some needed her signature; some were background reading she had requested about St. Jude's. Glancing at a short history of the place, she noted there had been a name change in 1932. St. Jude's had originally been called Resolve College. It had been founded in 1886 by a wealthy son of the Emerald Isle who, shocked by the depth of anti-Catholic politics in the region, had been determined that the immigrant lads would be educated. It looked as if Resolve College had served the community well. Just over a century later, the demographics had shifted. *Interesting.* Dee took her ever-present pocket-sized spiral notebook out of her bag and recorded some pertinent details.

Students: 1,250; 51% female; 10% minorities; 90% Catholic; well off, established professional family backgrounds; feeder schools northeast US.

Faculty: 120; 25% female; 40% Catholic; 5% minority; typically first generation professional in family; recruited US wide.

Alumni: loyal; 40% law and medicine; average annual giving $80.00.

N.B. Ask about name change: Depression, financial problems?

For Dee the field had always been a sensual place – the invigorating smell of blue-gray eucalypts in Australia, the comforting taste of yellow matooke in Africa, the springy texture of tightly braided hair. Here also, the smells, tastes and textures were evocative and descriptive of the place, but it seemed to her that at St. Jude's these things created a menacing and forbidding aura.

Cultural dissonance; trust your senses; look, touch, smell, listen, taste AND ask questions; the piquancy will fade with exposure - record now.

Unlike in her fieldwork in Australia, there was a literate tradition at St. Jude's for Dee to study. In the months to come she would explore the college archives, but for now she simply ran her eye down the list of items in the catalogue: annual reports, bulletins, minutes of faculty meetings, Orientation and Commencement programs, photographs of visits by dignitaries, and a collection of videotapes of St. Jude's in the news. It was an impressive resource but, to Dee's thinking, partial. Student newspapers were simply not archived. *Was this an intentional, perhaps even contemptuous oversight?* Student publications were usually a barometer of campus tensions. She guessed there would be little documentation on the secretarial staff, and probably next to nothing on the housekeepers, gardeners, and maintenance workers who kept the place running. Their histories, as in other communities where she had worked, were the stuff of oral history. Clearly, she would have to record them herself. She knew there would be plenty of opportunities as she settled into her office and apartment to tap into these traditions.

At 9 am Mary J – as Dee learned she was called to distinguish her from the other Mary in the office – arrived at work. She was carrying flowers.

"I thought you might like these for your office."

"Daffodils in January. How wonderful. Where did you find them?"

"There's a place, well a hole-in-the wall really, on my way to work. I'll show you sometime during a lunch hour if you want."

Mary J was a canny shopper. During the lunch hour the other secretaries scurried up the three flights to the institutional cafeteria where they brushed off the laminated tables, ate their packaged lunches, talked about their work woes and campus affairs, and plotted how their favorite faculty might advance and their enemies might get what was coming to them. But Mary J would nip out to the local mall and return with genuine bargains. Designer clothes that had been wrongly sized, silk scarves with a tiny run. Her specialty was shoes. And so it was that Mary J helped Dee buy her first pair of winter boots – happy, red, waterproof ones – which delighted the two of them, and confirmed for the secretarial staff that Dee was out of step with the codes of St. Jude's. These women were lifers, and loyal. They had worn their neat silk shirts, dark tailored suits, and sensible pumps for decades. They dressed for their Jesuit employers and, as far as possible, faded into the dark wood paneling of their offices, a faint trace of light cologne the only sign they had been there. It was unusual enough that Dee, a faculty member, had befriended one of them, but in addition there were Dee's brightly colored African prints, multi-string beads, scarves, shawls, and long hair. These things did not sit well with their ordered world. And now, red boots.

"Click your heels. You're not in Kansas anymore," Mary J quipped.

Mary J had processed all of Dee's paperwork and quickly become an ally. The others on the sixth floor had kept their distance. They were not accustomed to being close with faculty. Watchful waiting was a sound strategy for the St. Jude's secretarial staff. They knew how to bide their time and when to play the insider knowledge card. Some speculated Dee wouldn't last long. She was too foreign, too loud, too opinionated, too inquisitive, and too exotic to survive in this dour place. Most damming of all, she was outspoken about her feminist politics. She talked openly about the patriarchal basis of the church and, they learned to their chagrin, was fond of quoting from Mary Daly's *The Church and the Second Sex*. "The church must admit its past failures, accept its responsibility in the battle against the powers of darkness . . . or be seen as the inevitable enemy of human progress."

And it wasn't only her words that signaled danger. Dee was happy to work with a group of student activists who wanted to establish a Pro-Choice group on campus. On top of that, from time to time, private mail came to the office from Uganda from someone called Christian Olúfẹ́mi, certainly not the father of her two children. Wasn't the children's father in Australia? Something wrong there too. Dee was definitely trouble, they agreed. Back when the student body and faculty were all male, the rhythm of life at St. Jude's had been calm and steady. Those were the days.

January 6, 1995: The Epiphany of the Lord; a totum duplex feast of the first class; Twelfth Night, the manifestation of Christ to the Gentiles, represented by the Magi.

By week two Dee had emerged from jet lag, started to plot her research agenda for the year, and was ready to launch her new course on "Global Perspectives on Indigenous Women." She had began to acclimate to the short winter days – such a rude change from the brilliant, shimmering, equatorial heat of Uganda, and the balmy, lingering, twilight summer days in Sydney, her home town. The students seemed to crave the light as she did. She noticed that for the tiniest shaft of sunlight, they would burst out of the dull dormitories and dingy classrooms and spill out onto the bare patch of dried grass along the south-facing quad. There, armed with Frisbees and boom boxes and stripped to shorts and T-shirts, they would celebrate a mini thaw with full gusto. *But*, she reminded herself, *this is the northern hemisphere and it is winter. Better follow the lead of the older natives.* With some more guidance from Mary J, she bought a coat. Not one of the dark, padded, down coats popular among members of the faculty, but a vibrant red and green plaid cape that she wore with dark green knitted gloves and a scarf. The green matched her eyes and the red complemented her dark hair and the tan that was fading but still deep enough to give her a healthy glow on a gray day. Wrapped in her wonderful cape, she now walked purposefully across the campus from her apartment to her office every day.

"There's the new professor," a first-year student who had been to basketball practice at 6 am sang out to her teammate. "She's up wicked early. I know I'd still be in bed if the guys didn't get the best practice times!"

"Do you think she plays any sports? She's tall enough to be on our team."

Dee caught the last part of the exchange and smiled. She was often taken to be much taller than her 5 feet 4 inches, but she wasn't much into competitive sports. Taking care to place each foot squarely on the slippery wooden steps, Dee descended from the parking lot to Coyle Hall, the gloomy Victorian ivy-covered building where administrators, faculty and staff went about their daily routines in their neat little offices, classrooms, and studios. She hung onto the rail to steady herself as she reached the landing. There, for a fleeting moment, a huge ginger cat held her gaze. Then, as silently as it had appeared, the cat slunk into the low shrubbery. *Strange*, Dee thought, *the students are not allowed to keep pets. Oh well, one more flight and I'll be there.*

Ask about Title IX - the 1972 guarantee that "any educational program receiving federal funding must be equal for all".

Look into implementation of Americans with Disabilities Act - Anyone in a wheelchair? On crutches?

Dee spent her mornings on organizational tasks and the rest of the day and evenings preparing classes and setting up her apartment. She carried on in her usual can-do Australian style, but at times she allowed herself a few moments of self-pity and wondered what it would be like to be sharing this new life with Bruce. Although Dee and Bruce had divorced some three years ago, they had stayed friends and he had originally planned to join her and "give it another go." She was willing to try. They'd been such good comrades in arms. *Hadn't they laughed the day they'd thrown red paint on the stock exchange and then made love all afternoon? Hadn't they linked arms and sung protest songs during the Vietnam Moratoriums? Where had the passion gone?* Bruce loved Hannah and Ned but he had never really accepted the full responsibility children required. That had been her work. In those days, he wanted to stay late at political meetings, organize, picket, carouse. When the children were young, she had found her challenges within Australia; now they were independent, fieldwork in Uganda had become possible and relocating to the United States feasible. Now she could imagine a life elsewhere, live up to the "global" part of her title. *Flighty, eh? Why should I be grounded?* Bruce's words had stung. Dee had a long memory and a tendency to hold grudges. He had apologized for upsetting her but not for the words. She began the familiar inner argument cum pep-talk. *Learn to let go. There are no easy solutions. You tried to make the relationship work but there is no life-long guarantee of security in marriage, if there ever was. You're making the rules as you go along. Trust your own good sense. You'll be fine.*

Right now her own good sense was telling her she was indeed alone. It was unlikely Bruce would be joining her. She had better start to build a network in Resolve, establish a base, make friends, and try to have some sort of social life. So she had begun inviting faculty to visit her new digs. But getting to know her workmates in this small community was proving to be a slow process. Slower than in any of the other places she had previously landed, although some colleagues were obviously curious about her and revealed their strange ideas about the life of an anthropologist. She was, after all, the first of that breed on this faculty.

"Where do you sleep?" asked one of the political scientists.

"On a futon I borrowed, but I've bought a bed which should be delivered this week."

"Oh, we thought anthropologists slept on the ground and that's why you didn't need any furniture."

11

Dee looked for the hint of a smile and seeing none, continued anyway. "Well, if I'm doing fieldwork here, you'd better look out, or you'll end up in my next ethnography."

Anthropology is a stance on life.

Dee had written this many years ago in one of her little note-books. She still believed it.

Some of the natives were friendly and intent on making her feel welcome. Brian Baxter, in Religious Studies, delivered a comfy couch for indefinite loan. Over it she threw the two bold red and blue Massai blankets she'd bought in the airport store in Nairobi. It reminded her of the day Christian Olúfẹ́mi, her partner for the Ugandan AIDS prevention campaign interviews, had wrapped her fever-riven body in a similar blanket and carried her for miles to the nearest clinic. The machine-made blankets she had bought were not as strong or daring as the older hand-made ones, but they would do for now. Dee moved her few pieces of furniture around until she had created a small sociable space near one of the main windows. She bought a stark white table and chairs, the basics for her kitchen, and a deep blue potted hyacinth for the window ledge. Next she began exploring the aisles of supermarkets.

Many of the foods were new to her. Under the glare of fluorescent lights, the neat rows of packaged meats had a clinical appearance. Dee had never seen so many choices of what she called "minced meat" but which in this country was in packages labeled "ground beef" with various fat contents displayed in bold figures. She leant over to touch one and pulled back at the spongy feel of the plastic container and the squishy bloody meat. All manner of dark green vegetables – none of them silver beet, a leaf she did know – were heaped in dewy displays. And squash. Endless varieties. She asked her colleagues to join her as she experimented with these new foods. They looked a little surprised. "We could eat at the Chowder Pot, or the new Italian place," they'd suggest.

"No, I'd like to cook and have you over to my place, although it's a bit basic and I'm still working on it." She puzzled about why people were so reluctant. Later she figured out it was all about bathrooms. If they ate at Dee's, she would expect them to reciprocate. Then she'd see their bathrooms. Too intimate. No, better eat out.

By the end of her second week, Dee's first St. Jude's field notebook was full. She was getting a sense of who was where and when.

Staff: 9-5; mothers of school-age children vaporize somewhere in the late afternoon; work-related errands?

Faculty: minimal presence; much car-pooling from Hartford and from Springfield, just over the border in Massachusetts; exit after the morning rush hour and return before afternoon rush; productivity?

Students: midmorning to library close at midnight; but N.B. early morning sightings of young women in sweats, noon-day men in shorts and baseball caps with Frisbee; off-campus life?

Jesuits: on-campus community; inaccessible; home life?

Dee occasionally saw Jesuits driving a circuitous route from their castle-like residence on the hill to Murphy Chapel and Coyle Hall. She guessed this was to avoid the short but treacherous trek down more of those St. Jude's steps. Some twenty years of field-work in remote locations had honed Dee's powers of observation and taught her that the elders of a society might be elusive, cautious, retiring; might be protected from the outsider's gaze by appointed minders; might need to be courted. *In the service of others? Celibate men? Who are these men?* Patience was needed and patience, she acknowledged, was not one of her virtues.

In time, Dee would meet a number of the Jesuits; some were on faculty, some part of the administration, but most were simply living out their lives as men of the cloth, undertaking retreats and doing their spiritual exercises. She would see the inside of their residence at a formal dinner, make friends and allies of several, and enemies of others. She would hear of their sparse private rooms from her students. Looking back, a year later, she found it hard to imagine what might have prepared her for the suppurating vileness of much of their culture. The contempt for others she

13

would find so corrosive of the values espoused by the community was merely an inflection in her early encounters.

January 28, 1995: Jose Marti's birthday AND feast day of St. Thomas Aquinas, the "Angelic Doctor," patron of all universities and of students; resisted temptation of an impure woman and persevered in his vocation; rewarded for his fidelity by God with the gift of perfect chastity.

By the end of her first month at St. Jude's Dee felt a little less alien. She was now in regular phone contact with Hannah and Ned after finding that letters were too slow for their fast-moving, full lives. She knew most of the faculty and staff by sight, if not by name. Her students were hard-working and she found their earnest questions about justice in other cultures endearing. She had a running account with the local thrift store, was on first-name terms with the buyers at the bookstores, and had even ventured into Boston, to attend the symphony. Dee rather liked the easy access to neighboring states and planned to explore more of Massachusetts and Rhode Island when the weather improved. Her beloved books and papers had arrived and the limited shelf space in her office was overflowing. Winter seemed to drag on, but Phil, the famous groundhog of Punxsutawney, Pennsylvania, did not see his shadow on February 2, a good sign winter was on the way out. Brave crocuses broke through the snow. *If they can survive, so can I,* Dee thought.

Feb 2, 1995

Dear Bruce,

I often wonder about what it would be like if you were here, or if I had turned down this job and returned to Australia when the Uganda project was done? Could we have made it? Was it really as simple as me needing to settle down? We have a history together. Is that enough? What was it that kept us together? Keeps any couple together for that matter? Children?

Ideas about what the world might be? What else? Must there be something else? You once said I live in the world of ideas too much. Is that wrong? And for whom? And anyway, field-work is hard yakka and raising children is 90 per cent physical endurance, so I don't think I am lost in a world of ideas. Right now though I'd be happy to be lost in the idea of sleep. Don't laugh. The insomnia is back, big time.

I am enclosing some clippings from the local newspaper. Thought you'd like to see what happens in a real snowstorm.

Love Dee

A month later, a large manila envelope stuffed with newspaper clippings arrived. "FYI", said the yellow Post-it note, not in his hand. Dee looked inside for a letter. *Has Bruce picked up on my reflections on life, my acknowledgement that I am an insomniac?*

Feb. 12, 1995

Dear Dee,

I think those of us who care about Indigenous rights, women's rights, or the environment, need to begin building coalitions. This country is moving towards economic rationalism and the advances of the 1970s are fragile. There is a meanness in the air. Remember the Aboriginal women who fought so hard to protect their sacred places on Hindmarsh Island in South Australia? Who refused to reveal their secret knowledge of the traditions of the place but were prepared to have the story placed in a sealed envelope marked for women only? The envelope has landed, by mistake they say, on the desk of a member of the Opposition. I think this will explode in the media soon. I'm meeting with the local union reps to see what might be done to keep developers out of the area.

Bruce

Okay, so much for introspection, Dee told herself as she placed the clippings in a folder marked "Women's Religion: Australia", and

15

settled down to read a letter, which had arrived in the same post, from her fieldwork friend in Africa.

C/O Post Office, Kampala, Uganda

Feb. 10, 1995

How are you my dear friend? I think of you often. The situation in the southwest of Uganda remains critical. The political instability in Rwanda, Tanzania and Zaire continues to exacerbate the existing health crisis. What is the stance of the USA? I wonder. Do ordinary Americans understand the magnitude of the genocide, the dislocation, the horror of refugee camps? Water. No-one here wants to drink from the Kagera River. You can still smell the carnage. It is indelibly imprinted in my mind's eye, that April day last year, all those headless bodies floating downstream. You stood weeping on the roadside and I could scarcely control my anger and you said, "There will be a rush to lay blame and punish, but that will not stop the violence."

Yours in the struggle,

Christian Olúfémi.

Along with his letters, Christian sent tapes the local women had made of their latest adventures. He wrote of his work, of their friends, of his successes with the educational outreach programs, and of his continuing efforts to secure affordable drugs to treat his patients.

Dee looked forward to these updates and responded with carefully coded letters to confuse the African censors who checked all incoming foreign mail addressed to the Cuban-funded People's Health Depot. "Three inches of snow today," she wrote and knew he'd smile. Three more letters in support of the free pharmaceuticals for HIV-AIDS campaign had arrived. She and Christian, "CO" in her field notes, had worked together on a number of projects including the petition and she knew how desperately the drugs were needed. "Particularly hot this week," she wrote, and he'd know the talks with the Senate Committee had resumed. She hoped the censors didn't watch the weather channel.

She listened to the State of the Union address. "Our country is stronger than it was two years ago," President Clinton said and called for a "New Covenant," one of rights and responsibilities. "God bless you all." The campaigns for the 1996 election were already under way. "Family values" were being contested.

Map the gap between the ideal and the real, the local and global, equality and inequality; beware of binary oppositions; most people live on the mushy middle ground.

2

THE ELDERS MEET
Spring 1995

President Simon Firmitas SJ rose. The faculty followed. He read slowly and deliberately. "There was a man in the land of Uz, whose name was Job: and that man was perfect and upright, and one that feared God and eschewed evil."

Faculty meetings always began with a reading from the Old Testament. The President did not venture into the confusion of the gospels but rather found all he needed to communicate in the time of the prophets. Faculty was in little doubt as to what was required. Father Firmitas presided over faculty meetings as a strict patriarch over his own flesh and blood family. And, while there was much talk of the college being "one big happy family," when this patriarch spoke, his word was law. A meeting that began with "God judgeth the righteous, and God is angry with the wicked every day" from Psalms 7:11 was a warning to faculty that those involved in the campaign "Contraceptives for Catholics" would face sanctions. Similarly, when Alejandro Gómez SJ, from Mexico City, spoke at the Orientation Mass, the faculty knew the program in Chiapas would be funded.

Read the subtext.

President Firmitas was a scholarly man, tall, slightly stooped, of florid complexion and wiry build, precise in his speech and inquisitive by nature. His clerical collar seemed to bite into his neck and Dee wondered if he loosened it in the evening with his fellow Jesuits. Dee liked the man. His intellectual range was remarkable and surprisingly eclectic, a result perhaps of growing up in a household that was ruled by a stern Polish grandmother and frequently disrupted by her wild Irish husband. *Now there was a marriage worthy of anthropological study.* When Dee had admired the finely painted black lacquered box on his desk, "From my Polish grandmother," he'd said with some affection, and treated her to a short, informative explanation of Ukrainian religious symbolism and the naming of all eastern Europeans immigrants to Connecticut as "Polish." She would also hear him on the subject of his Irish grandfather and his membership in secret societies.

N.B. Check library for histories of Freemasons and Knights of Columbus.

Interestingly, in Simon Firmitas, now President of the prestigious St. Jude's, Dee saw little of the negotiator one might have imagined could have emerged from such a culturally rich family background. Rather he had little patience with those who carped and quibbled. If you were on his side, his decision-making style could be quite exhilarating; but if you fell from grace, there was no hope, you were finished and should start exploring the job market. Regardless of the recommendations of properly constituted committees, there would be no tenure, no fellowships, no course releases.

Dee recalled the story President Firmitas had told her during her interview the year before when she asked about the process by which the college had become coed in the 1970s. "Process, bah!" he'd said with a dismissive wave of the hand. "If you want to change an institution, don't look to process, or incremental change. It's too slow, and there are too many opportunities to get derailed. Once I decided it was in the better interests of the college to admit women, we set the mix at fifty-fifty, and went coed the next year. Sure a lot of people were upset, especially some middle-ranking male students, but the quality of the entering year improved with the women's scores and that helped our ranking. And the parents of the female students gave generously to the Annual Appeal. It was win-win."

Dee settled in to watch this man in action with his faculty. She playfully indexed these quarterly faculty meetings as "Council of Elders," but was beginning to think "Religious Rites" might be more appropriate.

Faculty assembles at 3 pm in the Coyle Theatre; Faculty

attendance taken by Father Abacus; President, Dean, and Recorder of Faculty on stage; Departments sit in blocks in tiered auditorium.

N.B. Self-policing. Read Foucault.

The President handed the meeting over to the Dean. First item: approve the minutes of the last meeting, fall 1994. There was some shuffling as the faculty members scanned the document. They waited to hear who would object today: Professor Bill O'Vafer, Head of Political Science, the largest department at St. Jude's, or Professor Henry O'Macer, Head of the English Department, the second-largest.

Ritualized behavior.

"Your turn, Henry," O'Vafer nodded.

"The report of Item 3, 'Alcoholism on Campus', does not reflect the spirit of the discussion. Could it be amended so that it is clear that I objected to any further research on alcohol-related violence? As I said then, the police statistics speak for themselves."

Dee had read this report. She knew that its author, Amy Nakamura, had suggested that the prevailing attitude of "boys will be boys" was no longer acceptable at a coed St. Jude's and that sexual assault was on the rise. Amy had been denied tenure last year, after she had submitted this report. She had concluded that the zero in the rape column on the campus police blotter reflected the reporting of crimes, not the incidence. "Listen to the tape and confer with Professor Scriba," the Dean said. Bob Scriba, the Recorder of Faculty, was all too familiar with the frequent amendments to his minutes required by Henry O'Macer and Bill O'Vafer.

Contesting of sacred texts. Remember the bureaucratic maxim: "It doesn't matter what is said, it is who writes the minutes that counts."

The Dean introduced the next item on the agenda, a report on tenure and promotion policy and procedures, and called upon Bill O'Vafer, the committee chair, to join him on stage. "We first met in spring 1993 with the President and Dean to clarify the terms of reference. We met monthly during the academic year. We met with current members of the Tenure and Promotion Committee and previous chairs. We interviewed all departmental heads, read all departmental annual reports, and . . ." O'Vafer's monotone monologue continued.

Why is he reading all this? Dee wondered. The report had been circulated. There were no surprises. It was a carefully chosen committee. O'Vafer was a safe chair, nominated by the Dean. Nothing was left to chance.

Why didn't they interview people who had been denied tenure? Or cases that had been contested? Has anyone ever sued?

There was that question again. Dee underlined it in her notes, pushed her hair back from her face, and looked up. She was sitting in the same row as her colleagues in the Religious Studies Department but had positioned herself at the end. If she leaned into the wall she could see most of those seated in the theatre auditorium. On stage she saw that O'Vafer was into a rhythm. He was sufficiently familiar with the report to be able to walk around the stage, which, on this occasion, was set for a production of *A Midsummer Night's Dream.* He leaned against a tree of the Enchanted Forest. *Might someone morph into an ass? Were there any mismatched lovers?*

"Candidates for tenure will have to prepare a file which covers three equally important fields – teaching, service, research and publication," he said. Dee doubted this. In her experience, teaching evaluations were only used punitively. It was research and publication that really mattered: The bigger the grants, the better the file; the more prestigious the press or journal, the greater the weight accorded. O'Vafer outlined the decision-making process from the departmental committee, to the college-wide committee, to the final arbiters, the Board of Trustees. He was winding up. "I won't read all the statistics. But you can see that we only award tenure to the very best. So number one: Our system is working and, as they say, 'If it ain't broke, don't fix it.' We are not recommending any changes in the committee structure and the

Dean will remain a member of the College Tenure and Promotion Committee and the Appeals Committee. Number two: We need to be recruiting more women and minorities. The Equal Employment Office is planning a weekend workshop to address that matter."

Who staffs the EEO? Who attends weekend workshops? Are there potential conflicts of interest for the Dean sitting on both committees?

Dee looked up from her note-taking to see that President Firmitas had risen and walked across to join Professor O'Vafer, who was now resting his report on the stage prop for Puck's speech, "I'll follow you, I'll lead you about around / Through bog, through bush, through brake, through briar." The President shepherded O'Vafer back to the table and tapped the microphone in front of Dean Simean, who was chairing the meeting. "The floor is open for discussion. Yes, Professor O'Macer."

"I congratulate my colleague on an excellent report," O'Macer began. "He and his committee have provided us with a blueprint for the next decade."

"Do you have a question?" asked the Dean.

"No, I am ready to close discussion and move that the report is accepted and forwarded to the Trustees. We have a full agenda today and need to move along."

Professor Annales, Head of the History Department, now rose and was recognized. "According to Robert's *Rules of Parliamentary Procedure*, the faculty can only endorse the report. It is the Board of Trustees that legislates."

Father Disputare, Head of the Philosophy Department, interjected, "Oh come on, Jack, don't stand on ceremony. The faculty is ready to vote."

Fellow philosophers, who were sharing the same row of seats as their departmental head, nodded vigorously. The History Department, sitting in the front stalls, began to close ranks around their leader.

Dean Simean rose and President Firmitas nodded approval. Simean strode into the Enchanted Forest, home of nymphs, satyrs, and fairies, and squinted across the footlights into the faculty audience. Despite his size – a full 350 pounds, the result of over-indulging in all those good red wines, heavy pasta sauces, and sumptuous chocolate tortes – David Simean moved with a certain lumbering grace. Like many powerful men, Dean Simean was a mass of contradictions: blustering, often abusive, comfortable with the locker room language of his contemporaries, but in matters of faith, humble, mild, and measured. His unshakable faith was an awesome thing. When he spoke of the presence of Jesus in his life, his whole demeanor changed. Clearly, his savior was with him in all he did. When he spoke of the Holy Father in Rome, his voice softened. When he referred to the college President, he called him "Father." His deference was suitably filial. As a father himself, he gave glimpses of what might be a "softer side" when he was with his wife and children. Dee was sure there was a studio portrait on the desk and a snapshot in his wallet. When his children were in trouble, as they were all too frequently, it was a source of deep pain for him, and the Dean took as conscientious an interest in the affairs of others as in his own. When one senior colleague had been seen dallying with a junior member of the faculty, the Dean had said, "Marry her." And so it came to pass.

Dean Simean now dominated the stage of the faculty meeting. He had the microphone. Dee noted the somber suit, nothing distinguishing there, but his bold block color bow ties, every day a new one, there was something to ponder. *Who dresses the Dean?* She made a quick sketch of his profile: broad forehead; receding hair, prematurely white; clean-shaven, deeply scarred face; half-frame steel-rimmed glasses worn low on his nose, and that nose. *Was he a boxer in his youth?*

Ask Mary J about the Dean's nose.

Simean inhaled slowly and exhaled loudly. Sneezed. The stage was still slightly dusty. *His handkerchief matches the bow tie. What attention to detail,* Dee thought. The Dean continued to stare down at the junior faculty in the stalls, who shrank into their seats. He stared into the theatre and found his old friend Bill O'Vafer. "Make a motion." And, turning to Professor Bob Scriba, who was half hidden behind the stage flap depicting magical, unearthly trees entangled with luscious vines, the Dean added, "Professor Annales will clean up the language for the minutes. Okay, Jack?"

. "Aye, aye," said Annales.

"Aye," said the faculty.

"Nays? Abstentions? Seeing none, we will move to the next item, the establishment of a Center for the Study of Catholicism at St. Jude's."

Father Parsimonia entered stage left via the stairs and past the small white string of stars twinkling through the forest trees. His voice was soft, his accent Southern. He argued strenuously that faculty needed a center dedicated to the study of values crucial to their faith. "We are living in Godless times. We need to return to traditional family values; to set aside all this talk of personal freedoms; to join together to protect the vulnerable, the unborn, the poor, the halt and the lame; to give substance to our mission of being 'In the service of others.'"

Dee, pencil poised, was watching faculty responses to his presentation. The push to establish this center came from a small mixed group of faculty, administrators and alumni and was backed by the Office for Development. This was a proposal that would attract generous gifts and keep conservative alumni attached to the college. The idea had been around for several years and Father Parsimonia knew there were many who objected. Some of the non-Catholic faculty feared this might be a move to introduce "loyalty oaths," and some of the Catholics feared it might ghettoize the study of Catholic faith.

Academic Freedom enshrined in the 1940 Statement of Principles and Ex Corde Ecclesiae - From the Heart of the Church - the Pope's 1990 apostolic letter of guidelines to preserve the Catholic identity of church-related institutions of higher learning; finally endorsed by American bishops. How much power does the local bishop exercise? Do the Jesuits accept his authority?

"Would this center invite fellows to visit?" Professor Vivisecare, Head of Biology, asked. He was thinking of colleagues who, after a comfortable stay at St. Jude's, might reciprocate with an invitation to their own center. This appealed to him because there were ethical debates about cloning and fetal tissue experimentation he wanted to pursue. The position of his colleague, the Dean, was well known. He was a prominent spokesman on the issue and had been since his graduate days. It was wrong and that was that. Vivisecare thought there was some middle ground.

"Would the center offer courses?" asked Professor Designare, Chair of the Curriculum Committee. "What would be their disciplinary base?"

Father Parsimonia had assumed it would be Religious Studies, but other departmental heads saw the weakness in that. "What of the historians who study Catholicism?" Professor Annales wanted to know.

Boundary maintenance; ambivalence about interdisciplinarity.

The discussion continued along predictable lines. Dee had begun to doodle on the agenda. She drew circles inside triangles and triangles inside circles. Her doodles marched down the page and onto the next. *Pay attention*, she told herself, but she had cracked the code. It wasn't hard. The same persons argued the same points regardless of the topic as they staked out their territory and metaphorically brandished their clubs at the elders of a hostile clan. There was an unarticulated speaking order based on the seniority of clan members and the ranking of the clans, based partly on age, partly on their centrality to the Jesuit mission, partly on their ability to deliver what the Dean wanted. This day, Father Parsimonia realized he had had his time. The matter was held over to a future meeting when he could provide written answers to the questions posed by the faculty. The meeting was almost done. One item remained on the agenda: The Office of Equal Employment and the Sexual Harassment Policy.

Professor Virginia Glacialis, Head of Religious Studies, joined the men on the stage. Dee had been waiting for this item. She did not yet have the measure of this woman. Dee resumed her doodling. It was all circles now, concentric circles, ones that interlocked and overlapped. *Circles, the kinship symbol for woman*, Dee thought and turned the page face down in her lap. *A woman's woman?* Certainly there had been more women appointed in Religious Studies while Virginia had been department head, but Amy Nakamura had been denied tenure and the previous occupant of Dee's office was gone. One thing was certain. For the President and Dean, Virginia was the voice of women at the college. They trusted her to keep them informed and expected her to still dissent. The sexual harassment policy she was about to introduce had the Dean as the gatekeeper for all faculty complaints. The college lawyers had warned the Trustees that an expert in this rapidly evolving area of law should be appointed. The President was interested in seeing where the discussion might go; the Dean was less curious and more concerned that new policies and appointments not add more paperwork to his already over-burdened office.

Trained as a biologist, Dr Simean had been a brilliant classroom teacher, but as Dean he was a bureaucratic nightmare. He disliked reading long reports, and he had little patience for qualitative research or for findings that were at odds with his goals. These were simple enough: first, to survive; second, to maintain the honor of the college. He preferred to be lobbied in person, and it usually turned out that the last person to offer an agreeable analysis was in a strong position to make policy. Given that his closest advisers were men like himself – men who had little experience of institutions other than St. Jude's – his policies tended to be conservative and involve as little change as possible.

"We are in compliance with state law," Virginia began. "But the committee to consider revisions has prepared three possible models for the consideration of faculty. Number one is a centralized model – that's what we have now. Number two is a decentralized model with multiple points of entry, formal and informal reporting procedures, and committees of faculty and students. Number three is the appointment of an expert to work with our existing policies and suggest revisions."

"Why do we need an 'expert' prying into our business?" Bill O'Vafer began immediately.

"What happens to the records of complaints?" asked Jack

Annales, who had a background in law. He knew criticisms of sexual harassment polices often focused on issues of due process. "Sounds like the accused doesn't get to confront his or her accuser." Annales was proud of his competence with gender-inclusive language.

"How are accusations investigated?" Jim Vivisecare added.

"What about frivolous accusations?" asked Father Sordes SJ of the Sociology Department.

Whoops, Dee thought. *He doesn't know the speaking order.*

Virginia noted each question. She valued order in all things, at meetings and in her private life. She had come to the college directly from Harvard Divinity School, where her outstanding work had caught the eye of her professors. She'd studied the classics, could read Greek, Latin, French, German, and a little Hebrew. Her writing was disciplined, her arguments tight, her prose spare, unadorned with adjectives and adverbs. To the outside observer, there appeared to be little in Virginia's life for which she had a real burning passion, save for her dissertation research. She had chosen a difficult thesis topic, "Pope Pius IX and his Encyclicals: 1846–78," not a subject that attracted many women. His papacy spanned an unsavory period in church history and most scholars shied away from it. But Virginia was attracted to that Pope's attempt to make lists and live by them. His "Syllabus of Errors" of 1864 was a case in point. It was a meticulous inventory of heresies. Error Number 80 captured the spirit of the man nicely. "The Roman Pontiff can, and ought to, reconcile himself, and come to terms with progress, liberalism and modern civilization, March 18, 1861." Pope Pius was having none of that kind of nonsense. Virginia had her own passion for lists. As a senior in college she had written on a yellow legal pad:

1. B.A.
2. Ph.D.
3. Tenure track position
4. Monograph – Cambridge University Press? Oxford?
5. Marriage
6. Tenure

7. Monograph No. 2 – Yale? Harvard?
8. Children
9. Full professor
10. First woman President of Catholic Liberal Arts College in the northeast.

"Well of course, we will need to engage in a college-wide education program to explain whatever we decide." Virginia glanced at her watch. It was 4:45 pm. Father Tempus, a senior member of the Religious Studies Department who was currently working with Development Office, rose and was recognized. "I move that, given the hour, the meeting be adjourned." Regardless of the issues under consideration, Father Tempus could be relied upon to keep time for faculty meetings. It was the only time he ever spoke up at meetings. Although there might be some grumbling, his motion invariably passed, and the faculty filed into the foyer where refreshments were served. Dee saw Virginia head towards the hallway that led to her office. *Was that a cat following her?* Virginia was around the corner and out of sight. There would be no opportunity for further conversation with her today. Small groups of like-minded persons stood around eating canapés, drinking a range of beverages – coffee, beer, wine, soda, it was all there – and exchanging clever commentaries on the performances of their colleagues over the previous hour and three-quarters.

Knowingly, Bill O'Vafer winked at his brother-in-law, Anthony Bufo, who had just joined the faculty and was slated to be the next Head of History. "We're in for a review of faculty workloads. Readings from Job mean a crackdown."

"What about departmental heads' workloads?" Anthony asked anxiously. He was hoping to get the revisions done on his book.

"Don't fret. With any luck, Jim Vivisecare will be asked to convene the committee. Let me catch his attention so we can talk. I know he appreciates the nuances of faculty governance."

Jim Vivisecare and Bill O'Vafer carpooled and thus had plenty of opportunity to gossip. Not a word they would have used, Dee imagined – women gossip, men politick – but in their three hours together each day as they drove from Springfield to Resolve and back, they made each other aware of the undercurrents at the college. Jim Vivisecare had studied biology at Harvard with David Simean, and made sure he kept close to his buddy, now risen to the level of Dean. For his part, Simean was happy to have a faculty informant who could keep him apprised of any untoward developments. Unlike the Dean, Vivisecare was a skilled negotiator – pragmatic, flexible, and well aware of the tightrope he walked being both faculty and friend of the administration.

David Simean, like many others on the faculty, had stayed close to his roots, a fact underscored by his distinctive Boston accent. Simean had been an undergraduate at St. Jude's during the turbulent 1970s, had stepped outside the college to earn his doctorate at Harvard, and quickly returned as a junior faculty member. Bill O'Vafer '62, predated the Dean at St. Jude's by a decade, and Bufo '70, had been a junior at Simean's Commencement in 1972. Another alumni pattern of the all-male St. Jude's was returning to teach at a coed St. Jude's, marrying a student, and then sending one's progeny to the college under the tuition remission available for faculty after one year's service. Bill O'Vafer had married Anthony Bufo's younger sister, Christine Bufo, '76. Bill O'Vafer Jr., very much his father's son, was a promising Political Science major at the college. Dee had heard that he had been living abroad for a year or so.

Is Christine the mother of Bill Jr.? She doesn't look old enough. Was Bill O'Vafer married before?

What about the Dean's wife? Where did she go to college? Career and motherhood? What's her story?

It was Bill Jr. who had told his father how a young English professor corrected him in class saying. "Bill, when you refer to adult women as 'girls,' you're diminishing their standing. A woman who has earned a seat on the Supreme Court is not 'the girl with the red ribbon.' She is 'The Honorable Justice . . .,' just like the men."

"Well my father calls Mom 'his girl' all the time and she likes it."

"And he calls women 'girls' at work?"

"Yes, at work too. He calls all women 'girls.' It doesn't mean anything."

Dee relished stories about St. Jude's. She delighted in decoding the webs of kinship and marriage of the St. Jude's community and the political alliances they generated. She drew genealogies, noted which wives had found love in which classes, then tracked the children of St. Jude's who, she learned, routinely took courses taught by their parents. If there was any discussion of the potential for conflict of interest in these arrangements, it was never mentioned in Dee's presence. In her field notes she sketched the patrilineal clans, which passed as departments, alongside the extended families, which provided the links and channels of communication between the clans. All this fitted with known anthropological models, but what to do with a community based on the concept of "family" whose head was a male sworn to celibacy?

Evans Pritchard, the Nuer, and segmentary lineage theory? Lévi-Strauss and alliance theory? Crow and Omaha? No, won't do. Classificatory kinship, maybe?

Dee's doodling and her kinship diagrams were beginning to look remarkably similar.

Intertextuality?

She walked back across campus and noted the smudges on the foreheads of other members of the community. Today, she was an outsider observing the rituals of others.

March 1, 1995: Ash Wednesday: first day of Lent, sprinkling of ashes on the heads of penitents.

3

WORKING STORIES
Spring 1995

Walking back to her office from the faculty meeting, Dee was playing a mental game of connect-the-dots where she plotted the links between people she knew, but who did not necessarily know much about each other. She would have dinner parties based on these reckonings. She liked to imagine the conversations that might ensue. The links among the male faculty were relatively easily mapped. But the women at St. Jude's were connected in more fragile and less obvious ways than education, the seminary, and field of study. Building a sense of community among women at the college would be a more difficult task, but it was one Dee thought worth pursuing. One of the things she loved about being in the field was the mutual solidarity women enjoyed. It wasn't that Dee disliked men *per se*; what she disliked was the way senior men spoke for their junior wives, or when men were called upon to speak and then merely repeated what a woman had said just a few minutes earlier, but this time to general acclaim. St. Jude's had potential. A women's support network was possible. After all, the enemy was not hard to identify, but the fracture lines among the women ran deep.

> *Patriarchy isolates women and puts them in competition with each other for men as protectors, sustainers, legitimators. Capitalism devalues women's work. Reread Eleanor Leacock on egalitarian relationships in band society. How far have we come? Where do we want to go?*

In mapping the connections and disconnections, Dee began with the women working on the sixth floor of Coyle Hall.

31

Virginia Glacialis, Head of Department, certainly knows her secretary Mary J, but how much does she know of her life, aspirations, family?

Mary J knows a great deal about Virginia, but plays it close to the vest. What does she have on Virginia?

Magdalena cleans all the offices, sees everyone's photographs and empties everyone's garbage, but has never met Mary J or Virginia. What does she make of their lives?

N.B. All three have aspirations for their talented daughters and all three have less than satisfying marriages.

This connect-the-dots exercise brought to mind stories Dee had recorded in other fieldwork situations. Dee's notes on the women of the sixth floor of Coyle Hall resonated with her notes from women in Australia and Africa.

June 10, 1984: Central Australia; Dry Creek; population 450: "Yes, Dee, we know that we can call the police when there is a domestic, but we know everyone here. There is no confidentiality. We're all related, all family. It's hard when you bring in the police and one of them's your brother-in-law."

October 5, 1994: Uganda, Mbarara Women's Solidarity Committee: "International Human Rights are all very well but we need clean water."

December 15, 1994: Uganda, People's Health Depot: "I know we'd be safer without Jacob. He beats me when he's been drinking. He sleeps with prostitutes when he's in town. He'll give me the HIV-AIDS too, but he is my husband, and he is the father of my children, and the Christian relief workers tell me it will be worse if I leave. And where would I go?"

High on Dee's agenda was finding ways of forging a future where women at St. Jude's might be able to share their stories.

32

She genuinely looked forward to her chats with Mary J, Magdalena, and eventually with Mary Kane, the Dean's secretary. Their wisdom, like that of women in her fieldwork, was grounded in their everyday experiences. Their stories of family, the church, and bureaucracies were prophetic, compelling, the stuff of feminist theorizing. Their stories reminded Dee of Patricia Hill Collins' African American narratives that had impressed her students so deeply. "When Collins writes about 'matrices of oppression,' it sounds so abstract," one student said, "but then I don't have to think all the time about my skin color. Mostly it is not an issue. It's invisible." "Collins brings it alive and I see it's not just about being a woman. Being black, working class, and a woman is a triple header," a perceptive classmate added.

> N.B. *shifting intersections of gender, ethnicity, religion, and class; compare women's stories of subordination and Catholicism with women's stories from the field.*
>
> *March 8, 1995: International Women's Day:*
> *1857 US garment and textile workers organize after devastating fire reveals inhuman working conditions;*
> *Australia - attend a women's dance;*
> *Russia - daughters give flowers to their mothers.*
> *See Robin Morgan's* SISTERHOOD IS GLOBAL.

Magdalena and Dee swapped stories of the Immigration and Naturalization Service: stories of anger, humiliation, and petty tyrants. "They asked how many sex partners I'd had and was I gay?" Dee said sharply. "No rights to privacy if you're not a citizen, eh? I was coming from Africa so maybe they thought that was an appropriate question. And this woman officer, she was so cold and humorless, and I wondered if everyone got asked these questions. She seemed to take a personal interest in my answers."

Magdalena looked embarrassed and nodded. "I know, they shamed me too with all that talk about sex. I've ever only been with one man, my husband."

"Supposedly it was about controlling AIDS, but I asked her how many partners was considered 'dangerous,' and she said 'three.' Good lord, many Americans have been married that many times," Dee chortled.

Magdalena spoke of her apprehensions about the INS and the shady financial dealings of her American-born husband. They had married young, when Magdalena, on a visit to their Miami relatives, had met Carlos, a friend of a friend of the family, and was overwhelmed by his glamorous lifestyle. "They were all so flash. Parties, expensive clothes, fast cars, money for everything." In order to accept his invitation to see the real Miami, she had told her chaperoning aunt she was tired and wanted to rest while the others went on a picnic. She had slipped out and the amorous Carlos, believing she was at least eighteen, had seduced the naive fourteen-year-old. When her family found out, they agreed the young couple could marry – indeed, according to their law, must marry. Carlos was torn. He didn't want to bring shame on his mother and knew that the only way to avoid charges of carnal knowledge and a family feud was to marry Magdalena. He complied, but did not cease his philandering ways.

> ESTUPRO, the crime of "ravishment", i.e. sexual relations with a consenting minor, male or female, providing the person is "chaste"; but ESTUPRO goes unpunished if, with consent of family, the infractor marries the victim.
> The law as guardian of women's virginity?

"Our marriage was okay at times," Magdalena said. "He could be charming and oh he was so cool in his black silk shirts and gold jewelry, but I hated knowing he was playing around with other women. And then he left. I kept saying a good father would do this or that for his children, but he'd shout at me, 'Stupid woman. What do you know?' and walk out. Sometimes he didn't come back for days. I was worried sick but my close family was a long way away. Who could I talk to? His mother was no help. 'That's the way of men,' she would say. He was always respectful of her, but towards me, oh no."

"But no divorce?" Dee asked.

"It's against my faith and my family. I just can't do it, but I needed money. Then this aunt – she lives near here and her husband died – well, she's old and needs help during the day, so I moved in with her. It's not too bad. She helped me get into classes to improve my English. Then I heard about this job, from one of the teachers at my kids' Sunday school. It works okay. I'm home for them and for her."

"All that's missing is sleep," Dee sighed. "I know what that's like. Do you get to visit your family in Cuba?"

"I want to, but it costs money and I don't want any trouble with those immigration people. I know Carlos has done some bad things, moving money around and who knows what else?"

On the subject of the INS, both Dee and Magdalena had a lot in common, and both proceeded very carefully in their dealings with this organization. Both watched the shifts in immigration law with far greater concern for civil liberties than most American citizens, who remained certain that their Constitution would protect them from arbitrary arrest and imprisonment. In their lighter moments, they spoke of expressions that confounded them – simple things like telephones and greetings.

"Call me," her colleagues would say.

"Call me what?" Dee joked.

"Have a good one," they'd say.

"A good one what?" Magdalena wondered.

Between Mary J and Dee, the subjects were local politics, families, and shopping. Mary J had married young, had six children, and now wondered when it was that her husband had stopped noticing her. It was not as if she had run to fat. She'd kept her figure, paid attention to her appearance, still longed for intimacy, but the relationship had cooled. The marriage lingered on, more as a residential arrangement for the benefit of the children than anything else. Mary J dutifully turned the other cheek and prayed for guidance when her husband stormed in and out of the house in one of his rages. But when her children were involved, she was anything but passive. She was determined they would have the best education possible.

"What's the story about my office?" Dee asked one lunch hour when she and Mary J were scouring the supermarket shelves for golden syrup. Dee had promised to make Anzac cookies, an Australian favorite, and needed this ingredient.

"You don't know?"

"All I know is the students say it is haunted, and it was empty for a bit before I arrived, and the paint and shelves are new."

"Well, Ms. Detective, what you don't know can't hurt you," Mary J said as she tossed six boxes of sale-priced cat food into the trolley Dee was pushing.

"Who was in there before me?"

"Jessie."

"No other name? This secrecy isn't like you." Dee stopped at the ethnic food section and pounced on a jar of Vegemite.

"Look Dee, you treat me decently and that matters. There are a lot of uppity people at St. Jude's but I am sticking it out here. I have my reasons. I like you, and I liked Jessie, so let's leave it at that for now." Mary J took charge of the trolley as they neared the checkout.

"Okay, tell me about your daughter. I'm guessing she is one of your important reasons. Is she coming to St. Jude's?"

"I hope so. She's smart enough."

"Like her mother," Dee laughed and the tension melted. As they walked to the car, Mary J showed Dee the photo of "Little Mary," as she was called to distinguish her from her mother.

"Who will she be?" Dee asked, looking at the sweet-faced child in her first Communion dress. She had her mother's face, bright blue eyes, generous smile, upturned nose.

"Someone with choices, I hope."

Industrial blackmail? Compare admission rates of children of staff to those of faculty.

Upward mobility? The American Dream.
Do the children of St. Jude's staff ever return to the college to teach?

N.B. Employees stay for the health benefits; to put their children through the college and to take advantage of the tuition benefits - one year's service for faculty; compare - five years' service for staff.

Like Mary J, Magdalena also had aspirations for her daughter. Another ten years of working at St. Jude's would see her youngest through college. On her second encounter with Dee, Magdalena had brought out her photographs of her children. "This is Consuelo, my baby, my consolation. She was born in 1981. And this is Mercedes, our graces, born 1980. And here, my first-born, my son, Juan, born in 1979. I was only fourteen."

Dee saw that they were obviously their mother's children. Their bright, clear faces stared out from the photograph. Magdalena had that same direct look, just older, more worldly, and chronically tired.

"What amazing red hair," Dee said, "like yours."

"And like my three sisters and my mother's four sisters," Magdalena nodded. "And those deep brown eyes – all my children have that – that's the Hernández side."

"It's a common enough name, but are you any relation to Melba Hernández, the lawyer, one of the two women with Castro in the attack on Cuartel Moncada?" Dee asked.

"You know about her?" Magdalena brightened. "I wanted to grow up to be like her. At school we learned about *compañeros* Ché and Fidel. I saw a photograph of Melba."

"When they were together in the Gran Piedra range?"

"*Sí*," Magdalena continued, her face alive. A smile formed at the corner of her mouth. "We all read the 'History will absolve me' speech. You know she hid his letter to the court in her hair, the one saying that the doctors were just following orders when they said he was too sick to appear in court. He was not sick at all. They didn't want him to speak. It was Melba who brought out the truth. What women can do, eh? Who would look in her hair?" Magdalena dug deeper into her purse. "Here she is. Melba. I heard her speak once. Her ideas swept me away. I wanted to be a lawyer too, but then I got pregnant. Maybe Consuelo will become a lawyer. She certainly knows how to argue."

Magdalena smoothed out the photographs and looked

expectantly at Dee who understood the message. "I do have some photos of my family," Dee reassured her, "just not handy." *Why not "go native" and display my photographs?* Dee asked herself. *Why does it feel like an invasion of privacy for me, and how come "the natives" seem to be so free with them?*

> *Photographs: Ubiquitous artifacts; sharing photographs a "getting to know you ritual"; expectations of reciprocity; a way of establishing rapport.*

> *N.B. Cross-cultural variations in demarcation of public and private space, potential case studies: bathrooms (intimate spaces) and photographs (intimate artifacts).*

As Magdalena returned the photographs to her wallet, Dee noticed a portrait of the patron saint of Cuba, the so-called "Black Madonna." *If she shows me her photographs again, I'll ask about the significance of this complex female figure,* Dee thought. Religious belief and practice in Cuba was such a fascinating field: Dee had hoped to find a student interested in pursuing doctoral research there, but it was not an easy field site for American students.

> *March 13, 1995: Anniversary of the 1957 attack on Batista's palace.*

The Amanda Cross paperback didn't take long to come back. Magdalena was clearly a hungry reader.

"Want another?" Dee asked.

"Anything about this place?" Magdalena replied.

"Not that I know of, but there are plenty of novels written about colleges, some funny, some serious, and some, well here, like Marilyn French's *The Women's Room*, it's set in Massachusetts."

Magdalena shrugged and half nodded. Dee was scanning the section of her bookshelf where academic novels were stacked. *David Lodge? He's deliciously disrespectful, but* Nice Work *will date quickly. Maybe A. S. Byatt's* Possession, *a good read, might make a good movie.* Magdalena was moving along the shelves. "I like the murder mysteries."

Dee went to her collection of novels about women sleuths. "Okay, what about one by Barbara Neely? *Blanche Among the Talented Tenth*, or *Blanche on the Lam*?"

But Magdalena was now scanning a different shelf, the one where Dee had stacked her books about Catholicism. She had skipped over the Mary Daly collection with their provocative titles, *Gyn/Ecology, Pure Lust, Outercourse*, and had taken *Of Love and Other Demons* by Gabriel García Márquez off the shelf. Maybe it was the cover that attracted her with all that luscious red hair of the virginal Sierva María, or maybe the name Márquez resonated. He was well known in Cuba and friendly with Castro. Magdalena flipped the pages and looked up at Dee when she reached a section highlighted in yellow. "Yes, I write on my books," Dee said. "I see you're at the part about the Yorùbá religion of the slaves, the ones who took care of Sierva María and taught her to speak Yorùbá." Magdalena nodded and kept reading. Dee had long been fascinated with the ways in which Catholicism had managed to take root in different cultures and reflected as much of the local folk beliefs and practices as it did the dictums of a distant Pope in Rome. *What might Magdalena think of such matters?*

Cuba: Santeria, the melding of stories of the lives of Catholic saints with those of West African Yorùbá Òrìsà.

N.B. Wonderful juxtapositions and combinations. Obàtálá, the creator of men and women, dressed in white, eats white food, now associated with Christ. Odùduwà wife of Obàtálá, known as god of purity, but also of unbridled sexuality, associated with the underworld and with the Virgin.

Dee recalled the time Christian's mother had come from Lagos to visit the clinic in Uganda. She had talked at length about the Yorùbá religion, about contacts with Muslim traders in the seventeenth century, the Catholic missionaries in the mid-nineteenth, and about the ways their religion had survived over the centuries.

"Now it's the Protestants who are telling us to give up our old ways and follow Him," the old lady had begun. "But why? What will happen to the òrìṣà? Who will feed them?"

Christian had softened and looked fondly at his mother, "When I was young, I loved going to the ceremonies, listening to the drums, seeing the dancers, waiting for the òrìṣà to come down and possess the priests and priestesses," he had said. "The òrìṣà were so unlike the flat, lifeless Catholic saints I was being taught about in the boys' school. The òrìṣà were real to me, and like the places and people I knew. Those saints with all their virtues did not inspire me, but ah, the òrìṣà had such a range of personalities and characters – lustful, vengeful, creative, reflective. They could even change sex at midnight."

Christian's mother nodded warmly and turned to address Dee. "Ah, my son, he was so clever as a little boy, and even at the beginning of his journey, at his *fi esè ntèlè*, the 'stepping into the world' ritual, the Ifá priest said travel and healing were in his future."

"I thought going to school with the Little Sisters of Perpetual Sorrow would be the travel adventure the Ifá priest had predicted. Well, it was travel, but notions of original sin and the inevitability of the final judgment were foreign. The nuns drilled us. And the wisdom of our experts? They called it pagan and primitive. I almost lost touch with the òrìṣà."

"I still ask the palm nuts for advice," his mother said softly and reached out for his hand. "You must keep the contract with your source of creation. I don't want the *eléèdá* to turn against you, my son. You will be a healer."

"Well, not like Jesus, and not like the traditional Yorùbá way," Christian had mused. "More likely something in between."

It was that "in between" that Dee now wanted to ask Magdalena about: Yorùbá beliefs brought to Cuba during the slave trade blended with the Catholicism of the Spanish masters.

> *Sòpònà: the dreaded god of smallpox, worship forbidden by the British colonizers; smallpox outbreak in Lagos in 1940s. Were thanks given to Sòpònà when the epidemic was over? Ask Christian's mother for details.*
> *Is there an òRÌṢÀ for AIDS?*

Dee's questions about the Yorùbá religious beliefs and practices and their manifestations in Santería in Cuba and the United States were now beginning to fill her "follow up" file.

Does Magdalena have a shrine to Cuba's patron saint, the Virgen de la Caridad del Cobre? What does she think about the asexual Mary of Roman Catholicism? Are there any BABALAWO experts to consult about Santería in Resolve?

Of Love and Other Demons took longer to come back from Magdalena and, once Dee was on east coast time, she was rarely in her office early enough to see anyone from the housekeeping staff. But then one night, when she had worked through until dawn on a journal article due the next day, Magdalena's key turned in the lock. They both jumped at seeing each other. "So late, and by yourself. It's dangerous you know," Magdalene said.

"Who is going to bother me here?"

"Well, things happen."

Magdalena shuddered as she said this and quickly changed the subject.

"That's a nice photograph."

"Oh, Mary J got stuck into me about not having a photograph on my desk. Made me feel 'shamed.' She said she'd spoken to my daughter on the phone and why couldn't she see her? I capitulated."

Dee passed the photograph to Magdalena.

"It was taken in Australia a while back, one Christmas when we were all together. That's my first-born, Hannah. She's thirty-two now, married, works for the BBC and lives in London. I had them young, like you – well not quite so young as you. I was eighteen when Hannah was born. And my second, Ned, he's twenty-eight and working in South-East Asia. The kids of anthropologists, eh?"

Magdalena relaxed a little.

"And their father?"

"Divorced. He's still in Australia. He took the photograph." Dee's tone did not invite further comment.

Magdalena was looking at a collage of photographs Dee had on her desk.

"These are from the field," Dee said. "I pulled out ten of my favorite photographs and put them into one big frame. They're like family too. That's one place I worked in Australia." Dee ran her finger along the horizon where the sand dunes met the wide blue sky. "Desert red. I love it. Makes me feel warm in the winter. And this one is from Uganda. The soil is red too, but there's water in the rivers and it's so fertile."

"And who is the good-looking *compañero*?" Magdalena asked.

"Oh that's Dr. Christian Olúfẹ́mi. We worked together on a lot of projects. His mother is a *babalawo*."

"*Babalú, sí.*" Madgalena collected her cleaning gear and looked around the room. "You asked about Mary J before. The one in Room 610?"

"Yep, she is my guide to Resolve, especially the shopping."

"Ask her about this room."

"I did. She said it was Jessie's."

"That was before my time. I only know what I've been told."

"And?"

"Jessie died after a hit-and-run car accident."

"Did they find the driver?"

"Not that I know. Some students were at the scene. They'd been drinking at the pub and the locker rooms in the Field House, but it wasn't one of their cars that killed her."

"You sound like you're not convinced?"

"Well, like I said, I only know what I've been told, and she made enemies – like she helped the students who were organizing protests."

What protests? Which students? Who was Jessie?
Why are people not telling me about her?
What is it about Room 606? Proceed with caution.
Magdalena does not need this trouble.
She needs the work.
N.B. All is not well at St. J's.

Magdalena turned to go. Then she looked at Dee, took a deep breath, and said, "Okay, can I ask you something. I'm not prying or anything, but you're not Catholic are you?"

"No, I'm not really anything."

"And it's all right to have all these books about religion?"

"That's my research."

"And it's okay to talk about the priests like that?" She was still holding *Of Love and Other Demons*.

"Sure. There's what they say and then there's what they do."

Magdalena had bookmarked one of Dee's underlined sections about this chaste, passionate, forbidden love. "They exhausted themselves in kisses . . . they writhed in the quicksands of desire to the very limits of their strength: spent, but virgin."

"Ah, yes," Dee smiled. "The priest bedeviled by love, the Bishop's uncompromising belief in demons, and a terrified girl. A sure recipe for tragedy." She took the book, turned it over in her hands, and read from the blurb on the back cover, "Father Cayetano Delaura, ordered by the local bishop to prepare the twelve-year-old Sierva María, who has supposedly been bitten by a rabid dog and is assumed to be possessed, for exorcism. He falls in love with her and her raging red hair instead." Dee returned the book to the shelves. "A tale of rigid hierarchies, self-serving prophecies and a grueling death for the magical María, eh?"

March 21, 1995: Spring Equinox - the Goddess rejoices in the fertilizing energy of the ram.

Dee knew that living in a community would allow her to document the difference between the rhetoric and the reality. She set about mapping them in earnest, taking a census, writing herself notes on the key players, and establishing relationships that would allow her to be both participant and observer. Figuring out the authority structures and identifying the cultural brokers was going to take time. After one year, she might be able to recite the ritual calendar, but it could take many more years before she could distinguish between what was idiosyncratic and what was routine. Several members of the college community were eager to help her in this task and, as she gained greater insight, she sought out others who might be expert in particular aspects of the life of the college.

One of Dee's most telling encounters had been with Charles "Chuck" Vernon Negotium, the Business Manager. His public posture was that the staff was "family" and that they were capable of solving their own problems. In this spirit, Dee had suggested in a memo that the staff might be given time to attend a workshop she had planned on work and family issues, such as the need to establish a childcare center at the college. This was not a problem that was at the forefront of the Jesuit consciousness, but it was being pursued by younger faculty. They sought alliances with the secretarial staff whose childcare needs were also pressing – perhaps even more so, because their hours were not as flexible. Christine O'Vafer had caused a stir when she spoke at a faculty reception. She generally left business to her husband Bill or her brother Anthony, but she had heard of the struggles of junior faculty and decided it was time to act. It was too late for her but this was a new generation. The story Lizzie Scriba had told at one of the spiritual retreats was a common one.

"All I wanted was time to finish my article that had been accepted by *Text and Context* with minor revisions. It would make my tenure file almost Board-proof. I was cooking dinner. Jack was working on the minutes of the last faculty meeting. The baby was asleep, at last. Then my mother called to say she was sick and couldn't take care of our son the next day. I told Jack that this time he'd have to stay home with the baby because I had to finish the revisions. Jack hadn't really thought about childcare much till then. I always took care of it, like his mother did." But stay home he did and the revisions got done.

In choosing her panelists on the childcare issue, Dee had been careful to include an economist who argued that childcare was cost-effective. She hoped to convince some men – like Jack – that childcare was their issue too. Although socialized in the 1950s, he was married to a woman of the 1990s and, quite apart from Lizzie's career aspirations, it was hard to survive on one salary.

Score one for pragmatic feminism.

When the fliers came out for the panel, Negotium had summoned Dee to his office deep in the bowels of Coyle Hall.

There was no natural light, just banks of harsh fluorescent tubes, and the halls were lined with notice boards covered with public announcements, and signs to the Campus Security service office further down the hallway which wrapped around the electronic heart of St. Jude's in a rough square. On the outside of the square were a number of offices, including those of Chuck Negotium and the newly appointed Director of Information Technology, G. A. Herz. Dee walked two sides of the square to the suite of offices occupied by the Negotium team. The outer office was visible from the hallway through a series of glass panels. Dee entered and gave her name to the secretary who gestured to a hardback chair. "He shouldn't be long," she said and then took a hard look at Dee, ending with a thorough examination of her red shoes. They had become something of a signature for Dee; by now she had red sandals and red sneakers as well as the pair of dressy, low-heeled, red patent leather shoes that were currently under inspection by Negotium's secretary.

Dee sat, crossed her legs and arranged her long black and red streaked skirt so that her shoes were clearly visible. She flipped through one of the pamphlets from the wall display unit. "Emergency Procedures" outlined the exit routes from the college and listed the phone numbers for Campus Security, Chaplain's Office, Health Center, but in a striking omission, there was no entry for the local police in Resolve. Dee checked all sides of the pamphlet and, finding no number, wondered why emergencies were to be kept on campus. Maybe Mary J would know. Dee slipped the pamphlet into her folder and ran her fingers through her hair.

The secretary had disappeared into the adjacent office. Dee was starting to explore a little, read more of the notices, and make a sketch of the suite, but Chuck Negotium appeared at his door, startling Dee. He motioned for her to enter and sit in the green faux-leather chair in the corner. It crackled nastily, like dry lightning, as she settled in and took out her notebook. Negotium kept standing, leaning back with his ample rump touching his desk. He folded his arms across his barrel chest and stared at Dee.

45

Does this man speak or just stare? she wondered as she took in the photographs on his wall – Charles V. Negotium with President Firmitas at the ground breaking for the sports stadium; Charles V. Negotium at the opening of convention center; and Charles V. Negotium with bishops and cardinals, all in full regalia. On his desk stood a bronze plaque on which was inscribed "The absence of doubt makes you strong." Next to it was a triptych of his son's christening, graduation and marriage – all of which apparently took place in the Murphy Chapel. This man was a St. Jude's lifer. Finally he spoke. "About this Helen Bishop," he began, in what Dee guessed was a tone meant to intimidate.

Dee responded in a helpful, cheery manner. "Yes, the Director of the Working Women of America. She is on our panel."

"I don't think we need her on campus," Chuck Negotium growled.

"Who is *we*? She's been invited to speak on a panel of distinguished experts on work and family issues," Dee continued in a matter-of-fact tone.

"She promotes unionization," he snapped, unfolded his arms, undid the gold button on his burgundy jacket and abruptly pushed himself away from the desk.

"She's been invited to speak as an expert on childcare. Have you looked at her résumé?" Negotium was now standing so close to her chair that she had to look up when speaking to him. *This man is a heavy smoker*, she thought and fought to repress a sneeze.

"The unions have been dying to get onto campus," he persisted, ignoring her question and continuing to tower over her.

"And you're afraid that in a fifteen-minute presentation she'll persuade your workforce to join a union?" *Wow, this is more than a touch paranoid*, Dee thought, *and I do wish he would just sit down.*

"Well, we're family here on campus and we look after our family." Negotium's narrow mouth curled into what Dee guessed was a smile. *This would be the family with a father who knows best; the family that never was; the family that keeps its own dark secrets.* "Humm," said Dee out loud. "But now that you've brought up the subject, there is that small matter of academic freedom here for

46

faculty." She stood up, ready to leave. "I realize it's up to you whether staff will attend, but childcare is not going away as an issue."

Negotium buttoned his jacket, squared his broad shoulders and walked to the door. His countenance changed to that of an overly sincere televangelist as he inclined his head and smarmed, "Take care." As Dee exited, she decided to follow the arrows to Campus Security. "You can go either way to the elevator," Negotium called after her. "Say hello to my good friend Sergeant Inservire. And have a good one." This last part, he said cheerily and loud enough to be heard in all the nearby offices. Dee turned the corner of the hallway and was again bathed in brilliant light and overwhelmed by the busy, regulation-laden notice boards of Campus Security. *Was that a faint whiff of kitty litter she smelled?* Dee exhaled in relief when she rounded the next corner and found the waiting elevator. *Now I can sneeze.*

Negotium must have known well ahead of her visit that the childcare issue was simmering. He must have heard the rumblings. Jack had told his story more than once at Happy Hour in Mick's Sports Bar, and there were other St. Jude's husbands who wanted to co-parent with their wives. Slowly the necessity for childcare on campus – or a subsidy for care – was becoming a front-burner issue for the old guard.

> *Hostility to outsiders entrenched. Who is communicating with Negotium about all this?*
>
> *N.B. fracture lines in old alliances opening up; positions being renegotiated; new generation, new interests.*

Negotium decided Dee should be monitored and, if possible, thwarted. It was under his watchful eye, and because of his good connections in local and state government circles, that St. Jude's had been able to "grandfather in" their renovations and skirt the expensive requirements of the Americans with Disabilities Act. He didn't want her meddling in his informal arrangements with local interests. And for her part, Dee had decided any future interactions with him would definitely require a third party to be present as well as careful documentation of verbal exchanges. He was holding the lid of the pressure cooker of this community much too tightly. If and when it blew, it could scald and scar all within its reach. Dee could always hoist the banner of academic freedom – she had tenure – but the secretarial staff was vulnerable. This was a man against whom she could easily hold a grudge.

Sunday April 9, 1995: Palm Sunday: The beginning of Holy Week; the wearing of small crosses made of palm; the triumphant entrance of Jesus into Jerusalem to celebrate the feast of Passover; crowds shout "Hosanna," lay down coats and palm fronds - later burnt, blessed, and used for Ash Wednesday the following year.

N.B. Similarities between the religious ceremony of Palm Sunday and secular rituals of the entry of royalty into a city. How many layers might be excavated with multiple readings of a seemingly simple religious experience?

48

4

It had been a long day. Getting through Virginia's packed agenda for their monthly departmental meeting had tested Dee's patience. Her doodling had become so frenetic that at one point Virginia had paused to ask Dee if there was something she wished to share with her colleagues. Tonight, Dee decided, she would listen to music instead of working on her lesson plans, maybe write a few letters or read a novel. Mostly she wanted to think more about her future at St. Jude's. *Should I get involved in the politics of the sexual harassment policy that Virginia was working on? If so, at what level? Who would become allies if I did?* She didn't want to alienate the college lawyers. They had managed to get her Green Card processed in record time and, no doubt, there would be other occasions when she would turn to them for advice and assistance. She definitely did not want the sexual harassment policy to be the issue over which she and Virginia clashed. *But if I don't get involved, does that mean I'm complicit in allowing abuses of power to persist?* Dee was no stranger to tough decisions and she had made some bad calls in the past – intervened when she should have remained neutral, let things pass when she should have resisted. Hindsight was always 20/20 she concluded. She'd try to be patient with those who could be brought on board, but Dee did not humor fools, and was particularly impatient with the willfully ignorant. The best survival strategy here was to proceed with care. *Hasten slowly,* she told herself as she filed the papers from the meeting.

Check the policies at other Jesuit colleges and universities. Build a database. Is compliance the only factor motivating policy at St. Jude's?
What about being in the service of others?

Dee had had some experience with the shortfalls of the sexual harassment policy: informal procedures didn't seem to have much effect on chronic offenders and she had noted a general reluctance to establish any kind of procedures that might fetter the administration at St. Jude's. When Dee had explained to Professor Taurus, who was always wanting to show her *National Geographic* photographs of bare-breasted African women, that she found his comments on their bodies to be racist, he had countered with "I know what you anthropologists do." He had looked directly at her breasts. "You love to go native. What about some photographs of you?" Dee knew she would have to be direct. After all this was the man who, on instructions from Dean Simean, had married the junior faculty member he had been "courting." "I consider your comments unprofessional and demeaning of women," Dee had said. "Kindly desist." But he didn't. He'd leave copies of *National Geographic* lying about in the general office and would try to draw Dee's attention to the photographs. In exasperation, Dee mentioned the matter to the Dean, who replied summarily, "I've known him for decades and I've never heard him utter a racist slur." Case dismissed.

Old boy network rules at St. Jude's.

Shortly after her conversation with the Dean, Taurus had stood menacingly in the doorway of Dee's office. He had spread his arms so that she could not get out, and had stormed, "So, I understand you spoke to the Dean about me."

"Yes I did, and that was supposed to be a confidential communication."

"Well, you can't just go around *accusing* me."

"No, Professor Taurus, what I can't do is *lodge* a complaint and *expect justice*, unless I know I will be free of this kind of *recrimination*." Dee had stood up, drawn her shawl around her shoulders and walked around her desk. The afternoon sun was at her back. The rays caught the highlights in her long brown hair. She had felt fortified by the warmth and knew that Taurus, because he was now looking directly into the sun, was at a disadvantage.

"You don't get it do you?" Taurus said, his eyes narrowing.

50

"All your work is in commie countries. This is America."

"Yes it is, and you can now leave my office," Dee had said stonily and sniffed the way she remembered her grandmother did when she was taking the high moral ground in a conversation with Dee's father about the propriety of drinking with his army mates on Anzac Day. She had stared unblinkingly at Taurus.

"I'll leave when I'm done. You're the sort who would have enjoyed the McCarthy era, because . . ."

Dee had broken in. "Your analysis of my motives is duly noted," she had said in a voice that even surprised her for its almost baritone resonance. This exchange had taken place during office hours and Dee's students could easily be coming from class in a few minutes. As Taurus further advanced into her office, Dee had picked up her phone, ready to call Campus Security. At just that moment, Frank O'Meara, a junior in her class on Global Perspectives on Indigenous Women, had darted in around the angry professor. Frank was slightly built, softly spoken, and stuttered when put on the spot in class. From his written work, Dee knew he was a serious student, interested in comparative religions and well-versed in feminist theory. Frank had stood between the two.

"O – O – Office hours?" he had asked and pointed at the notice on her door.

"Yes Frank. Come in. Professor Taurus was just leaving."

Hasn't anyone sued this place? Dee thought for the umpteenth time. Maybe there had been lawsuits and she had not yet learned of them. She doubted that her source for such information would be the Dean; perhaps his staff would talk to her about it. There was Mary Kane, the Dean's secretary, who predated his elevation to the Dean's Office, and would no doubt be there long after he had moved up or returned to his department. She kept order where order was resisted and kept the peace when conflict loomed. Faculty might profess their faith in faculty governance, strut and fret on the stage of scholarship, talk about tenure and freedom of ideas, but Dee knew that, like in many other institutions, the staff provided the real continuity.

Cultures change slowly. Can policy drive such change?
Do old soldiers ever change?

Dee looked at the doodles she'd drawn on the back of a flier for an upcoming speaker in Religious Studies – Marian Cults Through the Ages. *Might be interesting.* She noted the date, slipped the paper into her planner, and reached for her heavy wool shawl. In a hopeful moment she had put her plaid cape away with her heavy winter clothes and was experimenting with other combinations of lighter jackets and warm wraps to keep out the chill that was still in the air. *Enough for now*, she thought. *Time to go home to that novel.* As a reflex she checked her voice mail. At 5:30 pm Mary J had left a message: "I'm in the chapel. I'll be there till six." Dee threw her shawl around her shoulders, flipped her hair free of its embrace, and hurried to Murphy Chapel, a clean, square-cut house of worship where daily Mass and Masses for Orientation, Commencement, and other special occasions were held. Dee glanced at the well-tended flowerbeds which edged the gravel meeting area outside the church. The first spring bulbs were peeking through. She guessed that by Commencement, the whole area would be ablaze with color. She knew this was a favorite place for weddings. College graduates married in Murphy Chapel felt their unions especially blessed and were anxious to have the priests – who had taught and mentored them during their student years – christen their children. In times of trouble, sickness, and death, family members also turned to these same priests for solace. When the sun was at a certain angle, the gold cross on the spire of the chapel glowed warmly against the green hillside. A blessed site, to be sure.

Dee had been paying close attention to the intense religiosity of the St. Jude's community as the holy days of Easter approached. Each day, students, members of faculty and staff came to pray, to recite the Stations of the Cross, confess and take communion. Dee liked Palm Sunday for its association with peace rallies in Sydney. She was less sure about what would go on during Easter week but was looking forward to the quiet time and the length of the break from Thursday to the following Tuesday.

April 13: Maundy Thursday

April 14: Good Friday of the Lord's Passion

April 15: Holy Saturday, Easter Vigil

April 16: Easter Sunday, Resurrection of the Lord

April 17: Easter Tuesday

N.B. Dating based on old lunar calendar
- the first Sunday after the first full moon after
the Spring Equinox, formerly the "pregnant" phase
of Eostre - Easter - estrus.
Not called "Easter" until the late Middle Ages.

The chapel was poorly lit. Traces of stale incense from the Mass lingered in the air. Dee waited for her eyes to adjust and when she finally saw Mary J kneeling in a pew, quietly slid in beside her. Mary J took her hand. "Let's go to the little chapel. I need to talk to you."

They walked in silence past the confessional and down wide wooden stairs into the smaller, more intimate setting of the little chapel. Dee could still hear Bach playing above them in the Murphy Chapel. The organ, a gift from an alumnus from the 1920s, attracted the attention of organists, composers, and recording studios from many parts of the globe as well as from those seeking repose, solitude, reflection, or the fine acoustics of the chapel.

"Did Bill O'Vafer say anything about Amy's report from last year?" Mary J asked rather tersely. Amy Nakamura, a minority hire in the Religious Studies Department, had been sure that if she just reported the findings from her extensive interviews, focus groups and questionnaires, the message would be obvious: students were abusing alcohol and the situation was not being taken seriously. Student respondents to her survey had reported they drank to oblivion; they drank with the priests; they drank at parties that turned into orgies at the Field House; and they drank to be accepted by their peers. On these nights of sexual license, the boys were "just being boys" as far as the St. Jude's community was concerned. Amy had interviewed a number of alumni and uncovered a St. Jude's tradition. In pre-coed days, women were bussed in from St. Mary's, the sister college, in nearby Littleburg. The male students would line up, assess the potential of the women being delivered to the door, make their choices and, in the hope of scoring that night, ply the young women of St. Mary's with all manner of liquor. When it happened, the sex was nasty, brutish, and short. No need to acknowledge the woman the next day; she was safely back with the little sisters. All this Dee had gleaned from the report and the stories students had told her.

Mary J filled Dee in on more details. "Amy's report was like dynamite. At the spring faculty meeting last year, when she said that the tradition at St. Jude's of close-to-anonymous sex was ongoing, a lot of people were upset. They said, 'Not our students. They wouldn't do that.' Next, at their April meeting, the Board of Trustees voted down Amy's tenure case. This was after the department and the college tenure committee had endorsed her."

"Did they give reasons?

"Ah-huh. They said that Amy Nakamura was not sufficiently well published in peer-reviewed journals and that she wrote for journals of Asian Studies and that much of her work was in Japanese. Only Father Tempus has any knowledge of that language and I can't see him reading about psychoanalytical theory and the religious symbolism of Japanese women's dreams. Can you, Dee?"

"Oh, Tempus, Tempura. Time and food. I love it," Dee laughed and adjusted her shawl. It was quite cold in the chapel. Mary J had folded her coat on the pew. She didn't seem to feel the cold as much as Dee.

"I liked Amy," Mary J continued, ignoring Dee's wordplay. "She had a different take on things, growing up as second-generation Japanese in Seattle. I didn't always get all her theories, but what I did get is that it's easier to say women are lying than believe that abuse is widespread on campus, or elsewhere for that matter. But, there was some justice at the end. St. Jude's denied her tenure and then she landed a position at Yale. I was so happy for her."

Check Amy's Ph.D.; Reread Jeffrey Masson on the suppression of Freud's seduction theory in the 1890s - women's hysteria is not, as he had originally proposed, the result of seduction (today read sexual assault) but the girl's fantasy; see Shulamith Firestone's suggested rationale for the reversal - Freud was more palatable than feminism in the 19th century. And now?
Is sexual assault still understood as fantasy?
Check Juliet Mitchell's feminist critique of Freud.

Dee began to reconstruct for Mary J the faculty discussion that had occurred the week before. "Yes, Amy's report came up, but only as far as the minutes were concerned. Prof. O'Vafer was pretty insistent that he not be on record as endorsing any causal link between alcohol and violence. I think he was alluding to allegations that there have been rapes of women students at St. Jude's."

"Well, there have been, and Amy knew about them and so did Jessie. I think Jessie knew a lot more."

"The woman who died, who had my office?"

"Yes. Jessie Seneca."

That's better, Dee thought. Mary J had finally volunteered her full name. Of course Dee already knew the name because she had checked in the old catalogues and found the entry for Jessie K. Seneca, Ph.D., 1989, Santa Cruz, History of Consciousness Program. Jessie had taught classes which Religious Studies had variously cross-listed with Psychology and Art. "So tell me more," Dee said.

"I only know what I heard from Bill O'Vafer's secretary," Mary J said. "He is in big trouble. And he has a thing for younger women, really young women." There it was again, Mary J had shifted her conversation away from Jessie and Room 606. Dee let Mary J circle the issue a little longer. She was obviously upset and having trouble getting to the point. Dee probed, "He married one of his students, didn't he?"

"Yes he did, and he hangs out with the students at Mick's Sports Bar, especially the Friday Happy Hour. They think it is cool to go drinking with a professor and trash women."

Enough evasion, Dee thought. "So Mary J, what's the matter? Why did you want me to meet you tonight?" Dee realized her impatience was bubbling up, but Mary appeared not to notice. She was ready to talk.

"Well, this was last week. Bill O'Vafer was shouting that the minutes of some meeting had to be corrected and I walked in on him. He was furious and stomped into his office. His secretary was close to tears, so I asked her what was up. She was just about to go to lunch. We walked up together, and she told me she was scared. He'd told her to go into Amy's files and change the data. But she wasn't sure how to do that and, more importantly, she wasn't sure she should do a thing like that. So she asked me. I told her, 'Don't do it.' Then, today, the Business Manager, you know Mr. C. V. Negotium, called me in and said there were problems with my performance review. I think he's looking for a reason to get rid of me."

"Oh yes, I know old Negotium," Dee said, thinking back to her encounter with him. She half turned to look more closely at Mary J, who was holding her rosary beads loosely in her lap. Dee was ready to be somewhere warm. Still she owed it to her friend to listen and be supportive. Dee knew all too well how difficult it was to make a life while raising children, and Mary J had six. The St. Jude's Business Manager could spoil her daughter's chances of getting into a topflight law school. Little Mary needed to get into St. Jude's. "Why do you think he is out to get you?" Dee asked.

"Because there is a lot more to what Amy did. I went into those files."

"After you told O'Vafer's secretary not to?" Dee shifted in the pew and faced Mary J. Out of the corner of her eye, fleetingly she saw a black robed figure sweeping up the stairs to the Murphy Chapel. She was about to mention it but realized Mary J was intent on answering her question.

"Yes, I did. But I know stuff about Virginia and up till now it has kept me safe."

"Is she involved?"

"Oh, believe it. She's in knee deep. Trust me, I know how hard it is for her. She has been head of the department for the past five years and she makes it clear where we stand."

Dee had seen the secretaries stiffen when Virginia came into the office. They dreaded what would be on the list for the day – usually a combination of items to be located, meetings, memos, mostly desk-bound tasks. And for her part, Virginia had little sympathy with any mumbling that her lists interfered with the secretarial lunch hour. She considered these "briefings" to be gossip. Mary J, whose career at St. Jude's predated Virginia's role as departmental head, seemed to enjoy special privileges and took full advantage of whatever the edge was she had over her boss. Her lunch times were her own. "You know I only saw Virginia rattled once," Mary J said. "I heard her on the phone. She was sobbing, begging, 'No, I can't do it. Please don't ask me. It's too much.' She shut her door and flattened herself against the wall so she was out of my line of vision, but I could still hear her. 'But I have a daughter. I have to protect her. I want her to have more than I had.'"

Dee had not thought of Virginia as a mother who would protect her child with ferocity, or a person who regretted any of her decisions. "Did you tell the other secretaries?" Dee asked.

"I keep my own counsel."

"I've noticed," Dee smiled, "but now that we're talking about Virginia, I could do with some help in figuring out how to deal with her. She is never rude to me, or anything like that, just removed, never forthcoming. You know what I mean?"

"Well you can be pretty tight-lipped yourself when it comes to some things," Mary J said.

Dee smiled. "I do want to tell you about Bruce, but I don't want to blur the lines between work and home too much." She sat back in the pew, shuddered, and suddenly realizing how hard maintaining this balance was and how tired she was.

"I think we're past that." Mary J chuckled. "We're both in a 'spot of bother' as you Aussies would say, but not half as bad as the spot Virginia is in."

The organ music in the chapel above them had changed to an experimental piece, more discordant and disturbing than the Bach.

Mary J paused to listen, but then added, "Virginia was married in the chapel."

"I don't think I've ever seen her husband." Dee's curiosity temporarily took her mind off the cold.

"Well, he was part of her life plan. Probably on a list somewhere there was an entry that said, find a well-spoken, well-connected husband. But her life hasn't quite matched the plan. They hadn't been married long. I think Mandy was about six months old when he stopped coming to functions at work and became more and more withdrawn. All he did was write."

"What sort of writing?"

"I suppose it was his stories. He was a great storyteller. He could keep the young kids spellbound for hours on end. He made up these fantasy worlds with amazing, complicated rules. They were really detailed and there was all this religious symbolism. Good and evil, demons and snakes, ethereal and disfigured bodies, and they all fitted into the way he structured these marvelous make-believe places."

"And Virginia was attracted to the order of these worlds?"

"Oh yes. Can't you just see them with their lists?" Mary J laughed.

"So what happened?"

"It was gradual, but his fantasy worlds took up more and more of his time. He'd shut himself in their basement for days on end, wouldn't eat properly, slept at odd hours, and all the time he was writing and drawing on large pieces of craft paper that he'd pasted on the walls."

"How did Virginia cope?"

"It could all be managed. Maybe she wrote a new list. She didn't talk about it much, but I knew she was worried about her daughter. She kept ordering medical journals on inter-library loan. She did talk with Jessie a few times. Did you know that Jessie had some training in clinical psychology?"

"Yes, I know. I looked up her publications and she knew the psychoanalytical literature pretty well, I'd say."

"She had that in common with Amy," Mary J said. "They used

the same kind of shorthand in their papers. Not that I read much of them. I tried but they were dense."

"So what happened with Virginia's husband?"

"His family seemed to understand and made sure he had the best doctors, but Jessie had figured it out – she was the one who recognized the symptoms of schizophrenia."

"Did it run in the family? Is that why his folks weren't surprised?"

"Guess so," Mary J shrugged.

"And what about Mandy, her daughter?"

"Virginia watches her like a hawk."

"And she didn't have any more children?"

"Her husband is like her second child now. He hates the drugs and once fooled everyone into believing that he was taking them, but he had stopped. He told Jessie he could still hear the voices, muffled, but still there. He resented not being able to hear everything they were saying. They were his inspiration because they spoke the truth."

"So that's why he doesn't work?"

"Yes. He can't hold down a regular job. His parents help with the mortgage on that stuffy nineteenth-century brick colonial they bought."

"Have you seen his paintings?" Dee asked.

"No, but Jessie did. She got on quite well with him, just entered into his world as if it were real, the voices, and all the conspiracies they told him about. She just said, 'Okay.' Apparently his paintings are amazing. 'Intricate apocalyptic visions' Jessie called them."

"Well that makes sense of why Virginia wanted her daughter to have a life different from hers, but what was the threat? Was someone going public with the family history of schizophrenia?" Dee was now very interested.

"Don't know. Really I don't, but the question of a second child has something to do with it." Mary J was closing down now. "Okay, Dee, your turn."

"I really don't want to burden you with all this," Dee began, shifting slightly in the hard wooden pew. "Doesn't the cold here get into your bones?"

"I guess I'm used to it." Mary J wrapped her coat around Dee. "It's too early to shed your heavy coat just yet, you know. Take your cue from us natives. But look Dee, I know you got a letter from Australia which really upset you and I also know you've been a bit jumpy lately. So, what's up and can I help? Lord knows you've helped me through a lot of things lately," Mary J reassured Dee.

"Well it's about Bruce. Seems it's always about men, right? But Bruce is different, or at least I thought he was." Dee snuggled into Mary J's thick wool coat, one of her great recent bargains. It smelled of lavender. "Okay, I guess we all say that. It hasn't always been easy – we do fight – kids, that kind of stuff. I don't let go all that easily you know. I try, but angry words hurt."

Mary J nodded. She'd been there.

"He was going to join me here. I was prepared to try again, see if we could work it out, but then he changed his mind. I have been agonizing over what I did wrong and lying awake rerunning scenes from our marriage, having bizarre dreams filled with recriminations. I mean it was his idea to have another go at our relationship and then he cooled towards the idea, said he was going to 'move on.' Turns out Cheryl was moving in."

"Cheryl?" Mary J asked, although she knew what was coming. She reached out and held Dee's hand tightly. The warmth of her grip was reassuring and Dee squeezed Mary J's hand.

"Cheryl is the woman who worked as his research assistant a number of summers ago, a year or so before we were divorced. She used to drive him mad, and me right along with him. She was so unfocused, so shallow, and there was nothing about her I could relate to. He'd say, 'I'm so glad I have you in my life Dee, imagine living with someone who doesn't read or even care about the world beyond her safe little corner.' It was clear to me he was referring to Cheryl. But I didn't see the danger. Turns out he was finding out what it would be like and, guess what? He liked it well enough to stay. Now I wonder what Bruce and I ever talked about or had in common."

"Well, it's his loss," Mary J declared. "But what are you doing about this insomnia of yours?"

"I'm avoiding taking any medication and I'm redefining it as *wakefulness*. Maybe I'm in denial, but mostly I'm not tired."

"Not tired but tortured," Mary J said.

"Oh, is it that obvious?" Dee asked. She hated the compromises required of professional women. She knew well that any sign that she was preoccupied with her love life could be read as a weakness, but she also knew that by always appearing to be totally focused on work, she was living a lie that made life harder for other women whose personal lives unavoidably intruded into their workplaces. She felt safe with Mary J and was grateful her friend had asked. She needed to talk.

"I'm paying attention to the dreams. My subconscious knew that something was wrong. His letters were businesslike. He wasn't responding to my reflections about who we'd been or might be. Then I got the letter about Cheryl. I just don't get it. And *he* called me 'flighty.'" Dee paused, straightened up and looked directly at Mary J. "And now can we get back to Amy and Jessie?"

"Not too long. I need to get home and Dee, you're cold. Go home, have a hot bath, sleep."

"Okay, you're right and, by the way, I love this coat." Dee put her hands up the sleeves of Mary J's coat and hugged it to her body. "But before I go, tell me what you think is going on."

"What I'm guessing, well, actually I'm pretty sure about, is that Amy had access to Jessie Seneca's files. She uses initials for her informants and one is 'JS.'" Mary J had lowered her voice to a whisper, "Dee, there is some really bad stuff going on here and I'm sure that O'Vafer and his students are in the thick of it."

"Who else is involved? Who knows you've been into the files?"

"Well it won't take Virginia long to figure out and I think somehow Father Sordes in Sociology is caught up in this mess."

Conspiracy? How deep? How many?

April 27, 1995: feast day of St. Zita: patroness of domestic workers - her credo - a servant is not holy if she is not busy.

5

ALUMNI WEEKEND
April 1995

It was Alumni Weekend and St. Jude's fairly sparkled in the late April sun. The air was full of the scent of magnolias. Giant pots of purple trailing geraniums alternated with pots of pale pink azaleas along the divided road that swept from the ornate wrought iron gates to Coyle Hall and on towards the library. The banks rising behind the library to the Convention Center were ablaze with forsythia, some pruned, but mostly wild and sprawling over awkward sections between steps and retaining walls. The gardeners had been busy for weeks with mulching, mass plantings, shrubs and annuals, and arranging scores of potted plants. The cynicism with which students greeted the general cleanup before special weekends like this would undoubtedly evaporate after they graduated. The fine displays would validate their sense of worth as alums. The notice in the *Daily Dispatches*, to beware of lighting matches near the highly combustible, newly mulched, acrid-smelling garden beds, was expected by faculty used to seeing it each April and appreciated by some students who saw the bizarre in the mundane message.

Dee sat, looking out on the car park of St. Jude's, in her now – after Herculean cleaning efforts – almost wholesome-smelling kitchen, to index her first four months of field notes on St. Jude's. She was working on the annotations of her sketch map of the tiered grounds and stone buildings. The campus looked like a giant cross rising through a number of levels.

Level one: The Sports Center, Field House and Sports Field, top of the hill

Level two: Dorms, Bookstore and Convention Center and visitor parking

Level three: Dining Hall and Quad

Level four: Chapel, Coyle Hall, library, selective parking and main entrance

Level five: General parking.

Dee flipped back through her notes looking for further details for the map. The doodles had taken over a couple of pages – more of those triangles and circles, but they were growing more and more complex, quite unlike any kinship system she knew. The lines of descent connecting the generation of male triangles and female circles were not vertical. They careened all over the page. The equals symbol, used to denote marriage, joined all manner of individual and clustered triangles and circles. Dee turned down the corner of the page and looked up.

She could see small groups of middle-aged men making their way up to the Sports Center. They were probably going to see the new stadium, a facility Dee had decided was definitely a male domain. Dee had tried to use the swimming pool over Spring Break but found that the women's locker room was closed. To her chagrin, she learned this was the rule, not an exception for repairs or cleaning.

"Saves on operating costs," the swim coach said. "No call for the girls' locker room to be open."

"Well I'm calling for it to be open," Dee retorted.

"When you girls bring in money like the men's team do, then I'll listen."

Dee had spoken with Dean Simean, who had brushed off her concerns with a gruff "Sure he's out of step, but his teams win, and he is O'Malley's son. You know, *the* Thomas O'Malley III, class of '38, who endowed the new indoor basketball stadium in the Sports Center."

"Okay, if I'm so invisible to him, I'll use the men's locker rooms."

"Why does it always have to come down to discrimination and gender with you?" the Dean asked through a weak smile.

"Because that is where I live and work," Dee said. "I'm going to swim."

Before she reached the second level, the swim coach, looking somewhat flushed, had headed her off.

"Will you be swimming today?" he asked. *Wow! The Dean must have said something straight away,* Dee thought. *The boys can really move quickly when they want to.* "The steam room takes a while to heat up," the coach continued. "Make up your mind."

She swam every day, and every day this large, awkward man watched. His expression was set as if against a bitter wind. Above his bench where he sat watching Dee swim, the lap timer counted the minutes. The sign below the clock read: "The only way to swim fast, is swim fast."

Dee liked to walk up to the Sports Center in the early morning and watch the city of Resolve and St. Jude's come to life. The nineteenth-century foundations of the gray stone buildings of the college were dug deep into the hill where Native Americans had once guarded a sacred spring. The Jesuit community had imposed itself on that earlier Algonquin sacred site. From high on the highest of the seven hills, close to the powerful forces in the sky-world, holy men of both religious traditions had oversight of all below and, fortified against attack from outsiders, could assume a superiority of spirit. St. Jude's looked down on the scramble of houses, malls, parks, and schools of the town. The Algonquin, looking down from this same site, had seen the woodlands, waterways and plentiful game.

> *New World stratagem: Colonizer builds church on desecrated "pagan" site; more layers to excavate.*

Dee traced the line of the tall black wrought-iron boundary fence that encircled St. Jude's. In its early days as Resolve College, in spite of its physical aloofness, the college had been part of the local community. But, in the process of trying to achieve its dream of becoming known as the premier liberal arts college of the northeast, the institution had walled itself off from the increasingly diverse population of Resolve that looked up at the college but rarely visited.

> *Boundary maintenance and issues of identity: To keep out possible infidel invasions or to corral the faithful?*

64

Connecticut one of original 13 states that broke from England, Puritan, profoundly anti-immigrant.

1840s Irish Potato Famine, Irish immigrants marginalized, called "Slaves of Rome", Pope denounced Freemasons, formed their own fraternal organizations.

1880s immigrants from Romanov and Hapsburg Empires, work on farms and factories; Eastern Rite Catholics, resent imposed Latinization.

N.B. President Firmitas has family links to both Eastern and Western Rite communities: life history as a microcosm?

Each new wave of migration to this old manufacturing town had brought new challenges for a college dedicated to contributing to the common good. From its origins as a solid Irish Catholic town, like so many others in Connecticut and Massachusetts, the good citizens of Resolve were now confronted with different Catholic traditions, and more recently, a Muslim presence. St. Jude's favored a policy of tolerance about the beliefs of others. The school proudly showcased diversity in its publications. How the dominant Irish Catholic culture of the college accommodated "others" in Resolve and in their midst was quite another matter. There was little contact between the Ukrainian Orthodox Church and the well-established places of worship of the Irish Catholics. Spanish was now the *lingua franca* of the neighborhoods adjacent to the college, but these new arrivals had little in common with the wealthy Hispanic students who contributed to diversity at St. Jude's.

On Alumni Weekends, Resolve was a welcoming community; the three local motels and the best restaurants were booked solid. In season, Resolvites and fans gathered to watch the Apostles – the St. Jude's home team – play others in their division. It was a matter of some acrimonious debate that President Firmitas, so popular with alumni in so many ways, resisted all moves for the college to become a Division One school. His vision for St. Jude's was to promote academics over athletics, but this had not translated into any stinginess about the playing fields. They were lovingly maintained and continued to serve as a splendid site for Commencement ceremonies. As long as the weather cooperated, some eight thousand could be accommodated within the area: the dignitaries on a small dais, the faculty and graduating students on folding chairs, and the parents, friends and others in the stands.

Dee watched as one of the groups of middle-aged men, now walking back from the Sports Center, was joined by a younger woman. She seemed to be related to them. Dee folded her sketch map, grabbed a new notebook, and headed down to Coyle Hall. The group was standing on the landing halfway down the steps. "One of the original buildings," one man was saying to the young woman. "Named after your grandfather, the Hon. James Coyle. In those days it was part of the Jesuit residence." He looked across to the library that was on a scale befitting Harvard, save for the religious statuary of uneven artistry that kept vigil over the place. Dee had already sketched the modernistic waterfall flanked by banks of forsythia on one side and the sixty stone steps that led to the glass doors of the library on the other. It reminded her of the water feature outside the High Court in Canberra but this was no simple series of cascades. The source was an elaborate fountain that dominated the first landing of the steps. There, the baby Jesus, wearing a crown of thorns, lay in a crèche: the innocence of the birth of the Christ child and the deadly treachery of the betrayal of the Savior encapsulated in one image. The water gushed forth from the rock base. *Moses striking the stone?* Dee wondered. *What would the original owners of this site make of this artificial water feature imposed on their sacred spring?*

"Another generous bequest," said James Coyle II, indicating the fountain."Generations of alumni have made this college what it is today. Your uncle and I hope you will follow in that tradition, Jamie."

Dee saw the young woman referred to as Jamie grimace slightly at these remarks as she looked around. In addition to this admittedly powerful image in front of the library, the college grounds were littered with statues of a most eclectic nature. There were exquisite bronze castings, pedestrian pieces celebrating individuals and occasions of local importance, and the obligatory blue concrete grotto for the Virgin Mary. Dee had logged them on her map and tried studying the iconography of the various sites, but found that this yielded few insights. Rather, she concluded, the unifying factor for this mixed bag of metal, painted plaster and rock seemed to be that those bestowing the objects wished to have their names on a plaque in the college grounds.

The Coyle alums were now headed to the car park where each space bore a name: Firmitas, Simean, Negotium, Coyle. *So that last space is for an actual person.* Dee had often been tempted to park there but knew she'd incur a fine from the ever-vigilant campus police. This weekend parking regulations had been relaxed, but on all other occasions visitors to St. Jude's were vetted. Their only public access was by a road that passed through the ornate arch bearing the college motto, *Fiat Certum,* and the college shield with its depiction of St. Jude and his axe, a reference to the price he had paid for his faith. From there, the road divided and traffic was funneled past a sentry box where armed guards recorded names and the purpose of the visit, and checked license plates. Today all the gates were open and alums were enjoying the unaccustomed luxury of driving from one level to the next.

Dee walked over to the blue and white striped marquee set up on the lawn outside Coyle Hall. Jamie Coyle, wearing tailored slacks, a fine white over-shirt and a little straw peaked visor, was helping herself to a cup of the institutional pink punch and a chocolate chip cookie. Dee moved towards her. "I couldn't help overhearing your father and uncle," Dee said. "It must be quite a responsibility to be the third generation of Coyles at St. Jude's."

"You got that right. Coyle this and Coyle that. Recoil, that's what I do. I'm grateful for the education, don't get me wrong, but it was a hell of a constraint too. I was monitored all the time – even the courses I took, " Jamie replied.

"And if you defied them?" Dee asked, curious about the fact that American college-age students lived in these states of extended dependency into their early twenties.

"Well I did defy them, but in little ways. They were paying the tuition, room and board. I'm not stupid. I knew that with an education from St. Jude's I could get into the grad schools on my list." Jamie looked intently at Dee. "Are you the new professor in Religious Studies?"

"That's me."

"Good. I hoped I'd see you. I heard my father talking about how some of the alumni were upset about your courses and I figured I should meet you."

"I heard rumors too, but nothing to my face."

"The rumor mill is pretty active here, but then there are plenty of things that just don't make sense and trying to get an answer from Jebbies – that's what we call the Jesuits – is like pulling teeth."

"'Listen to the silences,' my old professor in grad school used to say. Find out what people don't want to talk about." Having said this, Dee took out her notebook. "Mind if I make a note on the Coyle lineage? Looks like it's James all the way down."

Jamie nodded, reached for another cookie, then pulled back. "No, damn it. I don't want any more of these cookies. They were comfort food for four years. Enough. Want to walk?"

"Sure. I've been working on a map of the college and there are some things I need to check out." Dee unfolded her sketch map.

Jamie looked with interest and said, "I used to be an official Apostle guide here. I took prospective students and their parents on the campus tour. We were drilled on what to say, but I've always wanted to do the Jamie Coyle version. Let me take you on a tour of the St. Jude's I know."

Rites of Passage, Arnold Van Gennep: separation, transition, incorporation, the rites renew energy of the society. Orientation and Commencement = rites of passage for these 20-year-olds.

"Great." Dee folded her notebook so she could write on the sketch map as they talked. Jamie pointed. "Let's walk up to the dining hall first. Its proper name is Tuck Hall, but can you imagine the jokes about that? And whatever possessed the Tuck family to endow the building?"

"In Australia we call food 'tucker.' It's British slang actually I think," Dee volunteered.

"The 'Tuck Hall' sign just disappeared one day. Well that was after the maintenance crews had cleaned off the caricatures of jovial Friar Tuck and scrawled messages suggesting one might 'tuck off' and 'get tucked.'"

Dee and Jamie entered through the heavy swing doors and walked to the back corner of the long rectangular room. "This is where I learned how deep the contempt for 'others' runs at St. Jude's," Jamie said. "We're supposed to be 'In the service of others,' but you should see this place when it is full." With a sweep of her hand she indicated the tables near the back, far from the windows onto the quad. "This is where the African American students would sit. If you feel carefully along the under ledge of the tables you can still make out the graffiti with the 'n' word cut into the wood." Dee had already noted the declining enrollments of African Americans, now offset by increasing numbers of Asian Americans and Hispanics. As a result, the 10-per-cent minorities target remained constant.

Jamie passed Dee several dingy brown plastic trays. "Here, look at these. As soon as they replace them, they're defaced again." Dee read the sexist, racist and homophobic inscriptions.

"Oh, these are intimidating."

"That's only the half of it. When I was here, the wait staff were called names, you know the classic Spick, Wop, and Slant-Eye epithets. One guy, who worked the salad bar, I think he was gay. He was called 'old fruit' to his face. It was a jungle. Faculty never ate here. The Jebbies don't eat here. It's real *Lord of the Flies* territory." Jamie was standing as if in line for dessert. "The guys would be scarfing burgers and the women would be picking at salads. And here, the women lined up for frozen yogurt, and these big hulking guys would rate their bodies. Anorexia and bulimia, that's what a lot of women were majoring in while I was here."

"Not only the students," Dee mused. "Do you think this is just part of being young and a woman, or is there something else going on?"

"The women here would kinda shrink, take up the least amount of space possible. Good girls don't want to call attention to

69

themselves," Jamie said, pushing her curly hair back under her visor. "Now don't get me wrong. There are some strong women here, but it's all inside the lines, and they are way too tough on themselves. Like Virginia and all her lists, how to study, teach, live. She was fond of telling us we needed order in our lives. We called her Ginny Frost. A good use for all those years of Latin," Jamie laughed.

Who else has nicknames?

Dee was intrigued but a little uncomfortable discussing another faculty member with an alumna, but she didn't want to interrupt such a good storyteller. Jamie looked straight at Dee. "Don't worry. I won't tell," she reassured Dee. "I know how to keep secrets, even some I'd rather not know." For a minute Dee thought that Jamie was about to cry, but she turned and did a comic impersonation of Virginia and her unmistakable crabwalk on the steps. "You know why she walks like that? Broke her ankle. Being on crutches is no joke at this place. I think she took up exercise because she was worried she might put on weight like women do after they have children."

"And did she?" Dee asked.

"A bit and I liked her look then, it softened her a bit. But it didn't last long. She would run every day. But she tripped on an uneven pavement and crashed down on her ankle. Notice how she always wears flat shoes?"

Dee guessed Virginia was around 120 pounds. If that was her target weight, she must be starving herself because she was at least 5 feet 10 inches. Some would have called her gaunt in her pencil-slim skirts and well-tailored jackets, but that was her look. Sensible shoes and a sensible haircut were her standards. She was blessed with a flawless complexion and thus her disdain for any adornments, jewelry, makeup, or bright colors, passed without comment.

Dee was pleased when Jamie led the way out of the Dining Hall onto the quad. She'd seen students passing through this well-tended space, but had never seen any large gatherings. To Dee, with her history of campus protests, it seemed a perfect location for a rally.

"Where do people assemble if they want to stage a protest?"

"Outside the library, I think. That waterfall is pretty inviting, green on St. Paddy's Day, detergent bubbles at Commencement, a cool spot to soak one's feet on hot days, but demonstrations? No. There hasn't been much unrest since the moratoriums. Then St. Jude's was in the thick of it. Registering conscientious objectors, offering safe haven, the best of the Jesuit tradition."

Swords to plowshares, Isaiah 2:4; Catonsville Nine: Daniel Berrigan SJ and his brother Phil Berrigan (Society of St. Joseph) burn draft cards, throw blood/paint on documents; accomplice Mary Moylan, nurse in Uganda 1959-65, testifies she is enraged by "accidental bombing" in Uganda and "justifiable homicide" ruling in police violence at home. Conclusion - a black man can't get justice at home or abroad. Burning draft files celebrates life, not death; Pax Christi and Jonah House. Which alumni were involved? With what repercussions?

Jamie glanced at Dee's earlier note. "You want to know if there are other nicknames? It was a game we played, finding the most perfect parody – even the name of the college. I suppose St. Jude and his lost causes could be fun to think about, but we thought the college would be better named 'St. Judas.' You know, Jude/Judas, mirror images, good and evil. Why was Judas the only disciple with nothing named after him? And what if he wasn't all bad, but was playing a kind of political game? You know, testing the strength of the populace, playing devil's advocate. Maybe Judas thought they would rise up and Jesus would be saved. Anyway, that's what comes of reading the Gnostics. You begin to get ideas."

Caution: Literate women at work.

"You got that right." Jamie glanced at Dee's note about literate women and laughed. She skipped up the steps to the coed dormitories at the next level. Jamie was slightly built and light on her feet. *A gymnast?* Dee wondered. They paused and looked back towards the town. "The college used to be called Resolve College, after the town but, during the Depression, the town went broke and so did the college. Then, my grandfather, the Hon. Coyle, of Coyle Hall, came to the rescue."

"And they named the building after him?"

"Well, the building was already there. He paid for the repairs on it and underwrote a series of loans that allowed the college to get out of debt."

"That was when it was renamed. Right?" Dee asked.

"Yes, and it was his suggestion that it be named for St. Jude."

"I wondered about that. It's not really a Jesuit name, but St. Jude was very popular in the late 1920s, I seem to remember."

"Oh, so you've been reading up on us have you?"

"Well, enough to know that during the Depression, many found solace in their devotion to St. Jude, and that his story was seen as hope that ordinary people could triumph over seemingly impossible odds."

"I think that's partly what my grandfather wanted to celebrate. He was the son of poor immigrants and he rose to be a Federal Court judge. His personal motto was 'Get the best possible education.' His mother was totally unschooled, but very religious. That woman would have been happy with the mystics, I'd say. It was her vision that inspired the fountain. She saw the crown of thorns on the baby Jesus in a dream. We heard the story when we were growing up, about how she'd go into these like trances and when she woke, she'd be unsettled and pray a lot for guidance. St. Jude was one of her favorites. She prayed to him that her son would prosper, not be cut down in his prime."

"So he wasn't a lost cause at all," Dee said as they walked along the path to the main entrance of the newest dorm. Later she wrote.

St. Jude; Saint of Hopeless Causes; National Shrine of St. Jude established in the Church of Our Lady of Guadalupe, Chicago, 1929.

N.B. Role of women's devotion in maintaining the shrine.

"St. Jude, glorious Apostle, faithful servant and friend of Jesus, the name of the traitor has caused you to be

forgotten by many, but the true Church invokes you universally as the Patron of things despaired of; pray for me, that finally I may receive the consolations and the succor of Heaven in all my necessities, tribulations, and sufferings, particularly St. Jude's College, and that I may bless God with the Elect throughout Eternity. Amen."

Dee and Jamie crossed the road that divided Dormitory Row. "What is that god-awful smell?" Dee coughed as she stepped around one of the grates on the path.

"Euwww, smells like sulfur," Jamie said. "There is a whole underground network of pipes and tunnels under this place, a regular catacomb. Those grates go down to the kitchens and the infirmary, I think."

"Nice combination," Dee shuddered slightly. "And while we're talking about weird stuff, did you ever see a huge ginger cat when you were here?"

"We called it Feles," Jamie laughed and pawed at the air.

Maybe acting, Dee thought. "Oh, cat," she said aloud. "Another of your learned Latin puns?"

"Ah-ha! Yes, but it also means like a thief. Feles hung around the kitchens sometimes," Jamie volunteered.

"Who owns it?" Dee asked.

"You got me on that. It used to appear at the strangest times and then disappear for long periods. It has never been that friendly. Even after it has left, you can smell a whiff of something dark and dense. Kind of like the smell in the chapel vestry. Maybe it lives there."

"I thought it might live down in the basement with Campus Security and Chuck Negotium." Dee watched out of the corner of her eye to see if Jamie would respond to this notion.

"Ha ha! Old Negotium. He knows the score, that's for sure. I've had one or two run-ins with him. Have you seen that obnoxious plaque thing he has on his desk? 'The absence of doubt makes you stronger.' Ha!" Jamie said with just the right degree of arrogance to evoke Negotium in his office. "The absence of doubt is more like rampant abuse of power. That man is soooo costly. And beware, he *is* dangerous. Maybe the cat is his familiar, not like for a sorcerer, but you know the servant of the Inquisition. And what is with those burgundy blazers he wears with the gold buttons?"

"I take it you don't like him," Dee said.

"That would be putting it mildly," Jamie said. "Have you seen the way he treats his workers and the general staff? Not to mention his contempt for women students – or, as he calls us, coeds."

"You know Mary J, in Virginia's office, was in his sights the other day," Dee replied.

"Doesn't surprise me. She helped me a lot," Jamie said. "And she knows the score around here too. Imagine Mary J with a Ph.D. I'd sign up for her courses. I hope her daughter gets in. I told her I'd write a supporting letter for Admissions. I figure the Coyle name should be worth something."

Jamie and Dee continued to walk down the dorm pathway. "Here we are. This one, Calley Hall, was dedicated to a substance-free dorm the year I left. My cousin Cissy lives in this one. Did you hear about the report by Amy Nakamura on drinking?"

"I've heard of it. Yes. It was discussed at the last faculty meeting. What can you tell me about it?"

"She's the one who brought it into the open and she paid for that, big time. Student drinking is just doing what the Jesuits do, and what their families do. It's private, hidden. Back when St. Jude's was all male and mainly Irish, alcohol was just part of the scenery. And the priests were treated with respect wherever they went," Jamie grimaced. "*Fiat Cella,* 'Let it be concealed,' that is what the school motto should be, not *Fiat Certum.* What a joke. Truth is a scarce commodity around here."

Dee knew these stories. If the priests had been seen weaving erratically down Route 91 and were a little tipsy when pulled over by a police officer, the mere sight of the collar was enough to evoke deference and solicitude. "Now you be getting along home, Father." The officer, most likely a Catholic, would have a great story to tell his family, and there would be no hint of disrespect. The laws that bound other mortals and kept them grounded were not for men of the cloth.

Jamie and Dee were now in the lobby of the refurbished college bookstore. "A souvenir shop really," said Jamie eyeing the sweatshirts with the Apostles logo and the postcards with the sun glinting on the cross atop Murphy Chapel. There were fliers for upcoming events on the windows of the bookstore. None was allowed to remain after the advertised event, and everything had to be from an authorized association. "Can we talk about this?" was a series sponsored by the Chaplain's Office. Its flier announced that dorm security was the topic of discussion next week. "No-one is supposed to be in the dorms unless they have been swiped in," Jamie explained, "but people just prop the door open if they're having a party. Dulcie McNeil tries to get these conversations going and she knows about women being second-class citizens here."

They walked along the path, cut through the bank of pink Andromeda that shielded the dorms from the Convention Center. Dee had not been into this building. "My father helped with this one too," Jamie said. "Have you been in the auditorium named for him? It's so different from Coyle Hall and the dorms. Look at the walls. Newly painted, all the time. Graffiti disappears pretty quickly in this building, like magic, within hours of its appearance."

"Was that stuff in the women's bathrooms too when you were here?" Dee asked.

"Some, but it was mostly in the men's. We weren't supposed to see it, so it didn't matter. Like I said, *Fiat Cella*. But I saw it. I went into one of the men's bathrooms when I was in a hurry one day and didn't want to run up to the women's on the next floor. It was really disgusting. I knew I was in classes with the people who wrote those things. What did they think when they looked at me?"

Bathrooms, again: Who cleans which buildings? Who does the work schedules? Who writes the work orders for maintenance?

N.B. Ask the Dean's Secretary about the bathrooms when St. Jude's went coed. What was it about immersing oneself in a bath that was considered the only

appropriate cleansing ritual for young Catholic women?
Transgressive behaviors and women's bodies; who is
inscribing what on whom? Read Judith Butler?
Too indulgent? Read Hélène Cixous? Too French?
Better still, Mary Douglas, she was Catholic and she
did write about purity and pollution.

Dee had seen the bathrooms in the basement of Coyle Hall. It would not do for visitors to see the racial slurs, crude representations of genitalia, suggestions of sexual services that might be rendered if one were so minded as to call a particular number. But apparently it was appropriate for the students, faculty, and staff to see these messages in their quarters. Jamie was upset now. "Well I don't like it any more now than I did then. It's not funny. It's not free speech. You're right. It is intimidation. The Women's Watch tried to do something about it and we made quite a splash before we graduated. We published the graffiti from the bathrooms in our newsletter, but then it was used against us – like we were the ones with foul minds. They said it was private and none of our business, so we printed the graffiti that we saw on the trays in the Dining Hall to prove that this was going on in public too. But, then it was the end of the year and we kind of just ran out of steam. We tried to work with the Black Student Alliance but they had issues too."

"Like?"

"We're the wrong kind of 'other,' I guess. You know, in the service of 'others.' Women have been over 50 per cent of the population for two decades, but this place is not ours. Oh sure we can study and socialize here, but there are still places we can't be, things we can't do, just because we're women."

Seven rites of passage: baptism, confirmation,
communion, confession, matrimony, last rites,
ordination. Sacraments: an outward and visible sign of
something that is inward and spiritual - water for
baptism, bread and wine for Holy Communion, rings
for Holy Matrimony. . ... Impact of the new Code of
Canon Law 1983?

"That's right," Jamie said. She was getting into the hang of Dee's note-taking and even paused between ideas so Dee could get it all down. "We get six of the seven rites and things did improve a bit with the new code."

"Was that when Dulcie McNeil was appointed to head the Chaplain's Office?"

"Good for you, you've done your research. Yes, it took a while for the changes to percolate from Rome to St. Jude's, till 1988 actually. That was my first year here and I thought things would really change. But it was all cosmetic. It was like there were not enough real priests to go around, so women could do some of the housekeeping. We could distribute Holy Communion, but not say the Mass."

"Did you take any of Pica Liberatio's classes?"

"Oh, yes. She arrived just after Dulcie. It was so great."

Dee had liked Pica the instant she met her. They had sat up late one night swapping stories of their undergraduate days. Pica's blue eyes lit up when she told tales of her training with the Sisters of the Immaculate Conception. Dee was entranced by Pica's earthy laugh that tipped her lips into a smile both sensual and mischievous. But Pica was also a scholar, the very model of a post-Vatican II nun and Dee knew there was much she could learn from this good-natured, smart woman. Pica dressed with a certain flair, modest but fashionable – boxy jackets in bold colors, paired with cheery, patterned skirts, set off by simple but stylish jewelry. She wore light makeup, kept her dark hair short, but the cut was professional and admirably suited her small Irish face. Many students were surprised when they learned Professor Liberatio was a nun. In their eyes, she was very "in the world."

Pica loved her church but used her reason to come to independent decisions on a number of ethical issues. She had seen women die in childbirth, seen mothers worn to the bone through raising more children than their economic situation could sustain. She'd worked with HIV-positive prostitutes. When pushed to explain why she could be so forthright in her criticism of the local bishop and of the bishop in Rome, she had once said, "I took three vows: one of poverty, one of chastity, and one of obedience. The latter was for obedience to God, not a power-seeking male in Rome." Pica knew her attitude probably qualified her to appear on one of Virginia's lists. Certainly Pica would have appeared on the Syllabus of Errors where Pius IX had proscribed thinking for oneself. Was it a sin of pride? She felt sure Jesus, who was a healer, would not have condemned women who had few choices.

"Say hi to Pica for me and tell her not to overdo it on that exercise bike."

"Will do." *Obviously this young woman knows a great deal about the personal lives of faculty*, Dee thought.

"Pica was my shero." Jamie did a little pirouette.

"So, gymnastics? Ballet? Acting?" Dee laughed.

"I was a Theatre major," Jamie bowed. "And if you don't mind my saying, you're well named as Scrutari. Do you come from a long line of scrutinizers?"

"Well, I am trained to ask questions," Dee conceded.

Jamie nodded. "Look I have to meet my father and uncle for dinner, but let's stay in touch. There's so much still to do at this place. There are all these expectations about what I'll do for the college, but I don't want my name on a building, and I don't want to give money to an institution that is so complacent with the status quo. *Fiat Certum* can go to hell. I want the truth because I can doubt."

"I think some of the students want to form a new women's group," Dee ventured.

"Cissy, my cousin, will be one of them. They'll have to get past Ginny Frost. She worked hard with us, but she won't rock the boat. That's why I was so pleased to hear about your appointment and to know that Pica Liberatio would have a colleague."

"It's even better than that. There are three of us now. Miriam Levi is with us too. We'll be working on some course development stuff for Women's Studies over summer."

"About time," Jamie sighed.

"You have to visit. I think we could stir up some good mischief." Dee smiled and shook Jamie's hand. "I loved taking your campus tour."

Dee watched Jamie set off across the campus. She was mimicking Dee, pretending to take notes as she walked along.

What does Jamie know about Jessie Seneca?

Dee walked back up to the Sports Center and, sitting on her favorite bench, watched the sun set over Resolve. She liked to think about the Algonquin sacred spring and the ceremonies that would have been celebrated on this site. The fountain outside the library was a poor substitute for the life that had bubbled from the rise behind the college. As a mark of respect, Dee tied a small fetish made of a twist of herbs from her newly established kitchen garden to the underside of one of the bushes, and took out her notebook.

Can institutions be evil?

Before coming to St. Jude's, Dee, a lapsed Presbyterian, believed talk of evil was just that, talk. There was good and bad, of that she was sure, and some people were very bad; but, in her view, there were no forces of darkness, no anti-Christ, no Satan, no inevitability that man's fall from grace doomed everything. Her approach was we make our own heaven or hell on earth. We have some choices, but mostly we make tough decisions. Certainly some of those decisions are circumscribed by the material conditions of our existence. A member of the Stolen Generations in Australia – the Aboriginal children who were taken from their families to be raised by the state in an "orphanage" or on a mission – had less opportunity than a white child of the middle class. But was the state evil for formulating and pursuing assimilation policies that destroyed families? Was the defense that a policy was in "best interests of others" sufficient? Careful historical research, including attention to survivors' narratives, was starting to suggest that a more sinister politic underwrote the assimilation era, one that advocated genocide and placed Indigenous people on a lower rung of the evolutionary ladder. Were the individual policy-makers evil? Could they plead ignorance? Good intent? "Just doing my job?" It was a different time and place. Again archival research was beginning to reveal that there had been dissenting voices, that there had been visions of shared humanity in which difference was to be

79

celebrated rather than eliminated. Why did one view become policy and another become philanthropy?

What are the subversive narratives of this institution? Jamie knows a number.

N.B. Read Hannah Arendt on the banality of evil.

May 1, 1995: May Day

maypole entwined in ribbons

phallus and vulva

tree-worshipping cults

workers of the world celebrate Labor Day

USA - National Day of Prayer

mayday = distress signal.

6

CONSPIRACIES AND COALITIONS
Fall 1995

Good mischief, that's what she had promised Jamie Coyle. On picture postcards of St. Jude's Dee wrote, "Remember, my place, tonight, 6 pm. Time to talk women's business." She slipped them into Miriam's and Pica's mailboxes and walked up to her apartment to do a few chores. Dee enjoyed these Friday evenings. During the summer, when they were drafting the outline for an interdisciplinary course to entice students into central debates in Women's Studies, the three had started meeting at Dee's place. It was so convenient. Their meetings had continued into the fall semester and evolved into a kind of ritual as they took turns cooking. Pica did a mean gumbo. Miriam made chicken soup for the soul, and Dee threw things on the gas grill that were simple and full of flavor.

During the summer, they had also made time to explore the countryside. Miriam and Pica were committed to introducing Dee to the delights of rural New England: the Berkshires for high tea, a concert at Tanglewood, a visit to Hawthorne's cottage, and a Mark Morris rehearsal at Jacob's Pillow; Salem for the history of the witch-hunts; Rhode Island for a wind-blown weekend; a tour of the Mystic Museum; a visit to the homes of Harriet Beecher Stowe and Samuel Clemens in Hartford; and a trip to the Pequot casino at Foxwoods. There had been some tensions on that occasion. "Don't be such a puritan," Miriam had exploded when Dee had expressed her distaste of such institutions. "They offer a way out of dependency," Miriam had argued.

"But at what cost?" *Must find a better way of approaching this topic with Miriam*, Dee thought. They agreed when it came to the right of self-determination but disagreed on how it might be achieved.

Dee knew her direct and candid speech was off-putting and that Miriam often tried to smooth over matters where Dee would rather have had a good shouting match and cleared the air. *I'm not a very good native when it comes to American resolution of conflict*, Dee had thought, *but damn it, I'm no puritan either*. Dee privately nursed that sting – it wasn't the first time someone had called her a puritan. She resolved she would have it out with Miriam another time.

Puritans: sought to purify the Church of England; 1630s Massachusetts puritans begin to settle in Connecticut; no other religion tolerated.

Apart from that moment with Miriam, their excursions into the countryside kept Dee fresh, and on most nights she had easily fallen into a peaceful sleep. Without students the campus was quiet and the high-domed reading room in the library was a perfect place to work – cool, natural light, and well resourced. And, as Dee learned more about the symbolism of the herbs presented to the baby Jesus at his birth and the thorns woven into his crown at his crucifixion, her curiosity about the pharmacological knowledge of Jamie's female forebears and the vision embodied in the fountain intensified.

Women's knowledge, passed down through the generations? Wise women? Healers? Witches? Reread A WITCH'S GUIDE TO GARDENING.

Dee's book on women and land reform in Africa was coming along nicely. She'd completed five of the six planned chapters and had gotten into the habit of sending her drafts to Christian for comment. He had responded with questions and suggestions, and in his last letter had asked: *Would you tell me more about your daily life? I enjoyed the first sketches you sent. And, tell me, what's happening with your children?* She put Chapter Five into a large padded envelope – ready to take to the Resolve Post Office in the morning – and penned a summer update for Christian.

Family matters. Hannah's visit was a great success. We had a traditional clambake on the Fourth of July and watched the

fireworks over the water. Ned hopes to be here for Christmas.
You didn't ask about Bruce, but he is settled with Cheryl.
I think I'm finally okay with it. The kids have been great, lots
of email and even some pics. I love this new electronic
communication. It has real revolutionary potential. I signed up
for the training sessions as soon as I heard St. Jude's was being
wired over summer. Would be great if you could be online too
but I understand the lack of infrastructure.

Work fun. Women's Studies syllabus coming along nicely. Mary
J and I have been meeting regularly for lunch – over summer
we even managed a movie or two. Sometimes we shop but
mostly we talk. I really like her but fear there is a fight ahead
over her daughter's hoped-for admission to St. Jude's.
Consuelo, Magdalena's daughter, also wants to come here.
She called in the other day when she was checking out the local
colleges. She is very smart. I think your mother would really
like her and I know she is very interested in *òrìṣà* and there is a
babalawo they consult locally. Who knew? I told her you spoke
Yorùbá and Swahili and Spanish. She was very excited.

News in a nutshell. I miss the summer. It goes out with a bang
after Labor Day.

Dee.

Dee took out her notebook and flipped back to her notes on the
conversation with Jamie Coyle. She was right; Virginia Glacialis
would be an obstacle to the formation of a new activist women's
group on campus. Virginia was the faculty mentor for the women
students in the Women's Watch, and had been since its inception
in 1980. It was a group with a noble purpose. It acted, not unlike a
number of amnesty groups, to monitor and spread the word about
women's lives worldwide, but avoided any domestic issues. The
Women's Watch sponsored talks, raised money for those in need,
deplored the one-child policy in China and the baby farms in
Romania. Dee had heard that, every now and then over the past
decade, one of the students would ask about the possibilities of

St. Jude's adding more courses that focused on women, minorities, and feminist critiques of the patriarchal basis of religion. But Virginia had always been able to assure the administration that there was no need for a fully fledged Department of Women's Studies at the college. A small interdisciplinary program relying on courses offered in other departments would do. But recently a group of determined students had approached Dee about forming a new kind of women's group on campus. Dee wanted to talk with Pica and Miriam about how they might support the group and not alienate Virginia in the process.

Dee did not want to undercut Virginia and she didn't want any fallout for Pica who was coming up for tenure a year early and whose research, Dee knew, made Virginia uncomfortable. On the other hand, she was not going to stand mute in the face of any perceived injustice. Virginia Glacialis could be a formidable foe. Her politics were complicated. Jamie Coyle had recognized this in their conversation over Alumni Weekend last spring. She'd seen Virginia's strengths, but had also seen the costs of her unflinching pursuit of her goals. Many of Virginia's colleagues at Harvard focused on feminist readings of the Bible, the matter of women's ordination, ethical questions around women's bodies and reproduction. Virginia did not.

What Dee didn't know was that sometimes Virginia had been sorely tempted to join the Harvard group because she yearned for their company and they seemed to be having so much fun together. In the end, though, she would think about her parents and the sacrifices they had made for her and give up the notion of a "frivolous" pursuit. She knew that working on the "woman question" in religion was no fast track to tenure and promotion. Besides, Virginia was often uneasy with all those intense young women, like Pica, who dreamed of changing the world. *Yes*, she would say to herself, for the thousandth time in her life, *it is better to carve out a piece of action, in an obscure period, and become the world expert in that field.*

Virginia Glacialis was the daughter of teachers – her father taught high school science and her mother taught French and German.

Her parents had done all they could to make sure their gifted only child was afforded every possible educational opportunity. When others were read nursery rhymes in English, her mother was reading to her in French and German. When it became apparent that Virginia had her mother's gift for languages, her parents enrolled her in a private school that taught Latin. They believed a well-educated person should know Latin. They sent her to voice coaches to smooth out those harsh New England vowels. It was not that affection was lacking in Virginia's family. Her parents loved their daughter and wanted to see her happy, fulfilled, and settled in a marriage as stable as theirs and they had a plan in place to get all that for her. They were sure she was on track when she was admitted to Harvard because they knew by then that Virginia was ambitious and would use everything she had to succeed. The Syllabus of Errors would serve her well.

Virginia had learned early on that the Coyle girls were a handful – first Jamie and then her cousin, Cissy. With the support of the Chaplain's Office, and backing of the Women's Watch, Cissy had led one of the "Can we talk about this?" sessions. The Watch had been upset when the Current Affairs Task Force in Political Science circulated an article from the *New York Times Book Review*, which purported to be about third wave feminism. In her overview, Christina D'Molish focused on the recent rash of books that argued that feminism was bad for women; that feminists fabricated facts; and that the word "feminism" was out of fashion. Cissy and her colleagues had been outraged. "This is backlash literature. Why not pair it with other more positive articles?" Cissy had demanded.

"Do they think we'll fall victim to the heresy of women's oppression?" MC – short for Mary Christine – had asked.

The women were accused of being divisive and male bashers.

"Who's getting beaten?" they countered and then the conversation devolved into a slanging match.

"Who says one in three women can expect to be sexually assaulted in her lifetime?" one student heckled.

"I don't know any women who have been raped!" another declared.

The Women's Watch approached Virginia. Cissy was insistent, "This is why we need a real Women's Studies program, a safe place to do this kind of work. And, we need an organization where we can advocate for women at home, not just in distant Third World places."

Virginia had smiled and not objected. She was a pragmatist and knew that the four-year life cycle of a student was a mere wink of the eye compared to the life of the college. She could wait out this group. On the other hand, she intended to derail the proposal for a free-standing Women's Studies program. She knew it wouldn't be difficult. She had allies and meticulous files.

Pica hoped that the "women's business" of Dee's invitation included some discussion of Virginia. She was wary of her department head and worried about her upcoming tenure case. Pica's scholarship was open-ended and sprawling. She was interested in Liberation Theology and believed that the "preferential option for the poor" included women, especially poor, marginalized, and working-class women. "I know where those students are coming from. You can't separate what happens here and abroad. Like it's okay if my work with HIV-AIDS populations is about pastoral care. I get lots of praise for that. But I get grief when I say you can't divide the sick into the deserving and undeserving," Pica's bright blue eyes blazed. "I mean you can't help the *innocent* victims of blood transfusions and neglect those who 'brought it on themselves' through their own drug abuse and sexual practices." Pica railed against the sanitized versions of sufferers and the refusal of the church to sanction condom use. "The Vatican position is tantamount to homicide. They'd rather have people die than allow condoms," Pica had said, "in which case they had better do more than pray for a cure. They had damn well better develop one!"

During the summer, Pica had taken Dee to visit the small cemetery behind the Murphy Chapel. She had pointed to a number of recent graves. They all dated from the late 1980s to the present. There certainly seemed to be a lot.

"These are all Jesuits, all from St. Jude's. Don't even try asking about the cause of death. I suppose there must be records some-where, but . . ."

"So what is it all about? You have my attention."

"HIV-AIDS," sighed Pica. "That's why the college insurance premiums are so high. It must cost a fortune to insure the place with this aging and vulnerable population."

The two women had fallen silent and walked through the rows of newer graves, searching for more information about the occupants. *What had their lives been like as Jesuits – men of the cloth – ill with a taboo, sexually linked disease?* Dee thought. *How would I even begin to track the statistics on AIDS-related deaths in the priesthood?*

Dee intended to draw Pica out on her research at the next departmental meeting – what better place than in a department that considered ethics to be central to its teaching? Now she hoped she'd be able to broach the matter over tonight's dinner and to do so without setting Miriam off on one of her "soothing troubled waters" trips. Fond of Miriam as she was, Dee hated being "managed."

Dee was in the kitchen listening to music when Pica arrived for their Friday Fest. "Is that Tracy Chapman's *New Beginnings*?" Pica asked taking off her deep purple jacket to reveal a soft silk fuchsia shell that topped a slightly flared floral skirt. "Listen to that guitar." Music was one of Pica's many passions. She played guitar and sang. Her range was wide. She played in the chapel. She played in class. She played at HIV-AIDS benefits. "I sometimes listen to Chapman's *Crossroads* when I work out," Pica said.

"Ha! Jamie Coyle said to take it easy on your exercise bike," Dee said.

"Oh, she knows all about that. She had quite a bit to say about eating disorders and holy anorexia in class and did a wonderful skit on 'Fat is a Feminist Issue' at St. Jude's."

"I'm sorry I missed it," Dee said as she took the marinated meat out of the fridge, flipped it over in her hands, and set it by the grill. "Do you think Catholicism sends different messages to women about their bodies than other religions?"

"Well we could start with the vilification of the flesh and the female body as the site of pollution. Maybe we need something about it in our course outline. The carnality of the Catholic tradition. Think of it. Catholicism is so focused on the body."

"How so?" Miriam said as she came through the door, threw her long knitted black cardigan over the back of a chair, and greeted her friends. She reached for the corkscrew, opened a bottle of Jacob's Creek merlot, and then began to slice the Camembert that was breathing on the window ledge. Miriam was not one to stand on formalities when good food and wine were concerned. She had never worried too much about her weight. It showed. She was on the plump side, with a sort of comfortable, healthy, tanned fleshiness. Her small, intense face was swamped by her long black hair, loose over her shoulders. Light makeup. Her large clear brown eyes needed no emphasis. "Go on," Miriam said, kicking off her black pumps. "Don't mind me."

"Well, to begin with, there is the resurrection; then there's transubstantiation, the blood as wine, and the wafer as the body of Christ. And I shouldn't forget the Word made Flesh, the crucifixion, the stigmata, and the virginity of Mary."

"In my family we eat. It's all about food and . . . How did we get onto this anyway?" Miriam asked, loosening the tie on her long black dress.

"I was just repeating Jamie Coyle's message to Pica about her exercise regime."

"We've been through this before," Pica moaned. "My bike is in my study and after a good dinner, a glass or two of wine, a little chocolate flan, I'd rather read a good book."

"I'm starving. It's been a long day for me. Virginia had me on one of her damn lists. When are we going to eat?" Miriam asked. "And Dee I must say you look very fetching in that butcher's apron."

Miriam Levi had joined the fledgling Judaic Studies program in fall 1992. The program was one of the significant moves in refocusing the department from the study of theology to that of comparative religions. Miriam was a quick study and she had some familiarity with Jesuit practices from her research in China. She had made quite a name for herself with her unconventional study of the roots of anti-Semitism, not as one might expect by exploring Hitler's Germany or Russian pogroms, but through a finely wrought historical ethnography of the relationships between the Jews and Chinese in World War II. It was research sparked by childhood experiences and her parents' stories of their life in the Hongkew Ghetto in Shanghai from 1938 on to 1946 and their arrival in Australia where Miriam was born in 1948.

When Miriam and Dee got to reminiscing about their life in Australia in the 1950s, Pica listened intently. Miriam was Melbourne born and bred and had been in the United States much longer than Dee. For the most part she could pass as a local, but when she was with Dee, her vocabulary and accent shifted. Dee, three years her senior, had grown up in Sydney, but their accounts of the years following World War II were very similar. Miriam had lived with her mother, father and brother, in a modest three-bedroom home in a bayside suburb. New, triple-fronted, cream brick veneer bungalows, all neatly aligned, each with its own swinging front gate and white picket fence, encroached upon the old-money, shabby chic of white stucco, deep verandahs, small lead-paned windows and rambling gardens hidden behind ivy-covered high walls. Dee nodded. "I know the places, but in Sydney we lived in a Housing Commission place, a concrete brick high-rise out in Parramatta in the western suburbs. It was miles away from all the fabulous beaches of the harbor, no garden, no fence – an experiment in creating communities where land was scarce."

"Remember your playmates?" Miriam asked. "Mine were all children of veterans."

"All proud members of the Returned Services League with all those hateful views on foreigners. Anyone who didn't look like us and talk like us was the enemy to the RSL," Dee said. "My dad used to say, 'Rice. I fought a war so that we didn't have to eat that wog stuff.'"

"Wog?" Pica asked. "Like in 'golliwog'?"

"Weird oriental gentleman," Miriam and Dee chorused.

"My dad would say, 'Wonder what the veterans think of us Jews?' Of course, I knew. I had heard them all by then."

Miriam had visited the homes of her school friends. She had seen enthusiasm for the idea of Israel, the vision of the new nation, and even heard one of these veterans explain the values of a kibbutz to his daughter. He said he had no regrets about fighting in a war that made that homeland possible. He did, however, have pretty rigid views about Jews and their financial dealings. He was fond of quoting from *The Merchant of Venice* with lines such as "the Jew is the very devil incarnate" and relished references to extracting one's "pound of flesh."

"My dad talked about that too," Dee added. "And he accepted that there was a secret Jewish plot to take over the world. He would never have bothered to look at the research that showed *The Protocols of the Elders of Zion* was a forgery plagiarized from a work of fiction by Tsar Nicholas II's secret police. And you know, come to think of it, I doubt he ever even met a Jew."

"Well, the Jewish population of Australia was pretty small overall. The White Australia policy made sure of that," said Miriam whose knowledge of the Jewish diaspora was extensive. "There were several Melbourne suburbs with large Jewish populations, but not in the newer suburbs. Your father was just repeating what *his* father and workmates had said. There was no-one to challenge them, nothing in their personal experience, education, or circle of friends."

"My dad used to say it was right and proper that Australia stayed a British country. As far as he was concerned the Yellow Peril, as he called them, could stay at home, eat their rice and smoke their opium. Same for the swarthy knife-wielding Mafia: they could eat their garlic and drink their red wine, but not in his house – beer and a steak on the barbecue were just fine by him. He worked hard for his house in the suburbs and resented the work habits of New Australians as we called them. In his telling they tolerated inhuman hours, lived in crowded conditions, and sponsored their families to join them in *his* country," Dee said.

"You know, at the reception after that forum we had on

90

multiculturalism at St. Jude's, the President was telling me a little bit about the history of immigration to Connecticut and religious intolerance."

Dee interrupted as gently as she could. She did not want to get into puritan history when they were about to eat. "Here Pica, help me with this grill. You know I'm much better on an open fire than with these gas gadgets."

"Okay, Bush Girl, you two do the meat and I'll dress the salad," Miriam laughed as she set the table. Then she poured more wine and passed the warm, crusty, sourdough bread to Pica.

"Where did you get such fresh lamb in Resolve?" Miriam asked. "Makes me homesick."

"I went shopping with Mary J the other day. She'd had another run-in with Chuck Negotium which I need to tell you about." Dee took off her apron, smoothed out the brown and green brightly patterned shift she was wearing, sat down at the table and patted the seat next to her. "Come on, sit down Miriam. Here Pica, try this chair. It's another of my finds.".

"But, first, what about the lamb?" Miriam persisted.

"There's a Middle Eastern deli on a lane off Main Street that has amazing lamb. Mary J showed me where but she says she never eats lamb," Dee said.

"Well neither do I, unless you cook it," Pica added settling into the chair opposite Dee. "This is comfy."

"So let's eat already." Miriam joined them and nodded to Dee as she tasted the lamb.

Dee smiled, grateful that Miriam was focused on food. *Maybe I'm being touchy about this puritan stuff,* Dee thought, *Miriam is so generous. Why can't I just let it go?*

"Now what about Negotium?" Pica asked. "God, it's hard to stay on a topic with you two."

"Mary J desperately wants her daughter to attend St. Jude's – it's one of the few things keeping her here – and he is making her feel threatened about that. First it was some bogus stuff about her performance review, and now it's about technology. He says she has to be literate in a number of software programs but won't give her the time to train. Says he'll reassign her somewhere to some office that doesn't need those skills."

"Can he do that?" Miriam got up to get another bottle of wine.

"He has up till now," Pica said. "It's a very brave person, or a very foolish one, who goes up against Chuck."

Miriam was frowning as she popped the cork. "What's his power base?"

"Chuck keeps the lid on. He knows the rules without being told. And, he's been here forever. 'Knows where the bodies are buried' as the saying goes," Pica said, pouring more wine.

"Sometimes I wonder whether that is literal or metaphoric," Dee said. "But, with Mary J, he has taken on the wrong person. She's very determined. And she'll work her butt off to get what she wants. I saw her in the library over summer, she was teaching herself how to do desktop publishing from a manual – and you know how obtuse those things can be."

After they had eaten, Dee suggested they move to the living room. "I have a couple of new lamps to show you. Can't get enough of them to chase away the darkness of this place. How do you think the Jebbies lit these rooms? There are no overhead lights."

"Who says they lit them?" Pica said. "My father, rest his soul, used to be happy sitting in the dark. Maybe the Jebbies were too. Maybe they were . . . well never mind. For my father, I think it was his way of getting some peace and quiet from us kids. He was kind, but rather remote and he hated Protestants – that was the Irish in him talking."

"Well from the little I know about the treatment of Irish in the colonies, there was some basis to his feelings," Miriam said and turned to Dee. "What about your dad?"

"A mixture. He was a bigot, no doubt about that. He told really vicious anti-Catholic and anti-Jewish jokes," Dee said, "but he was also a decent man, an ordinary man. He worked several jobs so that Mum could stay at home and raise us kids. That was what a man did then. I remember that he was proud when he had saved enough to buy her a washing machine."

"I knew about anti-Semitism and to be careful in what I said, but it's hard to think of fathers like that as people I should be careful around or avoid," Miriam said. "I remember my friend's father helping me oil the chain on my bike when it came loose. Yep, an ordinary man. Now I wonder what lengths such a man would go to protect a life he saw as threatened by outsiders, by others he neither knew nor cared to know?"

"Well my father had no intention of ever befriending any Asians," Dee said. "And then he turned around and bought a Toyota in the 1980s. Said it was safer, better value. Wouldn't touch a VW though. He'd actually fought against the Germans."

"My parents worried all the time about anti-Semitic attitudes. And it was confusing. Australia was pro-Israel, and yet rife with anti-Semitism," Miriam said. "They tried to strike a balance between telling me all the stories of our family and making sure I was well integrated into the local neighborhood."

Miriam had gone to a state school along with her neighbors but was excused from Religious Instruction, and was thus an object of curiosity – and some envy – for her classmates. She went to piano lessons after school. She went to Saturday School. She went to temple. Her family kept the holidays but not a kosher kitchen. They had no immediate family in Melbourne and had few Jewish friends because the Jewish community was concentrated in the older, more moneyed areas of the city. A couple of Jewish families lived behind the walls of the older homes in her neighborhood and their families celebrated Rosh Hashanah together, but those homes were formal and rather forbidding, and their children were grown. They spoke Yiddish with her parents and a heavily accented English with her. They spoke of the Holocaust and alluded to losses of family, friends, and property, but said little of their own arrival in Australia in the mid-1930s.

Miriam had read all she could and listened carefully when her parents and the occasional visitor talked of the old days. *What was it that fostered the growth of anti-Semitism in some places, like Germany in the 1930s, and mitigated it in others, like the Chinese in Shanghai in the same period*, she wondered? *Why did "perfectly ordinary people" express hatred of a people they hardly knew? What motivated the Holocaust doubters she'd seen on television?* Miriam had come of age during the flourishing of the second wave of the Women's Movement and took seriously the feminist maxim that the personal is the political. She had set about teasing out what could be known of attitudes towards Jewish minorities in various countries and began with what she thought she knew best, her own family history. Hers had been a long journey from Melbourne to Resolve and it was a story she anticipated sharing in greater detail with Pica and Dee. They were an unlikely trio – a Catholic nun, a Jew, and an agnostic – but when they sat together in faculty and departmental meetings, they saw their colleagues shuffle and stiffen a little at the sight of these well-organized, vocal, worldly women.

"Good," said Dee. "Nothing like getting a sense of what it is to be an outsider."

"They have good intent," Miriam added, "but they don't like stepping outside their familiar comfort zones."

"Watch how they break," said Pica, who often made references to playing pool, a sign, she said, of her misspent childhood.

"Time to get down to women's business," Dee said as she passed around a large bowl of fresh berries. "Three women students, Mary Louise, MC, and Cissy Coyle – you know this formidable bunch I'm sure – came to see me with a proposal for a reading group. Here's their draft. They plan to read Carol Christ, Cynthia Eller, Mary Daly, Morny Joy, and Rosemary Ruether. Then they want to stage a feminist litany about violence against women, at dusk, on the steps of the main library, near the fountain."

"Oh, I guess that's why they wanted a civil rights lawyer," Miriam said. "I asked Daniel and he told me that unlike other spaces – classrooms and foyers – this space was public space, so they did not need a permit to gather there, and they could not be told to move on."

"They are fired up and say they're ready to call the press if there were to be any interference. I sure hope no-one traces the advice back to your husband, Miriam," Dee said.

Mary Louise, Cissy, and MC had spent a good amount of time in

Dee's office, consulting her library and trying out various theories, strategies, and plans. Along with a couple of other outspoken women in the Women's Watch, they had joined Dee on a trip to Washington, DC, in order to participate in a Pro-Choice march. They were very taken by the orderly behavior of the crowds, the diversity of the protesters, and the intelligent fun of the slogans and costumes. This was not at all in keeping with what they had been taught to expect. Where were all the horrid, irresponsible, selfish women who killed babies? They had taken to wearing T-shirts that proclaimed their politics. "We Won't Go Back" and "Take Back the Night" were favorites, and Cissy seemed to live in her Rosie the Riveter "We can do it" shirt. The trio was working on their new organization to be called WOW, "Women of Worth", which would take up issues the Women's Watch avoided. They had also begun agitating for a stronger Women's Studies program.

"Guess what? That was an item on Virginia's list today. She knows that Women's Studies, such as it is, only works as a program because there are cross-listed courses. But that number has grown. The courses we teach are encroaching on the English Department, and we have this new idea for a truly interdisciplinary course. Up till now English has dominated the program, but that's changing."

"Well, it's about time," Pica said. "Knowing all the women in Shakespeare's plays is fascinating, but they need more. Like some of those great manifestos from the 1970s."

"My favorite was the *SCUM Manifesto*," Miriam said leaning forward to take another handful of berries.

"Oh, that's right." Dee jumped up to get her notebook. "It had all that great stuff about the sex division of labor. Hang on, I need to make a note."

> *After the revolution, who cleans the bathrooms?*
> *Housework: invisible in the home, poorly paid in the workplace; do liberated men clean bathrooms?*
> *Read the SCUM MANIFESTO.*

Pica and Miriam had grown accustomed to Dee's note-taking reflex and barely paused. "Do you realize each of us is teaching a course that counts towards Women's Studies?" Pica continued.

"Like yours, Miriam, on 'Women and Judaism'. The students all want to go to a feminist Seder. And how about yours, Dee, on 'Women, Religion and the State'? They love your stories about being in the Australian desert with Aborigines."

"Yep, they love hearing that biology is not destiny, that women have ceremonies closed to men that can shape men's fortunes. I talk about how missionaries reorganized extended families into neat nuclear families and as a result undermined women's power. I tell them how missionaries ignored women's economic role and just assumed men were the household heads. That stirs them up for sure."

"A bit more serious than 'stir,' I think," Pica said. "Didn't one student report you?"

"Yes, one did. He asked me who made me the judge and jury of missionaries. Accused me of religious intolerance. It was scary. Who knows where their advice is coming from? And it got really personal, and that is when I worry I'll say things I'll regret later. You remember that day at lunch – we'd gone into Resolve to get off-campus because I was so steamed up?"

Pica remembered well. Dee with a hangover from drinking at lunchtime was permanently inscribed on her memory. "You said, 'Life's too short to drink bad red wine' as you knocked back the second glass," Pica laughed. "You cussed in ways that were beyond my grasp of English."

"Good ole colorful Aussie slang," Miriam explained.

"They made me want to chunder," Dee said. "Well the wine too."

"Throw up, vomit," Miriam translated.

"Well apparently you made some very important people feel ill. I heard an angry alumnus had something to say about your course too." Pica looked across at Dee.

"It was one of the first stories I heard about your President," Dee said smiling, "And I must say I found it quite endearing. Apparently the alumnus asked why the college was teaching courses about pagans?"

"And no doubt our worthy leader said something along the lines of 'We're interested in teaching tolerance.'" Pica's voice captured the depth of President Firmitas's tone and she tugged at her neck as if her collar as was too tight.

"That's right, but the alumnus didn't give up that easily. He kept going and wanted to know why the college needed courses about women and, to add insult to injury, one being taught by a foreigner. Made him sick to the stomach."

"Oh, I heard about this," Miriam joined in. "The President said in that sharp tone he uses when he is finished with a conversation, 'Didn't the America First movement die a timely death in the 1940s?' and that was that."

"Dee. You are the stuff of legends," laughed Pica. "Tell Miriam about your encounter with Father Parsimonious. You know, when he thought you were a coed."

"I had only been here a week or so. I was getting out of my car and this frail, flinty, black robe says, 'Are you coeds permitted to park on campus?' 'Only when *they're* seniors,' I said. Then I told him I was the new professor in Religious Studies."

"I bet he was really confused," Pica interrupted.

"He sure was." Dee continued, "He asked if I worked on the Old or New Testament? I told him I did comparative religion, especially with Indigenous women, in Australia, Africa, Latin America. 'What? Women have their own religion now?' I decided to answer his question at face value and told him that in the central desert of Australia, women have rituals that are secret, closed to men and children, in fact very dangerous to men and in Africa, there are powerful women deities."

"And," Pica could now hardly contain herself, "you started to enumerate all those Marian cults, some with black Madonnas, like Our Lady of Guadalupe."

Dee was not sure how Pica knew the story but was enjoying the pleasure she found in the retelling. "When I'd finished, I simply said, 'So yes, I think I'd say women *have* religion,' and he looked at me and said, 'And you teach here?' I smiled politely and said, 'Sure do, and the students seem to be enjoying the classes.' But of course I know that could explode at any moment," Dee grimaced. "I know I push too hard sometimes."

"Well it's been worth it," Miriam said. "I like being part of what we've managed to build in Women's Studies. I like the eclecticism of the faculty teaching courses for Women's Studies."

"A big-tent approach, even if it is only a small program?" Dee asked.

"If we'd held out for doctrinal purity, the faculty would never have voted the program into existence," Pica said. "And there are always opportunities for widening their horizons – like that flier I circulated on Marian cults last semester. I suspect there was some discussion of that in the Jesuit residence." Pica had been on faculty for six years and, of the three, was the institutional memory. "Women's Studies faces the same structural problem as Judaic Studies. There are no tenure lines, except Miriam's in Religious Studies, and resources are always scarce. In Women's Studies we have to negotiate with those priests – they are so bloody sure their scholarship is critical to the program – and with others who exude hostility, but insist on attending the open meetings."

"Like that Father Paddy Sordes in the Sociology Department?" Miriam asked. "What's the deal with his research on the history of torture? He has all these terrifying images of men and women being subjected to unspeakable pain. From the Greeks to the present. And he seems to specialize in sado-masochism and torture."

"It's the pleasure of the pain . . ." Pica began.

"It's a nasty little perv," Dee spat out. Pica rocked back in her chair. She loved Dee's direct language but knew it disturbed others and could be a liability for her friend.

"There are really important questions to be asked about torture, sexuality and perverse pleasures. Look at the arguments of Page duBois in *Torture and Truth*. But no, he collects the instruments and manuals on how to use the torturers' tools." Dee took a deep breath. "And, do you know, I'm told that he has drinking parties with students?"

Miriam had seen him bundling four students into his car one evening when she'd been working late, but had not thought much about it. Now it occurred to her that it was probably the last time she had ever seen one of the students. "Do you have Mary Doyle in a class?"

"No, but I did last semester. She's smart and heading straight for a crisis of faith," said Dee. "Her generation of women has grown up believing they can all become the President of the United States, or a Supreme Court judge at the very least. They won't accept that gender-based inequality still exists."

"Do they know the statistics on women faculty?" Miriam asked. "Same qualifications, same rank, 80 per cent of the salary."

"I tell them that the starting salary for a woman with a college degree is the same as for a man with a high school diploma. When they ask the why and how questions, the answers they get aren't satisfying," Dee said.

"You know, Jessie Seneca did a survey on attitudes about family and career," Pica said. "And she found that an overwhelming majority of women graduates expect to marry, have children, and pursue a career. Their male counterparts also expect to marry, but assume that their wives will interrupt their careers to raise the children the two of them have agreed they want to have."

"Crisis of faith," Pica mused. "That is a good description and I'm not sure the Chaplain's Office is much help. Dulcie McNeil knows that women have been short-changed, but she operates in a pretty conservative environment."

"Can we talk some more about Jessie?" Dee asked.

"Be very careful," said Pica, "These are life and death matters."

"And Mary Doyle?" Dee asked.

"Oh damn. Daniel is out front. I have to go." Miriam looked about for her cardigan.

"Can I grab a lift?" Pica asked almost too quickly and began gathering her things.

As they disappeared through the door, Dee muttered to herself about what appeared to be more Jessie cover-up. She settled in her one really comfortable chair, bought in a yard sale over the summer, and opened her notebook.

Secrets. So many secrets. What does Pica know?

Dee had given a lot of thought to the role of secrecy in maintaining religious authority in Indigenous societies in Australia. There, knowledge was restricted on the basis of age, sex, clan affiliation, ceremonial roles, and a host of other more idiosyncratic factors. Recently she had been thinking about the issue in a wider comparative frame, in part because she was addressing aspects of secrecy and customary law in her book on women and land reform in Uganda, and in part because Christian had been pushing her to do so. They had been exchanging views on the pros and cons of various strategies for protecting knowledge.

Dee had started a letter to him with a question: Don't you think people have the right to protect their "inside stories," to prevent unscrupulous individuals from selling sacred objects, and to refuse to disclose the inner meanings of certain rituals? The trouble is that Western legal systems rely on knowing what it is that is being protected and the Indigenous systems rely on not letting everyone know.

Christian, playing the devil's advocate, had responded: Doesn't secrecy foster corruption? If we think about knowledge as the currency of the society, then if everyone knows, it is devalued. So those who control the resource are rich. Of course they need sanctions to prevent people speaking out of turn. So in Yorùbá secret societies, the rules of circulation of knowledge are known, and violations are punished and punished severely. Isn't that the same for Indigenous Australians?

Yes, Yes, Dee replied two weeks later when Christian's letter reached her. It was trying that letters took so long. Judgment is summary. You're taught right from the beginning about what can be said to whom, when, and where.

What about intent? Christian wrote back the following month. He hoped Dee had spent long enough with the Jesuits to be familiar with the intentional fallacy. In Swahili we say, "*Kuelekeza si kufuma.*" It translates as "to aim is not to hit" but it's more like "good intentions are not sufficient." There needs to be an outcome, something real.

I agree, Dee replied a week later. Christian's letter had arrived much quicker this time. Intent is irrelevant in the Indigenous systems I know. But I have been wondering about priests and the confessional, lawyer–client privilege, spousal privilege, doctor–patient confidentiality. Here it is sex, secrets and silence.

September 8, 1995: The Birth of Virgin Mary - Mary, Mother of God; mystery - of herself she is nothing - for our sakes God delighted to manifest His glory and His love in her; prayers for inner peace, family unity, the ills of our society and world peace.

7

SECRETS, CELEBRATIONS, AND SPEECHES
Winter 1996

December 1995, Dee's first white Christmas – so different from the long lazy summer holiday in Australia. In this cold and snowy corner of New England, the rituals made sense. The season was in harmony with the trappings. No need to spray shaving cream on the fir tree to simulate snow; no need to constantly water the hacked-off dead tree to prevent it from drying out and losing its needles in a heat wave. The owner of her favorite thrift store gave her fairy lights and a mock tree and, with some pushing and shoving, Dee got it into the trunk of her car. Ned flew in from Singapore bringing small silk dolls for the tree. Mary J had found some exquisite French glass ornaments on sale in G. Fox & Co. a while back, and Pica baked gingerbread men who sat cheerily on the branches. Dee strung strands of brightly painted Aboriginal beads around the base. When Hannah heard about the multi-cultural tree, she sent Dee satirical plaster British Beefeaters. Miriam presented Dee with an art deco menorah and Magdalena promised to fix *nacatamal*, a traditional Honduras Christmas food, popular with her family. Consuelo convinced Ned he should join her family for midnight Mass on Christmas Eve and the feast that would follow at their place. Dee went along too and, for the first time since her arrival at St. Jude's nearly a year ago, she felt the warmth of fellowship radiate in the ceremony.

Hanukkah - The Festival of Lights;

Kawanza, Swahili for the first fruits of the harvest - seven candles, seven letters;

Christmas; The birth of Christ; a candle in every window;

Winter Solstice - return of the light; virgin mothers give birth; Demeter to Persephone.

N.B. James Fraser and THE GOLDEN BOUGH; one ritual calendar imposed on another; peel back the layers; look below the surface.

Heavier than usual snow made driving dangerous so, apart from the obligatory trip to the stores on Boxing Day – an Australian holiday when one lay around in the sun at the beach, exchanged unwanted and inappropriate gifts, and perhaps attended a sporting event – one terrifying drive into New Haven to see *The Nutcracker Suite*, Dee and Ned hung around the apartment. They drank eggnog and watched *It's a Wonderful Life*. They played Scrabble and valiantly tried to use American spellings, till Dee cried, "Patronize, realize, harmonize . . . A plague on your 'z'. Give me an 's' please?"

Ned, who shared her love of wordplay, quipped, "Only if 'u' return the favour," spelling out the word with particular emphasis on the "u". He begged Dee to cook a leg of lamb with all the trimmings and together, feeling warm and comfortable, they declared this an excellent festive season.

Ned flew on to London to see Hannah and her husband William for New Year and Dee settled into revisions on her manuscript. She had ten days before school started to complete the revisions suggested by two readers from Beacon Press. They liked the manuscript but wanted her to expand the section on secrecy and customary law. Dee wished she could just pick up the phone and talk through some of her ideas with Christian, but phone connections to Uganda were unreliable and he was so often on the road. The post was slow and erratic. Their letters took weeks to be delivered and often crossed in the mail. Then Jay Suber, a mutual acquaintance who was going to Uganda the following week, offered to be a courier for her. That would speed things up a little. She hoped Christian might respond in time for Jay to bring a letter back to her.

Dear Christian,

I am thinking out loud in this letter. Writing to you helps me work through and I really appreciate the way your questions make me see problems in different ways. Your comments on my evolving manuscript have been very helpful and I'm sending the latest draft with Jay.

Following our exchanges over summer and into the fall, I've been turning over in my mind how to distinguish between the secrecy I find so destructive among the Jesuits and the secrecy I actively defend for Indigenous Australians. Is it wrong that not everyone knows everything, or must one always look to the context in which secrecy is asserted, expected, punished? Surely it is a question of who wields power over whom, with what consequence, and within what institutional framework.

Now, take the desert people of Central Australia. It is not a democratic society in the sense of having elected officials, but there are checks and balances. And there is no born-to-rule class. Well, older people do have more power than younger ones. And, it's an ongoing debate as to whether women enjoy the same quality of rights and privileges as men. You already know my position on that. But the residential units are small and there is no overarching government-like structure. Groups negotiate, alliances shift, new coalitions form. And it is the *assertion* that something is secret rather than the *content* of the secrets that is important. I know women know "men's business" and men know "women's business," but neither would *admit* to that knowledge.

I've been to sacred places with senior women and they've spoken in hushed tones, called out to the ancestors to warn them they are bringing me as a visitor, and swept the paths clean – you know, done all the things that indicate a place is really special. They've called the name of the place in that way that says, "Don't repeat this name outside this group. This is women's business." Then one time I realized I knew the place name already. I had read it in an ethnography written by a male anthropologist who had worked in the area and had published the book in an earlier era when Aboriginal people had no concept of the reach of the written word. Nowadays we all make sure that we don't publish secrets – the code of ethics says, "first do no harm" – and saying names out of turn is a serious affair. The men and women both knew the name and each kept it "secret" from the other. It's an oral culture. Words are powerful. I think the owners of those words have the right to protect their property – an imperfect analogy, but there you are.

But then, on the other hand, the secrecy maintained around the business of priests seems to be a cover for abuses of power and, further, a massive abuse of power upon which the church depends. It's so institutionalized, so beyond scrutiny. There is no accountability. Its reach is enormous. The stories of its abuse need to be told if the abuses are to be curbed. I understand the need for confidentiality in some circumstances, but should it be absolute? Should the confessional be completely beyond the law? One obvious question is: Why are priests excluded from mandatory reporting of abuse of minors and allowed to keep such things secret? Teachers, counselors, social and health workers are all bound to report any signs of abuse. Why not priests? If it is so unthinkable that a priest might abuse a minor, then making information known should not be a problem and could be included with all the others who must report abuse.

Then I think about the nature of taboos. They're a pretty good indicator of what is most feared in a society, and what behavior most disrupts the social order. Taboos say a lot about a culture. When taboos are broken and offenders are brought to justice, a society might heal. When taboos are broken and offenders are shielded by secrecy, a society can be scarred. But taboos are exercises in power too. Why are certain foods like eggs and red meat taboo to women and children in some places? And, come to think of it, why are so many of those taboos associated with foods that are really tasty and nourishing? Could it be that the old men are simply being greedy and, by calling the good stuff taboo, thereby keep it for themselves? If an outsider insisted the taboo was unjust, and that everyone should be able to eat the taboo foods any time of the year, the social order would be threatened. That's like what missionaries did when they decreed people should marry for love, not according to the custom of arranged marriage. It was a mess. No-one knew how to address anyone else; whose land was whose; who should perform ceremonies. People found ways of subverting the missionary rules, but the damage was done. So is it wrong to defend a society where people cannot choose their marriage partners? Or is choice itself illusory?

You know I favor open systems, open government. But maybe that is more appropriate for industrial society where there is no possibility of everyone knowing everyone else; where you can't specify the kinship relationship to your neighbor; and where there are written texts to support certain claims. In many Indigenous religions where there are secrets, there are no secret files that can be brandished, but there may be secret objects. In oral cultures secrets have to be committed to memory. And those with "inside stories" are not beyond the scrutiny of those without that knowledge. A person enjoys the status of elder as long as he or she behaves responsibly and as long as the elder's followers prosper.

At St. Jude's the "elders" – the priests – are not accountable to the laity. Vatican II should have changed that, but it only made partial and superficial inroads. Like the way priests now face the congregation during the Mass and the way the Mass is no longer in Latin but in the language of the people. Authority is supposed to be shared with the laity, but the hierarchical structure of decision-making remains very much within the church, the administration of the college, and departments. The power is still concentrated where it always has been. There is no sign that this will ever change unless there is a revolution from outside.

It's interesting to look at the way the departments work here, for the most part as self-determining units, with strictly hierarchical governance structures. The newer programs, like Judaic Studies and Women's Studies, are very different kinds of structures. They aspire to a form of democratic decision-making.

Do you think a system can be evil, or is it only people who are evil?

Dee

PS. The other day, while I was mopping up the weak rays of the winter sun in one of my favorite places – the hill overlooking Resolve – I thought about the way invading powers build on the sacred sites of the local population and made myself a note to ask you a question. Isn't Kampala built on seven hills also? Do you know what was on those hills before the mosque, cathedral, and so on?

Christian's response arrived ten days later.

Dear Dee,

In haste . . . I'm trying to catch the "courier" before he returns to the USA . . . I have an invitation to address the World AIDS Congress next month at UMass Medical in Worcester. Just northeast of you. It's the conference you wrote to me about. It's all happening very quickly. They want me to speak about "best practices". You know what works and how we've turned the statistics around here. They realize, at last, that our local knowledge is critical. Someone must have pressured the Global Fund and now I'm delivering the opening keynote! I think there is a real possibility of focusing international attention on the African crisis and moving the free pharmaceuticals campaign to the next level, like maybe real money, not just rhetoric. The conference details will be online but I can't access it from here. The week will be hectic but I hope you can come at least for the opening and stay for the reception.

Christian

PS. Your long letter – I have lots to say about secrecy and have been reading some of the early ethnographies on Yorùbá divination. The language is colonial but the texts are ones my mother knows. I want to talk more with you about this. And, closer to home, have you read Michael Taussig on the subject of Public Secrets? His work helped me think through how AIDS is represented on the political agenda. He was born in your home town, you know.

PPS. I will read your manuscript on the plane.

Dee had planned to attend the conference – just the regional section on Africa – and report back to Christian, but she had not been particularly optimistic about the chance of real change. The gulf between the so-called developed and underdeveloped countries was just too great. When it came to solutions, one size did not fit all. The grinding poverty of the vast majority of HIV-positive Africans had to be addressed. Now Christian was the keynote speaker. It was a brilliant choice. With his commanding presence, judicious turn of phrase, British training, African sensibilities, and wry sense of humor, there seemed to be real hope of shifting the priorities because, as Dee knew, he would not compromise in his presentation. Oh this was going to be fun, seeing Christian, being back in the action. *Steady girl*, she told herself, *take it slowly. This man is very task-oriented, maybe borderline imperious when pushed.*

Miriam offered to cover Dee's classes so she could attend the conference. But Dee insisted that Miriam also go to hear Christian speak. She wanted Daniel and Pica to go too if they could. "Never mind, Miriam, I'll show a movie that day," she said. "Mary J will make sure it's running and I'll give the students a work sheet so they won't feel too neglected. Hell, it's the first time I've ever skipped class."

"You don't have to justify it to me," Miriam smiled. "I'm dying to meet this Dr. Olúfémi." There was an insistent eagerness in her voice that Dee noticed immediately.

"Why the attitude?" Dee asked edgily.

"Well you speak so highly of him. You exchange letters. He's obviously important to you and . . ." Miriam's voice trailing off as Dee was beginning to flush.

The conference website was helpful and the bio on Christian was short but accurate. Born Lagos, Nigeria, 1949; BA, Ilé Ifè University, Nigeria 1966–9; University College, London, 1970–3; Junior House Doctor, London Teaching Hospital, 1974–5; Research Fellowship, Havana, 1976–8; Lecturer Ilé Ifè University, 1979–83; Medical Research Botswana and Zimbabwe, 1984–93; Director of the AIDS Africa Outreach Program, 1993– . Author *AIDS Africa: A community response*.

Dee emailed the conference organizers, explained she was a colleague, and offered to pick up Dr. Olúfémi at the airport, but she found that the arrangements for his arrival and stay were already in place. Clearly, he was to be treated as a VIP, flying into New York first for meetings, on to Boston for more meetings, then by limo to Worcester for the opening. She knew Christian would be networking as much as he could on his visit. Dee hoped he wouldn't be too exhausted by the long flight. *Funny*, she thought, *all the places we've been, and we've never been in a plane together.*

Miriam and Pica quizzed Dee as they drove to the Worcester campus of the University of Massachusetts. "I've seen his photo and I know he's been reading your draft chapters and all," Miriam said. "But what's he like?"

"Smart. Well read," Dee responded without thinking as she spun around the rotary. *Strange name. Why not roundabout? Rotary, sounds like a clothesline.*

"Smart? Well, duh," Pica said. "That goes without saying. Are we on the right road?"

"Married? Kids?" Miriam continued. "And, yes, Pica, we are on the right road, but we're not there yet!"

"Religion?" Pica added trying to be serious.

"Hang on," Dee said. "What is this, the Inquisition?"

"Inquiring minds want to know," Miriam laughed. "Sorry."

It was obvious Miriam was ready to ask more. *Doesn't like open conflict, but will probe my personal life*, Dee thought. *She's much better acculturated that I am to local speech styles but then she's been here much longer than I have.*

"Relax," Pica the pool player counseled. "No good comes of a hurried shot."

"Religion – complicated, I'd say. He went to Catholic school but I've seen him with his mother and he knows how powerful Yorùbá beliefs are. I know she hoped he'd go along with the marriage the families had arranged, but he was in London for five years and so that didn't work out." Dee began thinking of the way Christian interacted with women, always respectful, deferential to his elders, protective and solicitous with younger women – to a degree that sometimes verged on paternalism. *But with women his own age?* She wasn't really sure. Maybe there was a tinge of arrogance.

"Don't tell me he's so devoted to his calling there is no-one in his life," Miriam moaned.

"I've heard him talk about an Emma, a fellow student when he was in medical school, and I'm pretty sure they were close, but she wasn't with him in Cuba," Dee said relaxing a little. *If Miriam wants to know, so let it be. What is the harm of it? Why do I play it so close?*

"Okay, not celibate. Is he gay?" Pica asked with a tinge of mischief.

"Now there's a thought," Dee laughed. "Not that I know of. No, I'm sure he's not."

"How do you know?" Miriam pushed. "And I think we turn here."

"How do I know? Well, not from personal experience if that's what you mean."

"Turn here," Miriam and Pica shouted.

"And there's a parking spot," Miriam pointed. "Good, I think I can see Daniel's car. He had an early morning meeting with a client in Shrewsbury, and said he'd meet us here. We're going to split after the presentation."

"I'm sure you could crash the reception," Dee said.

"Maybe," Miriam said, "but that official invitation that came in the mail was all very grand and it was addressed only to you."

Dee knew they were determined to get back during daylight hours. She liked night driving. It was a chance to think, listen to public radio, sing along with her tapes. For this trip she had made certain to bring Ladysmith Black Mambazo Band. The rhythms and harmonies reminded her of Africa, and she was working on learning the words of "Wings to Fly," sung in a mixture of Swahili and English.

The auditorium filled quickly and they found four seats together near the back. "Like being back in Law School," Daniel said. "Big hall and projection facilities for boring overheads." Dee took off her coat and settled into the cold seat.

"I see you're wearing a 9 am to midnight dress," Miriam teased. "Take off that tailored jacket and you'll look just right for cocktails with the Chancellor in your little black dress."

"Well if you promise not to shout, I have a pair of strappy red sandals and a long string of beads painted with Australia desert ochres in my shoulder bag," Dee confided. *I'll try to be more forthcoming. Sharing this intrigue with Miriam is kinda fun – as if we were school kids again.* "Okay, here we go. That's the Chancellor about to welcome us all to UMass on this 'historic occasion.'"

Christian's address was stunning. He began slowly and deliberately with his own story of growing up in Lagos. He spoke of the power of Ifá divination, the long period of training for ritual experts, beliefs about sickness and health. He explained the importance of understanding the kinship system and family rituals. His delivery was clear and confident. Christian knew how to tell a story. Dee smiled to herself; he was his mother's son. The conference participants were enthralled. He drew contrasts and comparisons between Yorùbá beliefs and those he had learned in medical school. He outlined the strategies that delivered Western drugs in ways that were cognizant of African cultural mores. Then, ever so gracefully, he began to present the statistics. His tone didn't change. It was remarkable. He was having an intimate conversation with a room of some four hundred people. The lights dimmed and, instead of using the predictable overhead transparencies with graphs and charts, Christian was showing slides of people he knew. He was making the statistics personal. These were not numbers, but people with families, with hopes and fears and, he concluded somberly, a bleak future without access to drugs.

111

The lights came up and so did the hands. Christian answered questions patiently and expertly till the convener declared they were out of time. Along with others present, Dee, Miriam, Daniel and Pica were on their feet applauding. Dee worked her way to the front of the auditorium and tried to catch Christian's eye. He was surrounded by reporters, students, and fellow doctors, all wanting to ask one more question, but the convener was maneuvering him out of the room. Christian, who was not used to being managed, was scanning the crowd and finally saw Dee. He broke away from the mass of people around him, strode over, swept her up in a big bear hug and said, "I'm so pleased you're here. I've been on the run ever since I landed. Can you come tonight? Quick, tell me, before my minders tow me away to the next meeting."

"It would take an act of parliament to stop me," Dee laughed. "You were spectacular just now." The minder stepped up and reasserted his authority and Christian was whisked away.

Dee attended the next panel discussion, took notes and began doodling on the conference program. She was feeling vaguely disoriented. The doodles had broken out of their triangle and circle confinement and were now becoming an elaborate maze, like the one she had visited with Miriam and Pica last summer, and like the squares within squares in the basement of Coyle Hall. Then the afternoon session was over and she had an hour before the reception began. She found a bathroom, stuffed her sensible walking shoes into her shoulder bag, slipped into her strappy sandals, arranged her necklace so it fell in two loops, brushed her long hair, and took one last look in the mirror to assess the entire effect. She checked her coat and bag and walked down the long hall to Convention Hall A. Dee found a copy of the *Worcester Telegram and Gazette* and sat in one of the floral occasional chairs to read and write.

> *Who is the expert? Who has authority? Who gets to speak? Who listens? Who acts?*

She doodled for a bit and wrote, "Christian is really nice," but then scratched it out. *Now where did that come from?*

The reception was in a large room with an autumnal patterned carpet, heavy drapes, large floral arrangements and concertina doors that had been pushed back to increase the size of the room. Drink waiters held their trays high as they mingled with the crowd – red wine, white wine, or mineral water? Dee decided one glass of wine would be fine, especially if she could work her way to one of the tables where fine cheeses, dips, hot finger food, and bread were tastefully laid out. Christian came up quickly by her side and caught her elbow. "I'm really pleased you could stay, but so much is happening . . . I want to have a moment alone with you, but, oh, here comes the minder again."

"It's okay," Dee said, not really meaning it. "Maybe there will be some downtime and we can catch up."

"How about Friday?" Christian asked. "It's my last day and I told them I had to do some shopping for my mother."

"I'm not teaching Friday, maybe I can take you to the airport. I don't have a limo, but . . ." Dee turned her back to deflect the minder for a minute more.

"Great and we'll do a little shopping in Boston on the way." Dee relaxed and the minder moved in.

Christian introduced Dee to the "suit," Hans Gruff, but he was on a mission and didn't linger for small talk. Hans told Christian a representative of the CDC was waiting to speak with him and pointed the way to a private meeting room.

Dee struck up a conversation with a couple from Nigeria who had seen her with Christian after his speech and wanted to know how she knew him. They talked at length about the pharma-ceuticals campaign and land reform. Then Dee excused herself, found her jacket which she'd shed and thrown over a chair near the door, reclaimed her heavy coat and shoulder bag, changed out of her thoroughly impractical sandals and strode into the cold night to her car.

"Not so fast, Dee." Christian appeared out of the dark. "I'll walk you to your car."

"Where's your mate Hans?" Dee looked around.

"He thinks I'm in the bathroom. What is it with these people? Every minute has to be occupied," Christian laughed. "Well not to complain. I'm making many good contacts."

Dee unlocked the car doors and slipped behind the wheel while Christian climbed into the passenger seat. "Too cold standing out there," he shuddered. Dee watched as he dug into his pocket. "This is for you."

Dee carefully opened the little sachet of woven banana leaves. Nestled inside was an exquisite necklace of fine coral beads. "It's lovely . . ." she breathed and reached up to take off the Australian necklace she was wearing. She fumbled with the clasp and Christian quickly reached across, opened it effortlessly, swept her hair to one side, and slipped the coral strand around her neck. "Yes, lovely," he said as he kissed her on the cheek and then quickly extracted himself from her little car. "See you Friday, around ten?"

"Yep. Good luck with the rest of the conference," Dee called out the window and then quickly wound it up and turned on the demister. Her car had fogged up like a shower window. She drove home feeling strangely content. *This is good*, she thought as she turned up the Ladysmith Black Mambazo Band's "Journey of Dreams," and felt herself floating along awash in the sweet sounds and memories of Africa.

Friday was fun. Christian was still in high gear and full of ideas sparked by the conference. But he also listened carefully to all Dee had to say and questioned her closely about the intrigue at St. Jude's. "I know you can take care of yourself," he said, "but do be careful."

They bought presents for his staff in the People's Health Depot and for his mother. They strolled up Newbury Street looking in the windows. They ate at a small Italian restaurant and then it was time to go to the airport but they got stuck in the tunnel and Christian almost missed the flight. "Just drop me at the curb," he said, "and I'll make a dash for it." Dee got out of the car to yank open the over-flowing trunk. Christian held her shoulders. "Write, Dee. I love getting your letters and now that I have some idea of where you are, it will be all the more meaningful." He bent down to kiss her goodbye and said softly in Swahili, "*Safari hatua.*"

"A journey involves taking steps?" she called as he started to move quickly towards the terminal.

"Good literal translation, Dee," he looked over his shoulder and beamed. "But as a proverb, more like everything begins with small actions that build up to bigger actions, opportunities, and may involve unexpected twists."

And how many other layers of meaning? Dee thought as she watched him walk through the automatic doors and disappear. *What is his journey and how is it linked to mine?*

January 27, 1996: St. Angela Merici, founder of the Order of Nuns of St. Ursula, directed young girls in the ways of the Lord; Pope Pius IX decreed that her feast should be observed on May 31.

8

MISCHIEF AND MAYHEM
Spring 1996

Office Hours: Tuesday and Thursday 2–4:30 pm, or by appointment. St. Jude faculty were required to post their office hours. But Dee's students knew they could visit whenever her door was open. Cissy Coyle popped her head around Dee's door just before lunch and said, "Jamie sends her greetings. Wants to know what mischief you've been making." Mary Louise and MC followed Cissy into Dee's office and plopped into the two soft chairs. Cissy had the same dark curly hair and lithe form as her cousin, but her passion was English. Late in the afternoon she could be found curled up in one of the easy chairs in the library, reading and rereading nineteenth-century novels. Mary Louise and MC, also English majors, often joined her. These two could have been mistaken for sisters. They both wore their long blond hair tied back to reveal neat stud earrings. They both spoke quickly and with distinctive New Jersey accents. Like their peers the women wore jeans and sneakers. Their explicit feminist T-shirts – "Silence is Complicity" and "My Body My Choice" – seemed to be part of a shared wardrobe.

Cissy perched on the arm. "We're here to make some mischief ourselves and thought we'd give you an update. Our feminist liturgy is moving along. Want to come to a rehearsal? And we've got heaps of support for WOW."

"And we want a Department of Women's Studies, not just a Program," MC added.

"And on the seventh day?" Dee laughed.

"Will you be our faculty moderator?" Cissy asked.

"Of course," Dee said. "You could ask Miriam Levi and Pica Liberatio too," she added.

"Oh, don't worry, we already have."

"Okay, here's one for you. Do you know Mary Doyle? I haven't seen her this semester," Dee said.

They knew Mary Doyle all right. She had been going out with MC's older brother and there had been lots of talk at home. Her parents thought they were too young to be so serious. Everyone at St. Jude's knew they were an item, and that was unusual at a college where one-night hooking-up was the norm. Mary Doyle, being a responsible young woman, had made an appointment at the Health Center at St. Jude's, where she volunteered in the outreach program for health and nutrition, in order to get a prescription for the Pill. The nurse read the doctor's records and gave Mary a lecture about promiscuity, sin, pleasures of the flesh, and called her a slut. Mary Doyle was outraged by this treatment and shared her story with Mary Louise, MC and Cissy. She fumed, "I'm paying for health care here, not bullying. First the doctor won't give me the prescription and then I get a lecture from the nurse. It's none of her damn business."

"Just go to Family Planning in downtown Resolve," Cissy had advised.

Mary Doyle got the prescription, a check-up, advice about sexually transmitted diseases, and a copy of *Our Bodies Ourselves*. This she shared with her friends in the Women's Watch. All they'd been told in their Catholic schools was abstinence, abstinence, abstinence.

> *Teenage pregnancies, abstinence, peer pressure: What do these young women know about contraception and reproduction? Sex Ed includes carrying around eggs to simulate parenting. What happens if an egg breaks? One day of caring for a real child would probably be a much better lesson than carrying an egg around for a week.*

"Have you heard from Mary Doyle?" Dee tried again.

"She was at home this summer for a while and then was shipped off to relatives in Ireland."

"Is she okay? Do you hear from her?"

The three were getting very uncomfortable so Dee let it ride.

March 17, 1997: St. Patrick's Day: Green beer,
green bubbles in the fountain and gross behavior;
two students hospitalized with alcohol poisoning.

Lorica of Saint Patrick:

I arise today

Through a mighty strength, the invocation of
the Trinity

Through a belief in the Threeness

Through confession of the Oneness

Of the Creator of creation.

A week or so later, when Dee was sweeping the grass clippings from the path outside her apartment, Cissy stopped by. Mary Louise and MC were not far behind. MC's shirt said, "You can't beat a woman." It was a soft spring afternoon, thick with the buzz of insects. Dee had just squeezed some fresh lemons, and banana bread was in the oven. The young women sat on the porch, sipping their drinks and crunching the ice, as cars came and went in the parking lot. Cissy caught sight of the tall gaunt figure Father Sordes loping along and shuddered. MC sniffed. Mary Louise asked, "He comes to Women's Studies meetings doesn't he?"

"Yes, he does. We encourage anyone who teaches, or would like to teach, courses about Women's Studies to attend. Mostly it works well. Why do you ask?"

"Well, he's so fucking weird." Mary Louise flushed. She usually censored herself and didn't use foul language in front of faculty. Dee paid no attention to the lapse. She had good reason to agree with the assessment but did not want to stir the pot. If these women knew something, Dee wanted to hear it from them, free from her guidance and judgment.

"Shit. He's not just 'weird' and you know it," MC snapped. Dee kept quiet, waiting for more.

The sun was dropping behind the hill and Dee was ready to go inside. She could smell the bread was ready and invited the women inside. Dee held the screen door open and the three dove inside and quickly settled into the big chairs – a recent thrift store purchase. Dee turned out the banana bread and cut it into slabs. The steam rose. Perfect. She put it on her improvised coffee table – two crates covered with a red and brown Kanga cloth with a Swahili proverb, *Amani Kwa Watu*, "Peace to all." The students started eating and the story gushed forth.

Mary Louise began. "He is such a fucking bastard, makes my skin crawl just to say his name. He knew Mary Doyle was going with my brother and he invited them over for drinks. They thought it was a friendly gesture. He said he was very interested in my brother's photography – his portraits are really good, you know. He also praised Mary for her work with homeless women at the clinic. What a joke."

"Yes, he took me in too," said Cissy. "What did I know? He was so easy to talk to, always willing to help, full of ideas."

"Yes, but he had photos my brother knew nothing about, and it turned out he had found out about Mary going to Family Planning." MC was crying but she didn't stop talking.

"He wasn't interested in her confession. He wanted to know what kind of sex they were having. He wouldn't shut up. He talked about all kinds of sex, really kinky stuff. He showed them pictures and things he had in a locked box. 'His research,' he called it. It was really, you know, yucky. But he was being the Priest, a man of God. This was about all God's creatures. He said that such things were mentioned in the Bible, so how could it be wrong? He wanted them to show him what they did and all the while he was drinking, drinking, drinking. They'd had one cocktail. They thought that was cool, very sophisticated, you know, but he kept going and demanding they perform for him. He must have put something into their drinks because Mary said she began to feel woozy and my brother kept taking off his glasses and wiping them, like he couldn't see clearly." She paused and murmured, "Oh, we are really going to hell now. Mary said never to tell. That he would get us. That's why she was sent away, to protect her, and so she could recover from the attack. He really hurt her and my brother was forced to watch. He won't even talk about it at all. Then he . . ."

Dee had not expected this intensity but the women were not going to stop now that they had broken their silence.

"And then he forced himself on my brother. He was like an animal. He is a really sick bastard."

The group fell silent. Dee was struggling to find words that expressed her rage and that were appropriate for these young women to hear.

Cissy broke the silence, saying, "We don't want to get you into trouble. I'm sorry you know this now." But her gaze hardened, and before Dee could say anything, she continued, "He's done it before. That's what I heard in the Women's Watch. And anyone who gets in his way just disappears. Jamie knows more stuff, but she won't tell me."

And Amy Nakamura?

"Have you talked to your parents?" Dee asked. "Do you know if the police were ever called?"

"Oh the campus police. They're no use. They don't take us seriously. They leer at us when we wear shorts and make suggestions as they drive past and we think they make obscene calls to the dorms late at night. Mary didn't want to have them involved," Cissy said. "And my parents? When they learned about it they said, just keep quiet. You can't accuse a priest. They said an accusation would bring shame on the family and that I'd be the one with the bad name."

"Mary knew that because she was having sex, he could blackmail her," Mary Louise added. "And notice how they didn't even address the possibility that he was actually guilty and should be punished. Instead it is all about what he could do to us, no matter what. For them it's all about preserving the mystical powers of the priesthood. We're a threat to their way of life."

"Please don't talk about this,' MC pleaded. "For now, we keep out of his way and hang out together. Maybe we can do something after Commencement. Maybe if we have WOW, more speakers, more courses about women, more speakouts, other people might begin to understand."

120

Earlier protests and Jessie Seneca: What do these women know of that? Pica knows more than she is telling too. Why is she reluctant to talk?

Dee had seen reports about a priest in Louisiana who had molested young boys, and she knew the stories about the women who kept house for priests, quietly bore their children, and were well looked after, as long as they made no public demands. But this story about Father Sordes opened up a whole new set of horrors to her. She wanted to honor the confidences of the young women, but she also did not want this man to continue to prey on students. She wondered where to turn and not make it worse for the students. Clearly, the Health Center – and probably the Counseling Center too – were compromised. Dulcie McNeil in the Chaplain's Office was too close to the Jesuits for Dee to approach just yet. And, anyway, it would be the women's word against that of a priest. Dee wanted to share what she knew with Pica and Miriam, but she held off, not wanting them to be further endangered. *Am I jumping to conclusions by assuming his guilt? Maybe it's time to talk to Jackie Li again. She's a lawyer. She's the Equal Employment Officer. She has that file on Father Sordes from my encounters with him last summer.*

He wasn't all that young, but Paddy Sordes SJ could come across as very hip. He wore jeans and sneakers. His hair was long and tied back in a ponytail. His eyes were set a little far apart and gave the appearance of perpetual surprise. He listened to heavy metal music and hung out in Mick's Sports Bar with the guys. He invited students to call him by his first name and did not flinch when they cursed. He was interested in all that the students did and was known to criticize his fellow priests – especially those he considered very conservative. Little was known of his background. He sometimes spoke of his time in New Mexico, and he was fond of margaritas. In the summer he always had a jug of freshly made margaritas in his fridge ready to go.

Dee knew this because Pica had invited her to a wake. "It'll be in the best of the Irish tradition," she'd said. "You need to add this to your anthropological notes." It was an anthropological event and Dee quickly realized she could not keep up with drinking and concentrate on the stories that were being told. She was talking to an elderly couple, distant relatives of the deceased, who wanted to talk to Dee about their time in Uganda. They had been halfway through a story about their time in Kampala when Paddy Sordes lurched over to Dee. He had stood behind her chair, leaned over her shoulder, brushed back her long hair, and whispered in her ear. "I remember the first time I saw you. You were giving a paper at the American Academy of Religions. It was so sensational I almost came on the spot." Dee pushed her chair back, jamming his knee against the table behind them. He flinched, then shuffled sideways to join another group of boisterous mourners. She turned back to finish the conversation about Christian–Muslim relations in Kampala with the elderly couple. "I'll see you at work," Paddy Sordes managed as he resumed his seat.

On the following Monday there had been a plain manila envelope under her office door. Inside, on notepaper that bore the inscription "scratch note," was a sketch of a naked man scratching his backside, and the following note.

> Dear Dee,
>
> Great seeing you. When can we get together? I have an idea for a course on sexuality that might be of interest to Women's Studies.
>
> Paddy

Dee had not wanted to "get together" with him and hoped he wouldn't get the stamp of approval from Women's Studies for his course. She replied on plain paper:

> Professor Sordes,
>
> I took offense to your behavior at the wake. I trust you are not using this paper in your correspondence with students.
>
> Dee Per Scrutari

His reply was curt.

Professor Scrutari,

What a humorless person you are! Arrogant too. It is none of your business how I choose to communicate with students.

Father Sordes, SJ

Dee had taken the correspondence to Jackie Li, the Equal Employment Officer. Jackie had gone to school in Singapore where her parents ran an import-export business and she had the crispness of a person used to making hard decisions. She listened to Dee's account, read the correspondence, held it at arm's length and said, "Why do I feel like I need a shower?"

"What can I do?" asked Dee.

"I would like to take this to the President. It could be off the record. Or you could lodge a formal complaint, and it would be investigated."

Dee did not want Sordes to offend again. She wanted the college to have to deal with his behavior, but she also knew it would be very difficult. "You know that no-one will touch him. Nothing seems to stick, even though I suspect he's been in trouble for this kind of stuff before." She gave Jackie a long look. She took in the lawyer's dark blue suit, the padded shoulders, the hair drawn back in a high French braid, and noted the whimsy of the small diamond pin on the lapel. It was the symbol for woman. Jackie stared back. She neither confirmed nor denied the implied question, but Dee suspected she was right. This guy was an abuser.

"You would tell me if I was being puritanical, wouldn't you?" Dee asked.

Jackie Li gave her a quizzical look. "Where did that come from? Look, let's keep it on my record and the next time he offends, I'll come back to you if I need further ammunition. It's not a perfect solution, but I am going to be very vigilant."

Well, according to Dee, he had offended again, and this time it was a case for the cops. She outlined the story to Jackie Li who listened quietly, asking no questions but committing every detail she heard to memory. Jackie was a pragmatist. She knew if she was going to move against Father Sordes SJ, she needed a solid case. She knew that the church looked after its own. She assumed Mary Doyle had been quietly taken out of harm's way and that her parents had either decided not to press charges, or agreed to a sealed settlement. Either way they had been persuaded that their course of action was in the best interests of all parties. Maybe they'd been assured that the offending priest would be sent off for treatment. Jackie knew from an off-the-record conversation with a colleague in New Mexico that Sordes had already spent time there at the treatment center run by the Servants of the Paraclete, a small Catholic religious order, in Jemez Springs. Had she known of his extra-curricular activities during his sojourn, she might have moved faster. Jackie had little faith in the value of therapy and, in Sordes's case, there were multiple addictions – alcohol, violence, and sex. Alcoholism was not taken seriously by the church. Violence was wrong, but could be forgiven: women were counseled to turn the other cheek. Sex was a taboo topic. Celibacy was supposed to remove it from the list of potential problems for the priesthood. Sex was a sin, a mystery, a matter for the confessional, not the law. A man who had a calling was not to be sacrificed for such lapses.

In accepting the position at St. Jude's, Jackie Li knew she faced a particular challenge. There was plenty of good literature on male–female sexual harassment. There were good teaching videos designed to alert students and faculty alike of *quid pro quo* scenarios: sleep with me if you want an "A", a promotion, a better office, a grant. Even the "chilly climate" situation was not so hard to represent. No girlie calendars in offices, no derogatory comments about women as airheads, but what of the biology class where women were asked to locate their ovaries in front of other students? What of a literature class studying rape where students are asked to share their stories? Then there was same-sex sexual harassment. How to talk about the priest who invited young men to his room so they could study together and then made sexual advances? Jackie despaired. She had no real vocabulary to describe these kinds of abuse.

Even before she had met Dee and heard her story, Jackie had insisted there be a major consciousness-raising exercise at St. Jude's. It was one of her first actions in the newly constituted position. Jackie knew it needed to be more than voluntary discussion groups on the odd weekend, or memos to the heads of departments. There had to be many ways anyone who thought they were being harassed could seek advice and support. That meant there had to be plenty of persons around who were well versed in the policy. It was not enough to distribute literature to departments and expect informed discussion. She had sufficient reports from junior faculty who had tried to have an item on harassment placed on the agenda for their department meetings, only to be told that there wasn't enough time, or that it wasn't a serious matter, or that everyone already knew.

After weighing the pros and cons of raising the subject of sexual harassment, Jackie made a presentation at a faculty meeting. This, she reasoned, was her best chance of reaching all faculty members. The reading with which the President began that day had been from Genesis 4:16-17. "To the woman he said, 'I will greatly increase your pains in childbearing . . . your desire will be for your husband and he will rule over you.' To Adam he said, 'Because you listened to your wife . . . cursed is the ground because of you.'" Jackie had not been at St. Jude's long enough to think about the significance of this passage.

Jackie Li handed out the document she had prepared. It set out the best practices in St. Jude's market basket schools, the ones to which they liked to compare themselves. She discussed each in a businesslike fashion and then sat down. The President returned to chairing the meeting but something was out of kilter. The speaking order was not being followed. "About these confidentiality procedures, you mean someone could have complained about me and I might not know?" exploded Bill O'Vafer. "It's un-American. Anyone could make up anything."

"These young women just don't know how to take a joke," Anthony Bufo moaned.

"What about women who cry rape, say no and mean yes? That

goes on all the time. And what about women who harass men?" O'Vafer sat down. He had seen *Fatal Attraction* and had warned his male students about women stalkers. He had read the *New York Times Book Review* piece and knew that the often-repeated statistic – that one in three women would be sexually abused in her lifetime – was under assault. He agreed with that clever little Kate Roiphe. He knew three women and none of them had been raped.

The stage was set for *Iolanthe*. "Strephon's a member of parliament, carries every bill he chooses," Dee hummed to herself. Where was the brass band?

Enchanted Forests . . . A Forest of Symbols . . . Diana's sacred grove . . . And why do all these faculty meetings take place in Enchanted Forests? Traffic between the world of the spirit and the world of the flesh? Changelings?

Jackie Li answered patiently. "The college has to be in compliance with state law: the better the procedures, the stronger the defense." This was a standard position and the Trustees wanted to know the college was as well protected as possible. "These policies will safeguard both complainant and accused," Jackie explained, although she knew that there were many on faculty who thought students had way too much power already. "There has to be confidentiality so that complainants won't fear retribution and so that false reports don't take on a life of their own."

FIAT CELLA: Jesuits know how to stop rumors.

Dee was sitting too far back to make out the symbol of the diamond pin on Jackie's lawyers' suit but she was sure it was a statement on the proceedings. The woman seemed to have an inexhaustible supply of these small pieces. Unless subject to close scrutiny, they could pass for exquisite costume jewelry. Jackie was halfway through elaborating the difference between informal and formal complaints when Father Tempus raised his hand. "Given the time, 4:45 pm, I move the meeting be adjourned."

"Could the sexual harassment policy be the first item on the agenda at the next meeting?" Dee asked.

"Talk to the Faculty Board," Dean Simean said. Dee knew the board was a mere rubber stamp for the administration, but she was prepared to work through the process until it proved unworkable.

Due process, no arbitrary arrest, writs of HABEAS CORPUS, *trial by one's peers, the democratic contract, honored in the breach rather than observance.*

In the lobby O'Vafer and Bufo made a beeline for Virginia. She was looking flustered, not her composed self at all. Dee heard their questions about due process and saw Virginia Glacialis nod, smile in a perfunctory manner, and excuse herself. She had to pick up her daughter. Dee stayed long enough for O'Vafer and Bufo to corner her and ask about her role in the new women's organization on campus. "Why don't we have men's groups?" Bill asked, cradling a beer and looking around at his colleagues.

"Isn't it discriminatory to exclude men?" Tony asked, enjoying the moment.

"In this world justice only comes into question between equals," Dee said quoting Thucydides' *Melian Dialogues*. "The strong do what they can and the weak accept what they must. But remember those trampled by the power of the Athenians rose up." The two men weren't interested in this digression into ancient history. "Okay," Dee said, "First we need to level the playing field, then we can talk about equal measures."

"Well, what about having Men's Studies?" Bill persisted.

"You do," Dee conceded. "It's called 'Western Civilization.' Based on the syllabus I saw, it was produced and reproduced by men alone."

"I'd include women if they'd done anything of note," Tony said. "Name one great woman writer."

"Well considering literacy was systematically denied to women, those who we know about are pretty special, like Christine de Pizan. I could send you a bibliography of others," she added in a helpful tone and excused herself. Surely *her* bathroom needed cleaning.

Entries:

Abbess Herrard, Garden of Delights, 12th century.

Christine de Pizan, LE LIVRE DE LA CITÉ DES DAMES, 1405.

Do facts matter? Old patriarchs never die.
What hope for the next generation?

It was the end of another school year. The Commencement speaker was a woman for the first time in ten years, according to the St. Jude's archives. Maybe the President had decided this was the year to have a strong female presence on the official platform. Mary O'Legator, Dean of the Law School at St. Ignatius, the first woman Law Dean in its history, spoke with passion of her work with undocumented workers, of the promise of America, and of her good wishes for the graduates. Dee would have been on her feet cheering, had the Dean not felt it necessary to suggest that the battles yet to be fought, ones which this generation of students might address, included the incursions of medical science on the sanctity of life. Dee and Miriam exchanged glances. This was not a fight they could win. And Dee had lots to do and to think about.

What are the limits of protest? Choose your battles wisely.

Can institutions be transformed from within? Or can they only be reformed?

May 26, 1996: Pentecost: Whitsunday - fifty days after Easter, a holy-day superimposed on Shavuot, the Feast of Weeks, one of the three pilgrimage festivals, fifty days after Passover; Jews from many nations speaking many tongues were in Jerusalem on that first Christian Pentecost; white robes for those baptized on this day; the great liturgical Latin hymns VENI CREATOR SPIRITUS and VENI SANCTE SPIRITUS were composed for Pentecost.

9

NEW STEPS
Summer 1996

The campus was quiet as Dee's favorite season arrived. While others complained about the heat and sat in their air-conditioned houses, Dee luxuriated in the summer sun. She sat outside to read, write, entertain, and work on her herb garden. She popped into Massachusetts to the Brimfield flea-market and finally declared she had reached saturation point with floor lamps. There was no more room in her apartment. She planned to do some summer touring in her little car – maybe drive up to the Finger Lakes, visit Seneca Falls, see Elizabeth Cady Stanton's house. She'd decided to flex off – well, as much as she ever really did. She hoped her good summer sleep patterns would return soon.

And then there was the possibility that Christian would be arriving in July for an extended stay at UMass. After the conference an interdisciplinary working group had been formed to pursue funding for an intensive one-semester certificate program that would train medicos fighting HIV-AIDS in Africa. Christian had been invited to direct the program, but he was playing hardball with the terms of the appointment. In early June he had written to Dee:

> Why would I leave Uganda now, just when we are really getting somewhere? I am needed here. What can the West offer us? Education to be sure. Resources? Well it can move on the issue of free pharmaceuticals. They get cheaper by the day but are still completely beyond our reach. You know I met with several of the key players in New York, but they need to do more than talk. I've told them unless their talk is matched by action, I am unavailable. The stakes are high.

On a lighter note . . . here is a proverb for you. *Usiache mbachao kwa msala upitao* – literally, don't abandon your old rug for a passing mat, but like all Swahili proverbs it has a wider meaning. Something like "Treasure what you have and is more permanent rather than a temporary thing that is not yours, even though it might be more attractive than what you have."

Dee sat outside to reread his letter and puzzled over this new proverb along with the one he had left her with at the airport. With a start, she realized she had drawn doodles in the margins of his letter. *Where do these come from?* Dee turned the page around to try to make sense of the dense patterns. Maybe it was just a design from an old rug she was sketching. She was about to go inside to fetch her notebook when Pica came by.

"Got a minute? I was on my way to the lovely air-conditioned library and saw you mopping up the early morning sun."

"Sure, come inside. I do have a window fan you know. What's up?"

"I have an idea for an article and wondered if I could pick your brains on your African experience, particularly the interviews you did with HIV-positive mothers."

"I haven't written up that material. I tried once, but it was rejected. I won't bother with that journal again."

"Well that's okay for you," Pica said.

"Sorry," Dee said quickly. "Is this for your tenure file?"

Pica nodded.

"It could be fun to think it through together," Dee said. "There are all these ethical issues to be addressed if we want to use real case materials."

"An article in a refereed journal wouldn't go astray. You know how much weight is put on those kind of publications when it comes to tenure and I am coming up a year early," Pica said. "Is that your phone Dee? It's okay, answer it, I'm on my way. See you Friday for dinner, my turn."

It was Christian on the phone. He was very pleased. "They made an offer I can't refuse."

"Yes?" Dee was feeling light-headed.

"A pilot program with free drugs for Kampala for a year with an option for a further five, if we can develop a sustainable program."

"And what did they want in return?"

"Come to UMass, write the manual, teach, direct the new program and three built-in return fares in the first year so I can monitor the Uganda end of the venture."

"Where are you calling from and, my god, what time is it there?"

"The Ministry of Health in Kampala and it's early evening. We just broke for dinner. This whole venture has become very important in terms of East–West diplomacy."

"When will you be here?" Dee asked.

"Late July."

"Anything I can do to help?"

"Yes, but for now, here is my official government email – we can have almost real-time communications. Okay. I'm getting the signal I need to be elsewhere."

"Thanks so much for letting me know."

"Well, you have a role in all this you know. You've kept the pressure on with the petition."

"I'll email you tonight when I've had a chance to assimilate all the news. Bye, Christian."

"Bye, Dee. See you in cyberspace."

Dee walked down to her office to instant-message Miriam. Dee loved the possibility of real-time dialogue online and she needed help thinking this through.

DPS: Christian will be at UMass Medical in July, for a year!

ML: Let's have a party to welcome him.

June 21, 1996: Summer Solstice: Midsummer - the time to perform divination about affairs of the heart - renamed St. John's Day for the Christian calendar.

⚜

Christian and Dee got into a good rhythm with their emailing. He told her about his visit with his mother in Lagos. She told him about her visit with Consuelo and her growing interest in Yorùbá religion. She was learning Ifá divination, and already knew over 100 of the basic 256. Christian told Dee more about secret societies in Yorùbá culture. She told him about the article she was now coauthoring with Pica. He explained more about the courses he wanted to design and implement.

Then it was late July and Christian was about to take up the position at UMass Medical. She offered to pick him up at the airport, but he was to have a minder and meetings in Boston and wouldn't get into Worcester until late in the day. Dee kept her email turned on, hoping he'd appear online. It was nearly midnight when her IM lit up.

CO: Still up? Not sleeping well?

DPS: Kinda. How are u? What's your schedule for this week?

CO: I'll know more tomorrow.

DPS: Miriam's planning a welcome party.

CO: No parties yet, Dee. Tell Miriam thanks and I'm working on my schedule.

DPS: No worries.

CO: I still need some signatures on the contract to wrap this up.

DPS: Okay, 'nite.

CO: Sleep well. It's good to be in the same time zone.

Over the next week Dee and Christian had a number of cryptic IM exchanges. It *was* good to be in the same time zone but Dee wanted to actually see him. She was growing impatient with the disembodied nature of their electronic communications. She wanted him to get done with the business side of the deal. Dee confided in Miriam that she was feeling anxious.

"Have you told him?" Miriam laughed.

"Told him what? And what's so funny?"

"You are. You have such a sharp wit and can be so direct, but you can't just ask him when he'll be free?"

"Okay. Okay. I know it's the twentieth century. I could invite him to dinner. I don't know what's wrong with me. Not sure whose culture's rules I should be following."

Miriam raised an eyebrow, gave Dee a hug and said, "Try to get some sleep."

Dee hugged her back. She was learning to appreciate Miriam's concern about this relationship. *I'm direct about politics*, Dee thought. *And Miriam can be direct too, just on different matters. A little cultural relativism probably won't hurt me.*

Dee's "wakefulness" was back and her dreams mirrored her doodling – recurring mazes. Sometimes she was lost in those mazes; sometimes she could see the way out but then the light would fade and she'd be stumbling again. There was clarity in the mazes in her dreams that she couldn't reconstruct in her waking hours. Awake, the truth was there, taunting her, just beyond her reach.

August 15, 1996: Assumption (Feast of Mary) - Mass to honor the Blessed Mother; prayers will be offered for inner peace, family unity, the ills of our society and world peace; thirty-three dozen long-stemmed red roses will be presented to Our Lady.

CO: Dinner this weekend. I was thinking something special. The Publick House in Sturbridge maybe, or if that is too formal, how about the Inn at Ware. They cook tilapia.

DPS: I'm happy to cook.

CO: Dee, please. I want to take you out. I'll pick you up at 6 pm.

DPS: What, like a date?

CO: Yes, like a date.

Dee looked for Miriam online. There she was. Ping.

DPS: Christian asked me out on a date. Why am I feeling light-headed?

ML: Well if it was a dog it would bite you. I'm so pleased he has made a move. Time for you to move on. Bruce has made his decisions. That's history. Enjoy this. Whatever it is.

DPS: What am I going to wear?

ML: Something really simple, something it's easy to get out of, lol.

DPS: That dark green number I bought last year?

ML: There you go. Perfect. ☺

A date. Dee wasn't sure how to handle this. It had been a while, in fact, too long since she had gone on one. By Saturday she was in a state. She cleaned the apartment, did laundry, ran errands, and by late afternoon was beginning to panic. She was tired because her insomnia had been particularly bad the past week. Maybe a soak in the bath would revive her. It took some imagination to transform her bathroom into a place of relaxation. The dusty pink and glossy black tiles were cracked, the paint yellowed, the overhead light brutal. Dee lit several candles and without compunction poured the expensive musk-based perfume that Bruce's mother had given her into the bath water. Dee rarely wore perfume, and never anything as heavy and expensive as this one, but it was perfect for the bath. "Goodbye Bruce," she murmured as she emptied the bottle into the steamy water. She turned up the music. "Least Complicated" was one of her favorite Indigo Girls songs. They were right. Simple things could be hard to learn. Dee flicked the water in rhythm with the music. This was good. The scented steam filled the room and she felt the dead ache of her exhaustion beginning to fade.

As she got out of the tub she caught sight of her body in the worn mirror. It was not too bad – well, certainly not perfect, stomach no longer taut, a little extra around the middle, but no stretch marks, good muscle tone. Did she have time to braid her hair? Maybe just the top of her head, that would be about forty-eight braids. She

134

would tie those braids back and let the rest fall loose over her shoulders. Makeup? Light, but maybe that scarlet lipstick she'd bought on a whim. Lately, she'd been learning about cosmetics. They had not been part of her Australian or African experience, but in the United States they seemed almost compulsory. Dee threw the bathroom door open and the steam poured into the hallway.

She dressed quickly and remembered Miriam's advice. The dress was a simple, mid-calf shift in soft silk with a long back zipper. Who would know that underneath were her matching Victoria's Secret red lace bra and panties, a fun gift on her fiftieth birthday from her daughter? Dee picked up one of her favorite shawls, slipped on a pair of sandals, and carefully fastened the coral necklace Christian had given her. It set off the dark green of her dress perfectly. She threw her comb, lipstick, credit card and driver's license into a small purse. Should she include a condom? Why not? She still had some from her African days.

Christian was at the door. "These are for you," he said and handed her a loose bunch of deep blue irises. She walked through into the kitchen to get a vase and realized the walls were dripping from the steam left from her bath. "This place smells like a pharmacy. What have you been doing? No don't tell me. I just want to take all this in."

"All this what?" Dee felt a rising panic.

"Dee at home, no papers on the table. Dee dressed to go out. Great. I made a reservation for seven o'clock. We have enough time for the scenic route."

"Through the hills?"

"Yes, my minder grew up near Ware and gave me impeccable directions."

They walked to his black car, which looked pristine. Christian held the door for her and lent forward to make sure she was comfortable. *This feels good.* She glanced across at Christian. He was a very good-looking man. Tall, lean, loose-limbed, graying at the temples, and a smile that transformed his otherwise serious face into a mass of fine laugh lines, each one with a history; some she knew, and the rest she could only guess at.

Christian drove with a grace she hadn't paid attention to before, enjoying the road, effortlessly shifting gears as they wound through the hills. "Ah, music." He pushed a tape into the cassette player. "Ladysmith Black Mambazo Band. Listen to the rhythms," he said as he rapped on the steering wheel and sang along.

"You've got a really nice voice," Dee said. "I guess I've never heard you just sing."

"What about joining me? I know you know the words," he said looking across at Dee. She had not seen that face before – sort of serious but fondly amused. By the time they arrived at the restaurant, they had sung their way through the tape and Dee was feeling very relaxed.

The Inn at Ware is one of those New England places where dark wood paneling, wallpaper, and window treatments threaten to overwhelm any life that might venture indoors. Small muslin sachets of lavender were strewn on the counters. Quilted throw rugs and fussy hand-embroidered antimacassars adorned the Victorian chairs and couches crowded into the reception area. But the restaurant was a gem. It was pleasantly light and opened onto a small indoor garden where there was a fountain, climbing roses, hollyhocks, hydrangeas, and a proliferation of yellow, white, and pink daisies. The chef, who had decided to leave his high-powered position in Boston for this picturesque part of Connecticut, was quickly developing a reputation for his original, elegant cuisine. Dee had heard about the place from friends, but had not eaten there before.

Several people were at the bar, where she took note of the stuffed moose head. What did Christian make of all this? Very little it seemed. He spoke with the maître d'hôtel who said, "This way sir," and seated Dee and Christian away from the large family party and near one of the french windows overlooking the garden. The evening breeze played gently on Dee's still not-quite-dry hair. "I like the braids," Christian began, but he was interrupted by the wine steward.

"Champagne, please."

"Of course, sir."

They read down the menu. There really was tilapia, grilled with a fresh salsa sauce. "That's for me," Dee said.

"I'm going to try the garlic shrimp." Christian said and put down the menu. "Here's to you Dee," he raised his glass, "I have something to show you and it's partly yours." He pushed something towards her.

"The signed contract. Everyone? And the budget too. When did this get wrapped up?"

"Wednesday."

"And you kept it quiet all that time," Dee gave him a playful push. He caught her hand and pressed it to his lips. "No fighting. Here's to us."

"Here's to the CDC," Dee laughed. "I never thought I'd toast the Centers for Disease Control."

They ate slowly, savoring the simple but splendid food. Christian ordered a bottle of Rosemount cabernet sauvignon. They were almost finished with it when Dee said, "This is more than I usually drink, though I love the oaky touch to this red, even with fish." Christian moved his chair closer to her and pretended to breathe in the wine. "I think I'm slightly tipsy," she said.

"Maybe you are. Or maybe, you're just relaxing. You've had quite a year."

Dee found herself enjoying the playfulness of the evening and the feelings this man was arousing in her.

"What about dessert?" Christian asked.

"If they have a crème brulée, you could twist my arm."

"A liqueur, perhaps?"

Dee shook her head. "Just the dessert, thanks."

When it came, Dee cracked the sugar surface and spooned the lemony mix into her mouth. "Delicious. Want to try some?"

Christian nodded and Dee offered him some from her spoon. "I really like those braids," he said moving his chair further around to her side. "And I'd like even more to unbraid them."

Dee was feeling very good. She liked the way this man was flirting with her.

He tucked his leg around hers. She slipped out of her sandals, worked her way under the cuff of his trousers, and ran her bare toes up his leg.

"I think we should get the check," he whispered into her hair as he put his arm around her bare shoulders and pulled her towards him.

"Umm." Dee reached for her shawl and his arm brushed against her breast. She felt her nipples harden. Had he noticed?

"Excuse me for a minute Dee, I need to sign my card over at the register. I'll be back." She maneuvered back into her sandals.

They walked out into the garden hand-in-hand and Dee stopped to admire the deep blue hydrangeas. Christian waited and then took her hand again. "Have you seen the upstairs?" he asked. "It's quite something."

"I hear it's where people come for a dirty weekend," Dee laughed.

Christian ignored the comment.

Am I misreading this man? Dee thought anxiously and then reassured herself. *Patience, girl. Let the evening unfold.*

The stairs were wide. Gilt-framed bucolic scenes of New England broke the monotony of the fleur-de-lis wallpaper. Dee was busy inspecting the needlework of a wall hanging on the landing when Christian took her shoulders and turned her to the left.

"If you would do me the pleasure," he said, as he unlocked one of the doors and held it open for Dee. "Not a dirty weekend, Dee. There are wonderful baths here, and I'd soap you up in a heartbeat, but I think you've already had one bath today."

"Christian, are we doing what I think we're doing?"

"I hope so."

"Me too." Dee reached out and took his hand. The hint of nervousness in his voice was so touching.

He picked her up and carried her to the bed. "Remember that time in Uganda when you wrapped me in a blanket and carried me to the health center?" Dee asked.

"I was praying all the way. I called upon most of the gods known to man that day."

Dee half rolled herself in the quilt. "Oh doctor, do I have a fever?" she asked plaintively.

"Let me see the color of your eyes. Hum. Perfect match for your green dress." He kissed her eyes gently.

"Swollen glands?" Christian felt behind her ears. "No. They seem normal." He kissed her ears and she began to squirm. "Sensitive. I'll record that on the chart for future reference. Let me see your tongue. Looks delicious." He kissed her and her tongue was very healthy.

"Now about this hair. I think it needs loosening." Christian undid the clasp of her necklace, pulled it free, and began to unbraid her hair, slowly, deliberately, strand by strand.

"Don't stop." Dee was purring now. Christian, intent on the unbraiding, was humming softly. "Oh yes, sing to me." Dee intoned.

Dee shook her hair loose and rolled across the bed and out of the quilt. Christian caught her before she completed the turn, brushed her hair aside, and kissed the back of her neck. She kicked off her sandals and intertwined her legs with his. He pulled his shirt off over his head in one action. Dee loved that male move. God she'd missed being held so close. Christian was working at the zipper on her dress. He rolled her onto her tummy and inch by inch deftly slipped her dress down her body and then threw it onto a chair. He ran his tongue down her back and she shuddered. "Cold?"

"No, just coming to life," Dee half turned to face him. "You're wearing too many clothes," she said as she helped him out of his trousers, and threw them on the floor. They lay side by side, flesh to flesh, her freckled tanned body against his golden brown skin. Her whole body was tingling. He kissed gently, slowly. She ran her fingers down his back and up under his arms, and pulled him closer. She pushed against his groin. He was certainly ready. "Slowly, Dee," he said. "I've been imagining this for so long."

She propped herself up on one elbow and looked at Christian as if for the first time. He took the opportunity to undo her bra. "Nice red. The nuns said red drove men wild." Christian breathed deeply and kissed her shoulders, breasts, and down her arms to the tips of her fingers. "You are so beautiful. And brave. And brilliant," he said as he worked her pants down over her hips and kissed her toes, one by one, imparting a little blessing on each.

"And you are a great strategist and my god do you have a gorgeous body and can I have some of that?" she said as he kissed his way back up to her mouth and she worked his boxers over his hips and wrapped her legs around his.

"You can, and you may, but first, safe sex."

Before Dee could say, "In my purse," Christian had retrieved a condom from his trouser pocket and handed it to her. "Now it's your turn," he exhaled.

Their bodies rose and fell. They explored, murmured, sighed, cried out, and finally Dee lay back in the crook of Christian's arm and fell asleep, the first deep, non-dream-tormented sleep she had had for ages.

Dee woke slowly and it took a few minutes for her to adjust. The curtains were half open and the brittle early morning sun streamed in over Christian's shoulder as he sat reading the paper in one of the plush Queen Anne chairs. "Tea for my lady?" he asked and brought a tray with a pot and two delicate china cups over to the bed.

Dee pulled herself up in the bed, brushed her hair away from her face and ran her tongue over her teeth. Okay this is what I look like after a good sleep, she thought. Christian sat on the bed beside her, poured the tea and said as calmly as if they had been together all their lives, "Shall I read the paper to you?"

Dee nodded. This was very good.

10

Memorandum

To: All Department Heads

From: Office of the Dean

Re: Tenure and Promotion

Date: September 1, 1996

Since the tenure process for faculty leads to major career milestones and these decisions, difficult as they are, generally have major consequences for the College, it is important that the dossiers of the candidates be compiled carefully to facilitate what necessarily must be a very rigorous process.

As Department Head, it is your responsibility to nominate which junior faculty members are ready for tenure, form a committee, prepare a report, bring it to a vote in the department, and forward the recommendation to the college-wide Tenure and Promotion Committee.

Deadlines:

Feb. 7, Departmental Report

March 15, Dean's Report

April 20, Board of Trustees.

Of course everyone knew who was where in the tenure track. The ticking of the tenure clock was not easily ignored. Pica was in her fifth year at St. Jude's and it was her turn. If successful, she would become the fourth tenured woman in the Religious Studies Department, joining Virginia, Miriam and Dee. Virginia had been tenured for twelve years and had been Department Head for the past five, but was now on sabbatical, leaving Father Abacus in the chair. Miriam had been at the college two years and had gone through the tenure process the year before Dee arrived. She had brought five years credit with her from the University of Chicago and had thus come up for tenure early. Dee came into the college with tenure from her previous appointments in Uganda and Australia and did not have to run the gauntlet at St. Jude's. Both Dee and Miriam were eligible to serve on Pica's committee.

Pica worried about the kind of committee Father Abacus might form to make the preliminary report on her dossier. Certainly her service to the college was not at issue. She had been active at both the department and college levels. She had chaired the committee on departmental bylaws, had been active on the college education policy committee, and was generally considered conscientious and collegial. In terms of teaching, there was no doubt she was committed to her students and was innovative in the classroom. She'd team-taught courses in the freshman seminar program and forged links with faculty in History, Philosophy, and Sociology. Her courses were always over-subscribed and, with one exception, the student evaluations had been stellar.

It was her first course at St. Jude's that was in contention. A handful of well-connected Political Science majors, who were taking "Feminist Theologies" in order to satisfy a distribution requirement, heckled and harried her in and out of the classroom. These young men had taken an instant dislike to her, mainly for her advocacy of the ordination of women. She held firm when they appealed to President Firmitas, who dismissed their claims that Pica was a heretic with a brisk "I don't think so." He knew far too much of the internal divisions of the church to be caught in that one.

"But," the students had persisted, "how can women be priests? Didn't Paul say priests must look like Jesus? And Jesus was a man."

"You need to know the history of religious practices to know what is from God and what is of man," the President had cautioned. "Come back when you've read Elaine Pagel's *The Gnostic Gospels*. And you might want to delve into the history of Connecticut a little on the matter of married priests."

Pica had tried, ever so gently, to get her class thinking about such matters. "There is a difference between the historical Jesus and Jesus Christ the savior. As to the first, we don't know much about the everyday activities of the short life of Jesus of Nazareth. Was he a virgin? Did he have siblings? If he did, what does this mean for the virginity of Mary? As far as Jesus the Son of God, is concerned, we know about him and his teachings through the writings of the apostles, but their accounts were set down long after the events they describe and they contain inconsistencies and contradictions."

"But where are the women priests, apostles, and popes?" they demanded.

"Well, there is Pope Joan," she said lightly. "But you need to realize that in the second century the church had more centers in the East than the West, like at Antioch in Syria and Corinth in Greece. There is no direct line of apostolic descent from the Bishop of Rome to the present. In fact, it is not until the fifth century that the bishop of Rome was called 'Pope.' Until then any bishop was called 'pope' or 'papa.'"

"So what? I'm talking about Roman Catholicism, not some foreign tradition," Henry O'Macer Jr. had persisted. His father was Chair of the English Department and he used that as an edge in arguments.

"That distinction doesn't really work, Henry. The Catholic Church is the Church Universal and all the rites of the Catholic Church are equally effective. Latin, Byzantine, Alexandrian and so on. So, you see, if women were ordained as deacons in one of those rites, then 'we' have had ordained women."

"But Pope John Paul II said, 'The church had no authority whatsoever to confer priestly ordination on women.' We read the *Ordinatio Sacerdotalis* last year, and what the Pope says is infallible!" Henry O'Macer Jr. was not giving up.

"Well Henry," Pica began, knowing she was delivering a mini-lecture. "It has what many would call the 'aura of infallibility,' but is not supported by valid arguments from scripture or tradition. Papal infallibility has been declared on only two matters. The first, in 1854, concerned Mary's immaculate conception, and the second, in 1950, her bodily ascension to heaven. That's it. And, the doctrine of papal infallibility dates from the fourth century but wasn't really enforced until the thirteenth century. It does not come from apostolic times. I'm sorry Henry, all these things come out of particular political moments. You need to know something of the history of the ideas and practices."

"But the fall came through one woman, Eve," said Henry Jr., playing his last ace.

"And redemption came through another – Mary," Pica added gently. "And why couldn't Adam just have said, 'I don't eat apples'? Why did he blame Eve? Doesn't he have some responsibility for his own actions? And what about the story of Lilith?"

"Well, women are subordinate to men and that is that. The Bible says so. Women must cover their heads because they are not in the image of God. Women must remain silent in the churches. It is disgraceful for them to speak. If they have a question they should ask their husbands. And priests are men like Jesus." Henry Jr. was flushed now and Pica thought she'd give him one more idea before moving on with the class.

"But think about this," Pica, the teacher, continued. "When you say 'man' do you mean 'man' the generic, or 'man' the male of the species mammalian? And let's think, what kind of 'man' are we imagining? A white man? A black man? Bearded or clean-shaven? Long or short hair? Remember, Jesus was a Jew."

These were not questions the contentious students were willing to entertain. They had no interest in the possibility of gospels that were not part of the Bible as they knew it. They were hostile to any suggestions that theirs was a dynamic religion, shaping and shaped by the shifting politics of gender, race, nations, medicine, and ethics. They wrote about Pica's heresies in the *St. Jude's Review*, and claimed she should be silenced. They defended their attack on her as an exercise in free speech, but the contradiction in their position escaped them. They published other commentaries on "heretical faculty" that had already appeared in the *Dartmouth Review*, a student paper at Dartmouth College, which shared members on its editorial board with the *St. Jude's Review*. Both Dee and Miriam had been "featured" in the paper and wore the taunts as a measure of their success in raising controversial issues that needed to be aired. As far as Pica's case was concerned, they would vigorously support Pica should those early teaching evaluations be raised as a bar to tenure.

Pica signed off on her dossier. It looked impressive. There were folders for teaching, service, publication and research, and tabbed sections within each folder. She had solicited letters from colleagues who were familiar with her work, and was particularly happy that the letter from Beacon Press accepting her manuscript for publication had arrived in time to be included. *The Oldest Profession, the Newest Plague: Prostitution in the Age of HIV-AIDS*, was an ambitious undertaking, and Pica hoped her book would stimulate debate and be read by policy-makers. She left her dossier in the main office with Mary J and headed off to find Dee. It was Pica's turn to cook for their Friday Fest and she wanted to get the large container of gumbo into Dee's refrigerator.

Dee was in her office with the door open. She was working on what looked like a genealogy.

"Well it's done. I just handed it in," Pica announced.

"Great. We can drink to your case this evening."

"If you give me your key, I can run this food up to your apartment before my afternoon class."

"I'll be out of here within the hour, so just leave the key on the hook by the back door. I won't be far behind you. I have things I want to do at home before you guys come over for dinner."

Dee kept working. She was trying to figure out how the vote might go for Pica. Her colleagues in the department were a mixed lot: four women and fifteen men, among whom were ten Jesuits, one Jew, one Baptist, one Buddhist, and two devout lay Catholics. Four of the Jesuits formed a solid voting block, and they would be against Pica. That group would almost certainly be joined by the two devout lay members of the department. *Six against Pica.* Virginia was on sabbatical. That left eleven. Of those, two – Dee and Miriam – were solidly for Pica. That left nine, six of whom were Jesuits. She guessed Thomas Guye SJ would be for Pica. He had been willing to petition for childcare and seemed to get what sexual harassment was about. He often talked about his mother and sisters in ways that showed his pride in their accomplishments and concern for their well-being. *Three for Pica, but five Jesuits who might go either way.* Dee suspected it would be a matter of whether they were trained before or after Vatican II. Joshua Rosen would certainly be sympathetic to Pica's views, although he might recuse himself now that he was part of the administration. *Four for Pica?* Adam Lu, who taught Buddhism and was part of the China program, would take it calmly, but he might abstain. He really disliked making those kinds of decisions. *Five?* Brian Baxter, their Baptist colleague, could be brought on board. He had team-taught with Pica and told her he had benefited greatly from the experience. *Six for Pica?*

One woman: one vote

Women's suffrage 1920: But states fail to ratify the ERA.

Dee called Miriam. "Got a minute? I'm crunching the numbers for and against Pica and I think we should caucus before we eat tonight."

"Sure. I could be at your place around four. Pica is teaching then."

Dee looked for Christian online but realized he was probably still in his weekly debriefing meeting. She was hoping his advisory committee would sign off on the curriculum he'd designed and leave him free for the weekend.

It had been a month of negotiation, accommodation and some tension as Dee and Christian had settled into a sort of routine, in which they were together on the weekends with lots of email in between. This weekend it was her turn to drive to Worcester to visit him. But Christian had suggested a day in Cambridge to tour her favorite bookstores. This was fine with Dee – in fact she was really enthusiastic – but she wanted to suggest they meet in Cambridge and stay over till Sunday morning. She decided to email and leave voice mail. "Let's talk around 10 pm," she said. Christian knew that Pica and Miriam were coming over for dinner.

Dee was getting fonder and fonder of the man. And the sex, she grinned to herself, was better than she had imagined; in fact, it was fantastic. But could she live in the present? It was new for Dee, the strategist, to just go with the flow. And what about Christian? Could he? He was so accustomed to being the one in charge. She wanted to savor every moment of the relationship, but also knew she should heed the little voice that kept telling her to hasten slowly. Falling in love in one's fifties was fraught.

Dee left her office and walked up the steps that were thick with rain-soaked leaves. She pushed her door open and saw that Pica had left her keys on the kitchen table. *Why did she leave her keys here?* She put the kettle on for tea and glanced at her mail. *Funny, why is the mail pushed way back from the front door?* Miriam swept in and Dee thought no more about these irregularities.

"It's going to be close with Pica," Dee said. "Who do you think is going to chair Pica's committee? Does the departmental head appoint the search committee and the chair?"

"Well. It's on the agenda for our departmental meeting next week. How do you want to play this, Dee?"

"I guess we could push to get you elected chair, or hold our fire and, if necessary, write a minority report. Those sometimes get the attention of the Trustees, though Father Abacus has good ties to a couple of board members and he could easily whisper in their ear. 'Take aim carefully' would be Pica's advice."

"I'm for calling in some favors from our networks," Miriam said.

"Okay. Who do you want to work on?"

"I'll do Josh, he'll be our representative on the Dean's Committee. And you take Tom Guye and he'll serve on the departmental committee. It only takes six people, plus a chair at this level. We can argue the committee needs us for diversity. We'd have three who are sympathetic."

"What do you know about Tom?" Dee asked. "I like him. There's a story in there somewhere. He talks about his sisters a lot. He dotes on his older sister, Mary – why are they all called Mary? And I think he used to babysit a lot for his younger sister, Sarah."

"Oh, ask him about Mary and rock and roll. She must have been cool in the '60s. They had a record player their father had helped them fix up. It was in the garage, away from the house, away from Tom's mother. She was the Catholic, you know, another Mary," Miriam said.

"He told me about going to peace marches with his sister Mary. Sounds like she was very much in the world and convinced she could make a difference. She and Pica would get along."

"I think they already know each other," Miriam said.

"Okay, we can ask Pica what she knows about his background," Dee said.

"He reads a lot, all kinds of books." Miriam said. "He knew about Shanghai being an open port under the Japanese occupation leading up to World War II when Europe and the United States were closed to Jews fleeing Germany and Poland."

"And he knows a lot of the new literature on masculinities and sexuality," added Dee. "Just for starters, I happen to know that he's read *Refusing to be a Man* by John Stoltenberg."

Tom Guye came from one of those large Boston Catholic families that had made it from bog Irish to lace-curtain Irish in the two generations the family had been in New England. He loved hearing the stories of the Troubles from their feisty grandfather and knew that Grandma would then follow with her accounts of their newly found respectability. "To be sure, we were a wild crew, but now we's respectable, as good as any, mark my words, with God's help."

The Guyes wore public service as an honor. Tom's mother Mary had chaired the Annual Fund Drive year after year. She baked, she sewed, she arranged flowers, she cared for the needy and was remembered in the prayers of the faithful. Tom's father had fallen in love with Mary, that saucy young miss in the pleated skirt, lightly starched shirt, and straw hat who bounced past the gates of his school on her way to St. Mary's. He had courted her through the sweltering summer of 1945 and, despite the misgivings of his Protestant family, he had converted to Catholicism and had pledged to raise his children in the Catholic faith.

Even as children it was clear that Tom's two brothers, Luke and

Matthew, were set on the course of public service: Luke, who was the eldest, would take up the law and Matthew, the youngest, would go into medicine. His sisters, Mary and Sarah, as befitted young women in the 1960s, were destined to become teachers and nurses. Tom's life was similarly certain, or at least as far as his mother was concerned. He was destined for the religious life.

His mother had doted on Tom as a boy. He was a sickly child and, although it would have been fun to join the other boys in their games, he spent much of his time indoors reading. He read the books his mother brought to him of the lives of the saints. He poured over the illustrations: the pale, aesthetic face of the red-haired Son of God intrigued him. Was the savior truly cast in the image of God? The faded depictions reminded him of his Uncle Micky. However, Micky, being fond of a drop of firewater, had a red nose that became even redder when he drank. Tom read the books his brothers brought home. He read the books in his father's library. After a while, his mother gave up trying to monitor what Tom was reading. She was aware that some of the books in her husband's extensive collection were unsuitable for a boy and she guessed some were even on the Catholic Church's list of banned books. But it didn't seem to do him any harm. She wasn't committing a sin if she didn't know, and why should she pry into her husband's library? Tom was a good boy. He said his prayers. He loved his mother. He had few playmates but seemed genuinely fond of the boys in the neighborhood and wasn't interested in chasing girls.

"I'd be happy to be on a committee with Tom," Dee said. "He's so different from those closeted Jebbies. Maybe it's that he has healthy relationships with women in his family, maybe he has figured it out – whatever – he doesn't ooze contempt for women."

"No. He treats women with respect but I'm pretty sure he prefers men. There was a near scandal when Phillip Johans in English began flirting with Tom and I think Tom was attracted, but then, out of the blue, Phillip was offered a fellowship somewhere on the west coast and we didn't see him again," Miriam said.

Fiat Cella.

149

"Joshua Rosen. What do we know about him?" Dee probed.

"Well, apart from Elizabeth Stein and me, he is the only other Jew on the faculty. He has always been generous with his time. When I was first here, he was an excellent source on who was sleeping with whom, who was about to be promoted, and who was getting the axe."

"Don't you and Daniel sometimes hang out with him?"

"Yep. Josh writes on religious freedoms in the United States, particularly Native American issues, like the Al Brown peyote case, things like that. Daniel does lots of pro bono Civil Rights work. When the Religious Freedoms Restoration Bill was being brokered, we saw quite a bit of Josh and Ruth. But now that he's Associate Vice-President for Diversity, he's more distant."

Dee knew about that deep divide between faculty and administration. It was one she negotiated with enormous care.

"What about Elizabeth Stein in Chemistry? She has the President's ear."

"I'm not sure she is all that well disposed towards me," Miriam said. "She's a convert and her husband is extremely conservative. She's a much more traditional wife than any of the other Jewish women I know."

Elizabeth Stein was the prime mover behind the Judaic Studies yearly panel discussion sponsored by St. Jude's, and she was the spokesperson on the Gulf War. She was particularly proud that she had spoken at the dedication of the monument to Holocaust survivors that was in the garden outside the library. Elizabeth was always first in support of the President's plans for interfaith debates. For many years she had been the face of Judaism at St. Jude's, and she was vaguely resentful of Miriam's relaxed attitude towards her religion. She was not open to exploring a feminist Seder with Miriam. She spent long hours in her kitchen preparing kosher meals for her family. She kept separate dishes, pots and utensils for ritual occasions, as well for meat and milk. She would never join the others for a drink on Friday evening after work but rather hurried home before dark. "Mostly people here are respectful of my religion and seem to be supportive of the Judaic Studies

150

program," Miriam said. "I'm never really sure what Elizabeth might do, but she is not ill-disposed to Pica."

"Why would anyone be ill-disposed to me?" laughed Pica as she came through the door. Miriam popped the champagne, and the three drank a toast to Pica and wished her success with her tenure case.

"Have you two been plotting?" Pica asked and added, "Remember to keep a foot on the ground or the shot doesn't count."

"Just getting the stories and genealogies straight," Dee said. "What do you know of Tom Guye?"

"Why?"

"Just cos," said Dee.

"Well, sit down and talk with him," said Pica. "It's up to you, but I think he will have some insights on the matter of Mary Doyle, if you want to pursue it any further. Those big Irish families know how to keep their secrets and he was in the same seminary as Paddy Sordes, only later. My brother went there too."

"Slow down. Your brother . . . does he know anything about Paddy Sordes?" Dee asked. *Maybe the dots are connected more closely than I imagine.*

"Okay, enough. Time to eat, and no more talking shop. Agreed? Let's have some music," Pica declared. "I just bought *Yes, I am Melissa*. You know Dee, there is a place in town that sells used CDs, just down from your favorite bookstore."

"No. I'm on a strict budget and a new book regime," Dee laughed. "It's like AA, but for addicted book-buyers. I've been two weeks book-free. So don't tempt me with music. Christian is already undermining my resolve. I think we're doing the Cambridge bookstores this weekend."

"Did you two figure out what you're doing on the Columbus Day weekend?" Miriam asked. "I'm still up for a party."

"It's a fast-moving ball game," Dee said with just a hint of distress in her voice, "but I'll mention it." This was where she worried. Christian was always so busy – maybe he didn't have time to have a relationship, the little voice on her shoulder was saying. She wanted lots of negotiation. He tended to be pretty short about what he could attend and what not. That imperious note in his dealing with outside agencies sometimes spilled over to their relations. She had not yet decided whether to make an issue of what she was beginning to see as a sort of bossiness in his manner, and she was not sure she wanted to share her anxieties with Miriam and Pica.

Pica glanced up and saw that Dee looked edgy. "You don't have to shoot every shot hard to win," she said as she programmed the CD to play her favorite track.

"Hey, Pica. That gumbo smells great," Miriam said as she carried it to the table.

"They mature with age," Pica joined in the chorus with Melissa Etheridge. "Ah, love that dare not speak its name," she said to no-one in particular.

The departmental meeting to discuss Pica's committee was set down for Wednesday afternoon, in a time slot when, in theory at least, no-one had classes. On the walls of the seminar room in which they met hung dark, frowning portraits of previous presidents of St. Jude's. An image of Mary, swooning at the foot of the cross, was the only female presence in the room. Dee imagined the room being brightened with a representation of Our Lady of Guadalupe, ringed by roses or, better still, a piece by that brave Chicana artist, Alma Lopez. Our Lady in a bikini fashioned of roses. Our Lady with her feet visible, no longer held captive, but able to walk away if the endless petitioning bored her. Or, maybe a happy painting of the Virgin of Caring, from Cuba, glowing in a yellow sea, draped in diaphanous gauze, her sensual belly visible for all to admire.

Mary, roses, rosary, virgin, sexuality, swoon, birth.
Women with agency. Did Mary menstruate?

The department was assembled and seated by 3 pm. Father Abacus, sitting at the head of the large dark table, read from the memo. Then he turned to Father Babulus and announced, "I have asked Father Babulus to chair the committee and invited Father

Corbis, Brian Baxter, Father Decursus, and Father Venarius to serve. I was wondering whether Dee or Miriam might also assist?"

"Could we discuss the composition of the committee and the choice of chair? Maybe there are others interested in serving," Miriam said.

Father Abacus seemed a little miffed but didn't object. After all, tenure reports were onerous and no-one in their right mind would volunteer. Tom picked up his cue. "I'd be happy to be on the committee and I have already read much of Pica's research and know a little of the field."

Joshua followed up: "I'd also like to volunteer. Pica is an important voice at the college and her work is critical to bringing this department into line with other institutions."

This was an ongoing issue. Until quite recently the study of religion had been synonymous with Christianity and more properly the department had been a Department of Theology. Slowly departments around the country were looking outwards and finding much that was of interest and much that was to be feared. They saw cults of crazies, fantastical feminist rereadings, eclectic mixes in New Age practices, and all that syncretism. At St. Jude's they gestured to Palestine in their choice of speakers, prepared a registrar for conscientious objectors during the 1991–2 Gulf War, and deliberated on the concept of a just war. In the department there were traces of the different moments in its evolution. A story from the early days amused Dee. A newly appointed member of the Philosophy Department had proposed a new course, a study of Protestantism. "But we already have a course on 'Heresies,'" the then-department head had said at the faculty meeting convened to discuss course adoptions.

Heresy: literally "one who makes a choice"; once the Truth is revealed, one should not be making choices.

Syllabus of Errors - No 77. In the present day it is no longer expedient that the Catholic religion should be held as the only religion of the State, to the exclusion of all other forms of worship. Allocution, NEMO VESTRUM, July 26, 1855.

"I'd be delighted to sit on a committee with Josh and Tom," Brian Baxter said, "and why not have both Dee and Miriam join us?" Father Abacus saw he was being out-maneuvered and, in the absence of Father Tempus calling "time," he decided to defer. "Well thank you for these offers. Very generous, but now we have too many."

"Well, does anyone want to stand down?" Dee asked. "Or maybe we could vote on a slate of possible committee members?" Father Abacus was getting agitated. This was not where he wanted to go at all.

"Is there anything in the rules that says that a committee has to be of a certain size?" Dee asked. "Or is it just a matter of convenience and custom?"

"Probably the latter," said Tom.

"Well, let's be innovative," said Joshua. "We can have the discussion as a department and the committee can convene, bring us a recommendation, and we can all vote – the by-laws give a vote to all tenured members of the department of same rank or higher than the candidate. We all need to be familiar with the file for the final vote."

"Shall we begin with her research and publication file?" Father Abacus suggested.

Interesting, Dee thought, *he's accepted Joshua's collegial suggestion and passed over teaching and service and gone for the jugular. He's definitely flustered.*

Father Abacus was quick to reclaim his ground. He had dredged Pica's file from her mid-tenure review of three years earlier and found letters from outside experts that he wished to share with the department. He began in that low, sonorous voice: "I have read the proposal of Pica Liberatio and, in short, it is not the sort of scholarship that we at Loyola would find sufficiently rigorous for tenure."

Miriam was ready for this challenge. When she had first suggested to her committee at the University of Chicago in 1983 that she wanted to write about the Jewish Ghetto in Shanghai, she had been told it was too personal a quest and too politicized a topic. But she had persevered, and ultimately prevailed. Through her parents and their contacts, she had traced more survivors and attended their reunions. They told her about the guilt they felt in having fled Europe in 1938 and 1939 and found safe haven in Japanese-occupied Shanghai, while relatives had died in Hitler's camps. They shared photographs and memories. Eventually the stories began to coalesce and Miriam was confident that when she visited Shanghai, she would be able to find the sites they mentioned – the Ohel Moshe Synagogue in the Hongkew Ghetto, the kosher bakery, the place where the Mir Yeshiva students from Byelorussia had studied, the palatial residence of Baghdadi Jews like the Sassoon and Kadoorie families.

"I don't think we can dismiss Pica's research simply because it comes out of her deep commitment to the empowering of women," Miriam said to Father Abacus.

"But," Father Babulus interjected, "look at the work of Father Corbis. Now *that* is solid research. There is not a source or expert that he does not know intimately, and he has demonstrated most succinctly that women and their bodies are sites of pollution. I see nothing of that caliber in the work of this candidate." Father Corbis's entire *oeuvre* was devoted to the apostle Paul, and Father Babulus was happy to offer support from his own work on *Leviticus*. Father Babulus was into his sermon now and Miriam knew it was best to let it run its course. "A woman who gives birth to a son will be ceremonially unclean for seven days, just as she is unclean during her monthly period . . . after the birth of a daughter, for two weeks the woman will be unclean. Only after a burnt offering of a year-old lamb and an offering of a pigeon or dove will she be clean again."

Read Mary Douglas, PURITY AND DANGER, the abominations of Leviticus: the rituals of separation that contain women's potential to pollute also set out societal boundaries; the person in between threatens the order; the middle ground is confusing, dangerous, impure, must be contained with rituals and taboos.

"Be that as it may—" Miriam stared at the two black robes. She felt like telling them she was menstruating right now and that her

155

"unclean" condition did not diminish her sexual appetite, but thought she'd save it and share that image with Dee after the meeting. "One of the things Pica is trying to explore is the ways in which women have been cast as passive and subordinate, but then blamed for leading men astray. Jesus did not shun the prostitutes. He embraced Mary Magdalene."

Dee was waiting to share her insights from her work in Uganda. She had her sermons too. "Now there is a global epidemic of AIDS being spread by trafficking in women and girls, and reaching younger and younger girls as the myth is popularized that sex with a virgin will cure the disease. The epidemic is being exacerbated by structural adjustment programs. These programs create work for men in the towns, where they visit prostitutes while their wives remain isolated in the rural sector. When the men return they infect their wives and then beat them for having the disease. If the women ask their husbands to use condoms, they are called whores. The aid agencies don't want to talk about how married men are contributing to this epidemic. They want to blame the prostitutes."

"What has this got to do with Pica's research?" Father Abacus demanded. He was wary of these women who, almost overnight, had begun challenging the rules and traditions of the place. Like Fathers Babulus, Corbis, and Decursus, he had been at St. Jude's for his entire working life. The last five years had included too much future shock to suit him. And now this. First this woman working on the Shanghai Ghetto and suggesting that the Chinese were more accepting of Jews than were the Jesuits. Then that outspoken woman with all her research on cultures where women celebrate their own religious ceremonies and her suggestion that Christianity condoned domestic violence. And now, one of their own – well, at least the closest a female can come to being a priest – requiring that he read her publications on HIV-positive prostitutes.

"In Uganda there is a success story to be told about slowing the epidemic. It involves confronting the fact that men are spreading the disease among women. They are the main contributors to the spread of the disease. There are all sorts of ways in which women are being empowered, so they have options and can say no," Dee concluded.

"What has that got to do with the ordination of women?" Father Decursus asked out of the blue. He was just back from a sabbatical in California where he had heard Pica's research cited favorably and wanted to test the water with his St. Jude's colleagues.

"I guess she would say that where women are held in low esteem and culturally devalued, they have fewer resources to protect themselves than where they are treated as sages," Dee began.

"But we revere Mary, mother of God," Father Decursus said. "We pray the rosary."

"All true," Dee conceded. "But Pica's point is that only Mary gets to be a virgin *and* give birth. To become mothers, all other women must have sex and thus be defiled and in need of ceremonial cleansing. So Mary is a model of woman that only chaste women can attain."

"For Pica these are interrelated arguments," Tom began. "This is what I find particularly provocative and worthy in her research. I'd been thinking about Mary as the symbolic mother, and Mary as the divine mother. You know, the Good Mother, expressing loss and grief at Calvary, but offering a model of piety and compassion and a willingness to give birth." Dee wondered how long it would be before one of the older Jesuits cut him off, but Tom was into a rhythm and avoiding eye contact with Father Abacus, who was beginning to show signs of wear and tear.

Tom continued, "I was doing a survey of images of Mary at the Crucifixion. There is debate about the origins – the West in the thirteenth century or Byzantium in the eleventh – but in the mid-twelfth century there are frescos where Mary is no longer standing upright, as she had been in earlier representations. She is leaning against John. From then on images of Mary get less self-sufficient and more dependent. She is shown as human in her experience of the pain of childbirth and serenely sacred as the mother of God. She swoons as in childbirth. So we could say Mary at the foot of the Crucifix is experiencing this second birth – a rebirth of Christ. Or it may be seen as a rebirth of Eve's children, who are saved by Christ, and reborn by Mary. Or is it the postponement of pain spared at the Nativity, and now being experienced at Calvary?"

Tom leaned back. He'd been wanting to raise these questions with his colleagues and this seemed like an opportune moment.

Miriam and Joshua were fascinated by Tom's exposé of embodied Christian imagery. Brian Baxter shrugged. "Let's stay on topic here. I think we should each read sections of Pica's work and be ready to discuss it next week." Adam Lu, who had been silent throughout the discussion, picked up the paper on trafficking and AIDS that Dee and Pica had coauthored. "I guess I'll read this one. Last time I was in the field, I was overwhelmed by the number of young girls who had disappeared from the Yunnan province of China where I've worked for so many years. Prostitution yes, but trafficking, I don't know. Pica seems to be arguing that you can't call one choice and then call the other coercion."

Six for Pica.

29 September, 1996: Mass of Archangels Michael, Gabriel and Raphael.

Saint Michael, Archangel, defend us in battle.

Be our protection against the wickedness and snares of the Devil.

May God rebuke him, we humbly pray;

And do thou, O Prince of the Heavenly Host, by the power of God, thrust into hell Satan and all the other evil spirits who prowl about the world seeking the ruin of souls.

Amen. Pope Leo XIII

11

If she could die now it would be all the same to her. Her head was banging. Her body ached – a deep ache – and, no matter how she arranged the pillows and quilts, she was still miserable and uncomfortable. She alternated between deep chills and dripping sweats. Probably just a simple cold – she knew it would pass without medical intervention. *Please let that be soon*, she thought. Pica and Miriam wanted to bring food to the house. Christian recommended lots of bed rest and assured her it was a five-day flu. Mostly Dee just wanted to drink tea, gallons of it, hot, weak, stinging on her throat. Her ears had begun to pop and with each swallow she felt the swollen glands protest. All her joints ached. *Okay, concentrate*, she told herself. *This will pass. You will walk again. Your back is not really broken.* The vise tightened around her head. Her spine felt as if it could not carry her weight. She would try some aspirin with food. But what could she eat? She wasn't hungry, and nothing tasted right anyway. Nothing tasted good. Everything felt as if it was going straight to feed the engine that was pumping mucus into her sinuses. *What did I do to deserve this? Ha! Gotcha*, her rational self began to lecture. *You must be really low to be thinking this way. You know that illness is not a form of punishment for being bad.*

"Chicken soup for the soul," Miriam chirped as she came through the door of Dee's apartment. "I insist. This is my mother's recipe. Humm, more tea too?" Miriam shed her heavy coat, hung the spare key Dee had loaned her the week before on a hook in the hallway and busied herself in the kitchen.

"I hurt everywhere," Dee whined and pulled the covers up under her chin.

"Well, you had to crack some time. You've been running yourself ragged," Miriam said from the bedroom door.

"Yeah. I guess that new course has been hard work," Dee conceded, just a little peeved that Miriam was taking issue with her work habits. *Next she'll joke about the Protestant work ethic.* Dee was just on edge enough to respond "Weber's dead," but knew she would regret it. Miriam was not going to be put off. She sat down on the end of the bed. *Here it comes,* Dee thought.

"And what about driving up and down to UMass, helping WOW get off the ground, and I know Pica really appreciates you working with her on that article you did for *Women's Studies International Forum.*"

"Well yes, but I couldn't say no to her and I was still smarting from the rejection by *The Women's Review of Books* of my critical piece on postmodernism and HIV-AIDS. I don't forget this kind of thing and it wasn't hard to figure out who the readers had been who rejected it."

Miriam nodded and said, "I know. None of us is perfect, but Dee, take a deep breath."

"I know, I know I need to," Dee sniffed. She'd let Miriam be "mother" for now. *Maybe I can even enjoy the luxury of being fussed over.* "Do we have any softer tissues?" Dee asked. "I think my nose is almost worn out from these ones."

"What about a really soft cloth hankie? The sort we had as kids."

"Yes, please," Dee said and nuzzled the fine cotton handkerchief Miriam produced from her cardigan pocket.

"Dee I admire what you do, I really do. This may not be the time to ask, but I'm trying to figure out what keeps you going. Hang on, I can smell the soup." Miriam disappeared into the kitchen. "Come on Dee, out of bed." Miriam placed a steaming bowl of soup on a tray, plumped up the cushions of the couch, and handed Dee her dressing gown. "Come, sit down here, and I'll change the bed. Nothing like a clean bed to make you feel better, and I'm going to open all the windows."

"But it's cold outside," Dee whimpered and then added, "I don't think I'm a very good patient."

"That's okay, not many people are," Miriam nodded. "I'll turn up the heat." Miriam was trying to be stern and in control but was clearly worried about her ailing friend.

"My grandmother used to throw all the windows open. Everything was about fresh air, light, sunshine on the laundry." Dee settled into her couch and took the tray from Miriam. "Yum. This looks like really good soup. Wish I could smell it."

"'Feed a cold, starve a fever,' my mother used to say. Yes, I know you probably want to lie here and die, but we're going to cheer you up. It is a long weekend after all," Miriam said. "Daniel is bringing over our projector and our old Australian slides for a slideshow. Make you homesick. That'll take your mind off your cold. And Christian is bringing a special potion."

"Okay, so I get to be the party patient?"

"Yep. The doctor – well, the other doctor – will be here soon."

"More soup, please doctor. I think I'm going to live." Dee was starting to brighten. Miriam was a good friend and Dee felt a little ashamed of her earlier annoyance at being jollied along. "Thanks for getting me out of bed. I forgot how much that helps."

"Seriously, how do you do it, Dee? Keep up your good humor? You are always so focused, always trying to fix the world's ills."

"Well it seems that sometimes my body fails me," Dee laughed. "I think I've always had a sense that if one has the talent, one should use it. You know, if you're not part of the solution, you're part of the problem."

"No problem we can't solve," Daniel announced as he came through the door. "I have cider, Christian has the spices and we are going to banish that cold." The two men stood awkwardly in the living room, but Miriam took their jackets and shuffled Daniel into a chair. "She's sick. But she's not going to die," Miriam announced firmly as she took Dee's empty bowl and gave her friend an affectionate pat on the knee. "Now sit while I get soup for the hunters."

"Brought you some 'mums,'" Christian said, setting the potted plant of russet flowers on the small table by the couch, "No, the sign said 'hardy mums.' I couldn't resist because you are one hardy Mum." He sat down on a cushion at Dee's feet. She leaned forward and kissed the top of his head.

"That would be 'Mom' and the flowers would be chrysan-themums," Miriam translated for Daniel as she passed the men large bowls of soup and topped off Dee's teapot. Dee stretched out on the couch. Christian set the soup down, squeezed in at the end of the couch and began massaging Dee's feet through her thick woolly socks. One by one he separated and played with her toes. Dee flushed at the memory of the last time he had paid such careful attention to her toes, and said, "Um, not very romantic, my feet, right?" Christian continued the massage.

"Don't forget to eat your soup while it is still hot," Dee said dreamily.

"Okay, slideshow time," Daniel said, plugging in the projector and shutting off the lights while Miriam collected the soup bowls and began closing the windows.

"Enough fresh air for now," Miriam shuddered. The projector clicked and whirred into action, and a picture of young Miriam popped into view.

"This is Miriam when I first met her, in Melbourne, in 1972. She was twenty-four, and had taken a year off to work after finishing her BA, and before starting grad school."

"Then Daniel intervened. I didn't get back to study till 1980, after the kids were in nursery school and we were living in Chicago."

"I thought she was the most beautiful woman I had ever seen," Daniel said. "Still do," he added quickly. Dee was watching to see if Miriam flinched. She knew they'd exchanged some harsh words through the week, but Miriam had said it was now fine. *Does she ever crack? Harbor bad thoughts? Act out of malice?* Dee wondered.

"I remember that day," Miriam said without any rancor. "It was one of those brilliant late spring days where the twilight seems to go on forever, the warm earth hums, and every thing smells good, especially Mum's cooking."

Dee studied the slide. Miriam hadn't changed that much. True, she had traded the Indian wraparound skirt, a light white blouse, and sandals of the 1970s for a more tailored, professional look – the long black skirts, trousers and her hallmark cardigans – and maybe

162

put on some weight. Miriam did like food.

"Your hair smelled of apples," Daniel smiled.

"One of Mum's potions," Miriam added, chuckling. "Okay, here is Daniel, just as I remember him, standing at the front door. He's still got that lean and angular look, still wears jeans, T-shirts and sneakers. You guys are so lucky," Miriam joked looking at Daniel and Christian. "No angst over what to wear. That day Daniel had thrown a jacket over his shoulders, in deference to meeting my folks."

"What took you to Australia?" Christian asked.

"A conference – a bunch of lawyers, anthropologists, historians, and grassroots activists. We were looking for a fun place to meet and Aussies are great at partying." Then looking sideway at Dee, he smiled and amended his statement. "Well, most of the time, eh Dee?"

Dee nodded in acknowledgement of this concession to her health and said, "Oh, but those were exciting times. Just thinking about it makes me feel better." The 1970s had been the era of the Whitlam Labor Government, the promise of land rights. Passionate, articulate Indigenous spokespersons had started to build global networks. Dee already knew about the conference and the session Daniel had chaired on "Genocide and Human Rights."

"You know, Christian," Dee said, "It was all very new, using the language of human rights to refer to native peoples. We knew about the decolonizing of what we used to call the Third World, but we were struggling to make sense of the internal colonization of Aboriginal people." Dee shifted so that she was sitting up straight. "That was when the stories of the Stolen Generations began to surface."

"Oh, this is what brings Dee to life," Christian chuckled. "Methinks the patient is much improved."

"It was happening here too," Daniel said, "A wholly American Holocaust, that's what the Native American activists were calling it. I was working with some members of the American Indian Movement and we hoped to get an international dialogue going."

"And today is Columbus Day and here we are in Connecticut

where high-stakes gambling is generating millions for the local Pequot tribe," Dee sighed and immediately regretted having brought up the subject.

"A tiny tribe with big ambitions," Miriam added glancing at Dee.

"Yes, I need to learn more of how that all came about," Dee conceded. "It seems all wrong to me, but then the treaties here set up a very different framework for ventures on native lands than in Australia."

"Well there's plenty to learn. Daniel is a good source," Miriam volunteered.

"Things have changed a lot," Daniel said. "Do you all remember where you were during the 1992 quincentennial celebrations?"

"Massachusetts," Miriam said. "There were some great protests and speeches on this day four years ago."

"Like in Australia during the bicentennial in 1988, I guess." Dee was laughing. "Oh, remember Burnum Burnum? He did a reverse landing at Dover Beach in England, planted the Aboriginal flag, and said, 'We come in peace.'"

"Here. Look at these slides from the conference. It all seemed possible in the '70s." Daniel said. "That really was a revolutionary network in the making."

Miriam glanced at Dee and Christian, "Just tell us when you get bored. We never tire of these slides. They're a kinda turn-on for us. Heady times and all that."

"Well thanks for sharing that," Daniel laughed.

Dee settled back. She learned from watching this couple interact, disagree, make up, move on. She knew they quarreled and that Miriam could stand her ground, but the marriage was solid. *Did she and Christian have that staying power? Would they be able to balance their careers?*

"So who did you know in Australia at that time?" Christian asked Daniel. "Did you know Miriam's folks before you came to Australia?"

Dee already knew the story but was happy to hear it from Daniel's perspective. "Nope. I knew no-one, absolutely no-one, but one of my aunts used to talk about relatives in the colonies. I had no idea how that aunt fitted into my family, but I'd called her 'aunt' since I was a small boy. When I told her of my Melbourne plans, she immediately said, 'Look up the Levi family and take them this photograph.' It was an old black and white photo, fading to brown, of a street in Shanghai."

"Do you still have it?" Dee asked.

"Somewhere," Daniel said.

"It's in the hall closet," Miriam interjected. "Don't you remember I sorted all the photos last winter? It was my winter project."

Daniel looked embarrassed. "She's the archivist," he added quickly and bowed in mock deference to Miriam.

"Wait till you see the bill," Miriam said softly.

"I'll take that under advisement," Daniel parried and turned towards Christian. "It wasn't too hard to find Miriam's folks and I arranged to visit them on my free day. I brought matzos as a gift from my family. Passover in autumn felt strange, but . . . ."

"Dad was so happy, he just beamed," Miriam said. "He said, 'I made the best matzos in Shanghai. My bakery was behind the Synagogue.' Then Daniel took the faded photograph and placed it on the table. Dad said, 'That's the street we used to walk along to get from home to the Hongkew Ghetto.' Then Mum and Dad started calling the names of cousins, aunts, uncles. Look, there's the slide of the family in Melbourne at my brother's bar mitzvah. We had to go through the whole family. I'm still not entirely sure I have it all straight. So much happened in those war years."

"Oh, let me get my hands on the genealogy," Dee interjected.

"There she goes again," Christian laughed. "She loves being disruptive when it comes to people exercising authority in an arbitrary fashion, but give her a kinship puzzle and she worries away at it until order emerges."

"It's the scientist in me," Dee piped up.

"You should see Dee when she's with my mother. They'll sit for hours doing genealogies. They forget I'm there." Christian was looking fondly at Dee.

"Oh! Oh! Do you still have that photo of us all in Uganda?" Dee asked.

"When we turn the lights up. I've got it and some others. Miriam asked me to bring photos. I've been putting an album together," Christian said.

When? Dee wondered. *When did he do that and what's in it?*

Daniel was working through the slides of both sides of the family and trying to explain who each person was. Snippets of family history emerged. Daniel clicked on a slide of Miriam's parents at their daughter's wedding in Chicago in 1974.

"I got into a really heated argument with Miriam's father over the nature of genocide and who had the right to use the word."

"Usually it was Dad who had command of the floor," Miriam added. "He knew the stories. Then I watched Daniel, ever so slowly challenging, provoking, and dancing around Dad. I liked his style, his intelligence, and I thought he liked me. He didn't talk over or beyond me, just brought me into the conversation in ways I found wonderfully sexy." Miriam was smiling at Daniel.

Dee lay down again. "Oh yes, men who really 'get' strong women. It's such a turn-on," she sighed.

Christian felt her forehead. "I think the temperature is coming down. Hold that thought Dee. Will it be okay if I spike this cider with a little medicinal scotch?"

"Yes please."

"Okay, here are the kids when they were small." Daniel and Miriam had obviously both been very involved in their children's upbringing. "We took them back to Australia and all they wanted to do was see the kangaroos and koalas," Miriam was saying.

"Is that the Healesville Sanctuary, near Melbourne?" Dee asked. "I took my kids there. Now I'm getting homesick. I see eucalyptus and I want to be able to smell it."

"You will," Christian assured her.

Daniel was now working through the slides of Miriam's gradu-ation as she took up the story of her doctoral research, of documents lost during the Cultural Revolution in the 1960s and 19070s, of the difficulties after Tiananmen Square in 1989, and how she chased down survivors in Canada, the United States, and France.

"You know, I read Anne Frank, when I was young, but I knew

nothing about Shanghai," Dee said.

"Neither did I. Who ever talked about those 20,000 Jewish refugees who had found safe haven in Shanghai during the war?" Daniel said.

"Their testimonies were very powerful," Miriam said. "I remember Heinz Joachim Cohn saying, 'I have the Chinese people to thank for my life, because if it weren't for them, I wouldn't be able to tell this story.'"

"What was it that other guy said?" Dee asked. "You know, the one who said he never heard anyone call him a 'damn Jew' in China."

"You mean Eric Goldstaub?" Miriam asked. "The one I was talking about in our last departmental meeting?"

"Yes, that's the one," Dee said. "Father Decursus just didn't get the notion of family in China as a powerful weapon against anti-Semitism."

"I was only repeating what I was told. 'They were always good to us and they loved our children,'" Miriam said. "I guess it does fly in the face of the St. Jude's idea that it knows what the family is."

The slides kept coming and Dee, her sore throat mercifully dulled by the scotch, slipped into a gentle sleep. She woke as Daniel turned the lights back up and she heard Miriam talking about getting into Chicago University. "I knew identity was a hot topic, so I talked about my identity as a Jewish woman, mother, and scholar who had grown in very different circumstances from those of my mother and the grandmother I only knew through stories. I was lucky they took a chance on me."

Dee wandered off to the bathroom and caught sight of herself in the mirror. "God, I look terrible," she muttered. She washed her face, brushed her hair, cleaned her teeth, put on some lipstick and went in search of something warm and comforting to wear – her long purple wool skirt and matching sweater would do just fine. *Jewelry? No, a happy shawl would be more appropriate.* When Dee reemerged Miriam and Daniel were in the kitchen chatting away while doing the dishes. Christian was bringing something in from his car. "Look at you," he said admiringly as he put the box on the coffee table. Miriam and Daniel reappeared. "Who's the party girl now?" Daniel laughed as he came back into the room.

"What about you guys? How did you meet?" Daniel asked as he packed away his slides.

"I've been trying to reconstruct the chronology," Christian said. "I was clearing out my desk before I left Uganda to come here and found a number of clippings and old photographs." He passed the package to Dee. "This is for you – well, us, actually."

"How wonderful." Dee caught his hand and asked, "When did you get time to do this?"

"You're not the only one with insomnia," Christian laughed. "Yes, I know – wakefulness," he added quickly. "Well, call this my jetlag project."

Dee was studying each page. "That's a report about the Women's UN conference in Nairobi in 1985," she said.

"I think that's the first time I saw you. You were holding a sign that said 'Racism Kills: Sexism Kills'," he smiled.

"Well, little girls need an education too. No-one was paying attention to them in development plans. Look at the difference in Uganda now primary education is compulsory."

"You'll get no argument from me," Christian said holding up his hand. "Here, this is the craft market in Kampala, at the back of the theatre. All I could find was a postcard with a picture of it."

"All those wonderful little stalls," Dee said. "Ebony carvings of African animals, woven bags, mats, cloths, beads, musical instruments, and little banana leaf angels made by widows in the Ancholi district."

"What I remember about that day," Christian said taking hold of Dee's hand, "was that she wasn't haggling. She was carrying an *omweso* board – a game reserved for men – and was talking with the woman who was selling the little angels."

"Oh, I remember her. She was a really strong woman, an independent woman, a model for her daughters. Her parents were in a refugee camp, in the north of Uganda. I did buy some of her angels you know. I used to practice my Swahili with her."

"I was working in the clinic where a number of women came for help," Christian said, taking up the story. "Dee and I talked a lot

168

about global politics. We had similar ideas about development."

Dee continued turning the pages. "Oh this one with your mother is lovely, but where did this hand-tinted one come from? Is that your mother as a girl?"

"That it is. It was taken by my father, just before they were married. Such a romance those two had. And problems too. It wasn't easy for either of them you know."

"Your mother told me a little about that when we were doing genealogies together in Uganda."

"She gave me the photo that day," Christian said. "And told me to follow my heart. I think she knew before I did that we would be together. Think of it as her blessing."

"This is such a wonderful present. Thank you Christian."

"It's work-in-progress," Christian said.

So are we, Dee thought. *He's put all this thought into the album and I thought he was trying to hold me at bay by not being available. For now, I'm just going to enjoy the luxury of being looked after.*

"How did you end up at St. Jude's?" Christian turned to draw Miriam into the conversation.

"Well, Daniel was opening a branch of his practice in Springfield, so when I saw the position in the Religious Studies Department for an Assistant Professor with an interest in Judaic Studies, I jumped. I knew that St. Jude's had a fledgling Asian Studies program, and I suggested in my interview that maybe I could help them build a China program. Tiananmen Square was still raw, but I had hope."

"I have some of the China slides if you want to see them," Daniel said tentatively.

"I would like to," Christian said. "But what about our sick girl here?"

"Oh, yes please. Shanghai, the den of vice and iniquity, opium dens, prostitutes, imperialists. It must have been really something. Do you have any slides of the old city, and the gardens?" Dee asked. "And could I have some more of that cider, please?"

"What about some more food? Miriam asked. "I brought some potato knishes just in case you revived, and they are Daniel's favorite."

Daniel set up the projector again and dimmed the lights. The city of Shanghai as seen through the eyes of Daniel and Miriam was one of striking contrasts and enormous energy. In the narrow streets of the old city, food was being prepared and eaten on the streets, fish hung out to dry on the old stone walls, red and white barber poles dotted street corners, message boards carried pamphlets about good health, meetings, and community rules. Facing the river along the embankment, on the west shore of the Huangpu River, were the old Customs House, banks and other trading houses. It was a city ready to take off, but where to?

"This is us strolling along the Bund," Daniel said.

"It could be Vienna," Dee mused.

"Look," said Daniel, "This is the Ohel Moshe Synagogue refurbished. It has a wonderful history. It was a psychiatric hospital and then a book depository after the communists took control of the city in 1949, but it's all still there."

"And this slide is from 1992 when Israel–China diplomatic relations were opened, along with the possibility of academic exchanges," Miriam continued. "I took these in Shanghai, two and a half years ago. It was the fiftieth anniversary of survivors. At the ceremony one Chinese official said that the people of Shanghai 'will never forget the role of Jews in helping build our city.'"

"And that's a whole 'nother history," Daniel said. "The Victor Sassoon mansion is now the Peace Hotel. That's where Noel Coward wrote *Private Lives*. And here is the bronze and stone memorial inscribed in Chinese, Hebrew and English to Holocaust victims."

"And this one is of Pan Guang, Dean of Shanghai's Institute for Sino-Judaic Studies. He helped organize the ceremony, made possible the peace accord between the PLO and Israel, and the 1992 establishment of diplomatic relations between the People's Republic and the State of Israel," Miriam said.

"In another ten years, maybe we can all go to China. If things move along, there might be a functioning synagogue, and we could be there for Yom Kippur, instead of Columbus Day here. There is much to atone for," Daniel said.

"Amen," Christian said.

"But here we all are at St. Jude's in 1996. Well, it feels like we're all in this together. Do you think we have enough know-how among us to figure out what the hell is really going on at St. Jude's?" Dee asked. "But first, any more cider?

12

The mischief-makers had been hard at work. Women of Worth, WOW, was up and running, and the energy and optimism of the students encouraged and sustained Dee. They were reaching an ever-growing audience: the curious and the committed attended their meetings. The conservative newspaper, *St. Jude's Review*, edited by a group of well-connected seniors in Political Science and bankrolled by a right-wing think tank, ran interference when WOW organized a panel on Choice. The women had discussed their strategy at some length and had come up with ground rules for the debate: establish common ground, be civil, be accurate and rigorous, assume good will, admit the price of one's position, listen. Their interest in genuine debate had impressed most of those present, including Father Decursus, who had written congratulating them on their fine presentation. "I had never thought about moral choices as constructed in the way you outlined," he wrote. "Thank you, I think, for your thoughtful words."

St. Jude's Review carried editorials and cartoons ridiculing the WOW women, suggesting they were damned. On the list of the ten things the *Review* most reviled, WOW was number one and their advisers were listed as two, three and four. "Getting Back to Our Roots", an unsigned opinion piece, made the argument: "We are a Catholic college and those who speak of the devil's work threaten us all. Abortion is a sin. It is not a matter of social justice. It is murder. We call upon all right-thinking Catholics to put down this calumny. It is a misuse of our student funds to support WOW. If these evil-doers continue to promote their ideas on our campus, then the consequences will be dire. You have been warned."

WOW remained undeterred. The group was reaching beyond

the gated St. Jude's community. The members found a number of Women's Studies programs that were only too happy to network with them. The group requested copies of brochures, faculty profiles, and courses from college administrators. They sent announcements for their upcoming events to their ever-growing number of contacts. They were building networks and finding out that there were good speakers who were delighted to talk to their group. WOW began to visit nearby campuses and established good working relations with other Jesuit colleges in the area. Clearly, WOW was not alone in its frustration with the Health Center. There were many kindred spirits out there with similar problems. Just learning this, while disheartening, was nevertheless a source of hope for change. WOW was on a roll. Membership was increasing. The group petitioned the Curriculum Committee about the need for a proper Women's Studies program and asked to speak to the issue at the next faculty meeting. Jamie Coyle pledged enough to cover the cost of a Chair of Women's Studies and Social Justice. She had decided that would be her mark on the institution. Virginia Glacialis was still on leave. What could go wrong?

No good deed goes unpunished.

It didn't take long for the other shoe to drop. Several of the women in WOW told Dee of late-night phone calls they had received. The message was always the same, always spoken by a deep male voice: "You have been warned." The calls stopped after a week or so and, although they were annoyed, the women let it pass. After all, hang-ups and heavy breathing had long been part of the telephone culture for women at St. Jude's. Dee asked Mary J if she'd had any unusual calls recently. "Funny you mention it," she said, "I had one the other day. It was strange. The person started off as if he knew me, asked about the kids, and then said, 'You have been warned,' and hung up."

"Did you recognize the voice?"

"At first I thought I did, but then I realized it was just the friendly tone that seemed familiar."

"Have the other secretaries received calls like this?"

"I'll check at lunchtime. I haven't been to the cafeteria for a while."

Later that afternoon, Mary J reported that the secretaries in the Chaplain's Office and Dean's Office had indeed had similar calls and were not happy about it. "It's just like before," Mary J said.

"Before?"

"Well, back when Jessie was working with a group of women students who wanted contraceptives made available through the Health Center. There were a number of nuisance calls then."

"Did anyone figure out who was doing it?"

"No and we complained to Chuck Negotium, the Business Manager, but he said there was nothing he could do. So we all switched our phones over to our answering machines and he got really furious and told us it was our job to answer the phones and so on."

"And did you?"

Secretarial solidarity, what a moment! Nuisance calls or a well-orchestrated campaign? The same signature, "You have been warned." Who is calling the shots?

"I lasted the longest. The others gave in when they were threatened. But then the calls ended, so it wasn't an issue any more," Mary J said.

"And did they ever resume?"

"No and come to think of it, that was the same month Jessie died."

January 16, 1997: Martin Luther King Day: "I have a Dream. . .". The quality of justice of a society may be measured by how well it treats its minorities, the disadvantaged, the weak and the vulnerable. And women? Are women part of the dream?

Dee was reading the proofs of the article on trafficking in China that she had coauthored with Pica and Adam Lu, when Cissy, Mary Louise and MC appeared at her door. "Come in, come in," she said. "Sit down." MC perched nervously on the arm of Mary Louise's chair. Cissy pulled her chair up close to Dee's desk and said, "I found this stack of papers today in the WOW mailbox." She handed a large manila envelope to Dee. "We're not sure what

174

it means, or what to do, but we're sure it is important."

"Yes," MC said sharply. "And we want some answers."

"I see it has no return address," Dee said, inspecting the envelope. "The postmark is Springfield, Massachusetts. Know anyone there?"

"Just look at it," Mary Louise said, passing over Dee's question and growing agitated. She adjusted the clip in her blonde hair so that no stray wisps would cloud her vision.

"Someone has gone to a lot of trouble putting it together," Dee said as she emptied the contents of the envelope on her desk. It was a sheaf of news clippings and photocopies. "Okay, slow down and tell me again how you got this." Dee hoped she could calm them down a little and get a better sense of how to handle the situation.

"Well it's my job to clear the WOW mailbox," Cissy began. "I like doing it. I get to see the invitations to various events first. I feel like I'm the town crier. You know, 'Hear ye! Hear ye! Women rule!' Mostly the announcements in the mailbox are addressed to WOW, but this one was addressed to me care of WOW. It turned my stomach when I read it."

"Well, let me see what is here," Dee said, placing her hand firmly on the stack of papers.

"Look at the top one," Mary Louise said. "Who are all these people? Where did all these reports appear?"

Dee studied the elaborate cut and paste arrangement of newspaper articles. In the center of the page was the banner headline "Predatory Priests." Dee turned to the next page and read down the inventory.

Rev. Gilbert Gauthé, 1985, 11 boys, Louisiana

Rev. James R. Porter, 1993, 200 boys, Fall River, Massachusetts

Archbishop Robert F. Sanchez, 1993, 2 women, New Mexico

Rev. Paul R. Shanley, 1993, unknown number boys and girls, Boston

Father John J. Geoghan, 1994, 200 boys, Boston and environs

Father David A. Holley, 1993, 8 boys, Massachusetts to New Mexico

Dee began to leaf through the clippings. They were organized chronologically. There was the 1985 story of Gilbert Gauthé who was sentenced to twenty years, released after ten, and had offended again recently. For the same year there was an article about a meeting of the US bishops in Minnesota and a page from a report detailing some thirty known cases of sex abuse by priests. She read of a mother in Chicago who in 1991 established a group for victims. She read how, by 1992, the Pope was seeking to include attention to sexuality and celibacy in seminary education. There were articles about a number of treatment centers where priests with problems with alcohol and sex were being sent. So many places! She'd had no idea. The Servants of the Paraclete in Jemez Springs, New Mexico; the St. Luke Institute in Maryland; the Seton Psychiatric Institute, Baltimore; the Southdown Institute in Ontario, Canada; and the House of Affirmation in Worcester, Massachusetts.

In the 1993 account of the resignation of Archbishop Sanchez was a highlighted section about a sex ring that was run by inmates of a treatment center at Jemez Springs. "Have you ever heard of the place in New Mexico?" Dee asked Cissy.

"No," Cissy said. "Keep reading, Dee." The trio had long since dropped the formality of "Professor". *Why had all this been addressed to Cissy?* Dee wondered. She put the material down for a minute. There was too much to digest quickly. The young women were watching Dee closely. *Do any of these articles mention St. Jude's or anyone we know?* Dee began to scan the stories. She was getting a sense of the sickening sameness of it all. Then on the last page of the bundle of papers, staring at her from a photograph dated 1973, was Father Sordes SJ and he was in New Mexico. He had a beard and was considerably fatter than now, but it was Sordes. No doubt about it.

Dee read the text that had been pasted in underneath the photograph. "Recidivism is so high with pedophilia and exhibitionism that all controlled studies have shown that traditional outpatients' psychiatric or psychological models alone do not work . . . There is no hope at this point in time for a cure."

Dee flinched. Cissy leaned forward onto Dee's desk. "It's serious, isn't it? Will you help us?"

"I think I know who might be able to help," Dee said as calmly as she could. "Can I borrow the papers for a few hours?" Cissy was only too happy to hand them over. "Call in after class today and we'll see what can be done." The three young women left, feeling relieved.

Dee immediately called Jackie Li. "Do you know these places in New Mexico, Maryland, and Massachusetts and what they might have to do with Paddy Sordes?"

"Let's meet off campus," Jackie said.

"How about lunch at the Resolve Diner? No-one from St. Jude's ever goes there and they make great vegetable soups and fresh Italian bread."

"Okay, Dee. See you at noon."

Jackie was very tense when she sat down opposite Dee. She peeled off her dark blue woolly gloves and beret, put her coat with Dee's on the back of the spare chair and asked, "What do you have?"

"A stack of clippings." Dee said as she pushed them across the table. Jackie swallowed hard as she read the headlines. She put her head in her hands and began massaging it.

"You know this is dynamite?" Dee was sure it was but did not want the young women to be further harassed. "What do you think I should do?"

Jackie had regained her composure and was making notes. "I want to make a few calls before I say anything definite." That was fine with Dee. "Let's eat. I have a feeling you'll be needing sustenance to get through the day."

They ate slowly and with a growing sense of dread.

"I'll check in with you later," Jackie promised as they bundled up in their heavy coats and left the diner. Dee watched Jackie stride across the slippery path to her car. *How does she manage in those stiletto heels?* Dee wondered.

Dee knew that much of what Jackie might learn would be considered confidential or even privileged. She decided to do some of her own sleuthing with the online databases available through the college library. A Nexis-Lexis search of newspapers eventually turned up details of the report from 1985. It had been written jointly by the Reverend Thomas P. Doyle, a canon lawyer stationed at the Vatican Embassy in Washington, Michael R. Peterson, a psychiatrist and director of the St. Luke Institute, and F. Ray Mouton, a Louisiana lawyer who had represented the Rev. Gauthé. Doyle wrote that he was seeing an increasing number of sex abuse cases, had recognized a looming crisis and contacted Peterson and Mouton. Their report, drawing on the fields of canon law, secular law and psychiatry, detailed the cost of the known cases and predicted a much higher cost if the situation was not addressed aggressively. Dee read that only fifteen copies of the report were made and that it had arrived too late to be on the agenda of the bishops' meeting. Then the document had quietly "disappeared." *Who is now addressing the issue?* Dee wondered. Doyle had lost his job in the Vatican. Peterson had died of AIDS in 1987. Mouton, dismayed at the lack of response, had given up his law practice and his devotion to the church.

Wait them out; buy them out; harass them out.

Dee called Daniel at his office and was pleased when he picked up. "What do you know about sex abuse of minors by priests? Are there any public records I can scan?"

"I'll check with my 'deep throat' in the Attorney-General's in Boston," he said. "Stay off email on this one. The law isn't settled on the nature of privilege that attaches to electronic communications."

"No worries. I have a few other leads to follow up."

Dee thought she might be able to pursue the article from the *Hartford Courant*. Their back copies were all on microfiche. But she didn't want to drive into Hartford for an outdated technology she had grown to hate. Back to Nexis-Lexis. After some creative refinements to the search, she found an obituary for a Dr. Francis J. Braceland of the Institute for the Living, Hartford, Connecticut, in the *New York Times*. His credentials were impressive – Loyola, Chicago, a man committed to using psychiatry to heal good men of the cloth who had faltered. It appeared that the Institute of the Living in Hartford was a secular psychiatric hospital that had been admitting priests with 'disorders,' including molestation of minors, since the early 1980s. The professionals there were angry when offenders were put back into circulation against their recommendations. These doctors had broken through the silence maintained by the religious-based treatment centers. The *Hartford Courant* had followed the story.

Psychiatry as the secular cousin to confession; classic double bind - shift responsibility onto "experts" to heal the mentally ill, BUT the new "confessors" learn the extent of abuse and mechanisms of deceit, denial and deception . . . Church loses control of the story.

Daniel got back to Dee late in the afternoon. "Well, the Massachusetts scene is grim. Suits have been filed, but the records have all been impounded because the presiding judge – a good Catholic – ruled the particulars of the controversy ought to be kept from the public. Be careful, Dee, these boys play for keeps. The cases go way back and the church has been successful in settling and silencing. They know how to play the deference card. The judges and prosecutors are all Catholic. Their lawyers have shamed victims, accused parents of neglect, and suggested that the children who were abused were unusually seductive. Of this I am sure, what you have is the tip of the iceberg."

"I'm finding that out. Listen to this headline from the *Wall Street Journal*, no less. 'The Catholic Church Struggles with Suits Over Sexual Abuse: While it pledges compassion, its lawyers play rough defending lapsed priests.' And that was in 1993. I found quite a few others too."

A Catholic conspiracy? Who knows? Who is responsible? Who is accountable? How deeply is Sordes implicated?

Dee began making lists. These predatory priests were circulating through the various institutes and communities. Holley, Sanchez, and Porter had connections to Jemez Springs; Gauthé and Geoghan to St. Luke's. Maybe Geoghan was a link between those places and peoples. He had been in Hartford and Ontario. She began online searches on each of the priests. Where had they gone to school? What seminary had they attended? Had they been in treatment and, if so, where? Dee found connections. The biographies overlapped and intertwined. Dee called the number she had for the center in Jemez Springs, but found it had recently closed.

Dee called Jackie Li and asked, "How is your research coming along?"

"In a word? Scary. What do you have?"

"I have a chart that might interest you," Dee said, and explained about the interconnections she'd mapped.

"Would you be prepared to share?" Jackie asked with just a hint of humor in her voice.

"Do I need legal counsel?" Dee inquired.

"Okay, off the record."

"I have a feeling that it is not going to be an option for much longer," Dee said. "I'll drop the chart off on my way to the library."

"I'm going to try for a quick chat with our President," Jackie said. "His secretary says there might be an opening around 5 pm."

Jackie Li had a good working relationship with President Firmitas. He had hired her straight out of law school on the basis of the interview, where she had impressed him with her forceful, confident manner. "I come from a long line of strong women," she'd said. "My mother and grandmother back in Singapore, they might be diminutive, but don't be fooled, they think big." The President had jokingly called Jackie his "stealth candidate:" she could go under the radar. Jackie decided this was the time to test their relationship. She had asked for a ten-minute appointment and, by a stroke of good fortune, found he was free in an hour. So, on that miserable winter's day in 1997, Jackie Li took her worries to the President of St. Jude's and sparked a series of events she could not have anticipated in her wildest imaginings.

January 19, 1997: St. Margaret's feast day: virgin, daughter of King Bela IV, Order of St. Dominic;

180

distinguished by the virtue of her chastity, severity of
her penance, and charity toward her neighbor;
inscribed on rolls of holy virgins by Pius XII.

⁜

The next morning Dee was sluggish and found it hard to get moving. She hated these cold mornings, and the heating system was still clanking through the night. Sometimes she managed to block it out, but not last night. Her dreams had roamed wildly over vast terrains – from her conversation with Christian about Yorùbá secret cults to phone exchanges. Like her doodling, the design was there but not yet stable. It took an act of will to get out of bed. Dee lingered over her morning tea ritual and scanned the papers. An article on hate crimes by a young woman journalist caught her attention. She clipped it and decided to call the journalist later in the day. Maybe she could be a speaker for WOW.

Dee showered, dressed slowly and, still deep in thought, walked down to her office. The morning mail had just arrived. It was all routine: announcements of upcoming events, an overdue journal subscription, an inter-library loan slip, and an innocuous looking envelope, hand-addressed to Professor Scrutari. She opened it and read the big, black, block print.

THE PROBLEM: WOW

CEASE OR FACE THE CONSEQUENCES

YOU HAVE BEEN WARNED

At the bottom, printed large in blood-red ink, was "Terminator #126". Dee walked down the hall to show Pica. On the way out of her office she saw that a cross, made of twigs and carrying the same signature, had been attached to the 606 on her door. Before she reached Pica's office, Miriam caught her. "Cissy just called. She wants a lawyer. Says she has been threatened."

"Me too. Look at my door. Is Cissy coming up to see you?"

"I think I can see all three women," Miriam said looking down the broad sweep of the stairs. "I'll bring them into your office and get Pica."

Cissy, Mary Louise and MC had all received the same letter as Dee. Crosses had been placed on their dorm-room doors. Dee's letter looked as if it had been opened before she got it and so did Mary Louise's. "Okay, I'll begin at the beginning," Dee said. "I'll call the St. Jude's Post Office. See what they have to say for themselves."

"Yes, we opened them," Post Master Littera volunteered. "They were in the mail drop for student groups. There was a bunch of envelopes that were all the same, but there was no stamp identifying them as coming from a registered group. They have to go through a different mail slot if they're private."

"And you thought delivering mail that contained threats was okay?" Dee asked, trying not to shout.

"It's not our business. All I have to do is make sure there is not an abuse of the mailing system. I made a copy, just to be on the safe side."

Whose safe side? Where to start? Privacy? FCC?

"Aren't you bound by the rules and regulations governing employees of the US Postal Service?" Dee fumed.

"Yes ma'am. But this was internal mail and that is St. Jude's bailiwick."

Who pays his salary?

Pica was trying to stay calm by focusing closely on the handwriting on the letter. Miriam was making sweet hot tea and hoping Daniel would call her back soon. The women students were angry and a bit frightened.

"Okay, next step. I'll try the Dean," Dee announced as if this would bring an end to the outrage.

"It's just a note. Someone has been watching too many Hollywood movies," he exhaled loudly, as if he had been waiting for her call. "Anyone could have put it there."

"Well, the writing is backhand," Dee commented. "And smudged, as often happens with a left-hander."

He roared, "You want me to check handwriting? This isn't a police state."

"I want you to take this seriously. It is a threat. It is intimidation. These women have a high profile. They're being targeted."

"Well, I need a lot more to go on than what you're telling me."

Dee could feel the blood banging in her temples. She didn't want to terrify the students any further, but she did want them to know she shared their sense of violation.

Miriam brought in a teapot, cups and saucers, a little jug of milk and a bowl of sugar, carefully arranged on a big silver catering tray left over from a function in the department. The students were momentarily distracted by the formality of Miriam serving tea in this manner. "Everything feels better after a nice cup of tea," Miriam said as she spun the pot three times, shook it back and forth, and then poured a cup for each of them.

"We'll get to the bottom of this," Dee promised. Cissy, Mary Louise and MC had sipped their tea and were now standing, ready to leave.

"Are you okay to go to class?" Miriam asked in a motherly tone.

"What doesn't kill you makes you stronger," Cissy said. "We're not going to cave in to these bullies." And the three tromped out of Dee's office. Mary Lousie's T-shirt said "Uppity Women Unite." *A prophetic statement I hope*, Dee thought.

"They're gutsy, all right," Dee said to Miriam. "I hope their bravado gets them through the rest of the day."

"What about you?"

"More tea. And thanks for being a good mum to us all." Dee had given up trying to explain to Miriam that she found her nurturing impulses oppressive sometimes. Cultural relativism, she was learning, had its uses. There were different ways of mothering.

"I'll let you know as soon as I hear from Daniel. It's my intuition that we should not use email or IM about this stuff," Miriam continued.

"Yep, Daniel already warned me."

"Are you going to call Christian?"

"Later. He's in meetings and teaching this afternoon. Let's see how it pans out first." Dee didn't want to run to him with every little woe and she wanted to handle it her way – whatever that turned out to be. Sometimes his decisiveness left no room for Dee to find her own way. *I can handle this*, she told herself, *but a reassuring hug would be nice right now.*

> *January 20, 1997: St. Agnes' Eve: A girl might have a prevision of her future husband. Agnes, fourth century noble Roman virgin - martyred at the age of 13 after rejecting a well-born suitor; a duplex feast.*

✛

The women had almost convinced themselves that the threats were a one-day wonder. But then, a week later, a stone, with the same red Terminator #126 signature and cross, came slamming through Mary Louise's front window. She contacted Dean Simean but, because she lived off campus, that office offered no protection. "Move back on campus and we can protect her," the Dean said. "If she chooses to live off campus, she deals with what that neighborhood delivers."

Dee spoke with the campus police. "Keep it quiet," they advised. "It just fans their ego if you go public. We're in contact with the Resolve Police. We have our sources." Dee was not convinced that much was going on because each time she called downtown she got a different person and none seemed to know about the threats.

> *Safety? Emergency Procedures? Who is protecting whom and from what? What liaison is there between Resolve Police and Negotium's squad?*

The women were now frightened and furious. Mary Louise moved onto campus with Cissy, and the two invited Dee over. MC joined them soon after. "Should we call our parents?" Mary Louise asked as they sipped coffee laced with brandy. Dee let it pass that the women were underage and in the substance-free dorm. *After all*, she told herself, *they're not about to drive anywhere.*

"You know, my family is still upset about the stuff the Women's Watch published about graffiti in the men's bathrooms when my cousin Jamie was here. I can't see them being too thrilled that I'm involved with an even more radical organization," Cissy said. "But I could call Jamie."

Jamie was out, so Cissy left a message to call, no matter how late she got in. They then settled in to watch some mindless television. Around 10:30 pm the calls started. Not Jamie, as Cissy hoped but, "This is the Terminator. You have been warned." Dee stayed for another hour or so, in which there were two more calls of a similar nature. The group discussed their options – don't answer, disconnect the phone, call security. At Dee's insistence Cissy contacted Campus Security but was told that they could do nothing about phone calls. "Told you so," Cissy said, exasperated. "You have more faith in the system than I do, Dee."

"Well, it's where I start," Dee said.

"They said they'd protect us if we were on campus, but I guess we're on our own." Mary Louise was working her way through her little black phone book.

"It's okay, Dee, go home. We'll be fine. Mary Louise can stay here tonight too. We'll lock the doors and pull the phone out," Cissy said.

Dee asked MC if she could keep the stone – the police had demonstrated no interest in it. Dee wrapped it in a tissue. She'd put it in her desk drawer tomorrow, the one that locked. She hated being put in a position where she had to be on guard in her own office. Dee realized she was completely washed out. *Why should these young women have to suffer like this?* she thought as she walked up to her apartment. It was too late to call Miriam and probably too late to call Christian, but as a matter of habit she checked her messages. Miriam had called just to check on how she was doing. There was also a message from Christian. "Dee, call me. I don't mind if you wake me up." She looked at her watch. It was after midnight. *This will be a test*, she thought.

Christian answered almost immediately. "No, I'm awake. Tell me what's happening." Dee recounted what she knew and realized she was dead tired. "I have to sleep," she said. "I'm okay, really. I'll figure it out."

"Okay, but please be careful," he said.

WOW called meetings, circulated petitions, and wrote letters to the editor, including one from Jamie. They were ready to inundate the three student newspapers with copy. The *St. Jude's Review* editorial opined, "Too much press on this matter. And what did they expect, publishing all that obscene material from the bathrooms?" *Jude's Jottings* expressed outrage in one piece and accused the women of misusing college funds in another. *Daily Dispatches* noted that Pax Christi would meet the following week to discuss "Violence on campus." Some whispered they knew the source of the threats, but no-one came forward.

Words flew, but the administration remained silent. Although some combination of the Terminator #126 signature, "You have been warned" and the cross were evoked with each threat, Campus Security refused to see the incidents as related. There was the matter of the proper use of internal mail. There was the phone system. There were insurance policies for broken windows. The campus police said it was an "ongoing investigation" so they couldn't discuss the matter.

> *January 26, 1997: Martyrdom of St. Paula, widow, Bethlehem of Judea; renounced the world, distributed her goods to the poor; St. Jerome memorialized her virtues.*
>
> *Australia Day: Captain Phillip plants the British flag at Sydney Cove in 1788 and disenfranchises the Indigenous inhabitants in the name of the Crown.*

Christian insisted Dee take the weekend off, and go away. "I thought we could take a look at that place you told me about in the Berkshires. They have a vacancy. I checked online." Dee conceded she needed time off, but didn't like being told what she should and shouldn't do. She didn't need protection. Well not the paternalistic kind. *What if I made plans for him?* she thought and made a mental note to raise the matter later. She said with as much enthusiasm as she could muster, "The B&B near Jacob's Pillow? That would be a treat."

"Pack some sensible shoes and we'll go for a proper walk." Christian knew Dee loved walking, even in the frozen depths of winter.

"Will do," Dee said, trying to make light of it, but she bristled silently. *I can probably be trusted to do my own packing. Oh dear, I have to have this out with him and soon.* Christian had not caught the edge in her voice and continued, "We can pretend we're on a road trip, hide in all those feather down spreads, explore the town. There will be new bookshops, Dee. You can have a weekend dispensation from your AA book regime. We could eat blueberry muffins and buy little knick-knacks to send to Uganda. I'll pick you up around 10 on Saturday morning. We'll be there for lunch."

"Why is this so important to you, Dee?" Christian asked when they were settled in the guest room of the Old Village Square Bed and Breakfast in Lee, Massachusetts. Dee was sitting on the bed and checking out the local eateries.

"You mean the threats, or the bigger picture?" She put down the *Guide to the Berkshires* and looked up.

"The whole thing." Christian sat down beside her.

"Miriam asked me that too, I guess I just can't stand by, when there is something I can do. I think of all the people who did that during the period when Aboriginal children were being taken from their mothers in Australia, and in this country, with Native Americans too. I can't do much about that, it all started before I was born. But I can do something about the impact those policies have on people today, and I can help make sure the histories are not forgotten. I've seen the consequences of inaction. Miriam would say the same about the Holocaust, I'm sure."

"Yes, I know. Those who don't learn from history are condemned to relive it."

"So am I missing something here?" Dee asked. "It's not my culture, not my history."

"Is this really your fight?" Christian put his arm around her shoulders. "You're not going to change the church."

187

"I know, but these students are so brave. Surely I should be there for them."

"You are. They know it, but they have to figure some things out themselves too. I know you're strong. It's one of the things I love about you, but I also see the cost." Christian ran his fingers through her hair.

"You should talk." Dee drew back. "Look at your workload and the toll that takes."

"Yes and I'm not going to solve all of Africa's problems," Christian agreed. "I think I'm asking you to talk to me about what sustains you, deep down. I know it's not any belief in a super-power, or a life hereafter."

Dee relaxed a little. "I'm not sure I know, but I'm working on it. My notebooks are a riot of symbols and I'm sure that a pattern will emerge," she said. "But I know evil when I see it, smell it, touch it. I know hypocrisy and contempt for others too. There is so much meanness in the world, so much willful ignorance."

"And you're a gifted teacher and researcher." Christian looked at Dee.

"Flattery will get you almost anywhere," Dee said. This was not the moment to raise her qualms about his bossiness. "Can we continue this conversation over food? There's clam chowder on the menu at the little café next door. I think that's about what I'm up for. What about you?"

Christian laughed at the sudden change of mood. "Something light." He sat at the little desk, his long legs sprawled to one side and picked up the phone. "Shall I see if they do take-outs?"

"Please," Dee said and stretched out on the bed. "Then I could really do with some of whatever the doctor has to offer."

The following Monday, Dee made another appointment to see Dean Simean. Maybe she could appeal to him as a father of daughters.

He listened quietly as Dee outlined her case. "I agree the women need to feel safe. But as I indicated last week, they have to accept some responsibility."

"Are you blaming the victim?"

"Well, you can't go demanding that the Health Center offer reproductive counseling and not expect to upset people. You can't advocate the use of Family Planning and not expect some anger. You can't rehearse a feminist liturgy and not expect some outrage."

How does he know all this? Who is briefing him?

"Well, I think they have a case when they say they pay full benefits and get less than full service. And as for the liturgy, we do have academic freedom, don't we?"

"You are also at a Jesuit college and if you don't like it, you have options."

"Are you threatening me?"

"I'm just stating a reality."

"It might be your reality, within these walls, but the last time I looked, the laws of the land do not stop at the iron gates of St. Jude's." Dee's voice was raised and she suspected there would soon be a call from the outer office to remind the Dean of a waiting appointment. He was anticipating the call too. He stood fast and said, "We're *in compliance* with all laws."

"We should be more than in compliance. We should be leading the way," Dee pounded. That was it. She was out of there. But there had been no call from the outer office. As she exited she saw Mary Kane, the Dean's secretary, busily reloading paper in the copying machine. Dee knew there was a work-study student to do that. *Why was she away from her desk?* Dee caught Mary Kane's eye as she left and mouthed, "Thank you," and quickly stepped into the marble tiled hallway. *Had Mary acknowledged her thanks with a nod and smile?* Dee had not dared say any more.

Did Mary Kane's children go to St. Jude's? Ask Mary J.

Daniel called but his advice was not as clear-cut as Miriam had hoped. No-one had been physically hurt and conspiracy was hard to prove. He knew the Attorney-General in Massachusetts was engaged in some inquiries about gender and hate crimes and that maybe there could be some regional cooperation. He'd made some calls. "The personal costs will be enormous for all those involved," he warned Dee.

Dee was convinced there was a conspiracy and that the tight little group of students in Political Science was involved.

Connect the dots: Read Susan Faludi on the nature of conspiracy - you don't need a smoke-filled room, a coalescing of interests will produce the same results. What are the common interests at St. Jude's?

Sunday February 2, 1997: The Presentation of the Lord (Candlemas) Day: Celebrates the day Mary and Joseph brought the baby Jesus to the Temple, forty days after his birth - Purification of the Blessed Virgin Mary - as required by Jewish law; celebrates the arrival of Jesus Christ as the light and sign of hope beyond death and guidance to the world - candles blessed for the year.

13

DINNER WITH THE JESUITS
February 1997

It was time to talk more with Thomas Guye, and Dee didn't have to wait long for an opportunity. The department had prepared its report on Pica's file and it was positive. There was no need for a minority report. Tom had been superb in his management of the gang of four who seemed determined to prove that Pica had violated all scholarly norms with her research. Dee was already strategizing about how to persuade Dean Simean to see the obvious merit of Pica's work and thought she could have as a back-up argument that St. Jude's needed more minorities and women on faculty. After all, at St. Jude's, nuns and Jesuits were affirmative action appointments.

"We often invite faculty to dine with us," Tom said as he helped Dee put away the coffee cups that had collected in the seminar room, "And I would like to invite you to be my guest. Of course I have an agenda. I'll be visiting Uganda next semester and I want to pick your brains, get a background briefing on the culture, if that's all right."

"Sure. I'd love to dine with you and I want to pick your brains too," Dee laughed. "I think I need some background briefing on *your* culture."

"Okay, I'll meet you at the glass doors at seven o'clock. You'll need to be buzzed in."

"What do I wear?" Dee asked Pica a little later in the day.

"Whatever you want. They will be in black – well, not Tom. He'll be wearing slacks and a sweater like he always does. I think his mother must have knitted them – all that Fair Isle. Maybe you can brighten their dinner with one of those splendid long embroidered numbers."

Dee couldn't wait to share the moment with Christian. He was online.

DPS: Dinner with the Jesuits! Tonight.

CO: I'd love to be a fly on the wall. Full report asap.

February 14, 1997: All female faculty and staff at St. Jude's receive potted plants from the Office of the President - Happy St. Valentine's Day! What is being celebrated?

Brides of Christ?

Lupercalia, the Roman holiday of sexual license?

The day birds pick their mates?

The Valentine who was martyred by the Roman Emperor Claudius II Gothicus for defying a decree on wartime marriages?

The Valentine, persecuted for his Christian beliefs, who restored the eyesight of his jailer's blind daughter, and signed his letters "Your Valentine"?

Or Valentine, "Galantine," as in "gallant"?

N.B. In 1969, the feast was dropped from the Roman Church Calendar.

The dinner with the Jesuits was pleasant enough: creamed cauliflower soup with hot bread rolls, roast turkey with all the trimmings, some kind of sponge cake and berries topped with whipped cream, and wines – red and white, followed by an offering of sweet dessert wines. The coffee and liqueurs were served in an anteroom and there were those institutional cookies again, the ones Jamie Coyle had spurned. Tom brought Dee coffee and some port. The two sat in big overstuffed chairs, like the ones in Dee's office, and looked out over Resolve. The lights of the town winked at them through the bare trees and glistened on the snow-covered ground. This was her second Northern Hemisphere winter and Dee was beginning to anticipate the change of seasons and the rituals associated with each.

"Can I ask how you brought your colleagues around?" Dee began.

"You can, but I'd rather talk about Uganda. Tell me about the people you've been working with. Is it possible to make a difference? Or am I just wasting my time?"

"Well, let me tell you about Fatima. I met her in 1993, and in many ways her life reads like the history of her country in microcosm. Where people come from is important, you know. It's important to know what families, and what kingdoms, they belong to. And it is important to know whether they fish, raise cattle, or grow crops."

"And so?"

"Her father, from the southwest, near Mbarara, in the Ankole Kingdom, was killed by President Milton Obote's men from the Acholi Kingdom in the north. Then her mother fled when Idi Amin's troops laid waste to the area. She spent much of her life as a young widow in refugee camps in Tanzania, but the conditions there were really awful. A woman without a man was easy prey. The only negotiable good she had was sex. HIV-AIDS was rampant and younger and younger girls were targets, especially as the myth spread that sex with a virgin can cure AIDS."

"You really touched a nerve with that intervention," Tom said. "I know it rocked Adam. I don't think he would have taken much interest in Pica's tenure case otherwise."

"I'm sure you're right. It was great working with him on that article on trafficking, even though it had to go through so many revisions before it was deemed acceptable. You know I'd never connected the 'sex with a virgin' myth with Taoist notions of women's yin essence as inexhaustible but man's yang as expendable. All those emperors building up their yang, by getting the yin they needed from concubines and young wives."

"We probably have enough local expertise to organize a symposium around religion and AIDS," Tom said. "But tell me more about Fatima."

"Well, in many ways she was lucky," Dee continued. "She met Stephani and they married young. He was a good man. He didn't beat her. He provided for the children. She suspected he had another woman in Entebbe, but she could do little about it. She challenged him only once by asking, 'Why are you always so long in Entebbe?'

"'I'm working, that's my job, pick up clients from the airport, deliver them to Safari Tours,' was his easy answer.

"'Not seeing another woman?' and Fatima named a young woman about whom there had been gossip.

"He said, 'Okay. You think so. We will go and ask her today. But be careful. If I am right and you are wrong, the shame will be great. I will not continue to support the children for school fees. What then?'

"So Fatima gave up."

"How do anthropologists deal with situations like that?" Tom asked.

"You mean when the 'natives' violate our own cultural norms and values?"

"Yes. I mean, am I supposed to just pass it off by saying, well it's their culture and it's not my job to intervene?"

"Cultural relativism can be tricky," Dee smiled. "I don't stand by if women, children, or vulnerable people are getting beaten. And that gets me into trouble sometimes."

"What if Stephani had beaten Fatima?"

"Then I would have intervened, but I would have been as culturally sensitive as possible."

"Such as?"

"Maybe I could find a relative or friend who would be able to help – someone who had some responsibility to stop the beatings, to help the marriage survive. You know marriages implicate a wide range of family, on both sides. Maybe an aunt or uncle could have intervened. There were enough stresses in that marriage without having your friendly, resident anthropologist becoming part of the negotiations around your life."

"Or priest," Tom said.

"Indeed. We are symbols of Western power and our track record ain't that good. You know, bringing 'civilization' to the primitive pagans. I mean what are we doing about the AIDS epidemic?"

"Fighting over causes and costs?"

"Yes, but try to imagine a society where over fifty percent of the adult population is infected and where children are born under a death sentence. Who looks after the orphans and widows? Stephani's brother and sister-in-law died of AIDS and now Fatima is raising their four orphaned children."

"What about her own children?"

"They are grown, and like so many of their generation, they're rebellious, don't want to follow the strict Islamic family code. Fatima's oldest daughter has two children already, by different men. Stephani threw her out when she came asking for shelter after a particularly violent episode with the father of her first child. 'This is not our child,' Stephani had said. 'You may live here but the child must go to his father's family to be raised.'"

"Why?" Tom asked. "He took in his brother's children."

"Good point, but here is where you need to know something about the kinship system. Traditionally children inherit in their father's line, so Stephani's brother's children belonged to his clan, while his daughter's children belonged to their father's clan," Dee explained. "But – and this is a good example of how 'rules' can be bent because Fatima interceded – she asked her family to speak to her husband. 'For love of your wife and respect for her family, take them in,' her parents pleaded. He reluctantly agreed, but when his daughter became pregnant a second time, he refused to budge."

"So if I'm not prepared to learn about the history and culture and kinship system," Tom said, "I'll do more harm than good?"

Dee nodded and sipped at her coffee. "Good coffee," she said.

"The President has a taste for strong coffee," Tom said. "Sometimes on the weekend we have Turkish coffee. Now his family would make a marvelous anthropological study."

"True," Dee said and looked long and hard at Tom. *Who would he be if he had not joined the priesthood? He is really interested in others.*

"There is so much happening in Uganda," Dee said, bringing the

195

conversation back to Tom's original questioning. "I really hope they make it as a country. Ugandan democracy probably won't look much like Western democracy, but it will be interesting. Under the new constitution women have equal rights but they still live in families where all property passes through the male line. They should be able to inherit land, but that is in conflict with customary law. It gets really tricky when you try to make state laws work at the local level."

"It's not as simple as 'we're all equal before the law,' is it?" Tom asked.

"No, it never is," Dee replied. "Not even here."

"So what's to be done that doesn't make it worse?"

"Work with the local organizations. Listen to their goals. Don't impose your agenda. Like, all across the country there are local organizations, providing services for victims of violence and doing consciousness-raising around issues of violence against women. The global gag rule Ronald Reagan put in place really starved people, women in particular, of the information they needed," Dee added. "I know you're opposed to abortion, but women need to know about safe sex if they're going to avoid AIDS and unwanted pregnancies. And men have to take some responsibility."

Tom fetched the port, topped off Dee's glass and poured himself another, then glanced around the room. "Looks like we've got the place to ourselves now."

"Good, because I want to know how you got those four to get on board Pica's case."

"Well, I had to convince them that there is nothing tainted about research that involves passion and commitment. I told them about my research and why I do this stuff on masculinities. Mostly they have ignored my work, and as long as I don't embarrass them, it's okay with them. We live very private lives here."

"How so?"

"In the contemplative life, apart from dinner, we don't really sit around and talk about our everyday lives, families, experiences. But I figured I owed it to Pica, Jessie and to my sisters to speak out. I love my sisters."

Dee nodded, curious that Jessie's name had come up.

"Mary, my older sister, oh she would argue with me about Catholicism, be real serious, and then suddenly she'd be dancing. She could dance! I'd watch her quick feet in those white bobby socks and flat shoes and I loved it when she spun her head around. Her long blond ponytail would swirl around and around in front of my face. She'd coax me to join her, but I'd stumble. I couldn't throw her on my hip or shoot her between my legs the way she instructed. We'd collapse laughing onto the old couch our father had left in the corner of the garage."

"And you still enjoy her company?"

"Definitely. She's my best friend and one of the few people I can really talk to about things – things I can't talk about here."

"Like?"

"Well sex, for one." He looked at Dee who returned his gaze unflinchingly.

"My younger sister, she was different. I felt more protective of her. When our mother was off with the ladies in her church group, and I was not well enough to go to school, I'd read to her from books I knew wouldn't upset either our mother or father. She'd curl up with her favorite soft toy, a rather worn Pooh Bear. I'd set the cushions so she could fall asleep, head in my lap and then I'd wrap her in her blanket and carry her up to bed."

"I don't think I've heard any of the other priests in the department talk like this about their siblings," Dee said.

"Well that's part of the point of my research. I think that if you want to understand how men who have taken vows of celibacy develop sexual identities, you need to know a lot about their relationships with their sisters and mothers, not just as children, but into their adult lives too. So many young men – well, boys really – enter the seminary and are completely cut off. They have no male role models for how to behave with women. They are being drilled about obedience within an all-male hierarchy. I grew up having to negotiate with lots of different people, male, female, my age, younger, older, gay and straight."

"I saw a reference to a recent book, *Sex, Priests and Power*, when

I was doing a search recently. Doesn't the author talk about some of that? Dee asked.

"Oh, that book by A. W. Richard Sipe. Yes. He wrote about celibacy too. I wish I could get my colleagues to discuss his work. I want to talk about my religion as an embodied religion – acknowledge the eroticized mysticism of the early church. It's a secret, what your countryman Taussig would call a secret in plain sight. But sexuality among priests is a non-topic – well, celibacy supposedly means there is no need for theorizing sexual identities or desires. We're outside human sexuality. We see but we don't recognize."

"So, they don't want to know?" Dee said.

Tom looked hard at Dee. He had been watching her closely all evening. *Is he ready to confide in me?* Dee wondered. *Am I finding the right balance between listening and questioning?*

Tom broke the silence. "Next Sunday Father Humanitas from Georgetown will be delivering the homily. He is quite controversial and I'm hoping he'll touch on the issue of sexuality, however briefly."

Can I attend? I don't want Tom to think I'm being voyeuristic.

"You could come to the Mass, if you like," he said, as if reading her thoughts.

Dee was no stranger to the Mass. She had attended Orientation and Commencement Masses as part of the yearly ritual round. She had been to Midnight Mass on Christmas Eve with Magdalena's family but had, up until now, avoided "sitting in" on a Mass as a research task. For her the Mass remained mysterious and alien, a part of the culture of St. Jude's she needed to know more about, but she had not yet found the right moment to explore.

"I feel awkward," she said tentatively. "I don't join the line-up for communion and it feels strange just sitting down while everyone else files past."

"Well, there will be others like you at this Mass," Tom assured her. "Father Humanitas has quite a following, and Pica would probably be prepared to sit with you, cue you in if necessary. I'll be assisting Father Abacus. Come, Dee. Then we can talk about it afterwards."

"If you're sure." Dee was delighted. *The natives are inviting me to their rituals.*

"Great. There are so few people with whom I can talk about this stuff."

"Did you talk about sexuality with your brothers?" Dee asked.

"No, and at first, I wasn't sure how to describe my feelings. I would feel a sort of a rush when my brothers' male friends noticed me, a sort of churning in the stomach when they talked to me, a sort of dismay when they went off arm in arm with my brother to a football game. I know I am attracted to men, but to men of my own age. And, I don't act on it. I know that is my sexual orientation. I know many of my fellow priests entered the seminaries at twelve or thirteen and are emotionally frozen at that age. I am so relieved that I had the opportunity to figure out my own sexuality."

"What's this got to do with Pica and Jessie?" Dee probed.

"Does Pica ever talk about her twin brother, the one who was halfway through his novitiate and left the order?"

"She's mentioned him, but not in detail. She did tell me she taught him to play pool."

"He was in the same seminary as Paddy Sordes and I were, though he was a bit ahead of me. Pica's brother was young when he entered the seminary. He lived with other young boys and was taught by aging males. On their free day, once a week, they could go to town, but only to visit the drug store to buy personal supplies and maybe, on a special occasion, have a milkshake. There were no movies, no bookshops, and no eating out on their schedule. They were like a separate caste and they knew full well who were the untouchables – women. It was sin to even contemplate women. Any impure thoughts of women were to be purged. In the confessional, we were supposed to divulge our innermost desires but I wasn't thinking about women. I didn't know how to name my sexual stirrings. I did know that in the showers boys were checking out each other's bodies, but they were really careful not to be caught doing so. I knew that after lights out some boys crept into bed with others. I also knew that some boys disappeared from the dormitories at night."

199

"Where were your parents in all this? Pica's parents?" Dee asked.

"We were taught not to tell our parents what was happening in the seminary. It was God's business. At first there were only rumors, whispers, nudges and innuendoes about one father, I'll call him Martin. As the story went, Lennie, a boy who had entered around the same time as me, broached the subject of sex. When he was in the confessional with Father Martin, he mentioned that he'd wake up wet and sticky in the morning.

"'Is this a sin, Father?'

"'Do you touch your private parts?'

"'No. Is it a sin?'

"'It's a way to God, my son.'

"Then Father Martin had spoken gently and reassuringly about man–boy love as sacred. He'd instructed Lennie to unbutton his pants and masturbate while Father Martin said the Our Father. Lennie left feeling confused and curious. 'Might this play be a way to God about which only priests knew? Was this one of the mysteries into which he was to be initiated?' he wondered."

"Man–boy love," Dee mused.

"We were given paddles to tuck into our shirts so we would never have to touch ourselves. I tried that vilification of the flesh. All I got was a sore backside. But Lennie felt a thrill. Father Martin talked with Lennie about his family, about how he also had been one of a large family where his mother had worked to support the family. He spoke of the long hours alone, of the need for physical warmth.

"'Come to confession after dinner and we'll talk more.'

"That first 'talk' left Lennie bruised and sore. Could this sacred man–boy love, which Father Martin spoke of and was showing him, be what all priests did, Lennie wondered?"

"Man–boy love. I remember now," Dee said. "There was a mention of man–boy love in the articles in the *Hartford Courant* sent to WOW."

"I know you're good at figuring out how things fit together, Dee. Kinship and all that – this story is part of it."

"Okay, man–boy love. I'll be the cultural relativist. But I reserve my opinion on what I might do when I've heard the story."

"I was hoping you'd say that." Tom was speaking very softly now and watching Dee closely. "Father Martin had Lennie kneel before him in prayer. He lifted his black robe and pulled Lennie towards him until his bowed head was jammed in his crotch.

"'Take it in your mouth.' He crooned, 'Blessed are the meek for they shall inherit the earth. That's right, move and use your hands.'

"Father Martin's prayers grew louder and he groaned rhythmically. His engorged penis was choking Lennie, but the boy dared not stop. Father Martin now had his head in a vise-like grip between his knees. Then Father lay back, exhausted and Lennie could taste some fluid. He wanted to throw up.

"'Swallow,' said Father Martin. 'That is sacred fluid and will make you a Man of God. Now go to your dormitory and do not tell anyone of this. It is our secret. The power will be lost if you speak to anyone of this.'

"I guess Lennie lay awake most of the night. Later, he told me he had wanted to tell me the story because he thought I was more worldly than he was. But instead, he kept quiet and each night after confession Father Martin continued his instruction. First he took Lennie into the Sacristy, and later to his room on the pretext that they could study together in private. His room was like the other priests' – a simple bed, a chest of drawers, a small stool.

"'Lean over the stool,' said Father Martin. Lennie thought he was to be beaten as he had been by his parish priest when, as a child, he had watched the girl next door peeing and had an erection. After that he'd come to associate women's bodies and any thoughts of them with the pain of that punishment. But now he was bent over a stool. Father Martin pulled down Lennie's pants and underpants and began inserting an object in his anus. What was this? It was slippery. He moved to see what was in Father Martin's hands. But the priest was in a trance-like state. He began with the Beatitudes. 'Blessed are those who mourn, for they will be comforted.' Lennie knew the rhythm of this recitation well from earlier events in the confessional. 'Relax,' Martin said. 'You are moving closer to God. He is entering you. This object is one of the sacred relics of the church.' Then Lennie felt Father Martin's body against his rump. He was kneeling as in prayer but his frock was around his waist and he was penetrating Lennie, not with a greased blessed object, but with his stiff penis. He thrust so hard that he sent Lennie sprawling. Now he was on top of him, still thrusting. Lennie closed his eyes and held onto his rosary. He began to pray.

"'Hail Mary, full of grace, the Lord is with thee . . .'

"Then it was over. Father Martin was on his feet, smoothing down his frock and motioning for Lennie to dress and leave.

"'Tomorrow we'll study some more.'

"And so it was that Lennie became a Man of God, blessed by the Holy Relic and bound to secrecy. Now what does this have to do with Pica and why am I telling you all this? Think about it, Dee. Father Martin was from New Mexico."

"And now you work on masculinities?" *And Tom knows, or has guessed, I know about the facility in New Mexico. Who is speaking to whom?* Dee wondered.

"Yes, and am I going to keep quiet about the abuse?"

"You didn't threaten you'd speak out, did you?"

"No threats. I just told them my story."

"And what did they say?"

"It's not news to them. They all know about it. I think a number of them might have been abused and some of them might be abusers."

"And Jessie Seneca?" Dee asked.

"Well she knew about the man–boy love rituals and she knew about the drugs used on those weekend retreats. She knew a lot . . . but enough for now, Dee. Just promise you'll think about all this."

Secrets: Read Georg Simmel on secrecy and the Irish conspiracy; Michael Taussig on the public secret.

Christian didn't respond when Dee tried to IM him, so she rapped out a brief email. *Report on Dinner – Sex, silence and sin. BTW – the Valentine potted plant Firmitas sent me died. Is this an omen? Dee.*

14

HOMILIES, EPIPHANIES, AND LENT
February 1997

Pica was enthusiastic about the upcoming Mass and anxious to fill Dee in on what she might expect. "No, you don't need to wear a hat any more," an amused Pica assured Dee. "That's no longer required. And no need to dress up. I'll be wearing my usual workaday clothes, plain ones. It is Lent."

Dee grinned, "Well, at least I'll find some appropriately somber shoes to wear."

The two women were sitting in Pica's office. From the window Dee could see the students bustling up and down the stairs to the library. She wanted to ask Pica about the fountain on the library steps but she could see that Pica was still grappling with the complications of taking an anthropologist to a Mass at St. Jude's.

"And probably best to leave your notebook out of sight," Pica said. "The Missalette will give you the order of the Mass. If you need an *aide mémoire*, you could probably jot a word or two on the program – it's a special service so I think they'll have one."

"Can I ask you questions during the service?"

"Sure, well . . . within reason," Pica nodded. "But you know those limits from your work with Aboriginal people in Central Australia – the whole insider-outsider role – showing respect for their rituals even if you aren't a believer."

"You know, I don't think anyone ever asked me if I believed the stories of the Dreamtime ancestors. I was there. I think the people assumed that the rituals were sufficiently powerful to bring me within their sphere of influence. The really difficult part for me was that there were objects whose names one could not say aloud but people assumed that if you were present during a ceremony, you knew what was happening."

"I think there is that experiential dimension to Catholicism too – but for me, the more I know about the rituals, the symbols, the stories, the deeper is my sense of awe and mystery."

"Seriously, I do want to know what is at the heart of the Mass."

"You could think about the Mass as a holy meal, a sacred symbol for Christ's sacrifice. There is the sacrifice of Christ and the sacrifice of the Eucharist woven into one single ceremony. So the Mass is the representation or the re-presenting of Calvary," Pica explained.

"And the celebrant? What does he represent?"

"The Priest represents Christ and offers the Eucharistic Sacrifice in His name."

"Humm. I think there are some common threads here," Dee mused. "In Aboriginal ceremonies, the old people, the ritual experts, that's men and women of course, bring the power of the ancestral Dreamings into the present through song and dance and by painting their bodies with designs that tell the stories of how the world was made and ordered."

"Interesting. In the Mass we're doing a number of things also. We express adoration of Our Lord; ask for forgiveness for our sins and those of the world; petition God for favors; and offer thanksgiving to God for all the graces he has given us."

"But each Mass is different, isn't it?" Dee asked.

"Well, the structure is the same, but depending on the time of year, and on who is celebrating the Mass, yes, there are differences. Like now, during Lent, the Kyrie, where the priest and the congregation ask for Divine Mercy, and the Gloria, a prayer of joy and gratitude to God for our Redemption, are omitted. And there are no marriages celebrated during Lent."

"What about giving up things you like during Lent?" Dee asked. "I heard one of our colleagues say he had given up coffee for Lent and when I asked him if that was difficult – you know, given that you can smell the coffee brewing in Mary J's office all the time – he said not really because he didn't particularly like coffee anyway."

Pica was not amused by this dig at Lenten hypocrisy. This was a side of her that Dee had not seen before. "Well people can joke about it, but to me it is a way of focusing on the meaning of Lent, taking responsibility for one's life and transgressions. In my case, I have already taken vows requiring life-long abstinence so I guess you could say my options of pleasures to give up in Lent are more limited. But there are many things of this world that I enjoy – as you well know – so I still have plenty of scope for sacrifice."

Dee let that topic lie and changed the subject. Maybe Pica could give her some background on the homilist for the upcoming Mass. "Tom said Father Humanitas was a bit of a rebel."

"Oh yes. He has a reputation for being outspoken and using very direct language and examples to illustrate his points." Pica reached for a book from her shelves. "Here is a symposium he moderated on post-Vatican II reforms. It will give you some idea of how far ahead he is in his thinking about other religions. I mean, it was all very well to say 'there are many ways to God' but what did it mean in operational terms?"

"Like what to do with religions that have customs that are 'repugnant' to Christian values?" Dee asked. "Like polygyny? Infanticide? Homoerotic ritual practices?

"All of that and more." Pica opened the book. "See the list of participants. He invited dissenting views from within the church but mostly he wanted to encourage dialogue with voices from other cultures. Like, he wanted to see what we could *learn* from Buddhism. Not how we could *stamp out* some practice we don't like. And he has been very supportive of women – in the church, as reformers, as critics."

"Do you think he'll he say anything about sexuality or women?"

"Tom and I hope so," Pica said with one of her mischievous smiles.

"So," Dee continued, "who invites someone like Father Humanitas to visit and deliver the homily?"

"Excellent question."

"So give me an excellent answer," Dee parried.

"It could come from a number of quarters – the office of the President, the Chaplain, Counseling, Development – but it doesn't happen if the President doesn't approve."

"Have there ever been any unpleasant repercussions over the

choice of a speaker?" Dee was curious to know if Pica or Tom had a hand in this latest choice.

"Oh my, yes. Yes there have." Pica was now laughing out loud at the memory. "But Simon doesn't place much stock in that kind of trouble. Matter of fact, I think he secretly relishes it. He is often at odds with Bishop Rule."

Pica called the President by his first name, Dee thought. *Obviously they are on friendly terms.*

Sunday dawned damp and overcast. *A day in sympathy with the spirit of Lent,* Dee thought as she entered the dimly lit Murphy Chapel. The Bach organ prelude swelled, heavy and brooding, and it seemed to her that it filled every corner of the vast interior, pushing out all other sounds. She stood to one side and watched as each of the faithful dipped into the font of holy water, made the Sign of the Cross, walked down the aisle to a pew, genuflected, found a place in the pew, and knelt in private prayer. Dee saw Pica with her head bent over in the pew two back from the altar rail. She was reading. Dee joined her as quietly as she could and Pica handed Dee a hymnal open at "Amazing Grace." "I'm sure you know this one," she said into Dee's ear so as to be heard over the organ. "It is a favorite of Father Humanitas. We'll come to it later in the service. Did you see Mary J on your way in? She usually sits near the middle. I know she's so pleased you decided to attend."

"I was too busy trying to be inconspicuous," Dee whispered back.

"You're fine," Pica reassured her. "I see you've tied your hair back, looks good. I sat up here so you could see the details of the altar and the canopy. See how the statues are covered? That's for Lent. The Lenten altar is very plain – not the elaborate embroidered cloth you might have seen at an Orientation Mass. See the band around the altar? It's purple – that's the Lenten color."

"After black, purple is the secondary color of mourning for British royalty," Dee said. "Any connection?"

"Humm, interesting, but I don't know," Pica said. "See that altar rail?"

"It's very ornate."

"Yes, and now it's quite out of date. Since Vatican II, the priest has been required to face the congregation. The idea is that there shouldn't to be any separation between him and his flock. This rail was the gift of an alumnus and his family won't hear of it being removed. So we're stuck with this little bit of church history."

"Would it be okay if I sketch the layout of the sanctuary on my program?" Dee asked.

"Sure and I can give you details later. Okay, stand up. Here comes the procession. Sing if you want to. See, here is where we are in the Missalette."

Dee glanced to the back of the church and saw the Cross, blazed gold against the dark skies, framed in the open doorway of Murphy Chapel. The pure white surplice of the acolyte reminded Dee of the confirmation photograph of Mary J's daughter – a simple but powerful symbol of purity. Following the Cross were two more white-clad acolytes holding long gold candlesticks with glowing white beeswax tapers as they walked through the congregation. The Censer was swinging incense that completely overwhelmed the dry smoky smell of the candles that had just passed. Father Abacus, a man she assumed was Father Humanitas, Tom Guye, the Deacon carrying the Holy Bible aloft, and the choir completed the procession.

The singing continued as the choir fanned out into their positions in their pews to the side of the sanctuary. Father Abacus was at the altar. He bowed and kissed the altar stone. For a moment Dee was mesmerized. Sound, sight, smell, touch – this was a total assault on the senses. She began making mental notes of questions to ask Pica after the service. *What happens before the Mass? How do the participants prepare? Does everyone go to confession? How is the ritual paraphernalia prepared? Is there a ritual storehouse? What songs are sung over the objects? What prayers are said? What states of grace are required? Are there any speech taboos? Food taboos? Certainly some restrictions during Lent. What is the significance of the altar stone?*

Pica recognized the impact the entrance was having on Dee. "We begin the Mass with the Sign of the Cross," she said softly. "The majesty of the Blessed Trinity is present at the altar and our responses to the priest's greeting show our union with the Trinity." *Why didn't the early Christian missionaries recognize that same impulse in Indigenous rituals?* Dee wondered. *The sacred power of Indigenous ceremonies was also about bringing the past into the present and reliving the founding drama, of becoming the ancestors, of evoking their powers and wisdom, of retracing their travels that marked out the country and set down the law for all succeeding generations to follow. Once unleashed, those powers could be deadly. The rituals had to be done properly and regularly or the whole society would be imperiled.*

The choir was now in place. Dee watched as Father Abacus stepped forward. "In the name of the Father, and of the Son and of the Holy Spirit."

"Amen." The congregation responded as one.

"The grace of our Lord Jesus Christ and the love of God and the fellowship of the Holy Spirit be with you."

"And also with you."

"The Lord be with you."

"And also with you."

"Peace be with you."

"And also with you."

"The grace and peace of God our father and the Lord Jesus Christ be with you."

"Blessed be God, the father of our Lord Jesus Christ."

The comfort of repetition, Dee thought. *Evidence of roots in an oral tradition where stories have to be committed to memory.* There was a brief silence and Dee was aware of Pica's serious, calm demeanor. Dee looked down at the Missalette and followed the words of the Penitential Rite. It was a calling to mind of one's sins and a plea for mercy and forgiveness. As Pica was to explain later, "The rite prepares us for what is to follow. We express sincere sorrow for our sins in order to receive the full benefits of the approaching Mystery of our Faith."

Father Abacus stood in silence before beginning the Opening Prayer. Dee was aware of the profound stillness of the congregation. There were over two hundred people present, but she did not hear a murmur or a movement. She thought how different this was from Aboriginal rituals where dogs, crying children, wind, lightning and thunder could intrude and disrupt. The celebrant's words drifted by her. "Father, on this day in the third week of Lent we come before you . . . we rejoice that we have with us today Father Humanitas . . . we pray for all scholars such as he . . . open our hearts that we may hear . . . Grant this through Jesus Christ our Lord."

"Amen."

The stillness was broken. Dee was aware of shuffling as hymnals were being opened. She struggled to join in the singing, but the tune was unfamiliar and the key was too high for her. Pica smiled at Dee. "Drop down an octave and you'll probably make it." Dee finally found her range and by the last chorus was enjoying singing in unison with so many others. She wondered why they chose such difficult pieces. *"Lift every voice and sing." Now that is a hymn I love but the only time it's ever sung is on Martin Luther King Day.*

Dee was pleased when it was time to sit down. She wanted to study the Missalette and figure out where they were in the service. The Liturgy of the Word. Pica had told her about this. "The first reading is always from the Old Testament, the stories of the patriarchs and prophets, the anticipation of Christ." A reading from the New Testament followed.

"Thanks be to God," the congregation intoned at the end of each reading.

Father Abacus stood, head bowed, before the center of the altar and prayed silently. Dee noted his purple stole and chasuble, another Lenten symbol.

"The Lord be with you."

"And also with you," came the response.

Father Abacus made the Sign of the Cross on the book, and then on his forehead, lips and heart. The congregation followed and stood mute. Pica had told Dee about these silent prayers. Father Abacus was now onto the third reading. He concluded. "The Gospel of the Lord. Praise to you, Lord Jesus Christ." Father Abacus kissed the book and said silently, "May the words of the

Gospel wipe away our sins."

Dee checked the Missalette again. The homily was next. Pica touched Dee lightly on the arm and settled into the pew. "Here we go," she said. Father Charles Humanitas walked to the lectern. He was an imposing man, tall, straight, and light of foot. His voice was soft but carried well throughout the chapel. Dee listened to the accent: certainly not Boston or New York, more like the National Public Radio newsreaders she found so easy to follow.

"I'm sorry," he began, looking over his glasses at the congregation and back to the altar and over to the choir. "How often do we say 'I'm sorry'? What are we asking for when we say it? To be forgiven? That we will not sin again? To whom and for what do we apologize? To be sure, there is much for which we might be truly sorry in our personal lives, as citizens of this great nation, as members of the human family.

"Let us reflect on the simple apology, 'I'm sorry,' for a few minutes. Our readings for today are thoughtful signposts, guides to finding answers to our questions. Ezekiel 18: 21–32 tells us to repent and turn from our transgressions. In Luke 15:1–10 we read there is more joy in heaven over one repentant sinner than ninety-nine righteous persons who need not repent. 'He that overcometh shall inherit all things, and I will be his God, and he shall be my son,' says Revelations 21: 17.

"It is timely that we turn attention to the nature of apologies. Today is the third Sunday in Lent, and in the spirit of the Lenten season, I am asking you to think about the nature of forgiveness. In this period of forty days that begins with Ash Wednesday and ends with Easter, we observe Lent – a time of fasting and penitence for sins. We prepare for the events of Holy Week. We ready ourselves for the Easter celebration of the Lord's resurrection, when we might be absolved of our sins. Often, during the days of Lent, we give up something pleasurable as a penance for their sins." He slipped his glasses down his nose, paused, and looked deep into the congregation. "Give up something you really like. Not just that second order of French fries! They're bad for your health anyway. No. Give up something you really enjoy. How about sex?" He paused again and pushed his glasses back up his nose. "And don't try to cheat on God." Dee heard a slight sniff in the pew behind her. *Someone feeling guilty?* she wondered. *Or displeased with the earthy candor? Wasn't sex only for procreation? Was he suggesting sex might be recreational?*

"How useful and usable are our ways of naming evil, of understanding sin? Do they help us understand the destructive capacity of human beings? Let us look back for a moment to powerful forces that have shaped our own conception of evil. And here I must defer to my good friend and colleague Rosemary Radford Ruether and her thoughts on healing the earth, as a totality. I invite you to read her book, *Gaia and God*. There is much that will surprise and I hope much that will delight you in her work. She begins with the Hebrew view that Good and Evil are both part of human nature. There is no fall from original grace and hence there is no need for a redeemer. Rather there is a duality, a pervasive one, one we need to interrogate, which holds that which is pure apart from that which is defiled: the Sabbath from ordinary days, Jews from Gentiles, men from women. God is holy and must be approached from undefiled places. Violations threaten the cosmic order." Dee began thinking. *Anxiety about women's polluting power, the taboos about blood and reproduction. For men to approach God they must separate from women. Women are the unholy within the human family.*

"Then we have Gnostic notions where evil is in excesses, in unruly passions, like sex, which Plato tells us is the root of all evil. Virtue, on the other hand, resides in control and from it flows balance and harmony." *Will he embrace the full import of Ruether's thesis?* Dee wondered. *Will he name misogyny and patriarchal privilege as forces of destruction?* She looked sideways at Pica who was sitting with her hands in her lap. On closer scrutiny, Dee realized Pica's knuckles were almost white. Her hands were clenched. The message being delivered was close to Pica's heart and one that, if heeded, could generate radical change within the church.

Finally, Father Humanitas came to the Christian concept of the Fall, one that incorporates Jewish ethics and Greek metaphysics.

Once again he relied on Ruether as he traced from St. Paul's melding of apocalyptic and Gnostic modes of thought about the flesh and the spirit to the more fully developed concept of evil and sin in St. Augustine's thought. "If people have free will, then there is the possibility they will choose disobedience. From that choice comes evil and with it mortality." *The choice of sin by the primal parents . . . dooms them to death, sin and death . . . but it also generates the sexual impulse to regenerate and as a manifestation of the sinful nature of the fallen body. This is a flawed ontology.* Dee had read this part of Ruether when she had been working with Pica and Miriam on the Women's Studies course last summer.

Dee was only half listening as Father Humanitas began reviewing the catalogue of sins in Romans 1: 29–31. Then she realized he was yet again going to challenge the congregation. "The sins herein enumerated are violations of our relationships with other people. Let us think of our relationships with others in our daily lives. Think of the homeless on the streets of our prosperous cities. Do you avert your eyes as you walk past?" Father Humanitas looked out into the congregation. "Maybe you drop your loose change by the hand-written 'God Bless' sign at the man's feet, smile, and walk on quickly to the safety of your own home where you can lock out the dangers of the streets. Next time ask yourself, 'Who is this person? Why should God bless me?' Many are Vietnam veterans who fought for freedom and democracy and who are now spurned. Is saying 'sorry' and a few coins enough to heal our relationships with the homeless? It may make us feel better, but do not confuse charity with social justice. I want us to think again about the Hebraic understanding of evil as unjust relations between people and then reflect on the liberating possibilities of being advocates for the despised and downtrodden, for those victimized by systems of oppression. This is what Jesus meant when he spoke of the preferential option for the poor. This is at the core of Liberation Theology." Dee could feel the tension emanating from Pica.

"But it should not, it must not," – and Father Humanitas again looked over his glasses – "allow us to blame others for the existence of evil. In early Christianity we find tentative moves to greater sexual egalitarianism overwhelmed in later texts by woman-blaming, a despising of women as life-givers. Women become the source of death and sin, but it is not women's fault that we die. What we have is a capacity to enhance life or to stifle it. And yes, this is a moving target as we gain greater knowledge of human life and the lines between freedom and fate shift. Prayer, reflection, rigorous and open debate will strengthen our faith and guide us in making ethical choices, in a true exercise of our free will." *This is still pure Ruether. Remember to ask Pica how they all know each other?*

Dee was aware that the sniffing sounds in the pew behind her had become more pronounced. She heard a woman's hissy whisper and a distinctly male snort in response. She wanted to turn to see who was so uncomfortable and so brazen, but she was waiting for the next provocative Humanitas question. *Here it comes.* Humanitas removed his glasses, set them on the lectern, leaned forward toward the congregation and said, "How easy it is to say. 'She was asking for it.' But no-one asks to be beaten, abused, or raped. That is a myth, a convenient myth, one that demands an apology. But my brothers, we need to do more than say sorry. We must free our homes, our streets, our schools, and yes, our places of worship from all forms of abuse, especially by those who wield the power of the church." *Had he just alluded to predatory priests?* Dee heard the intake of breath from the next pew. *The air is being sucked out of the chapel. Surely the walls will implode.* But Humanitas was not just addressing the men present. "My sisters, sit not in righteous judgment of the woman who is hurt, abused, prostituted. Stand with her, be her ally, her advocate. Yes, say sorry. Say, I did not understand.

"Let us hold ourselves accountable for the distortion in relation-ships, for the skewing of power and the 'naturalizing' of it. Let us say 'Sorry' for that sin. But let us not stop there. Let us work to unmask these inequalities. The refusal to empathize with the oppressed and our willingness to erect systems of control and cultures of deceit to maintain and justify such power is a deadly sin. We can count the lives lost to such vanity." *Surely he is alluding to the spread of AIDS and the position of the church on condoms*, Dee thought. *But maybe others heard him differently.* Pica had unclenched her hands. She had heard what she needed. Dee waited to see if Father Humanitas would lower his glasses once more, but it appeared he had decided not to underscore his last point. He was now soothing and cajoling. "Turn to love, not hate. 'I'm sorry.' Such simple words. Such power to transform."

Dee was lost in thought as the Mass progressed from the Creed and General Intercessions to the Liturgy of the Eucharist. Father Abacus held up the paten containing the round, white host. "Blessed are you, Lord, God of all creation. Through your goodness we have this bread to offer which earth has given and human hands have made. It will become for us the bread of life. Blessed be God forever." The celebrant's hands were covered by the humeral veil. A small bell rang during the blessing. The faithful bowed their heads. Next the wine was prepared. "Blessed are you. Lord, God of all creation. Through your goodness we have this wine to offer, fruit of the vine and work of human hands. It will become our spiritual drink. Blessed be God forever." Now he was washing his hands, "Lord, wash away my iniquity; cleanse me from my sin. Pray, brethren, that our sacrifice may be acceptable to God, the almighty Father." He began the third Eucharistic prayer. Pica had explained this moment – the Eucharistic presence of Christ begins at the moment of Consecration. "On the night he was betrayed, he took bread and gave You thanks and praise. He broke the bread, gave it to his disciples, and said: 'Take this, all of you, and eat it: this is my body which will be given up for you,'" Father Abacus continued. "Take this, all of you, and drink from it: this is the cup of my blood, the blood of the new and everlasting covenant. It will be shed for you and for all so that sins may be forgiven. Do this in memory of me."

Blood that cleanses, blood that sanctifies, the very same blood shed on the cross two thousand years ago, precious blood, transforming and transformed blood. Ask Pica about feminist critiques of the sacred purifying blood shed by the son of God who dies so that the faithful might live, and the profane, polluting blood shed by women in the life cycle of species reproduction.

The congregation joined with the choir. "Christ has died. Christ is risen. Christ will come again." *This is a living sacrifice,* Dee was thinking. *We are reenacting the resurrection.* She realized the congregation was now chanting the Lord's Prayer. This chanting was unfamiliar to her, a Lenten practice. She listened as if for the first time and realized *this prayer contains all the petitions necessary for salvation.* Then came the Sign of Peace. Dee had been surprised during the first Mass she had attended at St. Jude's by the joyful spirit of this moment. People leaned across the pews to touch, to make the Sign of Peace, and to say "Peace." Colleagues, students, staff, parents, alums, sought her out and smiled warmly. There was a fellowship and communion in that gesture. *The peace that surpasses all understanding.*

Dee was thinking about the way in which ceremonies in various religions were broken into segments. There were extremely serious ones, and other contrasting, more light-hearted moments. In many rituals, in other religions, there were periods of joking and clowning that relieved the tension and further dramatized the sacred. There were moments of role reversal where the powerful were rendered powerless and the oppressed ruled. The Sign of Peace was a shift in mood but the authority structure remained clear. The Word of God was spoken by the priest. The faithful responded to him.

Dee stood to one side as those sitting alongside her filed past to receive the bread and the wine from the servers at the altar rail. Pica had told Dee that the period of thanksgiving following Holy Communion was a joyful one. "This is when we can listen and speak to Jesus heart-to-heart. He is alive within us waiting to give us many graces." Dee watched the faithful at peace with themselves and with their God. She wondered how someone like Mary J could reconcile this moment with knowledge of the abuses of power by those in authority. Dee, the anthropologist, could observe. Dee, the comparativist, could construct models of ritual action. But the Dee who had made friends at St. Jude's, who had become increasingly enmeshed in the life of the community, was feeling angry. *Was it possible to partake of this peace, this blessing, and yet remain critical of the institutionalized contempt these devout men had for women?*

"The Lord be with you," said Father Abacus.

"And also with you."

"Go in the peace of Christ."

"Thanks be to God."

It was all over. The priests, acolytes and deacon led the way from the altar to the grand double doors. Dee edged out of the pew and watched the chapel emptying. She stood waiting in the wide middle aisle for Pica, who was talking to an old friend from her graduate days. *Could that be the hissy, snorting couple?* Dee wondered as a pale, pudgy middle-aged man and his angular wife exited from the next pew. "Well, that takes the cake," she heard the woman snarl. "I've never been so offended, and in the House of God."

"Come on, Bertha," her husband said, taking her arm. "The Bishop will want to hear about this." The couple strode out of the chapel. Dee followed with Pica. "Did you hear that little exchange?"

"What? From old Abe and his wife Bertha?"

"If that's the couple who was sitting behind us, yes," Dee said.

"They routinely complain about the liberal excesses of St. Jude's," Pica smiled.

"Does it have any impact?"

"Not really. It's more of an irritant. Charlie was well aware of his audience. There are those you can challenge, those who can't wait to be out of the church and into their donuts and coffee, and all shades in between. Then there are anthropologists with their knowledge of comparative religions."

"This anthropologist has a thousand questions for you," Dee said as they walked out in the light. The sky had cleared. Mary J and her daughter were waiting to greet Dee, more than a little curious as to what she might say about the Mass. "Would you like to join us for lunch? We haven't eaten since last night," Mary J said. "And there's so much to talk about."

Pica excused herself – she was invited to dine with Father Humanitas. "We can talk later, Dee," she said.

"Great. And, if it is appropriate, could you tell Father Humanitas

I really appreciated the homily."

"Will do. Make sure you get Mary J's view on the service. I know she will be able to answer your questions as well."

Dee, Mary J and her daughter, Little Mary, walked up to the car park. "Oh wonderful. I can see Christian's car in the lot," Dee said. "His meetings in New York must have finished early. I wasn't expecting him till tonight."

"There's food enough for us all," Mary J said. "See if he wants to join us."

"Okay, we'll catch you up at your place," Dee said.

Christian was happy to accompany Dee to Mary J's for Sunday lunch. "It was a ritual I liked as a boy," he said. "Just let me get a jacket and I'll be right with you." He gave Dee a playful kiss on the forehead and grabbed his car keys. "We'd come back from church to a roast dinner. Very British and not particularly suited to the climate in Nigeria, but it had a certain charm."

"Well, part of the charm is that you put on the roast and the whole family can go to Mass while it cooks, but your mother didn't go, did she?"

"You're right, she didn't. She kept her distance from the church."

"So?" Dee teased.

"I know what you are getting at. She did things in her own way. Believe me, what she cooked was nothing like what they called roast beef in London. She might have been working as a domestic when she met my father, but she was nobody's servant, as you know." He held out the keys. "Want to drive?"

"Sure. I love this car and the way it holds the road."

"Good," Christian settled into the passenger seat. "Now I'm free to look at you."

Dee patted him affectionately on the knee and glanced in the rear vision mirror. "The homily was amazing," she said as she glided out of the car park and headed across town to Mary J's. "You'll no doubt hear more about it at lunch. This guy Humanitas was very forthright, just as Pica said he would be. She's off having lunch with him now. I think they're hatching something, but whatever, what he said should have been a wake-up call, especially in the

217

aftermath of the Sordes affair. But tell me about your meetings."

"More of the same. But the figures are coming in and we've definitely turned the corner on rates of new infections. They're going down."

"This calls for a celebration," she said throwing a quick look at Christian. "Maybe after lunch?"

"During Lent?" Christian asked.

Dee fell silent. She was thinking back on the homily and on the way in which talk about sexuality and bodies, especially women's bodies, was so carefully coded. She knew that regimes of the Catholic Church for "policing the body" had shifted through the centuries; celibacy had become institutionalized for the priesthood; witch trials had given way to attacks on feminists; portrayals of the Virgin Mary, Mary Magdalene and women's roles had undergone significant changes; but the fact remained: women's bodies were to be used for prescribed purposes and strictly controlled. The church was obsessed with how to control, define and manage women's bodies. Now, here she was, a feminist teacher with her female students in this Catholic college and what were they fighting for? Control: the right to control their own bodies. *How different are we?* Dee thought with a rising panic. *The church and feminists are both arguing over definitions of the body, and of sexuality. And, we're both focused on issues like HIV-AIDS, birth control, and abortion. Yet, we are so utterly different. My views on women's rights, women's bodies, and religion in general would be an anathema to the Jesuits. They would probably consider my ideas evil.*

Dee recalled Tom's insight that priestly celibacy conveniently closed off the possibility of debate on the matter of sexuality. No theorizing about the issue was required. The church could talk about AIDS. Priests could pray for the afflicted, but they could not follow through with any candid discussion of sex and sexuality. But celibacy did not eliminate sexuality as Tom had said. It remained unresolved, denied, a mystery. Priests had to find ways to displace their desires. Dee could talk about and work on AIDS campaigns. She could analyze, criticize, and theorize various approaches to AIDS. But was she also engaged in some kind of displacement activity? *What is the difference between us? They have institutionalized their displacement of their sexual desires and self-deception. I am constantly contesting and interrogating mine. But we are both absorbed by the AIDS issue.*

"Dee, where are you?" Christian asked. "You've gone frightfully quiet and serious."

"Don't laugh," Dee said, "But I think I'm having an epiphany – not a manifestation of Christ, but a clarity of vision, a whole new perspective."

"It must have been quite a Mass."

"I think I heard some of it for the first time. It's taken me so long to sort out the structures and the symbols of this strange tribe I've been living among and working with at St. Jude's that I haven't been paying enough attention to the emotions. I've been a participant-observer. I've been doing my fieldwork and taking notes. And all the while my dreams and my doodling have been running riot."

"I'm not cutting you off or anything, but isn't this where we turn?" Christian asked.

"Whoops, yes it is. There's Mary J and her husband and daughter. This is not going to be a good time to bare my soul, Christian. Can you help keep me on neutral topics?"

"For example?" Christian asked. "I was with the nuns during my early years so I know the vocabulary, but isn't Mary J going to want to talk about the service?"

"I'll take my lead from her. She and Frank have been getting along better these days. Nothing like having a smart daughter to get a man thinking about discrimination against women."

Mary J's husband stood on the porch. "Welcome to our home," he said, gave Dee a hug, and held out his hand to Christian. "Come inside. I've been looking forward to meeting you, Christian. I have a cousin who works at UMass and he says you have really kicked some butt there – excuse my French. What's your poison? Join me in a beer? I know the girls will have wine." Christian looked across at Dee to see if she had bristled at being called a "girl" but she was already in the kitchen with Mary J and Little Mary. By the time they brought out the food, Frank had an atlas open to a map of Africa, one where the British Empire was colored a dusty pink, and Christian was explaining how the borders and country names had changed over the last few decades. Christian winked at Dee as they sat down to eat.

"Would you like to say grace?" Frank asked Christian.

"We give thanks for the gift of food, the fellowship of friends, and the love of family," Christian said.

"Amen," Frank said loudly. "Let's eat. Mother really knows how to roast beef. Now Dee tell me about Women's Studies. Little Mary has been enlightening me. Maybe this old dog can learn some new tricks."

February 16, 1997: BOSTON GLOBE. Diego Ribadeneira reviews Thomas J. Reese's INSIDE THE VATICAN: THE POLITICS AND ORGANIZATION OF THE CATHOLIC CHURCH. Reese, a Jesuit priest and political scientist, recorded the perspectives of the Curia including: "Don't think. If you think, don't speak. If you speak, don't write. If you think and speak and write, don't sign your name. If you think and speak and write and sign your name, don't be surprised."

15

CONNECTING THE DOTS
Spring 1997

Winter was in retreat, and the Terminator had not struck for over a month. Dee had decided to move out of her apartment. She wanted more distance from St. Jude's and more privacy for the times when Christian stayed over. The two had been looking on the week-ends and finally rented a place that seemed perfect – a cottage on a "pond," as small lakes were called in this part of the country. Dee's teaching schedule meant she would only have to drive the ten miles to Resolve three or four days a week, and she imagined long weekends when she and Christian could cook together, work, and play.

They had been through a rocky period and Dee was pleased she had finally been able to have it out with Christian. Her simmering resentments around the way he made decisions for himself and for her had flared into the open when he had announced, over breakfast one Monday after he'd spent the weekend at her place, that he had been invited to stay on at UMass and needed to have an answer to the administration within the week.

"It's all about budgets and grant deadlines," he'd told Dee as if that ended the matter. Then he'd picked up his shoulder bag, kissed her goodbye and was ready to head out the door.

"Talk to me about the pros and cons of staying at UMass," Dee had insisted, her voice rising. "Don't just announce your decision as *fait accompli*."

"Are you angry with me?" Christian had put down his bag and looked truly perplexed.

"Yes, I am, and I have been for a while. Don't you see what is happening? We fell into this relationship and it's been good, don't get me wrong, but Christian, I have been living an independent life, so have you. If we have a future, we need to find a way to talk things through. What if I just up and told you I was taking on a new project in South Africa?"

"When did that happen?" Christian voice was now rising.

"I'm not saying I'm going to South Africa. I'm saying what if I made decisions like that?"

"But you don't."

"No, I don't and I don't think you do you either, not really. You take a whole lot of things into consideration, but could you please let me in on those deliberations?"

"I need to go," Christian had said. "Can we talk about this tonight? I'll call you as soon as I get out of my meetings."

Dee had thrown herself into her work that day. She had a brief conversation with Miriam, whose advice had been "Dee, you're both strong-willed and you're both articulate, you'll figure it out." Apart from that, Dee had managed not to think too much about what could happen that evening. It would be another five days before they could talk face to face, and maybe phone calls would remove the temptation to just fall into bed as a way of resolving the matter.

Christian called around eight. "Dee, I have thought about us all day. I want us to have a future and I *am* used to making my own decisions, but can we work on it, please?"

"Yes, we can." Dee happily repeated his emphasis on the "we."

"I'm going to start by trying to write out the pros and cons of this UMass decision – that's how I do it in my mind anyway – and maybe you could look them over."

Dee suppressed a laugh. She'd had a sudden image of Christian making lists like Virginia. "That would be great, but don't you have to decide by Friday?"

"I've got an extension. I told them I had some homework I had to do."

"Well the professor is very happy to grade your paper," Dee laughed outright.

"And the doctor would like to make a home visit next week, if that is agreeable to you. We could go over the list together."

Miriam had been right. They were strong-willed and independent and being a couple required work. Christian learned to joke about his over-determined schedules and Dee decided having "high control needs," Miriam's phrase, was better than being called a puritan.

"So, let's try this cottage life," Dee had said to Christian. "See what this future might look like." She planned to move into the cottage over the Spring Break. Daniel and Miriam offered to help. Pica said her twin brother John was going to visit and the two of them could help too.

Saturday March 8, 1997: International Women's Day.
Moving Day.

Dee sat in her apartment and surveyed the damage. She'd donned sweat pants and an old T-shirt for the occasion and to demonstrate she was learning the ways of the natives, she had bought a baseball cap and pulled her long hair through the opening in the back. She couldn't quite manage to wear it backwards as her students did. Pica, also wearing sweats and a cap, was helping her pack the kitchen and study. *Where did all these books come from?* Dee thought.

"What about your notebooks?" Pica asked.

"I always carry them with me," Dee said. "They're irreplaceable. For one thing, they're my way back into the intricacies of getting to know St. Jude's. God, remember when I arrived? It was so bloody cold. I just huddled by this radiator. It was even too cold to write that first night. And I still remember the smell. I think I still smell it sometimes after heavy rain."

"Didn't the maintenance crew fix your downpipe?" Pica asked. "Wasn't that part of the problem?"

"Yes, but a section of the pipe goes through the second bedroom, where it joins onto the back porch, and they only worked on the outside part of it," Dee said. "It floods every now and then, but I gave up trying to get it fixed. It certainly was not a priority for Maintenance, and I'm moving anyway. It's at a very strange angle, you know, like bits have been added onto it."

"Show me," Pica said.

"Now I know you can play pool, but don't tell me you have a plumber's license too."

"No, but my older brother has one, and I've watched him at work often enough. How hard can it be? Let's get a flashlight and see what we can see."

"Sure, anything but packing another box," Dee agreed. "Every time, I swear, it's the last move, and then here I am again, in moving mode."

Pica had worked the metal bracket loose and deftly swung the angle bend away from the down shaft. "Look," she said, rotating her cap around so the peak did not impede her view of the inside of the shaft. "There's a wad of something stuck in there. No wonder this place smells. Phew. Looks like the problem has come from the apartment above you."

"I never see the students who live there," Dee admitted. "They use the other entrance."

"Jessie Seneca used that place to crash sometimes, if she was working late," Pica said. "The apartment was used as a storage space mainly, but there was a little fold-out couch where she could sleep and nobody minded."

"You knew her before you came here?" Dee asked,

"Yes. We thought we'd be colleagues at St. Jude's, but she died December 1990 and I took up my position the following fall."

"So how did you know each other? Or don't you want to talk about it?" Dee added quickly, aware that Pica seemed uncomfortable.

"Big Catholic families. We all have our secrets. She knew my twin, John. She helped him a lot when he left the seminary. He loved to paint and she encouraged him. It was like therapy for him and she was very creative. Ask him when he's here. Now let's get back to this foul-smelling stuff we've dislodged."

"I'm going to see if anyone is at home upstairs. Maybe we can move it from there," Dee said as she ran up the stairs.

Ten minutes later, in the upstairs apartment, Pica and Dee sat looking at the mess they'd extracted from the old downpipe – the moldy remains of a bird's nest, and a tightly bound parcel. "That's

Jessie's writing," Pica said. "Oh my God, it's some of her notes. Strange. Do you think she stowed them here for safekeeping?"

"More likely stuffed them there in one hell of a hurry," Dee shuddered. "Pica, do you remember that Friday last spring, when we celebrated the completion of your tenure file? You brought gumbo and put it in my fridge. Can you remember where you left my key?" Dee asked.

"Where you told me, where I always leave it, on the hook on the back porch. Why?"

"I think someone was in my place that afternoon, maybe followed you up here, maybe trying to find something, and shot out the front when I came in through the back door. Who knew Jessie used to come here?"

"Mainly the maintenance crew."

"I think I'm catching a whiff of Chuck Negotium's work," Dee said. "Do you think we should try to read the notes?"

"Would you mind if I look first?" Pica asked. "I can read her writing. And don't even think of calling Campus Security. They aren't any good at following a forensic trail. The so-called Terminator left plenty of evidence but that remains an 'ongoing investigation,' as they say whenever I ask for a progress report. I hounded them over Jessie's death, but they closed that investigation: an accident, tragic, but an accident, and hey, it's dangerous out there on the roads, riding a bicycle after dark."

"Sure, take Jessie's notes," said Dee. "But watch your back. I have some thinking I need to do."

Dee had promised Tom she would think about what he'd told her after dinner. And there was the homily and the responses of various people to the message and mode of delivery. Then there was the matter of the Terminator, still unresolved. What did #126 mean? She'd tried all the number games she knew and none made any sense. She'd done a couple of online searches. But nothing seemed to fit. And now there were these papers, Jessie's papers . . . Thinking about it – all of it – made her head hurt. She reviewed her notes. The last week of January had been frenetic and frightening. The phone calls had continued steadily and then reached a crescendo the night WOW sponsored a talk on "Pornography as Violence against Women." St. Jude's parents were calling and demanding to know what was being done to protect their daughters against the threats. One, with connections in the FBI, called President Firmitas. Dean Simean was annoyed. He had written to the women telling them everything that could be done was being done. He had spoken with the President. They planned to set up a Race and Gender Task Force for the following year. "Why do only the fathers call me?" the Dean asked Dee.

"Patriarch to patriarch?" she suggested. "I hear from the mothers and alumnae."

The student newspapers continued their war of words. WOW was bloodied but not bowed.

Rehearsals and workshops for the upcoming feminist liturgy, planned by the three mischief-makers for Commencement, were attracting large numbers of women and an increasing number of men. The lampooning of the idea of a feminist liturgy continued in letters to the editor of the *St. Jude's Review*. When a jug of urine was placed on the table in the WOW offices, the women were sure it was a less than subtle message about how the harassers felt about them. Security was sure it was simply bad behavior after a rock concert, despite the #126 signature on the door.

Who, apart from the women and Maintenance, had a key to those offices? Negotium for sure.

Then there was Jackie Li's visit with President Firmitas. It took her a while to tell Dee – so much was happening so fast. "Sit down," he had said and joined her in one of the dark leather chairs set on an exquisite Persian carpet. "I've been meaning to drop you a line. You've been such a breath of fresh air and I know the Trustees are pleased with the sexual harassment policy you've drafted." The President had been impressed by Jackie's integrity and ideas. She was never sure whether he took note of her diamond pins. But that day, as she reminded Dee, she had been wearing one that was a tiny scales of justice.

"You may not be so happy when you see this," Jackie said and handed him the manila envelope addressed to Cissy Coyle at the WOW mailbox.

He read down the list of names of abusive priests and nodded. He seemed to be familiar with the rehabilitation centers and the 1985 report. He also seemed to know that Father Sordes had a checkered career. "Can this harm us?" he asked. "All the settlements were sealed."

"They could be opened if there were cause," Jackie said. "Is there?"

"Well, I must say I would prefer that our settlement with Amy Nakamura was not made public."

"That was before my time. So you'll have to ask the General Counsel to brief me, that way we'll be covered by legal privilege. But, this stack of documents," Jackie said laying her hand on the clippings that had been sent to Cissy, "are all in the public domain, and any competent journalist or lawyer could reconstruct a history of a complete lack of due diligence on the part of the church. Plausible deniability would no longer be an option. The college could be liable."

"I was prepared to give Paddy Sordes another chance and I acted on the written recommendation of Bishop Rule, who praised his dedication to his calling, but now I have to act on my own best judgment. I'll take care of Patrick Sordes," he said. "You make an appointment with General Counsel. Ask whatever you deem necessary. I'll square it with the Trustees."

On Friday January 21, after his meeting with Jackie Li, President Firmitas had given Father Sordes an ultimatum: "Get into a treatment program now, or resign." Sordes had been down this path before and was not at all worried about having another short stay in one of the centers. But President Firmitas was not about to be made a fool by the Sordes time bomb and was most specific with his requirements. "You have to get on the wagon and get treatment for your sex addiction and violent behavior. And you will have to stay in treatment until you can convince me you are no longer a danger to this community."

That was more than Sordes was prepared to pledge for his job at St. Jude's. He could reinvent himself. He'd done it before. He walked to his room and started to pack.

There were times when this President's disregard for process charmed Dee. He had acted true to form and according to his principles. For the most part, Dee endorsed these principles herself. Paddy Sordes SJ was gone, but there was still that matter of Mary Doyle. Dee had done some digging of her own. She had hoped that the canon lawyer, the Reverend Thomas P. Doyle, who had co-authored the 1985 report on sexually abusive priests, might be related to Mary Doyle's family, but she couldn't find a link. She also wanted to have another conversation with Tom about his sister's friendship with Pica. But, for now, she would have to bide her time. She knew Jackie would tell what she could, when she could.

The President had made it plain with his choice of reading at the last faculty meeting. It was Proverbs 31: 31, recognizing women's contribution. "Give her the reward she has earned and let her works bring her praise at the city gate." The Humanitas homily had stirred the St. Jude's pot considerably, and Dee suspected that President Firmitas was not unhappy with the discomfort a number of the St. Jude's family were currently experiencing as a result. The best news was that Dean Simean had said publicly that he wanted to see more women in tenured positions. This boded well because Pica's tenure file was now under consideration by the Dean's Committee on Tenure and Promotion. The difficult part, as always, was moving the Dean from rhetoric to action. Dee hadn't seen him since their exchange over the threats and attacks and she wondered how he might be feeling about her activities. He had been sick, or that was what his office said, so she had to wait for him to return to campus. Dee asked around, and Mary J suggested she talk to Mary Kane, the Dean's secretary. There was a story that Dee should know. Dean Simean was physically ill and in a desperate funk over his treatment.

"You need to know about the Dean's marriage and his children,"

Mary J began. "I can tell you a bit, but Mary Kane knows a lot more than I do. I know he was really close to his mother and sisters when he was growing up. They made sure that he had the best room in the house, prepared his favorite foods, did his laundry, folded and put it away. Spoiled him rotten, they did, but he was always there for them."

"What is it about these men and their sisters?" Dee said. "I heard Tom Guye talk about his childhood and it was very much focused on the women in his life."

"Ask Mary Kane about Dean Simean. She likes you. I gather she heard everything you said that day you had the fight with the Dean. She's on your side. Her daughter was treated badly by those students in Political Science who gave Pica such a hard time and she told her adviser – one of the priests – but he told her she had brought it upon herself. Mary was very angry but was reluctant to speak up for her daughter. It would have looked as if she was ungrateful, and she knows all about the wall of silence practiced by the priests and the church. She knew nothing positive would have happened."

Mary Kane and Dee arranged to meet off campus before work later that week. Dee ordered tea, hoping it would come steeped in a teapot for full flavor. Mary ordered black coffee and a bagel with cream cheese. Dee started. "I wanted to thank you."

Mary brushed her words aside. "It's strange. I wanted to tell you a while ago, but there was never a good time, and then the Dean had this crisis. It's never straightforward when it comes to his family. Background, you need some background."

"About his marriage?" Dee asked.

"That's a lot of it. You know he married his cousin, Mary Anne. Well, she's kind of a cousin . . .?"

"Which side? Mother's or father's?" the vigilant anthropologist asked.

"I think Mary Anne's grandfather and his grandmother were siblings."

"Oh, perfect," Dee exclaimed. "It's a most desirable form of marriage for people I worked with in Central Australia, matrilateral cross-cousin marriage, mother's mother's brother's daughter's daughter."

"Well you might tell her that one day," Mary Kane said, looking at Dee over her raised coffee cup. "Anthropology is such an exotic discipline."

"I think of it as more grounded than that. Like, you know how everyone has family photographs, and they are happy to talk about who's who. They're great ways of finding out about people without intruding too much. I don't have to pry."

"Well, those photographs are for public viewing and they're often quite posed, you know, studio portraits mostly."

"True," Dee said. "And it's not something we did when I was growing up. I notice it and ask myself questions about the significance of those photographs in your culture."

"And do you get any good answers?"

"Some. It's a way of bringing personal relationships into the workplace and kind of softening the formality of the office. The Dean really warmed when I admired the family portrait on his desk. He talked about Mary Anne with such affection."

"They've known each other all their lives, grew up together like brother and sister, holidays, and family outings, always together. They liked the same foods, movies, books, but then Mary Anne went away to college, it was a shock for him. I don't think he ever actually imagined a time without her, and when it did happen he couldn't quite figure out why he felt so agitated."

"Were they romantically involved?" Dee asked.

"No, they were both raised to believe that sex outside marriage was a sin and this was before the Pill was readily available. I think he was sexually frustrated – God weren't we all! Those were dreadful days for Catholics. But he didn't know how to name what he was feeling. Like all of us, he went to confession and asked for forgiveness for his sins, but these did not include lust or impure thoughts about his Mary Anne."

"But didn't they marry?" Dee ventured.

"No, they were too young. She went off to College at St. Joan's, a women's college in Pennsylvania, and he went to St. Jude's, when it was only for men. They grew apart. He didn't write, just moped. Then she broke his heart by announcing she was dating a young man from Penn State who would be visiting in June. He was pretty sure she was thinking of marrying this man."

"Do you think she knew that he cared about her?" Dee asked.

"Oh yes, and she cared about him. But they didn't know what to do. The boyfriend at Penn State was not Catholic and had no hang-ups. He just swept in and swept her up. Now, the rest of the story I heard from Mary Anne. We have daughters about the same age, her eldest and my youngest – both a handful – and we just got talking one day."

"At work?"

"Well that's funny actually. The Dean was away and Mary Anne came in looking for some papers he needed. We were in his office when she picked up the photo, and it all came out. I shut the door and knew we had complete privacy. She told me about that summer in 1970. She knew he had missed her and she suggested they celebrate the Fourth of July with his family, as they always had. He was deliriously happy. They were back in their old relationship – joking, confiding, sitting close together. But then she said, 'We were suddenly behind the water tower in the old park. I don't know how we got there. We'd been drinking, everyone had. And it was so easy, just being together. There was a kiss, another, and then, I don't know how it happened but we were half undressed and frantic. It was all so quick, not like I expected it would be at all. He was apologizing and I was reassuring him everything would be all right. What did I know? I was so naive.'"

"But she still married the guy from Penn State?" Dee asked.

"Yes, she did. He didn't see her again until her wedding at the end of that summer. Then she dropped out of college. His sisters whispered that it was a shotgun wedding."

"And was she pregnant? Was it his child?"

Mary Kane acknowledged Dee's question with a flick of her forefinger but was intent on telling the story in her own way and continued. "Mary Anne didn't say anything, and he says he just threw himself into his work, hung out with guys, went drinking on Friday nights, and got into a few scrapes. Even had his face smashed through a glass door once. You know his crooked nose? They say he was a real mess and that now he shaves every day so that he never forgets that folly. His sisters saw Mary Anne every now and then. They told him about the birth of her children, four children, all girls, in five years. Then, when he had almost finished his Ph.D. at Harvard, his older sister broke the news that Mary Anne was back with her parents. Her husband had deserted her. Gone.

"He told me how he composed letter after letter to her and eventually decided he would just visit. That summer he courted her. He was entranced. To him she was somehow even more beautiful as a loving mother with her four young children. He loved the wholesome smell of the babies after bath time, and he loved her. It's hard to get him to talk about his feelings, but I've heard him say Mary Anne was the only woman he had ever loved. He knew it would mean a divorce, but he was sure they should marry. Somehow their family knew the right people in the church and, presto, her first marriage was annulled. So he married Mary Anne the year he finished at Harvard and they moved, as a family, to Resolve, and he took up his appointment here in Biology."

"But they didn't live happily ever after."

"Well, he certainly loved Mary Anne and her children. Oh, sometimes he'd complain that he and Mary Anne didn't have any time to themselves. And then came the twins, Mary and Anne, so like their mother. You should have seen him with them. He wanted to protect all of them from the harshness of the world. His girls, his sisters, his Mary Anne, his home life was complete."

"The oldest one must be in her twenties by now."

"Yes, Marian, she's twenty-five. She was such a willful child, old before her time. She endured the marriage breakup and helped with the twins, till she went away to college."

"And wasn't she married in Murphy Chapel last summer?"

"That's right. You were away then, exploring the countryside. She was pregnant almost straight away, but miscarried, and that's where we are now."

"Where are we?"

"David had been feeling really tired and Mary Anne finally got him to the doctor's, their old family doctor, the same doctor Marian used. They did blood tests and then called him in. 'Come with me, Mary Anne,' he begged. 'I have a bad feeling about this and I want you there with me.'

"'The news is not good,' the doctor said, 'and I want you to get a second opinion, especially about some new treatments, but the blood tests show you have leukemia.'

"'What can be done?' Mary Anne asked. David was moaning by this stage.

"'Well there are the standard treatments – radiation, chemotherapy – but then there is another long shot, that's what we need to talk about.'

"'Tell me now,' David said, holding tight to Mary Anne's hand.

"'If we can find a match, there is some hope that with a stem cell donation, it's possible to grow a cure . . . umbilical blood.'

"'No. Not stem cells, nothing from a fetus, nothing from cells grown in a petri dish,' David said.

"'Can we at least talk about it?' Mary Anne asked, taking his arm and steering him towards the exit.

"They talked deep into the night about his ethical position on stem cell research. Mary Anne was firm. His position was noble, but abstract. For her, the real-life situation was that using the stem cells could mean that she and her children might continue to have him in their lives. 'Moral decisions aren't made in a vacuum,' she cried. 'Don't leave me and the children alone. If you won't do it for yourself, think of us.'"

"What a dilemma," Dee sympathized. "Pica wrote about a similar dilemma in her book and used Carol Gilligan's ideas, you know the feminist philosopher who talks about the gendered ways of thinking about and making moral decisions. Women are so grounded, while men tend to be more abstract. So what did Mary Anne do? Did she tell the children?"

"Only Marian. She begged her to reason with him. Marian was pregnant again and the doctors were worried about her. 'Please let my child have a grandfather,' she said to her father."

"And he still didn't know Marian was his child?"

"No, but it happened soon enough. Marian miscarried again. And . . ."

"There were cells available."

"Yes, and Mary Anne realized the possibility of her daughter's loss being used for something good. They were all at Marian's bedside: her husband John, David and Mary Anne. The doctor called David and Mary Anne aside. 'She'll be okay," he said, 'And now, will you please reconsider what I said about umbilical blood. She wants you to use it.' That's when Mary Anne told him, 'It's a match David,' she said, 'She's your daughter.' Of course he was speechless.

"'No, I couldn't tell you. I was engaged, and Alex was nearly finished with his degree, and he had a job lined up and you, you were just starting. Where would we have lived? Having a wife and child would have ruined you."

"So David had the procedure?" Dee asked.

"After much soul-searching and prayer, I gather. They decided the possibility of one tragedy providing the means for another's survival was God's will."

"So what do you suggest I do now?" Dee asked.

"Cancel your appointment with the Dean. Give him some space. Take some personal time, Dee. Do something nice for yourself. What about that fellow of yours? I hear he is making great waves at UMass."

"He is, but how do you know?"

"My husband works in Admissions at UMass."

How many degrees of separation?

March 28, 1997: Good Friday. Baltimore's Lesbian Avengers demonstrate at the Cathedral of Mary Our Queen over the role of the church in gay-rights bill's defeat; four arrests; 1979 Three Mile Island partial melt down. Have the stories been told?

16

OPENING THE CLOSETS
Spring 1997

Several stories were circulating about the departure of Paddy Sordes SJ, but when asked if they knew anything, Mary Louise, Cissy and MC offered no opinions. Jamie Coyle, however, was now ready to speak. She called and left a number with a 413 prefix.

Massachusetts, Springfield? Dee exhaled. *Dots are beginning to connect.*

"What are you doing this weekend?" Jamie asked when Dee returned her call.

"Not much, once I get this batch of papers graded," Dee said, looking at the file of papers from her Race and Gender class. It had been hard teaching about race at St. Jude's where the African American student population had shrunk to twelve. This low number seemed to have the effect of allowing the rest of the students to remain unaffected by questions of race. They considered themselves to be tolerant of others but resisted the idea that racism ramifies down the generations. To Dee, the students' racial consciousness and concern seemed far behind their peers at other, non-sectarian colleges. Responding to her unhappiness with this situation, Christian had offered to speak to the class about race, but Dee wasn't ready to broadcast their relationship just yet and had demurred.

Jamie sounded enthusiastic. "My family has a place at Pawcatuck, just on the Connecticut–Rhode Island border. No-one is there at the moment, so we could talk without interruption. Everything is there, so you don't have to bring anything. Do you sail? We could take my cat out, if there's a good wind. And I have someone I think you should meet. Say you can come."

Dee was taken aback but intrigued. Was such a visit as this

proper for faculty? It wasn't as if she were visiting the Coyles for fundraising purposes.

"Go," said Pica. "Please."

"Take a slicker," said Miriam. "How often do you think you'll get an invite like this?"

When she told Christian about the invitation he said, "Anything for closure. I have work to do here and maybe we can meet up on Sunday."

"Sounds good. Maybe I'll see a good fish place and pick us up something nice for Sunday dinner. I'm not teaching Monday," Dee said suggestively.

"Okay, so I'm definitely going to finish this paperwork and free up Monday morning. I love waking up next to you."

The Coyle compound was hidden from the road by the thick scrubby pines bent low to the ground by the stiff wind coming off the inlet. A dense yew hedge lined the driveway, and Dee could see banks of rhododendrons shielding a rather large house. Jamie, waiting on the back porch, signaled her into a sheltered parking spot and helped with her bag. The house, set into the dunes, was large, comfortable, and rambling. Perennial gardens separated by little stone paths fanned out from the wide side porch. The view across the water was spectacular. Behind the house were old stables, boat sheds, potting sheds, and tool sheds with long benches and plenty of evidence of use. Bird feeders hung from the trees.

As she walked up the gravel path, Dee could smell coffee.

"Come in, come in," Jamie said from the back porch. She was a gracious host. "Come through to the kitchen. We're having our morning caffeine hit. Amy, this is Dee. I think we have a lot to talk about."

Amy Nakamura was slight, with short-cropped black hair and brown eyes and, Dee noted, her intensity seemed to fill the room. Judging from the papers spread across the table, Amy had been working with Jamie for a while.

"Jamie told me she'd met you at the Alumni Weekend and has just been filling me in on WOW. Sounds as if you are determined to make changes this time around. It also sounds as if the forces of darkness and evil are regrouping."

"Dee, look at these statistics from Amy's report on violence and then look at the campus police reports. It doesn't add up." Jamie was flipping through the pages and stabbing the graphs of crime statistics with her finger.

"I haven't seen these. They're not in the report that came to faculty," said Dee, catching her breath. She was trying to figure out how to play this situation, what to disclose and what to keep confidential.

"Some of it comes from the work Jessie Seneca was doing," Amy said. "Before she was killed, that is."

"I was in the Women's Watch then," Jamie said, "and we did our own survey. It was anonymous, very straightforward. But we put a 'write in' section at the end. You know – where it asks if there is anything else you want to say? That's where one student said she had been made a 'Bride of Christ' by her priest when she was younger and that it had made her feel uncomfortable then and that she was still uncomfortable with it, but she'd been told to keep it secret. Jessie and Amy talked about how to deal with this information and decided to bring it up casually in their classes. A few weeks later, a student came to Jessie's office," Jamie explained.

"Jessie was angry, kind of confused, but ready to act when she heard the story," said Amy. "It turns out this priest, Father Beffin, would tell the girls in his confirmation classes that they should imagine themselves kissing and stroking Christ and that he, as the second coming of Christ, was an appropriate person with whom to play 'Brides of Christ.' He did everything short of having intercourse with them. He would say these sexual relationships were 'beautiful' and 'spiritual' and would bring the girls closer to God. 'Christ was human,' he would remind them and add 'This is our secret.'"

"Where is this Beffin now?" Dee asked.

"Back in a treatment center," Jamie replied.

"Was he ever in New Mexico?"

"Ah, I see you got the clippings," Jamie smiled.

Dee pulled out her notebook, cleared a space on the table, and showed her chart connecting the dots among the predatory priests and treatment centers.

"It all seems to come back to Jemez Springs," Dee said.

"Yes, Jessie figured that out too. I think she must have mentioned something about it to Pica, but she won't talk about it. Did you know they knew each other before Pica came to St. Jude's? Anyway, Jessie took a visit to New Mexico over the summer of 1989 and made some inquiries. The center was still open and Sanchez was in fine form. It was all in her notes. Like you, Jessie wrote stuff down all the time," Amy added. "She had a terrific ear for direct speech – her notes of conversations and meetings were almost as good as being present."

"Do you have copies of any of her notes?" Dee asked.

"We can't find them. All I ever found was an old file on the computer she used in the Political Science Department, where she had been doing some sort of statistical analysis. I guess they had software us qualitative types don't use," Amy said.

"And the 'JS' in your files refers to that material?"

"Yes. How many know about that?" Amy asked.

"Virginia Glacialis, Mary J, Bill O'Vafer, and after that I don't know," Dee answered.

"Well, you and Mary J could be next," Jamie warned.

"Next what?"

"Disappeared, dead, like Jessie. Who knows?" Jamie said.

"We need to find her notes. They might have been destroyed, but I think not. She was really neurotic about keeping them in safe places and making copies," Amy said.

"I think I know what happened to some of them," Dee said, no longer prepared to keep quiet about the bundle she and Pica had located.

"In the pipe, in the corner room?" Amy leaned back in her chair and asked, "Is it getting hot in here or am I having a hot flash?" She peeled off her zippered jacket and reached for the water jug from the kitchen bench. "Anyone want a glass of water?"

Dee held up her empty coffee mug.

"You know Jessie was always complaining about how that pipe was loose and one day we tried to tape it up, but it didn't work well. I remember we joked it would a good place to hide things." Amy took a deep swig of water.

"Okay. Let's try to figure out any other likely places," Dee said. "Tell me about her routines. I know she had my office, but where else did Jessie hang out, who were her friends?" She was making notes furiously now.

"Jessie liked that office. It suited her style. Lots of light, ample shelves, and big closets. You know Coyle Hall was a Jesuit residence and there are still bits of that past around," Amy said.

Dee recalled how on Alumni Weekend Coyle Senior had talked to Jamie about the earlier use of the building. "Closets?" she asked.

"Yes, places where the priests put their clothes and things," Jamie laughed.

"But there are no closets in my office," Dee said, quickly sketching the floor plan of her corner room.

"When Jessie used that office, there was one space under the stairs," Amy pointed to the sketch. "It even had a label – even the closets had numbers."

"It may be nothing, but I'll look closely next week. The room was painted and refurbished before I moved in. Shelves were put along the walls."

"It was empty for a while," Amy remembered.

"Okay, where else did Jessie go?" Dee asked and again took detailed notes as they described the routes she took to and from school, how she rode her bicycle, right into the winter months.

"She hated the snow," Amy said. "Not good for cyclists."

"Maybe we should take a walk before lunch," Jamie suggested. "The sun is out, and the wind is not too vicious, but grab your jackets."

The three women walked onto the sand and along the water's edge. Jamie was skimming pebbles into the waves. Amy was picking up shells. Dee was thinking about connecting her dots.

They turned around when they reached a rocky outcrop at the peak of the sweep of the bay and headed back to the house for lunch. Jamie had fresh fish, bought that morning.

"Maybe I can pick some up tomorrow and take it home with me," Dee said.

"We can call and order whatever you want," Jamie smiled.

Dee was happy to cook the fish on the outside grill and the others joined her.

"Where to now? What is to be done?" Dee asked. "And can I ask about the source of those clippings sent to Cissy?"

"You can ask," Jamie laughed.

"How much does Cissy know?" Dee asked.

"Some."

"What do you both know about Mary Doyle?" Dee asked.

"What do you know about Father Sordes?" Amy parried.

"Some," Dee said realizing she was in an ethical bind. She was bound to Jackie Li not to discuss his case, but she knew she could not expect Amy or Jamie to tell what they knew or suspected if she herself was cagey.

"Do you know whether anyone has ever sued St. Jude's?" Dee ventured.

"Over what?" Amy asked, a little too quickly.

Jamie was now very interested.

"Maybe Mary Doyle, or some other woman who was abused? Maybe you, Amy? Maybe Jessie? I don't know. I just get the feeling that Dean Simean is always so quick to crush any suggestion that the college might have a greater duty of care to its students or that its policies need to be revised. I just wondered. Well, for starters, look at the threats and attacks," Dee suggested.

"Tell me more about them," Amy said, "if you can, that is." If they were going to pool information, they needed to respect boundaries and build trust. Dee outlined the chronology and asked, "Am I being paranoid, or did those Political Science students who hang out with Bill O'Vafer bother you?"

"They bothered me plenty," Amy said. "Dan Dempsey, Marty McDuff, and now Bill Jr. is in the thick of it, I hear."

"What's his story?" Dee asked. "He's a bit older. Why did he take time off?"

Jamie sat quietly with a look on her face that Dee had seen once before. It was the face she saw when they had talked on the steps about Virginia on Alumni Weekend.

"He was drinking pretty heavily and . . ." Jamie trailed off.

"Okay, back to my dots." Dee pulled out her notebook. "We have Mary Doyle and maybe others who have been taken in by Father Sordes. And, of course, the Jemez Springs connection links a number of predatory priests. There is the so-called Terminator and the Political Science cabal. Add Jessie Seneca to the mix. Is it all part of one plot? Virginia knows something and so does Pica. WOW is now implicated. And maybe there are some lawsuits."

Amy nodded. So she *had* sued when her tenure case was overturned, and Dee was betting that the settlement was sealed. But, if what Amy knew could help solve Jessie's murder, could she be released from that undertaking? Dee felt certain that Jessie had been killed to silence her. The story of the bicycle accident had never really rung true. "Why did you send those materials to WOW?" Dee asked Jamie.

"Well they needed to be warned and they needed materials for their feminist liturgy."

And none of them is bound by any agreements to stay quiet.

Don't mess with smart women.

"I think we need to check out my office more closely," Dee said. "It's a quiet weekend at the college. There is some construction being done on the parking lot. No faculty will be around. Want to come with me?"

"Well, I have more food in the fridge for dinner," Jamie said.

"Bring it along," Dee said. "We can cook it at my place. Are you in, Amy?"

"I guess so. There was nothing in our agreement about my not visiting the college or having dinner with you."

As she drove, Dee thought back to earlier conversations. Magdalena had said the room had been closed for a while. Jamie mentioned closets. Jessie had been involved with a contraceptives campaign. That was in 1990, the year she died. It was winter, December maybe? December 6? The first anniversary of the Montreal Massacre? Marc Lepine had walked into a classroom and shouted, "I want the women." He had separated the men from the women, ordered the men to leave the classroom, and lined the women up along one wall. "You are all feminists!" he yelled and began shooting to kill. "*Alea Iacta* – the die are cast," he had written. "I'm sending the feminists who have ruined my life to *Ad Patres.*" She was worried. *Should she stop and call Miriam, or Pica? Ask Daniel for his advice? Tell Christian she was on her way home? Or was she the one being paranoid now?*

Dee parked in the space marked "Coyle." *Let the police argue with Jamie,* she thought. Jamie parked in Negotium's space. They ran up the stairs to Dee's office. Amy went straight to the space under the stairs that backed onto Dee's office. "There was a closet here. It had a number, something like 606A. The bookshelves are in the way now."

The three women began pulling books off the shelves and managed to dislodge the corner shelf from the wall. The patch was barely visible but Dee felt along the edge with her fingers.

"Do you think there's anything there?" Amy asked.

"We could pry it open," Jamie said. "My grandfather paid to have this building refurbished, I don't think he'd mind if we strip it back to its original form."

Dee pulled out her Swiss Army penknife and cut into the paint. "I'm going to need better tools," she said. "I have a good crowbar in my car." She disappeared through the door.

"Hey, don't leave us here," Amy cried.

"Stay at the top of the stairs. You can see me all the way down and back," Dee reassured them. "Better still, call Miriam and Daniel. The number is on my planner. We may need backup."

With the crowbar in use, the patch came off relatively easily. The space was full of bits of old carpet, masonry, and a box wrapped in plastic and taped shut.

Dee gasped. "What is it? Should we open it? Maybe it's some more of Jessie's notes."

"The ones I saw were in those upright box files." Amy said. "All carefully indexed."

"What about her rough notes?" Dee asked holding the bundle.

"Don't even think about opening that."

Dee swung around. "Pica, what are you doing here?"

"Don't worry. I called her before we left Jamie's house. It's time, please Pica." Amy said. "Tell them."

Pica started slowly, "Well, I knew Jessie long before she came here. We go way back to before I took my final vows. We kept our relationship secret, it's almost second nature to me now. I'm sorry if you feel deceived, Dee, but it really is my business. Jessie hated the church for making us feel like criminals, but she respected my choice, and we stayed friends, long after we stopped being lovers. We talked a lot about how we could work together if she took the appointment here and she thought we could handle it. Our lives were so entangled. Not just because of our affair, but because of my brother also."

"The one who was in the same seminary as Tom Guye?"

"Yes. How much did Tom tell you?" Pica asked.

"That Sordes was there too and about the rapes and the man–boy love cults."

"And Father Martin?"

"I got the impression that wasn't his real name."

"No, it wasn't and he's dead now, so let that rest. But my brother John is alive, in large measure because Jessie helped him so much," Pica said.

"So is that what Tom meant about owing you and Jessie a debt?"

"Yes. The seminary was transformed, and Tom felt Jessie had saved a number of young lives."

"And that was all before Paddy Sordes came to St. Jude's?" Dee asked looking for confirmation.

"He didn't come here till 1992. Jesuits are an affirmative action hire. They're an endangered species, you know. He arrived the same time as Miriam," Amy said.

"And here I am again," Miriam announced as she and Daniel appeared at Dee's door.

"Come in. I know we're a bit squashed, but can we finish this part of the story, before we move? Pica has just been connecting the dots for us – Jessie, Tom, Sordes – and look what we found." Dee pointed to the notes and closet under the stairs. "Pica do you want to recap for Daniel and Miriam?"

"Later, I think. Now, where was I? Oh yes, Tom had kept track of Sordes on and off. He told Jessie most of what he knew, and she spent a summer out in New Mexico in 1989. It suited her with the artwork she was doing, all that Georgia O'Keefe country and the fabulous sexual symbolism she depicted. Jessie found Sordes was still up to his old game. Incorrigible. While he was in treatment, he was running a sex ring on the weekends and trafficking in drugs. Can you believe it? He was visiting the sick in the hospital and feeling them up under the bedclothes. I guess he thought he had a good thing going."

"What happened in that fall semester, when Jessie was killed?" Dee asked.

"Amy can fill you in best on that," Pica said.

"She'd been working with some women students on forming a Pro-Choice group and they'd been petitioning the Health Center, and the usual crap was coming down from the conservative alumni. She got threatening letters and phone calls. Like what you were describing for WOW."

"And did they have the Terminator signature?" Dee asked.

"No, just a twig cross and #126. We never figured out what the numbers meant," Amy said.

"And did the Post Office open the mail and see that?"

"I'm pretty sure they did."

"What about our friend Charles Vernon Negotium? The man who thinks we're just one big happy family?" Dee asked.

"The man who helped clean up after Jessie's so-called accident, just keeping it in the family," Amy added.

"The man who renegotiated our health coverage plan," Pica said.

"The man for whom doubt is an oxymoron?" Jamie said.

"Where is your brother now, Pica?"

"He's in remission. 'Martin' died of AIDS. Lennie died of AIDS. But my brother is okay."

"Who else knows this?" Dee asked.

"Just us," Amy said.

"Just us had better be bloody careful," Daniel boomed. "Can we go to your place Dee?"

"I brought the chicken soup I had on the stove," Miriam said. "We can heat it up and talk about this some more in a private space. We need to decide what to do."

"Well, the electricity is still on in my old empty apartment. But there is the small matter of this hole in the wall and this bundle of papers."

"Oh shit," Pica said. "Don't touch the bundle. It might be poisonous. She wrote about an anthrax scare in the notes, the ones we found in the pipe. Jessie received threatening letters and one that said poison was being sent through the mail. It was around the time a number of Women's Health Centers had been sent similar letters, but the FBI wouldn't do anything about it."

"I'm shocked," Daniel said with heavy sarcasm. His work with Native Americans had soured him when it came to this agency.

"It was in women's publications like *Sojourner*. It's just another lost episode of women's history, and that was only 1989. The trouble was no-one ever knew if they were really opening an envelope with anthrax or talcum powder in it."

"Was that why this office was sealed off for so long?" Dee asked.

"Who knows," Amy said.

"I think our mate Chuck does," Dee said. "Here help me get this room back to normal."

"I think we should leave it as it is," Daniel said. "Don't disturb the evidence."

"I've done a pretty good job already," Dee laughed, "but I guess as long as we get here before the cleaning staff on Monday morning, it will be okay. Who is going to come in here?"

"Just don't touch that box," Pica repeated.

✛

Miriam, Daniel, Pica, Jamie, Amy and Dee sat on the floor in the near empty apartment. Miriam had found enough paper cups for soup and they sipped it while Pica continued her story.

"Jessie found that Sordes had contracted some venereal disease while he was in New Mexico and that he was super sensitive about what was kept in medical records, especially his."

"Did he have any access to the records at St. Jude's?" Dee asked. "That would explain how he knew about Mary Doyle seeking advice on contraception."

"He hung out at the Counseling Center for a while," Pica said. "Offered to help with troubled students, that kind of thing. He could be charming, you know."

"Yes, I've seen that side of him and it's appealing until you see what it masks," Dee said.

"He would have had keys to the Health Center, so he could well have read files after the offices were closed," Pica said. "No-one would have noticed, except maybe the Campus Security guys if they had driven past."

"Jessie knew those files were not secure," Amy said. "She told me about the way a major rape had been hushed up, and you're right Dee, your buddy Chuck was in the thick of it. He's always so sure he's right, never shows any doubt – and then there is Virginia too. The rapist was one of O'Vafer's students, and you know how he cultivates and courts the conservative sons of important alumni. Well, in fall 1989, the semester I joined St. Jude's and before Jessie died, there was a nasty incident involving a woman, who was a sophomore, and a graduating senior who was the son of an important member of the Board of Trustees. She got herself to the Health Center afterwards, bruised and bleeding. She'd been drinking. They cleaned her up, but they didn't do a rape kit. The Counseling Center was called. The attitude was 'Forgive and heal, move on.' But the girl was deeply troubled by the experience and started to lose weight. Her roommates had listened to her story and were furious that the guy was going to get away with it. And then they heard the guy was bragging that he could have any woman he wanted, any time. That was too much."

246

"How did Virginia get involved?" Dee asked.

"Bill O'Vafer was worried that he might be drawn into an investigation if the woman pressed charges. He had been drinking with the guy at Mick's Sports Bar and knew he was drunk and talking big about 'doing some chick' and what 'feminists really needed.' They'd all laughed about it. He asked Virginia to talk to the woman and find out what she was saying. So Virginia did."

"Why?"

"She badly wanted to be Head of Religious Studies. And lo, by the next year she was."

"That is some price to pay," Dee said. "If true, that explains what Mary J said about her. And Chuck?" Dee persisted.

"Chuck had to make sure none of the maintenance crew talked about the mess they'd cleaned up in the Field House," Amy said. "Remember, I wrote about how that place was the site for male violence against women, but they didn't want to hear it."

"And you wrote about this rape?" Daniel asked.

"Well, it was all in Jessie's notes and the first draft of my report, but it was expunged from the final report that went to the faculty and the Trustees."

"And that was what Bill O'Vafer wanted changed in the data-base," Dee said. "Okay, I've got lots of connecting dots now."

"If there was a cover up and your data was tampered with . . ." Daniel started. "We could get the files unsealed and then the details of your settlement could be made public. The woman who was raped probably doesn't want to testify. Who knows where she is in her life now?"

"I know," said Jamie. "Remember, I was at St. Jude's in '89–'93. We all knew the story of the rape. It was a cautionary tale. Not only are women treated as second-class citizens by the church, we couldn't get justice when we were sexually assaulted. We'd get fobbed off and then called sluts. And we are supposed to be 'In the service of others.' Some joke. We were being served up!"

"I heard women in WOW say, 'He's done it before and anyone who gets in his way just disappears.' Is that reportage part of the folk memory?" Dee asked.

"Yes, and the tight circle around Bill O'Vafer keeps it alive," Jamie said.

"Do you think that's who the Terminator is?" Dee asked, "Bill? A student in Political Science?"

"I'm not sure, but they're certainly implicated. Bill Jr. is a strange one. Christine is not his mother, you know. He started at St. Jude's when I was there but then he was sent abroad – trouble with alcohol – having blackouts and stuff like that," Jamie said. Amy and Pica nodded their assent.

"So where is the woman now?" Daniel asked. "The one who was raped and left the college?"

"She was in therapy for a while, but she decided that wasn't getting her anywhere. She needed to finish school at a local college, near where she lives in Massachusetts, and now she works as a paralegal."

"And she helped you put the file of clippings together?" Dee asked.

Jamie nodded.

"And what about man–boy love?" Dee asked.

"Jessie and I both heard stories about that. Drug taking on the weekend occurred before Sordes arrived at St. Jude's. He wasn't the only one on that kick. Secrecy is so pervasive and so destructive. There were others who were his protégés. Just doing the Lord's work."

Christian called. "Dee, are you okay? I've tried all the numbers I had for you. What's happening? Daniel left me a message that you were back in Resolve." He sounded worried.

"I'm okay, really, but this whole St. Jude's thing is unraveling."

"Do you want me to come up?"

"I have Miriam and Daniel, and Pica and Jamie and Amy," Dee began.

"Dee, I'm asking if you want *me*. I know you can look after yourself."

"Yes. Please come," she said. "I do want you here. I think we'll go over to Miriam's and Daniel's place soon. Can you meet us there? Oh, and bring some of that white gloss paint we've been using on the shelves in the cottage and a brush. And do you have a way to test for anthrax?"

"Not really. But it can be deadly and can survive in the soil for decades," Christian said. "And I have something to tell you that might be helpful."

"Daniel, what did you say in your message?" Dee asked.

"Men's business," Daniel said. "Men who *get* strong women . . . you know? We need to *share* every now and then."

Miriam mouthed to Dee, "I'll tell you later."

Pica continued to talk about Jessie, and little by little Amy talked about the settlement. By the time Christian arrived, Dee was in high spirits. "I think we've got it sorted out."

"Listen to this," Christian began. "There is a group at UMass Medical who are working with art therapy. You know, like what Jessie was doing? And their focus is schizophrenia. I see stuff on their grants at meetings sometimes. But they have an exhibit of some of the work of the patients in the main foyer and it is quite amazing. Some of it is titled, some not. Some has the artist's name on it, some doesn't. There are a couple I think you all should see."

"And whose would they be?" Amy asked expectantly.

"Howard . . ." Christian began.

"Howard Roberts? Virginia's husband." Amy was on her feet. "Yes, I love it when it all comes together. Pica, in Jessie's notes, did you see anything about his paintings?"

Pica weighed the possibilities that live anthrax spores might be released by opening the package of notes. The notes had lain dormant and, to her knowledge, no-one who had been in the office had contracted anthrax but, on balance, she decided not to take the risk without the benefit of some expert advice. The notes could go back whence they came. For now the paintings could speak for themselves.

> That's it. R.D. Laing was right. "Insanity - a perfectly rational adjustment to an insane world. There is very little difference between genius and schizophrenia."
>
> April 5, 1997: Feast day, St. Juliana of Liege (1192-1258). Vision of a dark ringed moon, 1208;

revelation it denoted a missing sacrament; bring the body of Christ into public view; the Feast of Corpus Christi celebrated in 1246; suffered greatly for her beliefs; St. Thomas Aquinas worked on the liturgy.

17

CALLING THE NAMES
Spring 1997

The race was on. Rehearsals for the feminist liturgy were now held almost every night. Dee offered to attend a rehearsal, but the women of WOW said, "Let us surprise you. It will be our graduating present for you, and Pica, and Miriam."

"And for Amy and Jessie," Cissy added. "So, Dee, just promise you'll be there, and Christian too." Cissy, Mary Louise and MC had met Christian one evening when he had ventured within the gates of St. Jude's, and now they were conspiring with him to keep Dee out of the planning and rehearsing for the event. Christian enjoyed the intrigue and had given them his email address at UMass so they could continue the plot to keep Dee away until the actual event. He was pretty sure she wouldn't see this as him being imperious.

Magdalena had walked in when Dee and Christian were putting the books back onto the newly replaced shelves blocking the secret closet, and noticed the fresh paint smell. "Good idea, painting this place," she said and returned her most recently borrowed books to Dee's shelf. Magdalena continued, "Consuelo has something to tell you. She's been working with the women in WOW as part of her senior project in high school. She has learned a lot about the courses that you, Pica, and Miriam have been teaching."

"I hope I will have the pleasure of teaching her," Dee said. "We could do with more comparative insights into Marian cults."

"I don't know about that but she's been asking me all sorts of questions about Santería in Cuba. The wise old *babalú* in Resolve says she is a natural. Her memory is amazing."

"Humm, I know what you mean. An outstanding memory is a prerequisite for an Ifá diviner. Christian's mother has that gift too."

"Consuelo showed me the paper she's writing on the Patron Saint of Cuba, the Virgen de la Caridad del Cobre," Magdalena said glowing with pride. "It's been so good to be able to talk to her about those things, and she told me some things that I wish I'd known earlier. She'll tell you. It's her story. I'm not going to spoil it for her."

Pica's twin John arrived and helped Dee move the last of her things to her new home. He had Pica's sense of humor. The two had obviously played a great deal of pool together and seemed to share a private language, as twins sometimes do. John and Christian quickly became friends. They talked about the politics of AIDS activism late into the night and ended up with plans for a joint presentation at UMass. John had also been spending a lot of time with Tom Guye and had ordered from the local bookstore the books for Tom's course on Masculinities for his reading group.

Tom's older sister Mary decided she wanted to meet the formidable women in Religious Studies. Mary turned out to be a lot of fun and accompanied Dee, who was putting finishing touches on the new "pond house," as she scoured the local thrift stores and planned a house-warming party. This felt like family. This felt like the fieldwork she loved. Commencement exercises were about to begin.

"We hold these truths to be self-evident; that all men and women are created equal; that they are endowed by their creator with certain inalienable rights; that among these are life, liberty, and the pursuit of happiness . . . The history of mankind is a history of repeated injuries and usurpations on the part of man toward woman, having as its direct object the establishment of tyranny over her. To prove this, let facts be submitted to a candid world."

Cissy Coyle, dressed in the white and purple robes of the suffragettes, with WOW embroidered on her gold satin sash, was standing on the top step. Behind her rose the granite columns of the library. The sun was dropping in the sky and the fountain, stark on the first landing of the steps, caught the last of the natural light. The soft sound of the waterfall soothed the crowd. Sixty or so students stood mute, listening intently.

"I read from Elizabeth Cady Stanton's *Declaration of Sentiments*," Cissy continued. "He allows her in Church, as well as State, but in a subordinate position, claiming Apostolic authority for her exclusion from the ministry, and with some exceptions, from any public participation in the affairs of the Church . . ." Cissy looked up from the text. "This was a grievance in 1848 and it continues unto today."

"Pray for us," came the response from the women and their supporters who had been rehearsing the liturgy for months. The growing throng was quick to add their voices. "Pray for us," they echoed. Dee could see faculty standing on the sidelines, not sure what was going on, but prepared to stay for a little while. The sun was almost gone. One by one the women, and a few of the men present, lit their candles. The vigil had begun.

"We begin with a reading from the Old Testament, Psalms 55: 14." Cissy's clear voice carried across the steps. Dee could see she was in her element.

"Genesis, Chapter 1, Man and Woman were a simultaneous creation. Genesis, Chapter 2, Woman was an afterthought. I ask the same question Elizabeth Cady Stanton asked, *Which is true?*" Jamie continued, "I say unto you, Jesus was a feminist, he believed in the equality of men and women."

"Amen," came this response, stronger than the last. Dee could see the crowd was growing apace. From the floor-to-ceiling windows of the library a weak light played on the steps and provided a dramatic backdrop for Cissy's presentation. For people sitting on the steps and the grassy slopes and looking up towards the library, Cissy was in silhouette. The women of WOW, also dressed in suffragette robes, moved through the crowd and offered candles for those who wished to join the vigil. Soon a sea of small white candles dotted the steps and slopes.

Cissy held a book aloft. "*This is the work of women and the devil,* said the clergy of Cady Stanton's *The Woman's Bible*. And what did our sister Cady reply? *His Satanic Majesty was not invited to join the Revising Committee, which consists of women alone.*

"Pray for our sisters," Cissy called to the crowd.

It was now completely dark outside and the whole slope beyond the library and the steps twinkled with the candles that illuminated the faces of the earnest young women and men. The crowd continued to swell, and Dee could see more students, faculty, and administrators arriving by the minute.

Cissy Coyle stepped forward. "I commend the words of this foremother to you." And with that she stepped forward and placed a copy of *The Woman's Bible* within the crèche with the Christ child. "May the Lord be with you."

"And also with you," came the crowd's emphatic response.

Jamie Coyle stepped forward. "I hold in my hand *Malleus Maleficarum*, also known as *The Witch Hammer*. This handbook for witch-hunts was first published in 1486 and, because the language is strange to our ears, I will paraphrase. *Are witches real or a matter of superstition?* the authors ask. Their answer is clear. *Maintaining beliefs in beings known as Witches is so central to the Catholic Faith that contrary beliefs savor of Heresy.* Now listen for the resonances with contemporary attitudes, and here I am drawing on the writing of our sister Mary Daly in the 1980s. 'The witch-hunter sought to purify society of those indigestible elements – women – whose physical, intellectual, economic, moral, and spiritual independence and activity profoundly threatened the male monopoly in every sphere. The purge was a cleansing of the Body Politic, but more specifically of the Mystical Body of Christ . . . the body which included all members of his church.'"

"Pray for the women burned in purifying paternal fires," Jamie called out.

Jamie stepped forward, drove a copy of the *Malleus Maleficarum* onto the crown of thorns and placed a copy of Mary Daly's book in the crèche.

"Pray for all our sisters," the crowd responded.

Mary Louise stepped forward. "I read from the *Syllabus of Errors* prepared by Pope Pius IX, in the mid-nineteenth century. This is the Pope who abducted six-year-old Edgardo Mortara from his Jewish family and never returned him; the Pope who blamed

Rome's Jews for what he believed was a conspiracy to defeat the papacy; and the Pope who condemned freedom of speech and religious tolerance. This is also the Pope who is on his way to beatification. His list of errors is extensive. His mode of expression is somewhat contorted, so I paraphrase.

"Error 47 of Pope Pius IX addressed the matter of public education. He opposed theories of civil society that held that schools should be freed from all ecclesiastical authority, control and interference.

"Error 56 of Pope Pius IX addressed moral laws. He asserted they stand in need of the divine sanction.

"Error 77 of Pope Pius IX addressed the status of the Catholic religion. He affirmed the position that it be the only religion of the State."

Dee scanned the crowd for Virginia but could not see her. Mary Louise continued. "I now read from Vatican II, Declaration of Religious Freedoms, *Dignitatis Humanae*, as promulgated by his Holiness, Pope Paul, December 7, 1965. 'A sense of the dignity of the human person has been impressing itself more and more deeply on the consciousness of contemporary man, and the demand is increasingly made that men should act on their own judgment, enjoying and making use of a responsible freedom, not driven by coercion but motivated by a sense of duty.'

"This is where the church lost its way, say voices of conservatism." Mary Louise's voice was deep and stern. *"This is where the church must move,* say the liberals." Her tone became more insistent. She stood tall and declared with passion. *"This is not enough,* we say. *It will not be enough until we can participate in all the rites of the church."*

"Let it be so."

Mary Louise stepped forward, drove the Syllabus of Errors onto the thorns and placed *Dignitatis Humanae* beside *The Woman's Bible*. How many people are out there? Dee thought as she heard the rousing response.

"Amen."

MC was now standing on the steps. "I take my inspiration from our sister Elaine Pagels. In the *Gnostic Gospels* she writes of finding oneself profoundly affected by Christian symbols while at the same time in revolt against the institutions. The discovery of the Gnostic texts in 1945 has provided a powerful alternative to what we know as orthodox Christian tradition. We echo her question as we ask: What is the relation between the authority of one's own experience and that claimed for the Scriptures, the ritual, and the clergy?"

"Pray for our sisters."

A slightly stooped, white-haired woman joined the women of WOW on the library steps. She spoke slowly. "In 1968 we burned draft cards in Catonsville, Maryland. Pax Christi at St. Jude's offered us sanctuary. For that I honor the institution." *This must be Mary Moylan,* Dee realized and thought back on what she had read in the college archives of the Catonsville Nine and their protests against the war in Vietnam. *I had no idea WOW had been in contact with her.* Mary Moylan, dressed all in black and backlit by the library lights, was now standing beside the fountain. "I repeat what I said at my trial. It is time to stand up. We are called to act on what we believe. This is what it means to be a Christian. This is what Christ meant when He lived. As a nurse, my profession is to preserve life, to prevent disease. But I see us turning away from violence in communities at home and abroad. During the Vietnam War, I took a stance on the napalm bombing of children and women. Today I take a stance on violence against women – physical, sexual, psychological." Mary Moylan stepped forward and placed a dove in the crèche. Dee watched it circle the chapel and fly off into the inky sky.

As she returned her gaze to the library steps, Dee noticed that the assembled crowd was being encircled by the campus police. They had carefully parked their cars along all the exit routes. They were positioned in such a way that they could completely control the growth of the crowd. Dee stared into the darkness, beyond the grassy slopes and the library steps. She was hoping to see Daniel. Nothing. The organizers had not yet realized what was being attempted and Dee feared how the crowd might respond. Then a voice came over a loud speaker. "Don't move. No-one will be hurt. We are going to have an orderly end to this unauthorized meeting." Dee caught sight of the glow of a cigarette.

"It's Chuck Negotium," Dee said out loud to no-one in particular. "What the hell does he think he is doing?"

Joshua Rosen, Associate Dean for Diversity, stepped forward and spoke out. "This is a peaceful assembly, in a public place."

"We are checking IDs," came the voice of Negotium. And with that the entire area was suddenly bathed in bright light as the headlamps of the encircling cars came on. Dee blinked as she felt the pain of her pupils dilate and then, for the first time, saw the extent of the crowd. There must have been at least six hundred people present.

"Don't do it, Chuck." It was Dulcie McNeil from the Chaplain's Office. "Joshua and I have copies of your email about the accident."

"This is my jurisdiction," Negotium roared.

Oh, the pressure cooker has blown. He's finally lost it. Dee was desperately trying to figure out a safe way of defusing what was becoming a very nasty situation. But then, one by one the women from WOW sat down and others followed. "Thank God they know about peaceful resistance," Dee said and realized that Christian was by her side. "I'm going to sit too," he said. "What does that man think he is going to do with those cars?"

"I don't think he is thinking. He is terrified. Did you see who is lining up to speak out? I'm sure I saw Jackie Li and the Dean. This could be really interesting."

"Students, faculty, fellow administrators, alumnae, friends, welcome. I entreat you to join with these brave, creative women."

"It's Dean Simean," Dee exclaimed. "Now what is he up to?"

David Simean walked over to Chuck Negotium, took the loud speaker, and said, "Let the stories be told." Beside him stood his wife Mary Anne and his daughter, Marian. All but one of the beams of light from the encircling cars dimmed.

A slight young woman, flanked by Mary Louise and MC, emerged from the crowd. The trio moved into the middle of the library steps and into the glare of the one remaining headlight. "I am Mary Doyle. I was raped. I was raped by a priest. Then my boyfriend was raped by the same priest. These rapes took place at

St. Jude's. When I reported these rapes, I was blamed for them and counseled to keep quiet. I left. The priest stayed. He was counseled too but it didn't change his behavior. He left St. Jude's earlier this year, but he hasn't been forced to leave the church. He is still out there and he is not the only one. The church knows who these men are but the church remains silent. It is time for us to start calling the names." Mary Doyle was joined by Cissy and together with Mary Louise and MC they skewered the newspaper photograph of Paddy Sordes SJ onto the crown of thorns.

"Buenos noches. Mi nombre es Consuelo Hernández. I know about this man," Consuelo said and pointed to the photograph. "Here is my story for you. From when I was a very little girl, my aunt told me stories about him and his friends, David A. Holley and John J. Geoghan. They were in the treatment center near where she lived. During the week and on the weekends they had parties. They had drugs. They had sex with young boys from the boys' club – like my cousin Philippe. My aunt said, 'Watch out for those *demonios*,' and she prayed to the patron saint of Cuba. The Virgin of Caring helps anyone who has faith – black or white, revolutionary or conservative. I pray to her that I may be the first of my family to go to college." Consuelo placed a small image of La Virgen de la Caridad del Cobre in the crèche.

Mary J's daughter, Little Mary, stepped up and put her arm around Consuelo. "Here is my story. I too will be the first generation in my family to go to college. My mother has worked here all my life to make that possible, but late one afternoon, when I was waiting for her in the car lot, one of those boys in Political Science pinned me against the fence. He pushed his hands between my legs and he hurt me. When I cried he said he would make trouble for my mother if I told. He did but she only worked harder.

"I prayed to Our Lady of Guadalupe. I love her story, especially the part about how her image appeared on the cloak of Juan Diego. This happened on December 12 – my birthday, her feast day. On that day in 1531, in the dead of winter, Juan was gathering roses – beautiful, fragrant Rosas de Castilla – on Tepeyac Hill, northwest of Mexico City, the same place where the temple to the Aztec great

Mother Goddess once stood before the Spanish tore it down. Our Lady appeared to Juan and told him to build a temple for her on that site. And so it came to pass. You can tear down our places, but we will rise again." Little Mary placed six full pink roses beside the baby Jesus, scattered petals so they cascaded down the waterfall and stood looking out into the crowd.

"Let her through," Dee could hear people in the crowd saying. Mary Kane's daughter, Lina, appeared and joined Little Mary and Consuelo on the steps. "I too have a story. One day there was this graffiti on my dormitory door. It said, 'Lina goes down for a dollar.' And then, when I was in my Political Science class the next day, there was dollar note on the desk. That night I got obscene calls through the night when I was trying to study. The campus police wouldn't help me. They said I was making it all up. I told my adviser and he said to drop Political Science and take Botany instead, because that's better for a girl."

Other students were coming forward. They stood and testified about the silences, intimidation and cover-ups. Frank O'Meara, the student who had stood between Dee and Professor Taurus two years ago, stepped up. "I have a story also," he began. "I heard stories about which women were targets and I heard stories about how powerful that gang of guys in Political Science was. Then one day, I was in the library and I surprised this senior. He had a coed pinned against the stacks and she was trying to push him away. All I heard him say was, 'You have been warned.' He glared at me and walked off. I wanted to report him but my friends told me that he could really make trouble for me. They said that he knew how to get into the system and could change my grades. I didn't believe it at first, but others told me it was true. Then they got to my kid sister. I was terrified about what he and his followers might do. I backed off. I'm so sorry. I know Father Humanitas was speaking to me at the Lenten Mass. I have to act. But who can I tell?"

"Tell us," Cissy and Jamie said. "Tell us," the crowd roared. Joshua Rosen intervened. "You can tell me and we will investigate properly but with regard for due process. I promise, before all of you, this will be done. I too am so terribly sorry. I just didn't know how deep this went."

"It goes very deep," Amy Nakamura said as she stepped forward. "Here is the report I submitted and here is the report released by the Trustees. You can see one is considerably slimmer than the other. Let me read a section from my original that was disappeared from the Trustees' version: 'As part of its Annual Report, the college is required to disclose the crime statistics for the year. Prospective parents pay attention to these statistics and the excellent safety record of St. Jude's enhances its reputation. Each year there is a zero in the column for sexual assault. We heard a different story. There *had been* complaints. Many women students knew not to believe that zero statistic. We followed as many leads as we could but, given what a sensitive matter this is, the desire of young women to move on with their lives, and the way women who bring charges of sexual assault get treated, we had little success. What we did learn was that the Trustees would not discuss the matter in open session.'"

Dee watched as a young woman – one she didn't recognize – approached Jamie. The two women obviously knew each other. They were hugging and crying and Dee heard Jamie say, "Of course I'll stand with you. We all will." Amy paused, and turned. "And some of us are very brave," she said holding out her arms.

"I am Mary D'Madre," the young woman began. Dulcie McNeil from the Chaplain's Office was instantly at her side. "It is time to speak, but I have lived with the shame, the silence and the guilt for too many years, and in breaking my silence, I want to know there will be an accounting beyond an official apology. I need things to change. It runs deep as Amy says." Mary D'Madre looked around. "And it runs wide." Dee could see Daniel and Joshua had linked up and were in an intense huddled conversation with Jackie Li. *Ah, the lawyers confer*, Dee thought. "Yes," Mary D'Madre continued. "There are legal consequences to naming my abuser and to naming those who worked on the cover-up. I am not naive. I have spent the last four years learning the law. I have legal counsel. This matter is not going to be disappeared like Amy's report. The Attorney-General is ready to investigate the cover-up. The recent attacks on WOW have convinced her there are grounds for an inquiry. I am not going to prejudice that process. Let it run its course. But know this . . . I stand before you. I will continue to do so. I survived. That has to mean something."

Joshua Rosen and Jackie Li were now talking with Dean Simean. "Yes, Mary, our lives do have meaning," the Dean said, coming forward and standing in the lee of the fountain. "This is something I have learned through personal experience. Cissy, Jamie, Amy," he said spreading his arm out in their direction. "All of you who have spoken, I need some time to work out the details, but I am endorsing the promise made a few minutes earlier by our Associate Dean for Diversity, Joshua Rosen. There will be a thorough investigation. We will cooperate fully with the Attorney-General. We will go back to the original of Dr. Amy Nakamura's report. Mary D'Madre is correct. We have to ensure due process, but you have my word, as the Dean, as the father of six daughters, and most particularly my first-born, Marian, who has taught me so much, and as a devout Catholic, we will not hide from the consequences of the stories you have told today. Thank you, WOW. You are aptly named Women of Worth." The Dean retreated to stand with his wife and daughter. "Peace be with you," he said gruffly and scattered the rose petals Little Mary handed him.

"And also with you," the crowd responded.

"What now?" Dee said to Christian. "What can possibly happen now?"

"Watch," he said and the laugh lines played around his eyes.

Cissy, Mary Louise and MC stepped forward. "Sisters and brothers," Cissy began.

"We are gathered here in the spirit of truth," Mary Louise continued.

"And full of hope for the future," MC concluded.

"Amen," said the crowd.

"The night is mild. We invite you all to stay. We haven't quite finished what we planned. When we first suggested a feminist liturgy, we had no idea how hard it would be, or how much we would learn about ourselves and about others. The stories and readings were to be followed by singing. We'd like to complete our program. I think we all know this one."

Pica stepped forward with her guitar and began to play the first bars of "Amazing Grace." The crowd stood and began to sing:

> Amazing grace, how sweet the sound
> That saved a wretch like me.
> I once was lost, but now am found;
> Was blind, but now I see.

Consuelo joined Pica and sang:

> *Sublime gracia del Señor*
> *Que a mi pecadora salvó*
> *fui ciega mas hoy miro yo*
> *perdida y el me amó.*

Tom Guye, his sister Mary, and Pica's brother John sang:

> Through many dangers, toils and snares,
> I have already come;
> 'Tis grace hath brought me safe thus far,
> And grace will lead me home.

"I didn't know they were going to sing that one," Dee said to Christian. "That's a favorite of Charles Humanitas."

"And one of yours too," Christian said affectionately. "I've heard you singing it to yourself when you're concentrating."

Cissy moved forward and stood in front of the fountain. "One of the things we have learned from our research for this project has been that there are many ways to be 'In the service of others.' There's the Seder."

Miriam joined Cissy. "I enumerate the Ten Plagues.

1. Patriarchal oppression
2. Capitalist exploitation
3. Environmental plunder
4. Imperialism
5. Ethnocentrism

6. Universalism
7. Silence in the face of abuse
8. Genocide in Europe: The Inquisition, the Holocaust, Kosovo
9. Genocide in Africa: Rwanda, Biafra, South Africa under Apartheid
10. Genocide in the United States, Canada and Australia: The Stolen Generations."

"Let the youngest person present ask the four questions," Miriam said. Consuelo stepped forward.

"Why are we here?"

"Why did we do it?"

"What did we learn?"

"What is still to be done?"

"Let us make the presentations," said Miriam.

"An apple for Eve," said Cissy, Mary Louise and MC.

"An orange for the Seder Plate," said Miriam, Joshua and Daniel.

"Sixteen kola nuts for the Divining Board," said Consuelo and Christian.

"Roses for our mothers," said the daughters of Mary J, Mary Kane, and Mary Anne Simean.

"Let us close with a song of triumph, hope and remembrance," Cissy said. Pica began to play "Lift every voice and sing." Dee, already deeply moved by the thoughtfulness of the young women who had planned the liturgy and those who had spoken so forthrightly, began to choke back tears. "This is my absolute favorite," she turned to say to Christian, but he was standing next to Pica. His voice filled the air.

> Lift every voice and sing,
> Till earth and heaven ring.

The crowd joined in. *The Black National Anthem. Hope. Courage. Promise. This is a beginning.* Dee sang with joy and purpose.

> Facing the rising sun of our new day begun
> Let us march on till victory is won.

18

Dee, suntanned and relaxed, walked hand in hand with Christian up the steps to the library. They stood quietly to read the plaque on the fountain.

> Women of Worth
> Aptly named.
> Your sacrifice was not in vain.

They smiled at each other and continued on into the library, where the welcoming roar of the air conditioning could not drown out the scream of delight from Mary Doyle, who was sitting signing books at one of the long tables in the reading room. Mary Louise was helping set up the display, the focus of which was an enormous poster. There, against a grainy black and white photograph of the vigil of May 1997, the scarlet lettering of the title, *Marys' Story*, was both a challenge and an invitation to read the book. Mary Doyle bounded forward. "It is so good to see you both. I can't believe you're actually here. I know you said you'd come, but . . ."

"But nothing. I wouldn't miss this for the world," Dee laughed and hugged Mary. "I am so proud of you."

Mary handed a copy of her book to Dee and said. "This is for you." Dee held the book in her hands as one would hold the delicate bloom of a camellia. *Humm, that wonderful smell of fresh paper, the feel of the shiny dust jacket, the crisp new paper*, Dee thought as she turned the book over in her hands. "I do love books," she said. "And the Women's Press has done a good job on this one." Dee opened the book and read the dedication page. "For Dee, our shero."

"Mary that is so sweet of you," Dee began, but was interrupted by Cissy and her cousin Jamie who had exploded into the library and were hugging, kissing Mary Doyle and admiring the book.

"Hi, Dee. Hi, Christian. Hey, you two look terrific. Great outfit Dee – wish I could wear those colors. Africa definitely agrees with you. And I know from your website that the work is going well. I'm so happy for you both. When will you come back to cold old Resolve for real?" Cissy's and Jamie's questions tumbled over each other.

Dee, still holding the book, was about to respond, but Mary Louise burst in. "Isn't it terrific?" she said and hugged Dee. "Don't you love the title? And, Mary has told the story of all us Marys – me, MC, little Mary, Mary D'Madre, Mary Kane, Mary J, Mary Anne, Marian Simean, and of course Mary Magdalene, and Our Lady of Guadalupe and . . ."

"Yes, yes. I get it. I get it," Dee laughed. "And I see you've all got new wardrobes – no more T-shirts."

"Whose idea was it to have a book signing here?" asked Christian who was enjoying watching the women and the obvious affection they had for each other.

"Pica insisted," Mary Doyle said.

"That would be Dean Pica Liberatio," said Cissy. She had recently taken a job in the Development Office at St. Jude's, where she was stirring up all kinds of good controversy with outreach to forgotten women alums. There were those whose names had just fallen off the lists, those who had chosen to distance themselves from the institution, those who had been outspoken in their criticism of the church. "The Dean will be along in a minute or so. She was just finishing up with President Humanitas," Cissy explained.

"I want to hear all about it," Dee said.

"You will, you will. We have a dinner planned for after the book signing. Everyone will be there – Miriam is just finishing up with her summer session and Daniel is on his way. MC too. And Tom Guye. He loves living in your cottage by the pond."

Dee nodded. "It worked out well. He needed somewhere to live when he left the priesthood and I needed a tenant while Christian and I went to Uganda."

Mary Louise continued. "Well, he still has some privileges at the Jesuits' residence, and he invited us to have our dinner there. We thought you might enjoy the irony, but in the end we wanted a place with better vibes. There is this new restaurant in town. The chef is a protégé of the guy who was at Ware. Really good food. Even some of that fish you like, Dee. Okay with you?"

"More than okay." Dee glanced at Christian to see if he was savoring the idea as much as she was.

"Can we help to set up the display?" Christian asked.

"No thanks, just make yourselves comfortable," Mary replied. "We won't be starting for another ten minutes or so."

Dee walked along the wide marble hall to the newly expanded college archives. She had heard they now held the records of WOW, copies of student newspapers, and the originals of Amy Nakamura's report and supporting documentation. Even some of Jessie Seneca's notes had been archived. The tests for anthrax had proved negative. With more than a little "help" from the Attorney-General's Office, St. Jude's had negotiated a new settlement with Mary Doyle, part of which specified that all the materials be available to future researchers. The earlier agreement, negotiated at the time of the rape of Mary and her boyfriend, had been unsealed, as had the settlement with Amy Nakamura, and Paddy Sordes, now defrocked, was serving a prison sentence of twenty-five years to life. His outbursts in the court had demonstrated that he still didn't get it, but apparently some of the inmates did. He had been severely beaten and placed in solitary confinement for his own safety. *At least his power to poison is neutralized*, Dee thought. *Not a perfect outcome, but probably the best we could expect under the circumstances.*

Miriam had just come from teaching a class and joined Dee for a walk through the Archives. As they strolled past the portraits of previous presidents of St. Jude's, Miriam pointed to the portrait of Father Firmitas SJ, 1961–1997, and said, "Remember the day he resigned?" Miriam was still wearing her teaching cardigan – the one with the deep pockets where she kept sticks of chalk and marking pens. Daniel, wearing a suit – *must have been in court today*, Dee thought – joined them and paused to look at the painting.

"We were just talking about the day Firmitas resigned." Dee smiled and kissed Daniel. "Miriam is looking awfully good, Daniel. Don't you think? Being Head of Department must be agreeing with her."

"Sometimes." Daniel winked at Miriam.

"I'd love to know what went down in the President's office the morning after the feminist liturgy," Dee said. "I do have some ideas. I think that his speech at Commencement must have been a reflection of what he said to the Board of Trustees when he tendered his resignation."

In a close imitation of President Firmitas, Daniel intoned, "I no longer believe I am the right person to lead this great institution. Yesterday the Board of Trustees agreed to accept my resignation. Wisely, they have asked Father Humanitas to step in and I hope he will be persuaded to stay. As we approach the new century, as we confront our past, we need new ideas, and we need new leaders. I ask you to pray for Father Humanitas and St. Jude's."

"Don't leave out the nice things Firmitas said about Dee," Miriam added. "You know, about how it had taken an anthropologist to explain our culture to us and how there would always be a position for her at St. Jude's. I loved it when he quoted a Swahili proverb."

"*Safari hatua*," Dee supplied the words. "I had offered to resign, you know, but he was adamant that the Trustees would not accept it. Actually I don't think he even asked them." The three fell silent and continued their walk.

"Jackie Li will be joining us later I think," Daniel said. "Dee, you know she's been heading the Task Force on Hate Crimes in the Attorney-General's Office. She was a witness to what went down in those presidential briefings and board meetings. You women really set the wheels in motion."

"Well, I hope Jackie is able to talk some," Dee said. "It seems the Attorney-General runs a tight ship; not much gossip gets out of her office."

"What a stroke of good fortune that Lucy Kelly was Acting AG

267

at the time," Miriam said. "She and Daniel knew each other from their student days. She was one feisty, no-nonsense, redhead, quick-witted Irish woman from Boston."

"And good that the *Boston Globe* reporters have been keeping tabs on the unfolding church scandal. They should be able to connect the dots I couldn't," Dee said. "I saw that Mary D'Madre, now practicing law herself, was quoted in a couple of the articles. There is a woman I admire for her insistence on due process, even though I sometimes wish for more summary justice." They all laughed. "Oh for the good old days of President Firmitas and his dismissive 'Process, bah!'"

"Come on, I think Mary is ready to start," Miriam said.

As they walked back, Dee saw that Christian was already seated in the front row and had read the first chapter of *Marys' Story*. "Some of this is hard to take in," he said as Dee and the others joined him. "She has tackled some very big questions, ones that implicate all of us and, if you know the background, there is more to be read between the lines. Who provided legal advice? Was it you Daniel?"

"Not exactly," Daniel said. "There were some potential conflicts of interest."

Dee was about to ask for details, but Miriam was looking directly at her and shaking her head. *Something is not right here,* Dee thought as she recalled the huddle of lawyers the night of the feminist liturgy. *They are a breed all of their own. Might be an interesting tribe for an anthropologist to study.* She settled into her chair and took in the details of the crowd.

The reading room was almost full when Pica swept into the room. She'd taken to wearing trousers with long tailored over-shirts, still in solid colors, but certainly more trendy than her skirts and boxy jackets of pre-tenure days. Pica had put on some weight since Dee had last seen her. *No more exercise bike,* Dee smiled to herself. *She's busy being Dean.* Father Humanitas, who had decided he too should be part of the book ritual, joined Dee and Christian. "Welcome back to St. Jude's," he said shaking Dee's hand. "And what a pleasure that you were also able to join us Christian," he continued. "I've been following what you two have been doing and hoping we'd have some time to talk. But this is Mary's moment."

Pica's introduction of Mary Doyle was warm. She praised Mary's courage and spoke of how silence in the face of evil destroys the soul. "I have learned a great deal from our students," Pica said. "I like to think that as teachers we are here to facilitate open dialogue and to search for the truth. But we failed in the past. We failed for different reasons. Some of us feared that our own story, if known, would get in the way of our careers; some of us feared rejection and sanction; some of us believed that the ends justified the means. The silences have been damaging and deadly." Pica paused and took a sip of water. Dee noticed that Christian had his copy of Mary's book open to chapter three, "Blaming the Victim."

"By breaking the silence around the sexual abuse of young women at St. Jude's, Mary has shone the light of truth on the darkness of evil," Pica continued. The reading room, bathed in the late afternoon sun, seemed to affirm this. "By insisting that the abuse be understood as part of a wider abuse of power, she has made it possible to speak about the abuse of young boys and men with a theoretical precision lacking in the sensational media coverage of pedophilia. She is right to ask. 'Why now?' Why now indeed? Why are we so shocked and moved to action by the abuse of young boys and men, yet remain unconvinced that women have been and continue to be abused? Mary is right to insist we take a hard look at the ways in which contempt for women and women's bodies has been institutionalized and 'normalized.' She draws our attention to the dynamics of what she calls the 'fault lines of race and gender' that run through American society. Can we see the invisibility of the abuse of women and minorities and the new visibility of the abuse of boys and young men as related? Mary suggests we must, lest, in our zeal, we attempt to eradicate the one and disappear the other. The abuses of power are so deeply woven into the fabric of the life of the church that to merely name them is a radical act. The crisis of sexuality is not about celibacy *per se*, it is about the refusal to acknowledge that we are all sexual beings."

269

Dee glanced around and saw that Tom Guye had arrived and was standing quietly in the back of the room with a man Dee didn't recognize. Maybe this was the person about whom he had written so lovingly to Dee recently. Tom had described to her how he had met Michael in the local outreach center that counseled troubled youths. They had made quite a splash in the media when they announced that they were not trying to "cure" homosexuality but rather to create safe spaces to talk about sexuality. Tom had said their center had received some funding from the AG, and she assumed some of their advice concerned how to deal with hate crimes. *The hand of Lucy Kelly?* Dee wondered.

Pica was winding up. "Mary's book is a great gift to us all and I want to thank her personally. Not a day goes by when I don't ask myself, 'Would Jessie Seneca be alive today if we had been open about our relationship?' I don't know the answer, but I am so grateful that in the telling of Mary's story, other stories may now be told." Pica sat down quietly, her hands clasped tightly in her lap. Dee recalled the last time she had seen her sit this way. It was in the church during the homily of Father Humanitas, now President of St. Jude's. *Had Pica just come out to the St. Jude's community?* Dee asked herself. All eyes were on Mary Doyle as she rose, buttoned the jacket of her well-cut linen suit, and walked to shake Pica's hand. There was no time for further reflection.

"It is strange to be standing here with my book . . ." Mary Doyle paused and opened it to a page that was already flagged. "Before I read some of it to you, I want to thank St. Jude's – Dean Liberatio and President Humanitas, in particular – for making this possible. Three years ago I would have said it was impossible for me to be here reading to you from my book. But change is possible. It takes good people with strong hearts and I thank all my friends who are here this afternoon."

Dee, ever the ethnographer, was making mental notes of who was sitting where and with whom. *Where was Virginia Glacialis?* She had seen Virginia's husband, Howard Robert, and their daughter Mandy slip in and sit together in one of the overstuffed couches near the entrance to the reading room. Dee and Christian had bought one of Howard's paintings at the exhibition at UMass. It had been a strange kind of farewell present for Jackie Li in 1997, but it seemed appropriate. Jackie had always understood and been revolted by the unseemliness of Paddy Sordes. Howard's painting of Sordes as a multi-headed hydra at play in an Elysium Field captured the dark contradictions of the man nicely. But like all his paintings, including one of Chuck Negotium as Feles, a misshapen thieving cat eating the rotting carrion flesh in a brightly illuminated sewer, it had a twist. Sordes's Elysium Field was also a force field, an invitation to dialogue between religion and physics. On closer examination Dee had noticed that all the paintings in the Negotium series – there were several of them – had a small twig cross hidden somewhere on the canvas. Howard had also been connecting dots and drawing on the wide range of symbols he had studied in his long intense periods of comparative mythologies. Negotium's cat was almost certainly an allusion to "The Cat Monster of Obake," a nineteenth-century Japanese woodblock print. The intertexuality had not been lost on Amy Nakamura. *Remember to get a copy of Mary's book signed for Amy*, Dee told herself. *Jamie will be seeing Amy when she visits her in the field in Japan later in the summer.*

Dee focused on Mary Doyle. The vulnerability of three years ago was gone. Today Mary looked radiant. "I thought I'd read from the section which talks about the steps you climbed to join us here today," Mary began. "Many of you were at the now-famous feminist liturgy. Some of you spoke that night in May 1997. Try to remember the exhilaration we felt as the stories were told and then consider what followed." *The difference between law and justice?* Dee mused. She and Pica had been in close communication via email and phone and she was well aware of some of the compromises that had been made in the aftermath of that fateful night.

Mary read in a pure, clear voice. "The morning after dawned overcast. The papers skewered on the crown of thorns and lying within the crèche were damp from the dew. We knew that as soon as the fog burned off we would face blistering heat. We were waiting for a representative of the Attorney-General to arrive and were not prepared to surrender the papers to anyone else. We had kept our vigil on the library steps and were not about to be moved or to have the papers disturbed. We understood that a number of people were extremely anxious about what was contained in those papers. Had we named individuals? That is a secret that we have kept to this day. The mere possibility that we might have named names was enough to set the ball rolling." *The power of secrets.* Dee thought back on her conversations with Christian on this topic. *It's not the content so much as the power and authority secrecy evokes. Can secrets serve the common good?* Mary was into her storytelling mode and her audience was with her.

"At about ten o'clock that morning, we heard the police sirens and saw that the police were engaged in an intense exchange with the guard who was on sentry duty. He had no idea what to do. His boss, Charles V. Negotium, was in custody and, we later learned, had negotiated a deal with the Attorney-General. There was no way Negotium could protect his incriminating email correspondence concerning the cover up of the 'accident' that killed Jessie Seneca. It would all come out. It would lead to questions about the night I was raped and the role he had played in the cleanup after the rape of Mary D'Madre. For decades Negotium had been cleaning up messes made by students, faculty, and priests. The absence of doubt had made him strong, but the security of that world crumbled quickly in May 1997. He had panicked during our feminist liturgy, and had thought he could control the situation as he had on other occasions. But this time it wasn't working. Members of his maintenance crew were ready to speak out. He was doomed. But Charles V. Negotium was, above all, a Business Manager and it was time to manage his own business. He was ready to cooperate with the Attorney-General in her investigations."

Was Daniel implicated in building that head of steam? Dee wondered. He certainly had contact with some of the maintenance crew. Did he have a hand in brokering the deal with the AG for Negotium? That would explain his pleading potential conflict of interest in advising the women of WOW on what to do with the documents on the fountain. Lawyers

272

also hide behind a wall of secrecy and protect their clients. What or who had Daniel kept from public scrutiny? Would that story ever be told? How much of these negotiations had Miriam known about? Was that another source of tension in the marriage?

Mary read about how she had pieced together the story of Jessie's accident. Her book explained how Bill Jr.'s father, the Head of Political Science, had whisked his drunken son away before the police arrived at the accident scene and had then convinced Bob Boyal, a junior, who was slightly less inebriated, to say he had been driving Bill Jr.'s car. Professor O'Vafer had reassured the lad that, should the matter come to court, he would have the best counsel, but had been equally certain that the matter would not. It so clearly had been an accident. According to the evidence Bob Boyal gave when, following the investigations of the Attorney-General, the matter had come to trial, O'Vafer had also said, "Bob, I must say I found your recent paper on the shifting politics of the Supreme Court to be quite outstanding. We're talking about top honors here. Any law school you want."

From the evidence of Charles V. Negotium, Mary Doyle had learned that the Business Manager had prepped a number of his workers to provide "eye-witness accounts" of the accident. It was a dark night. The street lamp was broken. Jessie Seneca, pushing her bike ahead of her, had stepped out, not seen the dark car allegedly driven by Bob, had been hit, thrown to one side and run over accidentally by a speeding car in the next lane. Being a responsible citizen, Bob Boyal, much shaken, had stopped and rendered such assistance as he could. Tragic, but an accident. Bob had been sent for counseling and the police had thanked the campus police for their assistance. That was the story until the email had surfaced. Negotium was having trouble containing Jake Rose, one of his workers who had not been promoted as he thought was his due, who was threatening to expose his boss. The email Negotium fired off to <u>J.Rose@StJudes.edu</u> had gone to <u>J.Rosen@StJudes.edu</u>. One keystroke, one letter, had brought the story of intrigue and conspiracy into the open.

Mary Doyle was now reading of the moment that was

emblazoned into Dee's memory, the arrest of Professor William O'Vafer. "The bewildered sentry called the President's office and let the police cars through. What else was he to do? The arrest warrants were valid as far as he could tell. The two cars, sirens blaring, drove up to the entrance of Coyle Hall. Two uniformed Campus Security guards met the police, inspected the warrants, and together proceeded into the building. Faculty, who were already in their offices, where they were finishing up their grading for the semester, had their windows open to catch the last of the morning breeze before the sun hit the south side of the building and made their rooms unbearable. Several faces appeared at opened windows, others leaned out to get a better view. Across on the library steps we could hear raised voices and then we saw it was Bill Jr.'s father, Professor O'Vafer, who was being taken into custody. He was cuffed. He glared across at us and didn't drop his gaze even as the police pushed his head down, bundled him into the car, and drove away.

"I stared back through all the pain I remember of the night I was raped. I stared at him across the years of hiding the truth from myself and others. I stared at him long after he was actually there. It was then, for the first time, that I allowed myself to cry. Cissy, Mary Louise and MC stood with me and stared also. Mary Louise hissed, 'You've been warned,' and we turned back to look at our documents on the crown of thorns. We could hear the sirens as the police cars drove away. About five minutes later the Attorney-General emerged from Coyle Hall with President Firmitas. It was at that moment I knew I had to write this book, for all the Marys. As Professor Dee Scrutari would say, I wanted to connect the dots." Mary looked up from the page and smiled at Dee.

Ah yes, the President had cooperated. This Dee knew. The women had handed over all the documentation to Lucy Kelly, who had shown herself to be a woman of extraordinary diplomacy and legal know-how. She had secured all she needed from Negotium who, for his cooperation, was allowed to plead guilty to a lesser charge of interfering with a crime scene and was doing 1000 hours community service in the local soup kitchen. His testimony regarding the vulnerability of the mail and telephone system at St. Jude's to tampering had prompted the Board of Trustees to overhaul the systems to protect them from misuse. Dee suspected that General Counsel at St. Jude's had outlined to the Board the dire consequences of preserving the status quo.

Lucy Kelly had spent many days at St. Jude's and had spoken with many different individuals but, in the end, O'Vafer was charged with being an accessory after the fact in the death of Jessie Seneca. It was a pragmatic decision that gave Lucy Kelly little joy but, as Dee had observed, Lucy ran a tight ship. There was some gossip at St. Jude's about why the investigation of his tampering with records had not been pursued in the courts. There was some speculation that the Trustees had brought pressure to bear on persons higher up the food chain than Lucy. But it was only rumor and innuendo. What was clear was that Professor William O'Vafer's teaching career was over. Pica had sat through the short trial. Negotium's testimony had been damning. Yes, he had cleaned up the site but, no, he hadn't actually seen the accident, or Bill Jr., but he had seen the crumpled bike and his crew had helped rearrange the scene. All he could say by way of justification was that he had acted to protect the college. He was just doing his job. At the sentencing, Pica caught Negotium's gaze and stared him down.

Shaken by the arrest of his father, when brought in for questioning, Bill Jr. confessed to having been the driver of the car that killed Jessie Seneca, but claimed that he had blacked out. On advice from his lawyers he agreed to plead guilty to manslaughter and was appropriately remorseful in his allocution of his guilt. The women of WOW attended his sentencing where he received five years. Although Dee thought this not enough, she was reassured that his dream of practicing law was ruined by the felony conviction. The instigator of the Terminator threats remained untouched and the potentially incriminating documents remained secret. *Was the trade-off worth it?* Dee wondered while Mary continued her reading. The women were not made vulnerable to defamation charges. But the identity of the Terminator remained a mystery. *If the conditions that made these threats and attacks possible no longer existed, would the evil evaporate?*

Mary Doyle had finished her reading and was now signing books. Jamie was buying a bundle. "Guess what the Coyle family is getting for Christmas this year?" she laughed as Mary signed book after book for all those "J" Coyles. Pica was buying one for Dean Simean, who had been in ill health. The experimental treatment had given some relief, but he was not expected to live much more than a year. He had established a scholarship for students on financial aid who could not afford the extra expenses of summer travel. He wanted the students to be able to reach beyond the gated community, to learn more of the "others" whom the college was dedicated to serve. Consuelo and Little Mary had taken advantage of the grants and were enjoying a six-week educational field trip to Cuba. Mary J and Magdalena, with some help from her aged aunt, had scraped together enough to visit their daughters. The postcard addressed to Dee and Christian care of Miriam was full of joy at the Hernández homecoming.

"Want to walk in the grounds before we join the others to eat?" Christian asked Dee. "Mary will be signing for a while."

"Yes, let's do that. Lay a few demons to rest," Dee said, grateful to be moving. "This place still gets to me."

"It's not the place it was three years ago," Christian said, glancing through the copy of *Daily Dispatches* he had picked up in the library. "It seems to be more connected to the local community, not as walled off. And look, there is some signage on the buildings. Must be easier to find one's way around now."

"How deep can that kind of change be?" Dee asked.

"Ah, you're so impatient," Christian said gently and paused on the steps. "The church is very old, Dee. It can't change fast enough for you. But look down there, see the space outside Tuck Hall, seems like there has been a public meeting."

"Yes," Dee conceded. "Miriam told me students have been more open in their demands for greater diversity on campus. Their protests are respected, even encouraged by the administration." Dee and Christian walked on in silence.

"So, was it all worth it?" Dee stopped as they rounded the corner to the Murphy Chapel and turned to face Christian.

"You got involved. How could you not?" he replied.

"I know," Dee said. "After such knowledge, what forgiveness? I had to act on what I knew."

"And that made it possible for others," Christian said, brushing her hair from her face. "I guess we should be joining the others for dinner," Dee said. "I'm going to have the tilapia if they have it."

"Humm, I guess I'll have some unbraiding to do." Christian put his arm around Dee and she did the same as they walked in companionable silence back down to the car.

The Resolve Restaurant was a perfect place for their dinner. Mary Doyle had booked a private room with a round table that was supposed to seat twelve, but they squeezed together to fit thirteen – Mary Doyle, Cissy, Jamie, MC and Mary Louise, Dee and Christian, Miriam and Daniel, Tom and Michael, Jackie Li, and Pica. "I propose a toast to Mary Doyle," Dee said lifting her glass. They drank to WOW, to each other, to the future. "Before I get too tipsy," Dee said, "I want to say something. Three years ago, I was worried that the emotional high we were all on after the feminist liturgy would dissipate, that the momentum necessary for change couldn't be sustained. We needed the liturgy as catharsis, but we needed a plan that could be carried through and I didn't know who would do it. I always thought I had figured out what a just society might look like. It was a dream, but a dream I wanted to pursue. I think I've learned it's always becoming, it's always different, we're in this together, for better or worse, a strange kind of a union, but there you have it."

Miriam was silent as Dee finished. "Here's to idealists," she said, raising her glass and looking directly at Daniel. "What?" he said softly. "What was that for?"

"And here's to pragmatists," said Jackie raising hers. *So she was part of brokering a deal among Firmitas, the Board of Trustees and Mary Doyle,* Dee thought.

"And to those who can work together." Christian bowed slightly to Dee.

"And to all the Marys," said Jamie.

"Jackie," Miriam said somewhat sternly, "you were there. What happened that morning with the President?"

"Well, as you know, he had just come back from an exhausting overseas trip but he insisted we all assemble and that he be briefed on every last detail before he met with the AG. My most immediate concern was the legal status of the papers 'tabled' during the liturgy. It would have been in the interests of the college if they'd blown away in a storm, just disappeared, but we'd had too many things disappear. I knew the women were reading from printed texts, but I didn't know how much more might be in the papers on the crown of thorns or within the crèche. Had they named individual students, faculty, administrators, priests, or Trustees? Who else? Of course I warned him that our conversations on the subject could be subject to scrutiny," Jackie said. "He said, 'Well I am working hard to make sure it doesn't come to that, but I want us to be as open as we can. I know that will mean walking a fine line. As President I have the interests of St. Jude's to protect, and I am sure the Trustees will remind me of where my duty lies. But I am also determined that we will root out this evil. I want the truth. I want a just outcome, not merely a legally defensible one. If anyone here has a problem with that, speak up now. If anyone feels that they need their own legal counsel, get it.' And then he dismissed us."

"And, the rest as they say, is history," Daniel said a little too quickly.

"Whose history?" Pica said. "*Marys' Story* will be read carefully. The archives are open for research. The *Boston Globe* is not about to give up. What about you Dee?"

"I think there is hope. Of course I want it to be neat, like a theoretical model, but it isn't. I know kinship diagrams are abstract forms, but I love their promise of order and structure. Real life is messier. Yes, I do believe that it takes time for change. And, I know I'm impatient," she added with a laugh. "But now I'm fading fast. We did only fly in late last night."

"How about brunch tomorrow?' Miriam asked. "Our place, everyone is invited."

"Good, so we won't say goodbye," Dee said.

"We'll talk more then," Miriam said as Dee and Christian made their departure.

Pica stood up, followed them to the entrance hall and embraced Dee. "There is something I need to say," she said so that only Dee could hear. "Need a bathroom break?"

"Sure," Dee said and turned to Christian, "I'll catch you up outside. Okay?"

Pica sat on the floral couch in the women's room. "I'm so sorry it took so much hurt for the stories to start to be told."

"Me too," Dee said and put her arm around Pica's shoulders. "If only you'd trusted me earlier, perhaps some of the violence might have been stopped."

"I know. I was scared. I'd seen what happened to Jessie. She moved fast, maybe too fast given the entrenched nature of things at St. Jude's. I thought your impatience might push things through too fast too. Perhaps I was wrong, but I couldn't bear another death. And I was scared that somehow they would find out about Jessie and me and use that to discredit me completely."

"Well, if you'll excuse the pun, you set them straight today," Dee said and she felt Pica relax a little.

"I'm not sure they heard it," Pica said. "But that won't be the last time. That was just my opening shot. Remember I'm a mean pool player."

"One vacation, I want you to teach me to play pool," Dee laughed.

"You're on," Pica said. "See you tomorrow at brunch, and thanks."

✢

Dee caught up with Christian and they walked out into the evening, still warm, the air full of cicada songs. "I'm not really ready for sleep yet." Dee said.

"We could walk up to your favorite lookout, near the native

spring," Christian suggested. "It's a clear night, we can gaze at the stars, and if you're up to it, you can connect some more of the dots for me. I want to hear what is going on in that amazing brain of yours."

"Thanks, talking it through some more would really help. You know what you said about reading between the lines in *Marys' Story*? Well, I think the lawyers have done their own little deal to keep this whole mess inside lines that they can control and that they understand. Even Daniel is implicated. They did a deal the night of the liturgy – him, Jackie and Joshua – and they did a deal the morning President Firmitas met with the Attorney-General. Jackie was part of that and I'm sure Firmitas was not particularly delighted with the compromise but went along with it for the sake of the college."

"You'll probably never know the whole of it. Can you live with that Dee? Can you move on?"

"It's the layer upon layer of half-truths masquerading as the solution that sticks in my gullet," Dee said. "Like this site up here. It was a native spring, a holy place. It had a story, but the Jesuits built on it and erased that history. Have the lawyers built their structure on the foundations laid by WOW?"

"We could go over the whole thing, piece by piece, the conspiracies, the lies, the evasions, the intimidations, but each was at a different stage of evolution, and Dee you're the one who identified those pieces and made many of the connections in your doodling and your analysis. Who but you, with your incredible memory and your notebooks, could have figured out the connection between the Montreal Massacre and Jessie's death?"

"It was easy really," Dee said. "Jessie was killed on December 6. That's the last date for grade changes at St. Jude's. Jessie knew Bill O'Vafer had been tampering with grades. His son was failing in 1990 and he was young for college anyway. He was drinking and out of control. And at that time, women all around the world knew that date.

"Like April 19, the day of the Oklahoma bombing, has become a rallying point for local militia?"

"Yes, I'd say Marc Lepine's vision of doing away with all feminists was well known to a number of parties, both supporters and opponents of affirmative action. We all wore red armbands to mark the date. Jessie was easy to spot that day. Pica has helped me piece a lot of this together over past couple of years. There are things Jessie recorded in her notes that are still hidden. Pica is holding onto them for now."

"And the #126?" Christian asked.

"That was the hardest and it was one of those secrets in plain sight. I did read Taussig as you suggested – remember back in the early days when we were exchanging letters? And I reread Simmel on the Irish conspiracy. It started to make sense. You know the Irish used numbers instead of names to disguise their membership in secret societies? I did more online searches about the Montreal Massacre, and I realized the connection. The # was a mark. It was a reference to Marc as in Lepine and the 12/6 was the date. December 6. I always write the date the other way around as 6/12, so I didn't see it." Dee paused. "Enough?"

"No. Keep going, please."

"When I searched on the Lepine name, I found a number of sites that praised his actions. They openly supported terminating all feminists. Free speech is a wonderful thing, eh?"

"At its best it is," Christian said. "I've seen what dictatorships do."

"Well yes, but free for whom?" Dee parried.

Dee and Christian sat looking out over Resolve.

"It was good to talk Pica tonight," Dee said. "Email isn't as satisfying as eating, drinking and talking together."

"She told me how much she missed your Friday night potluck dinners and conversation," Christian said.

"I miss them too," Dee said. "But the conversation I was thinking about this evening over dinner was how Pica had described the fallout after Professor Bill O'Vafer's arrest. Tongues were loosened. Secretaries, who had known all along that their boss was playing around with women students, but were not prepared to talk openly, suddenly had quite a bit to say and, no doubt, Mary J had a hand in opening those floodgates. Christine, Bill's wife, also opened up and that helped Pica make sense of some of Jessie's notes. The best I can reconstruct it, there was a nasty scene in the O'Vafer household one night in late November 1990, about a week before Jessie was killed. Christine heard Bill Jr. saying, 'Well you're the professor aren't you? You can fix it.'

"'Fix what?' Christine had asked naively.

"'He ran up a bill on my credit card at the liquor store,' her husband said. 'Let's leave it at that.'

"'No, Dad!' Bill Jr. had raised his voice. 'We won't leave it at that. The deal was that if I got A or A minus in all my mid-term exams, you'd let me use your credit card. My GPA was 3.75 at midterms. So what's the beef? You don't care if I drink. We do it all the time at home.'

"'That's different,' his mother had interposed. 'You're not driving. And what about your final grades this semester?'

"'Christine, please let it go. I'll handle this,' Bill O'Vafer said firmly.

"'Mom, stay out of it,' Bill Jr. said. 'The grades don't matter. Dad knows how to fix those.'

"'No, Bill. He has to earn the grades,' Christine O'Vafer had said as she walked out of the room in tears.

"'I do, Mom. Ask him how I earn them,' Bill Jr. had shouted after her. 'Ask him.'"

"But she didn't, did she?" Christian asked.

"I guess not," Dee said. "She knew that as father and son they were tight. She had heard them once in the basement – that was where they went to drink and play poker. 'Men's business,' they'd say to her. She had heard them plotting and scheming about what they would do with those who caused them trouble. She had written it off as high spirits, but now she wondered if it wasn't something more sinister. Her husband had told her not to worry her pretty little head about it, but she knew he was a complex man and that he had secrets he would guard to the death."

"And you've got an inkling about what some of those might be?" Christian asked but then reassured Dee. "Tell me at your own pace. I always like hearing how your mind works."

"Well, Jessie's notes were confusing at first," Dee said. "Pica had me read some of them, but she only told me tonight about the phone call she had from Jessie the week before she died. Pica told me that Jessie had been very angry and that she had said she was going to stake out the Field House. Again, as best I can reconstruct it, the ex-girlfriend of Marty McDuff, a Political Science major, had come to Jessie with an account of the drunken revels at the Field House on Friday nights. Initially she had not taken Marty's dismissal of opinionated women too seriously, but then he had started pushing her around. She had showed Jessie the yellowing bruise on her arm. By then I think Jessie had figured out the Field House was where Mary D'Madre had been raped. She decided that the following Friday, she would hide in the Field House and listen in. There was a temporary lean-to on the north side of the building while some construction was going on and she was sure she could squeeze into the shed without being seen."

"I think you and Jessie would have got on well together," Christian said. "She was tenacious, like you."

"Thanks. That beats being called a puritan. Anyway, so apparently Jessie settled into a corner against the wall that was being repaired and heard a lot of what was said that particular Friday night. It must have been the same night that Bill Jr. had stormed out of his parents' place. So, when he arrived at the Field House to join Eddie Casey, a fellow freshman, Bob Boyal, a junior, and the two seniors, Marty McDuff and Dan Dempsey, they were already pretty drunk but calling for more.

"'Here, let's get serious,' Bill Jr. had said as he unloaded the 'hard stuff.'

"'How'd ya get it?' Eddie had asked in awe.

"'On my old man's credit card,' Bill Jr. had bragged.

"'Cool,' Eddie said. 'Now what are we going to do about this Jessie Seneca bitch? She is getting too fucking close for my likings.'

"'Ya and she's whipping up those dumb-ass women in that student group,' Bob had added.

"'They're going to protest about the violence on campus,' Marty had said placing his hands on his hips like a teacher scolding a naughty child. 'I'll show them some fucking violence,' he had said and punched his fist up into the air. 'Bunch of fucking dykes. I know what they need.'

"'You think they'd fucking learn. Maybe they weren't paying attention to what happened to the last bitch who got in our way,' Dan said in a low hiss.

"'Jesus, I even called them up and told them, "You have been warned." Left them little crosses. Do they need a fucking diagram?' Dan had said and made a crude drawing of a woman's body in the beer spilled on the makeshift bar. As he leaned back to admire his handiwork, the stool on which he was perched slid sideways and he crashed to the floor. Jessie, on the other side of the thin wooden paneling, flinched and bumped into a discarded paint can as she felt the reverberations. 'What was that?' Bob, at that point still capable of standing up unaided, had asked.

"'That was Dan falling off the stool, you idiot,' Marty replied.

"But Bob pursued the matter and ventured outside. 'Shit, it's cold out here,' he said and looked across the campus. 'Oh, it's that cat. Must have been under the bar.'

"'Here, warm up, have some more tequila,' Eddie said and passed the bottle. 'Now where were we? Oh yes, our sacred purpose, upholding the law of the Red Knights. Maybe we need to remind a few of these bitches about little Mary D'Madre.'"

Dee wrapped her shawl around her shoulders and continued. "Bill Jr. had heard about the vicious rape of Mary D'Madre in the fall of '89 from Dan who, along with Martin, was the keeper of the sacred lore of the Red Knights. Not *Alice in Wonderland*, but the predecessors of the Knights of Columbus. I'd made a note to myself to check out the Freemasons, and I found all kinds of websites devoted to documenting the history of the Catholic secret societies. And you know Firmitas's Irish grandfather had been a member."

"So those Political Science majors were identifying with a time when Catholics were persecuted?" Christian asked.

"Yep. They saw themselves as endangered and feminists were the latest enemy. The arrival of women at St. Jude's and post-

Vatican II reforms, all threatened to dilute the St. Jude traditions they held dear. Over the years, there had been several women faculty and administrators who had needed to be brought into line when they threatened the rules, but Jessie Seneca, the Assistant Professor in Religious Studies, seemed to be impervious to their warnings. Bill Jr., who was being groomed to take a leadership role in the Red Knights, thought he could teach Seneca a lesson she wouldn't forget."

"And he had good reason to think he'd get away with it," Christian said.

"Yes, he did. Their society was known to a select few but their impact was felt across the campus. 'Know your Trustees,' was one of the principal rules of this elite group, as was 'Know your faculty.' Being related was even better. Jessie Seneca, these young men had discovered, was a persistent, dogged researcher and she was known to hang out with well-connected women students like Jamie Coyle. The possibilities of this gynecentric networking sent a chill down the spines of many pre-coed alumni. And, as Dan had suspected, Jessie Seneca had no intention of limiting her research to faculty and students. She had even begun asking questions about various priests and their students who were known as teachers' pets. And, if that wasn't enough, she was teaming up with a newly arrived faculty member, Amy Nakamura, on a project about alcohol consumption and violence against women. Dan knew from his nights of drinking with Father Venarius that Jessie had begun to get on the nerves of a couple of the Jesuits too. She'd come back after her summer sojourn in New Mexico with questions about 'man–boy love' that, as far as they were concerned, were inappropriate and none of her business."

"'She will not go quietly,' Marty had said. 'She's one of that breed of feminazis who think they have the law on their side. We've tried phone calls, threatening letters, even some fake anthrax. She takes all this attention as a compliment. It's up to you guys to teach her who's boss,' and Marty looked at Bill and Eddie. 'You're good soldiers and you know how to keep a fucking secret. Time to do her so she gets the message. So Bill?'

285

"Jessie, crouched down inside the small shed, was starting to feel numb. She'd worn her warmest clothes, but it was one of the clear, cold nights and the chill was getting into her bones. As quietly as she could, she pulled the hood of her duffle coat over her head and tucked her hands under her arms. She was concentrating so hard on not sneezing that she missed parts of what they were saying. Of course, we know now, from Bill Jr.'s testimony, that they were planning an 'accident.'

"But you know," Dee said, her eyes shining, "I think that both Bill Jr. and his father are carrying enormous loads of guilt. Each thinks the other really ran Jessie over. Bill Jr. blacked out, but he saw another car hit Jessie as she lay on the road. I'm guessing he thinks his father was driving that car but he covered for his father during the trial; and I think his father thinks Bill Jr. killed her and he covered for his son. The truth may be even more tragic. Had they got medical assistance straight away, Jessie might have lived. The Medical Examiner testified that she had lost a lot of blood and gone into shock. It was a very cold night. Had they not been so busy cleaning up and had they paid attention to Jessie, it might all have been different."

"The sins of the fathers?" Christian began. "Bill O'Vafer, Bill Jr. . . ."

"Something like that," Dee said. "But it gets even more complicated, and here is where we come to the secrets of big Catholic families . . . I had been playing with that genealogy, Bill, Christine, and Bill Jr., and it just didn't work. But then I remembered the secretaries saying that Bill O'Vafer had a thing for younger women, really younger women. I wondered which really younger woman might have been Bill's mother. Where was she?"

"Get thee to a nunnery?" Christian asked.

"That's what happened to many girls in the '70s. But it wasn't until I saw the photograph that Chuck Negotium carries in his wallet – not the ones on his desk, his private ones. It was quite by accident that I saw it. His wallet was lying open on his desk the day I went to see him, just before Commencement 1997. I needed his signature for the grant I'd got for that summer. I saw the two of them, brother and sister, I guessed, and she looked just like Bill

Jr. No wonder Negotium and O'Vafer were tight. They're like 'brothers-in-law.' Chuck is Bill Jr.'s uncle. All those doodles I was drawing suddenly made sense."

"So the mother disappears. Bill marries Christine straight out of college and they adopt Bill Jr.?" Christian said.

"That's my guess. Maybe one day we'll hear more of Christine's story. It can't have been easy for her, but she seems to have come out stronger. She has gone back to using her maiden name and is in private practice as a marriage counselor. Pica told me about how Christine had confronted her husband with evidence of his many liaisons with female students and had insisted, 'It's not consensual sex, Bill. You're old enough to be their father and look at the power you have over them. It's harassment, pure and simple. And to implicate your son in covering up these dirty little affairs, makes me sick.'"

"And Chuck's sister? Another 'Mary's Story'?" Christian asked.

"Maybe. I think Pica knows more. She is just coming out about so many things and she always said big Catholic families know how to keep their secrets."

"Seems your tribe of 'non-reproducing males' found a way to reproduce," Christian said. "But you also figured out the anthrax threat."

"Oh, that was almost too easy. Those threats had been around for some time. Intimidation. All the women's organizations had well-developed protocols for dealing with suspicious mailings. Jessie knew that. She knew she was a target. She kept the envelope she received that day. It was carefully sealed. But she knew. She knew about Bill's indiscretions and his tampering with records. Negotium was bloody lucky he didn't have that added to his charges."

"So you think that Firmitas negotiated a deal to protect the college? That he cooperated on the understanding that certain things were off limits as long as there were arrests for the rapes and murders?" Christian asked.

"Something like that," Dee agreed and looked up quickly. "You know what I never did figure out?"

"What?"

"Why the Dean always wears those stunning bow ties. I guess I'll just have to live with that. Oh, and the cat. I did figure that out. Negotium had one redeeming feature, he fed the cat. The clue was in one of Howard's paintings. I didn't read that level of the symbolism. Pica told me she now feeds it. He'd left her a note about the brand of food Feles liked best."

"And what about Paddy Sordes?"

"About as close to evil incarnate as one gets, but Jackie Li told me a wonderful thing – well, wonderful in the sense that there is hope. Sordes packed in such a hurry the day he left that it seems he overlooked a couple of items. They finished up with Lucy Kelly, the Attorney-General, and in an old battered photograph album was one of those posed baby pictures. Little Paddy Sordes, quite angelic, on a bear skin rug. He wasn't born bad, he learned it. So I will hold onto that hope. If it's learned, it can be unlearned." Dee scanned the horizon. Clear sky. No clouds. She turned to Christian, shuddered a little and drew her shawl tighter around her shoulders. "So, why does the evil persist? Is it so entrenched in the structures, the silences, the secrets, that it triumphs? You know all that is needed for evil to triumph is for good men to do nothing," she said but, as a reflex, held up her fingers as she said "men."

"There is hope, Dee. Look at those *women* today," Christian said, acknowledging her wordplay. "And Dee, you did something. You acted on what you knew." Christian took her hand and folded it through his crooked arm.

"I know I'm impatient," Dee said, drawing nearer and feeling the warmth of his body. "The history of the church reaches back across the millennium. But I come from a young country, with a very long past. We're all still trying to write our stories."

ACKNOWLEDGEMENTS

Without a sabbatical from The George Washington University, 2002–3, which gave me the time to undertake research in Uganda, China, Singapore and Australia and the time to write, this novel would still be a bunch of notes and folders. I am grateful to a number of friends and colleagues for their comments on various drafts of *Evil*, for sending me media clippings and recommended readings, and for listening to me as I talked through my ideas: Barry Alpher, Genevieve Bell, Ellen Boneparth, Sally Brinkman, Alison Brooks, Giulia Cox, Martha Cox, Celeste Duffy, Ian Fairweather, Deane Fergie, Amy Gardner, Colette Harris, Susan Hawthorne, Leslie Jacobson, Jean Fray King, Renate Klein, Heidi Lindemann, Sally Levinson, Rod Lucas, Garnet Marsh, Marilyn Merritt, Dan Moshenberg, Jane Perkins, Cassandra Pybus, David Le Sage, Mary Anne Saunders, Bryan Smith, John von Sturmer and Kristin Waters, thank you for your thoughtful assistance. I am particularly indebted to Nina Mikhalevski for getting me going and to Tansy Blumer for her extreme generosity in providing fine-grain comments on draft after draft after draft. As always the Spinifex team have been marvelous. Thanks to Janet Mackenzie for her careful copy editing, Claire Warren for her design and typesetting, Maralann Damiano for keeping our communications in order, and Deb Snibson for the wonderful cover. And to Renate Klein and Sue Hawthorne – friends, colleagues, feminist publishers in an increasingly conservative world – thanks for still being there and bringing this project to print. I take responsibility for the final result.

I gratefully acknowledge the permission of Dutton, a division of Penguin Group (USA) Inc., to quote from "Lift Every Voice and Sing", from *Lift Every Voice and Sing: Words and Music* by James Weldon Johnson, illustrated by Mozelle Thompson, copyright © 1970 by Hawthorn Books, Inc.

*If you would like to know more about Spinifex Press,
write for a free catalogue or visit our website*

Spinifex Press
PO Box 212 North Melbourne
Victoria 3051 Australia

women@spinifexpress.com.au
www.spinifexpress.com.au